Ed Adams
Touches The Stars

by

Art Myers

To Yuja Wang, and all the pianists and musicians that
bring the music to life for the rest of us to enjoy.

Other Books by Art Myers

MY STORY
How A Young Boy From California
Ended Up An Old Man In Florida

ADREW'S PIANO

ED ADAMS CHASES A DREAM

A NEW LIFE FOR ROBERT JOHNSON

10,000 YEARS – Before Present

Ed Adams
Touches The Stars

Preface

This is a work of fiction. I started writing it in the fall of 2019. Shortly after the new year several medical problems came about for my wife and I, thankfully none related to COVID-19, which are now mostly in our past.

That is my excuse and I will stand by it. In the first paragraph I wrote of a real place, person, symphony orchestra and time fictionally. So when you read about Ed Adams entering the stage of the Walt Disney Concert Hall, followed by the conductor of the Los Angeles Philharmonic Orchestra, Gustavo Dubamel, on Thursday, March 24, 2022 at 8:00 pm please understand that at the time I wrote those words the 2020-2021 L.A. Phil season had been canceled due to COVID-19 and I chose the date thinking I would have the book written and published for you to read before then

Alas, on this most important real day which will arrive before my work here is finished, Gustavo Dudamel will be conducting the Philadelphia Orchestra in the Verizon Hall and at the Walt Disney Concert Hall, Seymon Byhkov will be conducting the L.A. Phil.

I will repeat this is a work of fiction so I ask for some liberty with the events that occur in the real world. Please enjoy and if you happen to find out about the above you can know that I told you about it already.

Chapter 1

Ed Adams was waiting in the wings of the Walt Disney Concert Hall. It was just before 8:00 pm Thursday, March 24th, 2022 and near him was Gustavo Dudamel, the conductor for tonight's concert. Gustavo was pacing back and forth as Ed stood calmly by the door to the stage. He was always that way, even before a major concert as it would be tonight. The difficult Rachmaninoff Concerto Number 3, to be followed after the intermission by the popular Concerto Number 2. The Los Angeles Philharmonic Orchestra members were in position and awaiting their entrance. Gustavo nodded to Ed, opened the door and motioned for him to make his entry as he would follow a few steps behind.

Although the concert hall was not full, it still was a large crowd. The Covid-19 pandemic of 2020 had finally run it's course and this was to be the start, hopefully, of a new season for the LA Phil. It had been a long wait and a severe strain for everyone, both those on the stage and those in the audience. For the musicians and the classical music lovers it was a chance to restart their lives again. The orchestra now had a number of new members but fortunately had been able to keep most of the principals. Dudamel remained as director and conductor. Ed Adams was being paid a modest fee and expenses for the rehearsals and the performance. It had taken almost a month, and four rehearsals, to prepare for tonight's concert but he felt ready for the challenge. He had spent a good part of his fifty-six years seated in front of a piano to attain this position as a premier concert pianist.

The applause was much greater than usual as Ed crossed the distance to the Steinway Concert Grand piano, with Gustavo following behind. Ed Adams was a tall man, six foot two, with the build and manner of an athlete, and was by any standard a handsome man. His entrance some what dominated the scene as he and Gustavo made a cursory bow to the audience and then took their respective positions at the piano and the conductor's podium.

He glanced toward the first row balcony seats opposite him and smiled at those there. His wife, their two children, his grandfather-in-law and his wife. They acknowledged his look with smiles and discrete waves. None in the audience really noticed except an attractive couple seated a few rows behind the family. Later that night Ed, and his wife Julia Renquest Adams, would meet them at a special post Concert party and new friendships would develop. It would, in turn, lead to a most interesting twist in their lives.

Gustavo raised his baton and tapped the stand. The applause died to silence and the musicians were poised and ready. He looked down towards Ed who nodded back indicating that he was also ready. The first quiet notes by clarinet, bassoon and strings were sounded and Ed softly entered to what is thought to be the most technically difficult and nuanced concerto ever written. Rachmaninoff

Number 3 was underway and the next forty-four minutes would require everyone involved to do their very best, especially the soloists and of course the pianist.

Sergei Rachmaninoff was thought of as being the best pianist and composer of his day. He had exceptionally large hands and almost all his music was written to challenge anyone who chose to play it. He did not shy away from including multiple chords demanding spans leaving those with small hands to suffer. Ed had large hands, long strong fingers and superb coordination. In piano speak he could easily cover an "eleventh", meaning with thumb and little finger he could cover eleven notes. He had also been playing Rachmaninoff compositions for years, mastering Concerto Number 2 while still in his teens. Number 3 had come later in his life and this performance was his first playing it at a premier concert level.

The third movement, which is played without a break between it and the second, ends in a triumphant cadenza which many claim to be Rachmaninoff's musical signature. As the sounds slowly faded in the hall there was a long moment of silence. Those who didn't understand what had just happened started the applause first and then the rest joined in. Gustavo, eyes moist with emotion, stepped down from the podium and went to Ed with a firm handshake and clasping of his arm. They moved forward to make their bows to the patrons and then moved to face the orchestra, hands out stretched with palms up signaling their approval of their fine playing. They knew, Gustavo and Ed knew, that something magical had just happened. It would be later be posited that it had been the finest performance of Concerto Number 3 that any one present that evening had ever heard. Fortunately it had been professionally recorded and for years to come royalties would be coming to the L A Phil.

Following the long applause and the intermission, the more popular and loved Concerto Number 2 was performed at an equally high level. Again Gustavo was beyond ecstatic with the outcome as the orchestra had been perfect and Ed had played beyond great. As the bows were taken and the applause accepted and given, all in the hall knew they had witnessed musical history. One could only hope that Sergei Rachmaninoff had somehow been able to hear it.

In the balcony seats behind Ed's family Sandra Williams clasped Robert Johnson's hand and whispered in his ear, "You have to find someway to tell Edward Adams about your Rachmaninoff visit."

Chapter 2

The audience was reluctant to leave. All knew how special this night had been and the atmosphere had been electric. Slowly the Concert Hall emptied except in one of the side halls where a special party for the donors, principles and especially Gustavo and Ed was forming. Ed had Julia at his side as they began their mingling with the over two hundred invited guests.

Outside, in the hall near the entrance, Robert was waiting for Sandra to return from the Ladies Room. They were hoping to find a way into the party and make their introduction to Ed. Then Sandra showed up with an rather portly, finely dressed and bejeweled elderly lady hanging onto her arm who was talking non-stop. A quick introduction to Robert and they had been invited by Margret Markum to be her guests.

"What a sweet lady you are to help me out. I can't thank you enough." She spoke quickly to Sandra and then looking at Robert continued, "What a handsome man you have, my dear. You better hang on to him tight. There are a lot of us lonely widows in here." She steered them into the gathering and to Sandra and Robert's relief Margret was quickly surrounded by a number of others and whisked away. Margret Markum was one of the dozen two hundred to five hundred thousand dollar donors.

It was a large room and nicely furnished with a number of comfortable chairs, all of which were occupied. In one corner was a Steinway Parlor Grand piano. Ed had seen it immediately and was trying to guide himself and Julia in that direction. He had already had as many congratulations as he wanted but knew it was important to graciously accept every one with a smile and a thank you. Once they got near the piano they saw an elderly lady seated in a wheel chair next to it seeming to be half asleep. Julia knelt down and took her hands in hers, introducing her to Ed as she looked up and smiled.

"Edward Adams, my goodness you can certainly play Rachmaninoff. I knew him, you know," was said with a sparkle in her gray eyes. "I was fifteen years old the last time I saw him. It was in the Fall in 1942. My father was an auto mechanic and took care of his cars. He was also a pretty good pianist in his own right. They were friends and we were often invited to his house. One time Vladimir Horowitz was there. Mr. Rach, as I called him, had two Steinway Concert Grands in his living room and they would play having competitions with each other."

Wilma Herman leaned back in her chair, closed her eyes for a moment then was back. "It was such a good time. He would have liked the way you played tonight. Let me see your hands."

Ed placed his hands in hers and she massaged them and smiled. "Almost as big as Mr. Rach's. Show me a few elevens," nodding toward the piano.

Ed moved to the bench, arranged the seat and demonstrated several leading into them with the more familiar passages. The room went quiet. "That was well done Edward Adams. Well done! A twelve?" was asked for and Ed complied. "You cheated using the pedal and an extra touch but well done anyway." Ed took a closer look at Wilma, gave her a smile and said, "You do know a lot about playing a piano."

Wilma smiled back, then looking at Julia asked, "You are Julia Renquest, aren't you?" again closing her eyes, then opening them wide and asking, "Would you sing *The Way We Were* for me?"

Ed picked up on this immediately and Julia sang the song with his accompaniment. As they finished most of the party had grouped around and Wilma made another request, *The First Time Ever I Saw Your Face.*

After they finished Wilma smiled but had tears in her eyes. "Mr. Rach died a few months after my last visit, in 1943. He was already sick then but never let us know until near the end. He was such a nice man. He would have liked you Edward Adams. He would have liked the way you play his music."

Ed was saying his thanks when a young woman came up and told Wilma it was time to go and that the van was waiting. "I know, I know. Just when I am beginning to have a good time with these nice people I have to go home. Thank you two for being here. Memories are what I have left and you brought back some of my best ones." Julia gave her a kiss on the cheek, Ed took her hands in a gentle squeeze and then Wilma Herman was wheeled out of the room.

Sandra and Robert had watched this and after hearing most of the conversation approached Ed and Julia introducing themselves. It was Julia that recognized their names.

"You two wrote the "Visiting History" stories. The TV series is Grandfather's favorite. We watched all of them, two or three times. It is a pleasure to meet you," Julia saying this as the four of them sought a more private space.

Sandra lead the conversation that she thought they may have some mutual interests that might be enjoyable to follow up on. She mentioned that Robert had written the first three manuscripts of the first season before she joined him and that Ed might enjoy how he researched and wrote the Rachmaninoff visit. When Julia and Ed found out they were on their forty-seven foot sailboat at the California Yacht Club in Marina del Rey for the next week they agreed that it would be a nice place to meet and would like to accept. The weekend brunch at the club at 11:00 am and a lazy afternoon on board was arranged for the coming Sunday. If the weather was nice maybe a short sail would be possible.

Chapter 3

It was well passed midnight by the time Ed and Julia were snuggled up in their bed at the hotel. Both were tired but wide awake from the excitement of the evening. Ben and Jennifer Shea, Julia's grandfather and his wife, had headed home to Palm Desert. Their son and daughter, BJ and Jan, made the short trip back their college condo at UCLA. Ed and Julia were in no hurry to make the trip back to their home, also in Palm Desert. They had first met there some twenty-eight years ago. Julia was living at her grandfather's house and it would become their home as well as their romance matured. Much had happened in their lives before that time that guided them to meet, fall in love and then eventually arrive at where they were now.

Ed was thinking how good he felt at this moment. He had played Rachmaninoff the best he had ever done and Gustavo and the L A Phil had out done themselves. Julia looked at Ed, smiled and speaking in a whisper asked, "What are you thinking? You can't look at me like that without telling me what is going on in that handsome head of yours."

"I shall have to be very careful about this," he started and then continued, "I am happy. Much happier than just satisfied. It comes when you are successful in having done what you have wanted to do and have the one person you want to be with when it happens next to you. I think I touched the stars tonight."

Julia sat up saying, "I like that! Touching the stars. Do you remember the first time I kissed you. You know, the day we met and what happened a few days later?" Her smile got even bigger and she repeated her question "Do you?"

"How could I forget the best day of my life. Seeing you for the first time putting a golf ball with an antique golf club on the carpet in the back of the Golf Museum. Meeting your Grandfather and Little Willy after buying the Cornith golf clubs from Harriet, pretending to be Morris's wife at her supposed garage sale. Dinner at Pedro's that night. You first taking my hand as we walked to your grandfather's house and then outside the door pulling my head down and kissing me and saying, 'Don't you dare break my heart' as you turned away, going inside and leaving me alone on the porch."

"I think that maybe you do remember that just the way I do. And two days later something else happened and this time you don't have to tell me about it as showing me will be much better."

Ed did her bidding which made him think that he had finished the evening quite satisfactorily. The requested encore was decided to be done later, but not to be forgotten.

The next morning they found an envelope placed under the door and in it was an invitation to have lunch at Wilma Herman's at eleven that morning. She had something she wanted to show Ed and more to tell them about her visits with Mr. Rach. Ed called the number, accepted the invitation, got the address and confirmed the time.

With a few hours to spare and no need to hurry, they took a short walk around the Walt Disney Concert Hall. It was a strange looking building but it did hold a magnificent hall. They packed their small suitcase and hanger bag, checked out and put the bags in their 2010 Porsche Panamera S. Ed's much beloved 1959 Porsche Coupe was left at home now days as it had become a collectors item and too valuable to risk in other than short drives around Palm Desert. It seemed getting two sets of golf clubs and enough luggage to do overnight golf outings was more trouble than when they had been younger.

Chapter 4

As Ed started the Porsche, adjusted his seat belt and checked the mirrors, Julia entered Wilma's address in the navigation system. She seemed to be able to do it faster than Ed and seldom made a mistake or end up in something other than navigation. The friendly voice gave the first instruction as they exited the underground hotel parking garage. They would arrive in thirty-two minutes at 11:00 am.

Almost exactly on time, they came to near the end of La Collina Drive and to the left were confronted by a weathered wooden gate, covered in vines, that looked like it hadn't been opened in over ten years. Just as they stopped it swung open and Ed drove very slowly down the narrow lane, almost overgrown with trees, that appeared to end at the foot of the front porch stairs of a small California bungalow. Half the front steps were covered by a wheel chair ramp and on the porch was Wilma Herman, supported by a walker, waving a welcome. To the right was a van and room for one car which Ed turned into.

"You are on time! How nice. You must have one of those navigating things or it would have taken you a lot longer," Wilma said in such a welcoming way that Ed and Julia were both sure this was going to be time well spent with someone worth spending it with.

A hug for Julia and grasping of hands for Ed got things started.

"I am so glad you could come over this morning. Every morning counts for me now when you know there aren't going be many more left. Cindy is in the kitchen preparing lunch. She is such sweet heart. I'm so lucky to have her with me," Wilma was saying this with such enthusiasm that it set up what was to come next. "The only way to surprise you is to invite you in. Come with me!"

She turned and adroitly managed with her walker through the front door and moved to one side. Julia stepped in first and exclaimed, "Oh my! Ed look at that!" Ed was just behind and was caught speechless by what he saw. Filling the entire living room was a huge, ornate and glistening Model D Steinway Concert Grand Piano. In beautiful high gloss rosewood it's eight foot nine inch length left just enough space to walk around it. There was no other furniture, other than the piano bench, in the room. Wilma was almost dancing with the excitement of sharing this magnificent piano with some one who played as Ed did. It was a New York build of 1896 and denoted as a Victorian Fancy D.

Julia stood next to Wilma with her arm around her as Ed slowly began his inspection. The lid was up and looking down over the golden frame, pin block, strings and the action was always a thrill and this piano did not disappoint. He let his hand slide along the case, the cool smooth feeling of it's surface making it seem almost alive. The legs were huge and carved in ornate Victorian style.

Even the pedal arbor was ornate. It was probably the most beautiful piano Ed had ever seen.

Completing his circle he moved the bench back and sat down. The keys were ivory and in superb condition. He turned and looked at Wilma.

"Go ahead. Maybe start half through Paganini, including Variation 18 of course, will do for right now," Wilma spoke as if she would love what she knew she would soon hear.

Ed started with Variation 16 and played through to the end. He adjusted to playing solo in a small space and the sound and tone was perfect. Cindy had quietly brought in two chairs from the dining room for Wilma and Julia who sat close together holding hands. It was a wonderful few minutes and Variation 18 is so well known that even those having no interest in classical music would always recognize it. It was universal and Ed played it as it should be played.

"Let's have lunch, talk a bit and then Ed could play a little more Rachmaninoff if he wishes. I usually tire out by two o'clock so let's plan on that."

Cindy had prepared a salad with broiled salmon steak, asparagus tips and french bread. White wine was offered and a small glass each poured. It was simple but excellent. The conversation was likewise. First was about how the piano had gotten there.

It was a story Wilma loved to tell. She first told how her family came to be in Los Angeles. Her parents were German and her father was working in Russia when she was born in 1927. As the mid 1930s approached the stirrings in Germany had started and his boss at the time suggested that he get himself, his wife and daughter out of Russia, and not return to Germany. The company he was working for had a connection to one in Los Angeles and they arranged for them to immigrate. The move went well but the job didn't.

Her father could build and fix almost anything so they settled in this little bungalow and he worked out of the small garage in back of the house. His reputation grew and when Rachmaninoff first visited the area and his car had broken down a few blocks down the street he was told to seek out her father. He could speak Russian, fixed his car and they were close friends from then on. Ernst Herman, the son of one of his friends, met Wilma and that was that. They had no children but it had been a good and exciting life. Ernst was just like her father and they worked together. Ernst had passed away five years ago.

The piano had arrived in pieces and disrepair in 1941 having been bought on a whim by Rachmaninoff and was placed were it now is to do the renovation. It was almost finished when he passed away in March, 1943. It seemed no one in the Rachmaninoff group had any interest in it so they just told her father to keep it. It took over ten years to complete the renovation as World War II had taken it's toll on most things. It now stands right where it was when Ernst had it finished. It had never been moved.

"What a lovely story that is, Wilma. Did any of Rachmaninoff's family or friends ever see it as it is now?" Julia asked.

"Only twice and it was Vladimir Horowitz that came by. It was in the early 1970s. He was famous by then and very busy. According to him, Mr. Rach had asked him to go see what it looked like and to see if any progress was being made on the restoration. It was on his to do list and years later he called one day and asked if he could come over for a look. He only stayed a few minutes but played it and said how very pleased Mr. Rach would have been."

Wilma then continued by describing Horowitz's second visit. "Can you imagine a dozen people in the house with great music played. Horowitz was, of course, the center of attention. His group of friends stayed all afternoon and into the evening. They had brought wine and picnic food and the music was all Rachmaninoff. It was so much fun. He never came back but for Ernst and I it was a highlight of our lives. I can remember every detail like it was just yesterday that it happened."

"Mr. Rach, his wife Natalia, and their daughters Tatianna and Irina, always treated us like friends. We were friends," she whispered as tears came down her cheek.

The early afternoon shadows were showing. Ed played several more of his favorite Rachmaninoff themes and then it was time for them to leave. Plans were made for another visit soon. Ed and Julia had another important person in their lives and were looking forward to developing a friendship with this lovely lady that would become a part of their future.

Chapter 5

They had made the trip from Palm Desert to Marina del Rey in just under three hours and were waved in by the attendant at the gate to the guest parking area of the California Yacht Club. The traffic on Sunday morning was not bad until they reached the last twenty miles. Then it was stop and go for a while but tolerable. Ed thought he would never want to live in this area unless he could see the Pacific Ocean from his house and then would never leave home.

The trip back to Palm Desert after leaving Wilma Herman's place had been just the reverse, and home sweet home never felt better. It was actually Julia's grandfather's house with the later addition of their house next door. It was purchased in the Spring of 2000 by Ed and Julia, just after the birth of their twins. A boy and a girl both so smart and good looking that it would seem to to be unfair to the rest. It was the Spring of 1994 when Ed met Julia. He was unemployed, lonely and could be described as a lost soul. He was a Junior at Stanford attending on a golf scholarship, majoring in mathematics, when his parents were taken from him in a horrific car accident. He gave up all he was doing, including his first love of playing classical piano. Only happenstance had him find and purchase a set of unusual golf clubs at a garage sale while in Palm Desert which lead him to what became his future and gave real meaning to his life.

At that time Julia was living with her Grandfather during a break from attending UCLA where she was studying for an advanced degree in International Studies. On that special day she was tending the Golf Museum at the College Golf Center when Ed had stopped in to look around. Julia had also been dealt a serious blow to her life earlier, loosing first her mother to breast cancer and then a year later her grandmother to the same disease.

Their meeting was accidental but the golf clubs were not. Julia's grandfather and several other elderly friends of the late Morris Cornith, who had designed and built the clubs, had promised his widow they would try to find a golfer that could use them such that his efforts could be recognized. Ed and Julia found true love that day, and the small group of Morris's friends helped Ed make it onto the PGA Tour. A number of top ten finishes did get the Cornith name known but it was the discovery of the lost putter that made the name known with TaylorMade buying the production and sales rights.

As playing the Tour began to wear on Ed and Julia the revelation of Julia's singing talents and Ed returning to his musical skills on the piano had them begin a new career together as entertainers. It had brought fame and wealth well beyond their needs. This had then allowed Ed to get back to his classical music. His playing with the L A Phil three days ago placed him at the pinnacle of con-temporary concert pianists and another of his life's goals had been accomplished.

As they approached the steps leading up to the California Yacht Club's main floor and dining room Sandra was there and greeted them at the entrance. Ed took a second look, as did Julia. She was a remarkably good looking woman. Maybe an inch taller and a few years younger than Julia, with shoulder length light brown hair. Her eyes were brown with flecks of gold and her complexion clear and tanned. Dressed in soft colored slacks, shirt and jacket she and Julia, also nicely attired, looked like runway models as they crossed the floor.

Robert greeted them at a window table set for four and stood for a handshake with each. He too was handsome, about ten years Ed's junior, had a good smile and a pleasant demeanor. They settled into their chairs and the server arrived promptly with the menus. The Belgian waffles topped with fresh fruit and powdered sugar was the choice of each and orders were placed. Fresh orange juice followed by coffee made the order simple and it was quickly served.

The view was over a field of boats, most of which were sailboats. Robert pointed out their boat, a forty-seven foot Tartan with *Du-eT* on the transom. They settled into a comfortable conversation and soon the meal was finished. The dining room was not crowded and they were not rushed so they enjoyed a second cup of coffee and more talk.

After a quick visit to the restrooms they slowly wandered down to the dock level and onto to the dock where *Du-eT* was tied up. As they approached the boat Julia had taken Ed's hand, started smiling and turned to him. "Does this bring back any memories?" she asked in a way Sandra and Robert knew they were included in what Ed's answer might be.

They had just reached the stern which had the big letters spelling *Du-eT* and Ed stopped to answer. "Just after we had left a meeting with Laura McKenny and Lalo Schifrin at the Rusty Pelican, in Newport Beach, Julia and I took a walk along the docks. Laura was an agent and Lalo a music director, conductor and pianist that we were meeting to see if we should become entertainers. It was the beginning of Julia Renquest with Edward Adams. Julia spotted a yachting poster showing a beautiful boat underway with sails full. The couple at the helm could have been the two of you. Julia said something like it would be fun to do but there wouldn't room for a piano and I suggested that an electronic keyboard would work just fine. That was in the fall of 1994 and here we are about to step aboard that beautiful boat."

Sandra smiled a smile that was something very special. "What a nice story. Welcome aboard *Du-eT,*" was said as she stepped aboard and offered a hand to Julia. Ed followed and Robert then stepped on board. Once in the cockpit they shared looks and it was obvious to each some kind of special relationship was forming. The possibility of a good friendship was in the air and it was a nice feeling to have on a beautiful day in beautiful Marina del Rey.

Chapter 6

They sat in the cockpit on comfortable cushions. There was enough breeze to cause some singing in the shrouds and occasionally a clank or clink would sound. Ed could almost visualize an orchestra of sorts trying, not successfully, some type musical score. The sun felt good and they were relaxed.

Robert finally spoke to the purpose of their invitation. Ed could sense a change in his demeanor and also could see an appearance of concern on Sandra's face as she looked his way.

"Ed, hearing you play Rachmaninoff Thursday made me think I must tell you of my visit with him. That maybe a strange thing to say but four weeks ago I received three CDs from a friend telling me to enjoy them and if I wished I could share them with others. I was to be careful and not let it go any farther than just entertainment for close acquaintances."

Ed and Julia were unsure of what Robert was trying to tell them but waited for what would be next. Sandra watched the three of them and then gave Robert a nod that he should go ahead with his story. She reached behind her and then placed a beautiful bound leather presentation notebook on the cockpit table facing Ed and

Julia. On it's cover in gold embossed lettering was:

Visits to History as it Happened

Abraham Lincoln, November 18, 1863

Leonardo da Vinci, April 29, 1519

Sergei Rachmaninoff, March 22, 1943.

By

Robert Johnson

Robert opened it to about two thirds into the pages and then showing it to Ed and Julia. The title was *A VISIT WITH SERGEI RACHMANINOFF.*

"This is the manuscript for the third episode of the Visiting History series. I wrote this in the two weeks following my visit on the evening of Sunday May 24, 2015. You can take a quick look but what I want is for you to hear is on one of the CDs I have below. It takes exactly thirty minutes and I think you will find it of interest."

They went below and sat around the salon table. Robert had a portable CD player on the table and took a CD from it's slip case and showed it to Ed and Julia. In felt tip ink was printed *Rachmaninoff - March 22, 1943.* He inserted it in the player and touched the play button. A raspy, annoyed and accented voice said, "Who are you!"

Then Robert's voice said, "Mr. Rachmaninoff, my name is Robert Johnson and I am visiting you from seventy-two years in the future."

"You're what! Is this some kind of joke! I am dying and you are from the future. Go away!"

Robert stopped the CD and paused. Ed and Julia sat transfixed, not knowing what to think or say. Sandra smiled. She had heard it played through twice and had known for over seven years what it was and what her roll was in why it had happened.

"That is Rachmaninoff speaking, translated into English and speaking to me as if I was actually there in person. I can't tell you how it was done but I was there. March 22,1943." Robert said this in a manner that Ed and Julia would have to believe it to be true. It suddenly became very quiet below, even the outside noises seemed to have diminished.

Robert then touched the play button again and his conversation with Rachmaninoff continued. It included him telling Rachmaninoff of the ending of World War II, his compositions still being the most popular of works played throughout the world by the best symphonies, and that Russia now claimed him as their own. He kidded him about his height and his dower demeanor when he was in public. He told him about all the books, films and stories about him. His helping Igor Sikorsky keep his company going. He asked him about his cars, his fast driving and his Villa Senar in Lucerne, Switzerland. Also about the two Steinway Grand Pianos downstairs in his living room and his relationship with Vladimir Horowitz.

Part of the conversation about Horowitz was Rachmaninoff saying, "We became best friends. He can play my third piano concerto better than I can. I love the man."

Near it's end after Robert had told him, at his request, how long he had to live, he said, "You're an honest man, Robert. I appreciate that. This has been the best thing, this visit, that has happened since I found out I was going to die. Thank you for stopping by." There was a pause and then it was over.

No one spoke. Ed and Julia were stunned. It seemed it couldn't be real but there was no reason that Robert would be trying to deceive them. They had seen the TV production several times and the CD followed the script exactly. Or more accurately the TV script followed what they had just heard exactly.

Ed was first to speak. "That was Rachmaninoff? You know that except for a very short take added to an old home movie film there are no recordings of Rachmaninoff speaking."

"This was translated into English from Russian as Rachmaninoff preferred speaking in his native language," answered Robert and then adding, "Technically it is as it would have sounded if he had been speaking English. Don't ask me how it was done."

Julia then asked "Did you also visit Lincoln and da Vinci? Did you go there, too?"

"Yes," and a frightened look came over Robert's face.

Julia then asked in a whisper, "What happened?"

Chapter 7

There was an awkward silence. What had been an exciting revelation of an unbelievable adventure by one there was now a quiet that none of the new acquaintances knew how to handle.

Sandra solved the problem. "Go ahead Robert, tell them. All of it."

Robert hesitated, took in a deep breath, and spoke slowly. "It started the late afternoon of my last day at my apartment in San Francisco. I had lost my job with a high tech start up company. My stock options were worthless and the love of my life had left me," saying this last in almost a whisper while looking at Sandra. She smiled back at him with a loving look and reached for his hand.

"I had dropped my iPad from the balcony a few weeks earlier and had bought a replacement on an eBay auction which had just been delivered the day before. The last thing I did in the apartment was to set it up and when I had that finished a strange icon appeared in the lower right hand corner. I touched it and on a dark gray screen was, in blood red italics, you have the chance to visit history as it happens, do you have the courage to go there. I touched the enter button and a legal agreement of half a dozen pages came up. I read it, twice, and just above the agree button was a box asking for questions. I typed in that I was interested and could I have some time to think it over. Five days came up and then the screen went blank."

Robert stopped and his tanned face had lost most of it's color. Sandra looked as if she was about to cry and held his hand even tighter. "Go ahead, Robert. It was the last of the three visits that they need to know about now. Rachmaninoff. The rest you can tell them later."

"The next day, unplanned, I ended up in Point Reyes Station running a gas station for two weeks and staying in a small house provided by the owner. Online, before the five days were up, I agreed to their terms and a demonstration visit of their choosing was offered." Robert got this out but he was now struggling with the words. "It was a surprise ten minute visit with my parents on my first day at MIT. A few years after this my mother died from cancer and later my father lost his life in a mountain climbing accident. I was alone and didn't really care about what might happen. I even thought it may be a clever hoax of some kind. It wasn't. It was so real and was exactly as it had happened. It was an experience I will never forget. I then agreed to make the visits which would be of my choosing."

Sandra had teared up and looked like she might not be able to bear what was coming next. She gave Roberts's hand another squeeze. "Tell what happened when you came back from the Rachmaninoff visit. That will be enough for now," Sandra said this with such emotion that Ed and Julia didn't know how to react.

"The first two trips were truly magnificent, as was the one with Rachmaninoff. It was coming back from the hypnotic state they put me in that was the problem. Coming back from the Lincoln visit it was just noticeable. A little light headed, just feeling uneasy and a hint of nausea. Back from da Vinci it was worse and I felt when I first stood up I might fall, having to grab my chair for support. It took 15 minutes for me to feel good enough to stand. Coming back from Rachmaninoff was very bad. I almost couldn't move without thinking I would pass out. I felt I had lost complete control of my senses. I was truly scared that I wouldn't be able to come back to be myself. It was several hours before I completely recovered and I knew then that would be my last visit."

Robert had to stop at this point. He was reliving this again and was having trouble speaking. Sandra finished for him. "He did come back as you can see. The group of anonymous scientists, six of them, all agreed three trips were all that were safe. That they had all the information they needed to validate their program. They then told Robert he had been their only traveler. There was more for him of course, and then for me, as they set up the Visiting History TV series. We wrote the fictional visits based on the model of the three actual visits."

Again there was a lull in the conversation. Ed's curiosity overcame his hesitancy so he offered, "Robert, I would like to know more. A lot more. Not just about Rachmaninoff, which really intrigues me, but about you and Sandra."

Sandra answered first, "We are taking the boat back to San Francisco next week. Probably leaving Thursday morning. Would you and Julia like to join us. It may take five days, or a few more depending on the weather.

We don't like to be out in bad conditions and try not to be out overnight. You can disembark at almost any port along the way, get a one-way car rental and be back here to your car in a few hours."

Julia didn't hesitate. "That would be fun Ed! Let's do it. You have some free time now and it would be a good break after the last few months."

Ed thought it over and quickly agreed. They asked what they would need to bring on board but Robert and Sandra left it pretty much to tooth brushes and some warm clothes. They had extra foul weather gear and they were similar enough in size for it to fit them. They could leave their car in the Club's parking lot and get the one-way rental in San Francisco for the return.

It was time for Ed and Julia to head home and Robert and Sandra walked them to their car. Hand shakes and hugs were exchanged. The prospect of a new adventure, with new friends, was in the air with all the excitement that it implied.

Chapter 8

Even though Ed knew better, he commented on the light traffic. And then before he even finished the thought the Los Angeles's afternoon ritual drive began. Over an hour to go twenty-five miles before the traffic again lightened up enough to relax and a conversation could be comfortably carried on.

"They are not that much younger than us. Not enough to make much of a difference as far as being able to share in likes and dislikes," Julia said somewhat hesitatingly, then continued, "I feel pretty comfortable being with them. Not thinking anything unwanted will happen if we spend a week or so on the boat."

Ed answered, "I was thinking about that too, at least a little. I think it will work out just fine. What I was really thinking about just now was the day we met up with Laura McKenny and Lalo Schrifin at the Rusty Pelican in Newport Beach and our drive back to Palm Desert."

Julia's face brightened with a smile. That had started five whirlwind years in the entertainment world until the twins were well underway. About a year was taken off for maternity and was followed by three years making more recordings and having several big concerts. This had set them up for life as far as finances were concerned and they decided that they had enough of that world. Parenting came next and then Ed began his turn toward his desired objective of classical piano.

Julia started to laugh and reaching over gave Ed a friendly punch in the ribs. He liked it when she did it as it often was the start of a little more rough housing. It brought a wave of other good memories and pretending to concentrate on driving he allowed them to flow through his mind for a few minutes.

Julia knew what was going on with Ed's silence as she was having the same thoughts. Their life, since they had first met, had been so good she could hardly believe it could of happened the way it had. Love at first sight. The excitement of professional golf set around a bunch of special golf clubs, designed and made by an old friend of her Grandfather, that only Ed could use. Finding the lost putter that could be used by others and the production and sales rights sold to the TaylorMade golf company. At that exact time, through another chain of circumstance, having Ed reunited with his love of the piano and her finding her talents as a singer and entertainer. Both had been set aside in similar ways and they had come back together to provide them years of fun and fame. The birth of their twins, now in college, having success and the promise of happy lives to live. They had consumed much of her and Ed's time early on but have lives of their own to live without needing much of their time. Ed then reaching the pinnacle as a concert pianist just at the right time. Now Wilma Herman and Robert and Sandra, with their extraordinary connections to Rachmaninoff had come into their lives.

Ed had glanced at Julia several times and finally said, "We have had a wonderful time together, haven't we? I think something is about to happen which may add even more excitement to our lives. Something involving Robert and Sandra. Something to do with Rachmaninoff. Do we want to go there? Should we go there?"

Julia looked at Ed for a few moments and slowly replied, "I don't know. Something really strange happened, first with Robert, and then later including Sandra. I think on the boat trip we will find out and I am not sure I will want to go there. Even not knowing where there is yet."

Chapter 9

Sandra and Robert walked back to the boat holding hands. It was always nice approaching *Du-eT* along the dock as their side tie gave them the stern view with the original name which they had kept. Sandra had been the owner for several weeks in a convoluted way as had the previous owners. The first owner was Conrad Engstrum who had been Robert's boss during the one year his technology company had been in business. When a fatal flaw was discovered in what they were developing, Engstrum Technologies collapsed. This left Robert nearly broke, unable to keep his apartment and Sandra deciding crewing for Conrad on his new Tartan 4700 might be more secure than staying with him. Without the apartment her job with the bank was in jeopardy as she couldn't afford, by herself, even a small place in San Francisco. She knew it was selfish on her part but Conrad, who was gay, had always treated her properly, almost like a father.

The original plan was for a experimental cruise up the coast towards Alaska and if that proved successful an around the world adventure was possible. The onset of Conrad's pancreatic cancer changed everything and his sudden death, just short of their reaching Alaska, found Sandra bequeathed *Du-eT.* Robert by this time had made his three trips to visit history and had written what would become the first episodes of the Visiting History television series. Sandra had called him for help and he was by her side two days later. They handled Conrad's affairs in Campbell River, British Columbia and Sandra found out about her ownership of the Tartan there. A couple by the name of Jackson, who had wanted to buy *Du-eT* when Conrad purchased it, were willing buyers and an immediate sale was made. Robert and Sandra were back together bonded even closer than before by these events and started co-writing the television series which was both enjoyable to do and eventually brought them significant income. A little less than five years later *Du-eT was* back on the market and they purchased her from the Jacksons in Hawaii.

Robert let Sandra board first as he always did. He enjoyed watching her take the big first step aboard, then two more into the cockpit. She always ran her hand over the wheel in a caress that indicted that she was the master of this big boat. And she was. Robert could manage the helm and sails but the true sailor was Sandra. It did not bother him in the least and what she had brought to him in life he could only try to repay in kind.

"Robert, let's go below so we can talk in private. I want to know how you feel about having Ed and Julia with us on returning to San Francisco. We need to make sure this will turn out right." Sandra said this without any doubt in her voice and Robert knew exactly what she was asking of him. They went below, getting themselves comfortable on the settee.

Chapter 10

"Robert, you know me, all about me. My childhood. What I went through that has me now sitting here with you. You know I want no more from life than what I have now. What happened two years ago as we approached San Francisco after our crossing the Pacific from Hawaii was one of the most exciting adventures one could have in life. However, I don't think I want to do anything like it again. Meeting Ed and Julia and the chance of a new friendship is something I value. But the combination of your visit with Rachmaninoff and Ed's becoming one of the premier concert pianist of his music has me thinking that John is going to be involving us in another adventure. If his group is still operational in visiting the past program he wouldn't be able to resist another visit to Rachmaninoff and that would involve Ed Adams." Sandra fell silent and waited for Robert to respond.

"I really like them both. Nice people with such talent. They are about ten years older than we are but that has no bearing on a relationship. I understand what you are saying and think you may be right. We will just have to see what happens and decide on how to handle it if it does. John must be in his seventies and the other five are some where near that too. I don't want to go back in time again and I can't imagine Ed or Julia would want to. They have too much to lose. I didn't the first time with my three visits. John sent us back and then convinced us of the possibility of exploring the San Francisco Peninsula, and it's earliest inhabitants, 10,000 years ago. I don't think he would try something like that again. We will just have to wait and see."

They sat looking at each other for a few moments and then broke into smiles. Sandra spoke first, "It was some kind of three weeks, wasn't it."

Robert's phone then played his incoming call melody and he answered with a concerned look on his face and then realized it was Ed Adams.

"Hello, Ed. Seems like almost thirty minutes since I last saw you and Julia. You didn't leave her here did you?"

"No chance of me ever doing that. In fact, Julia is setting up a visit with Wilma Herman, the elderly woman we met at the after concert party. We were talking with her when you and Sandra came up and we met. We are planning to visit her Thursday morning before we show up at your place. She knew Rachmaninoff when she was a young girl and would love to hear the CD you have of your conversation with him. She lives less than an hour from Marina del Rey and we could pick you up first. We plan to be at her place at eleven o'clock. Cindy, her helper, would prepare a lunch for us and we would need to leave about two as she naps about that time. You and Sandra will love her, she has a Steinway Grand piano in her living room and you will get some entertainment. Would that work with your schedule?"

Sandra could hear the entire conversation and was nodding her head in the affirmative. Robert was just as enthusiastic and answered that it would be a great way to spend the day. All would be ready for the early Friday morning departure so that would be no problem.

Julia took over the phone and had just started her conversation with Wilma and Ed could hear the excitement in her voice. The time and date was set, Cindy would fix lunch and the piano bench would be in place.

Julia finally broke the connection and a few tears showed on her cheeks. "What a precious lady she is. Our grandmother. Part of our family now."

On board *Du-eT* Sandra looked at Robert and whispered, "It has started. I am sure it has started."

Robert answered, "You are right about that. I am ready, are you?"

"Yes!" Sandra said with no doubts in her voice.

Chapter 11

As Ed maneuvered the Panamera through the entry gates of the California Yacht Club he remarked to Julia that it had just been a week ago that they were in their hotel room readying for an early lunch, preparing his being the featured pianist for the opening concert of the Los Angeles Philharmonic season. He was smiling and she gave him a light punch in the ribs. "You do make my life most interesting, Edward Adams. How do you do that?" It was a question she knew wouldn't be answered but was amazed on how it seemed to be a never ending series of pleasant surprises.

Robert and Sandra were standing in front of the entrance to the Club so Ed wheeled up to it and stopped. Robert opened the rear passenger for Sandra and she entered and was buckled in and had the door closed by the time Robert had settled into the seat behind Ed. They were exiting the gate by the time he had his seat belt fastened and had set his brief case behind him in open area of the hatch back.

"This is a Porsche sports car? I don't think I have ever sat in a seat this comfortable," was Robert's greeting to Ed and Julia. They laughed at this and Ed mentioned it was a luxury sedan that had a four hundred horse power engine and a top speed of 175 miles per hour but that he would cruise along at the speed limit and they should arrive at Wilma's right on time.

They approached the vine covered gate at exactly 11:00 am, it opened and they drove up the tree lined lane to the small California bungalow where Wilma was on the porch, with her walker, to greet them. Julia turned toward Robert and Sandra and said, "Get ready for a very special visit with a very special lady. You are in for a treat."

The greetings were made on the porch and before Robert and Sandra could be introduced to Wilma she started with, "Robert Johnson and Sandra Williams! I am so glad to get to meet you both. I love the Visiting History programs you wrote and I have watched all of them. I didn't get a chance to meet you at the party after the concert last week but I saw you patiently waiting while Ed and Julia charmed me. Have they told you yet that I knew Sergei Rachmaninoff when I was a young girl? No one has ever played two and three better than Ed did that night. Come in, come in," Wilma continued as she led the way.

It was the same for Ed and Julia, and a new experience for Robert and Sandra, as the huge piano glistened, filling the entire living room of the small house. The smile on Wilma's face showed she knew what the sight of this magnificent piano had on every person who was lucky enough to see it. This time she escorted her guests to the small table in the dining room and with Cindy's help her guest were seated. Wilma couldn't suppress her smile and she didn't waste any time. "Julia told me you had a surprise to show me. Let's do that right now! Cindy will then serve lunch after which Ed will play some Rach and then Julia will sing some songs. Is that okay with you two?" she asked addressing Robert and Sandra.

Robert spoke first, "I think that is just what we should do." He placed his brief case on the table, opened it and put the small CD player in the middle of the table. Next he placed the leather covered presentation notebook on the table in front of Wilma. She ran her hands over the fine leather and read the gold embossed titles silently. She then read aloud, "Sergei Rachmaninoff, March 22, 1943." She read it out loud a second time and a few tears rolled down her cheeks. "I knew him, you know. I was fifteen when he died. He was such a nice man. My father met him when he first moved out here to California. He took care of his cars, fixed things around his house and became one of his true friends. Mr. Rach treated us as friends. As family. He was such a nice man." Wilma saying this in almost a whisper, wiped her eyes and fell silent.

Sandra reached over taking her hand with a gentle squeeze. "Robert has something he wants you to hear. He will have to explain what it is and why he has it. When you feel ready he will play it for you."

Robert then picked out the disc that was labeled Rachmaninoff - March 22, 1943 and held it so Wilma could see the inscription. "Wilma, I can't tell you how this happened as I don't how it happened. It did. I visited with Rachmaninoff this day, six days before he died, in the upstairs bedroom at his home in Beverly Hills. You probably know the room, at the top of the stairs when you first reach the landing. How ever it was done I was suddenly in the room looking at him laying in bed. This is the recording of our conversation as it happened. Any time he spoke in Russian it was translated into English and I spoke only in English. I am told his English was exactly as it would sound as if spoken by him. This was used almost word for word in the television production so you have heard it before. But this is Rachmaninoff himself. Are you ready to hear it?"

Wilma was sitting next to Julia on her right and with Sandra on her left still holding her hand. She looked toward Ed and then back at Robert. "Yes," was whispered in answer to Robert's question and he inserted the disc and pressed play.

"Who are you?" were the first spoken words in a raspy, accented voice. Wilma cried out, "That is Mr Rach. Oh my God, that's Mr. Rach!" and her tears started to fall in earnest. Robert quickly touched the pause button.

Chapter 12

Wilma's distress bought an immediate quiet to the room. She was obviously shaken by hearing just those three words. Cindy had come in from the kitchen and put her hand on her shoulder. Wilma reached up with her free hand, covered Cindy's and looked toward her with a loving smile through her tears.

"I am sorry to make such a fuss. Old ladies do that, you know." Wilma then straightened in her seat and with a handkerchief provided by Cindy dabbed her eyes. "That is Mr. Rach speaking. It has been almost eighty years since I heard his voice. He was the first person I knew that died. You will never forget that when it happens. It was hard on all of us. Natalia, and the girls, knew it was coming. My father and mother knew but only told me he was sick. I think the day he died was the saddest day of my life. I couldn't stop crying and here I am crying again."

Robert reached over to touch her arm and said, "We can do this later but there is much you will enjoy and hearing his voice during most of our conversation will be enjoyable. You have heard the words before but these are the ones he spoke."

Wilma smiled, wiped her eye's once more, and nodded her head to go ahead and Robert touched the play button. It was his voice that said the next words as he introduced himself by name and that he was visiting from seventy-two years in the future. Rachmaninoff's fiery response of, "Go away!" brought a chuckle from Wilma and she commented, "That's Mr Rach!"

Wilma had expressed herself several times on how good it was to hear his voice again and how much it meant to her now to hear him talking. As the CD neared it's end and Robert, at Rachmaninoff's request, told him of his final days all around the table grew quiet. Each of them had watched the TV series and all but Wilma and Cindy had heard him say his final words of the visit. "You are an honest man, Robert. I appreciate that. This has been the best thing, this visit, that has happened since I found out I was going to die. Thank you for stopping by."

No one spoke as none could think of what to say. It was Ed that broke the silence. "Robert, this is the second time I have heard those last words. What an honor it is for us to have you share them with us."

Wilma couldn't hide her tears and sat perfectly still as Julia and Cindy tried to console her. She suddenly smiled and commented, "Cindy it is time to feed these people and after you have it set up I would like you to play some Rachmaninoff for us to enjoy while we eat."

Cindy blushed and glancing Ed's way said, "I can't do that!" with Wilma retorting, "Yes you can. You are a much better pianist than you think and it is time for others to know about it."

Cindy scurried off to the kitchen and soon returned with Coquilles St. Jacques served in large scallop shells, sided with fresh garden salads and sliced baguettes. White wine was offered along with tumblers of ice water. Wilma knew already but the others would discover that it would be one of best meals they had ever experienced.

As this very contented group of five new friends took their first taste of this special meal the soft melody of Variation 18 of Rachmaninoff's Rhapsody on a Theme of Paganini drifted into the room. It was followed by half a dozen more Variations followed by Concerto 2 played in a manor to not disturb those at the table but to complement the food. Only Ed Adams had stopped eating so that he could concentrate on what he was hearing.

Chapter 13

The conversation continued at the table. Julia and Sandra shared a few details of their lives and Wilma had a few of her favorite stories to tell. She was describing the visit of Vladimir Horowitz and his friends one afternoon in the late 1970s for a picnic and the playing of her Grand Piano. It was while she was telling this story she saw the expression on Ed's face that let her know he had suddenly recognized what he was hearing being played by Cindy in the other room. A sly smile crossed her face which had nothing to do with the event she was then describing.

Ed had been enjoying the meal as it was spectacular in taste and presentation. It reminded him of a similar one that Julia had prepared for him and her Grandfather early in their courtship. He was also listening to the playing of Rachmaninoff by Cindy when he realized she was playing only parts of the scores. She was leaving out the Russian dynamic scoring playing only major melodies, knitting them together in an almost melancholy way that was so soft to the ear that you wouldn't have noticed if you weren't paying close attention.

Ed finished eating in silence, then excused himself and approached Cindy, stopping first to watch her play. She was in a different world as was her music. The very best of Rachmaninoff with such a soft touch as to be dreamlike. She floated between the melodies in a way that he could only marvel at as she wove together the different compositions of even the most familiar strands. Ed sat down on the piano bench to her right. She turned her head, acknowledged his presence with a weak smile and kept playing. Her eyes were damp and a few tears were sliding down her checks. As she lifted her hands away from the keyboard and looked into Ed's eyes she whispered, "He must have been a kind and loving man. How else could he compose such music? Why did he have to hide so much of it in the grand themes of the concertos?"

She started to stand and Ed asked, "Stay here for just a few minutes. I don't know what has happened in your life to have this talent and to hide it here taking care of Wilma. It is none of my business but I want you to know that Julia and I are becoming family with Wilma and you may be included in that family if you choose. For right now let's keep things as they are. You are too important to Wilma to harm that relationship in any way but I would like you to become part of our life. Will you consider it?"

As if to solve this awkward moment Wilma called out to Cindy that it was time for dessert and nearing the time for her guest to take their leave. Cindy looked again into Ed's eyes and said in a calm voice, "I think you may have come into my life at just the right time. We will see if that is as it should be. Thank you for being here."

Cindy quickly headed for the kitchen and as if by magic small glass dishes of vanilla ice cream topped with chocolate syrup and raspberries arrived. A plate of light cinnamon cookies was passed around.

As they finished the fine dessert Wilma announced it was time for her guests to depart as she was tiring and it was time for her afternoon nap. Hugs and kisses were made on the porch and Wilma was radiant with the happiness of meeting such extraordinary people with such interesting lives. She knew she now had new friendships which would last her through the time she had left. The thoughts of dying alone and having no one to remember her was no longer a concern. As Cindy cleaned up the dining room and kitchen she stated, "They are such nice people. To befriend an old lady in her last years is so nice of them. It is Mr. Rach, you know, that brings us together. It has brought you and Ed Adams together. You mind me now, he is a man worth knowing. He is like Mr. Rach in a way, such a kind man. You already know that, don't you Cindy. I can see it in your eyes."

"Yes Wilma, I think he will help me find a way to have a second chance. To have a family again. Thank you for making it possible." She gave Wilma a hug and Wilma then, using her walker, headed to her bedroom for a much deserved rest.

Chapter 14

As they drove back to Marina del Rey the conversation was light. How much fun Wilma was, Cindy's cooking skills and how well she played the piano. At this last Julia gave Ed a rather long look and he knew she had picked up that something had transpired between them. It would most certainly be discussed tonight when they had some time alone. Ed also wanted to learn a lot more from Robert about his preparation and visit with Rachmaninoff. There was much to be learned and that would happen a few hours after they boarded *Du-eT.*

Sandra asked, her question directed to Julia, if there was anything she or Ed needed to get before they got to the marina. They planned an early morning departure to try to get to Santa Barbara before dark. Nothing could be thought of so they drove straight to the yacht club parking lot. Ed checked about the car, locked the doors and a few minutes later they were on board the elegant Tartan 4700.

They had time before the evening meal for Sandra to give some boating safety instructions to her neophyte crew. Robert brought up the life jackets from the storage locker. These were ocean jackets and Sandra explained their operation in detail. All four were donned and Ed and Julia's adjusted. The Jack lines running along the deck on each side were explained and the tethers were attached to the harness's on each of the jackets. Next, Sandra demonstrated how to attach the tethers to the Jack lines, exit the cockpit and walking about the deck. She spoke clearly to her new crew. "When we are at sea and moving, no one on this boat is to leave the cockpit unless they are tethered to a Jack line. That is a standing order. If the boat is not moving and at least one other person is on watch you may go on deck but you must have your life jacket on. If we are at anchor or docked you may go on deck without the safety gear. Do you understand?" A yes from Ed and Julia was accepted and it was on to other instructions from assisting in docking to operation of the heads.

As dinner time approached a glass of wine and some cheese and crackers were offered and accepted. A nice sunset was appreciated as they sat in the cockpit and as darkness fell they retired to the salon. All four were tired and after canned clam chowder and fresh salad were served, cookies were offered for dessert. Ed caught smiles exchanged between Robert and Sandra and knew that there was some connection to cookies for dessert that they shared. He would ask them about this when the time was right and their answer would turn out to be part of a much larger story.

Ed had noticed a nice small wooden shadow box showing off a simple arrowhead. It was used as a paper weight on the navigation table and he picked it up and asked Robert what it was. He smiled and shared a look with Sandra that made Ed certain it had a much bigger meaning than that of it's size.

"That is an arrowhead I found on a hike we took in the Santa Cruz mountains a few years back. It is estimated to be 10,000 years old and made by a native American Indian. It has great significance for me, and for Sandra. It was made by one of the first inhabitants of North America as they migrated from Eastern Siberia, across the Beringia Land Bridge following the last glaciation. Do you have interest in that period and peoples?" Robert asked this in a manner to find out whether he should continue to tell Ed and Julia about how and when he found the arrowhead or just let the subject die. It was Julia that answered his question.

"I do! I spent an entire semester studying that time and wrote an extensive paper on the subject. It was about the most fascinating subject I studied in college. There is a really good book on the subject, if I remember correctly it was titled The Last Giant Of Beringia. Lots of archae-ology, geology, science and history. Is there a connection to that arrowhead?"

Again Robert and Sandra exchanged looks and Robert answered, "When we are comfortably docked with nothing important to do I will tell you both when, how and where I found that arrowhead. It is best we now turn in and get ready for tomorrow as it will be a long day."

As Ed and Julia got settled in the aft cabin a feel-ing of security in this small space came over them. This was going to be an all new adventure and they were beginning to have confidence a true friendship was de-veloping with Robert and Sandra. It had been an a very nice day. Julia reached over to touch Ed's shoulder and he slid closer to her on the comfortable queen size bed. He kissed her, fluffed his pillow and asked, "Aren't you going to ask me what I was talking to Cindy about when I was with her at the piano?"

Julia gave him the familiar punch in the ribs he was expecting and answered, "Of course I am. What were you up to out there?"

Ed smiled. He and Julia had such a good relationship and were as close now as they were when they first met some twenty-eight years ago. Maybe the youthful passion had lessened just a bit but it was still there. Only rarely were they apart for more than a few days and he always felt that even those days would have been better spent with them together. He knew what he was about to tell her may cause some concern but he was sure she would agree with his thinking.

"Cindy is just about the age of the twins, maybe a few years older. I have no idea what happened to her that brought her to hide from life taking care of an old woman in decline such as Wilma. Something must have happened as she is attractive, smart, an excellent cook and a truly gifted pianist. She also is a kind spirit. What she does with Rachmaninoff amazes me and I have never heard anyone interpret his works the way she does." Ed paused for a few moments as he had arrived where he would have to carefully word what he wanted to say.

"I told her that you and I were finding Wilma to be such a nice person that we wanted to be closer to her. Like becoming a family member. I trust you agree with that. I then told her that we didn't want to in any way jeopardize the relationship she had with Wilma but we would like to include her in that friendship." Ed had to pause again as he had made a very big assumption in using we without confiding with Julia first.

He shouldn't have worried. "Oh Ed, that is so like you. You are the kindest of kind men. Remember when Jennifer, just before she moved in with Grandpa, said you had this special gift of making the lives of others better. That is so true. I can hardly wait to see how Cindy's life will change because of her meeting you through Wilma, the newest member of our family." A very good kiss and embrace was followed by, "Now get to sleep! We have a big day tomorrow."

Chapter 15

Robert and Sandra knew that as they prepared for *Du-eT*'s five o'clock departure their guests would soon be up to help. As Robert brought in the offside fenders and stowed them next to the lifeline stanchions Sandra set up the Chart Plotter and started the engine. She checked the oil pressure and temperature gauges and they looked normal. A quick trip below saw the alternator was charging the batteries as they had brought in the big AC cord and stowed it last night. The electric panel checked out and she was greeted with a good morning from Ed as he entered the salon. Julia was a few steps behind and asked what she could do. All was ready so she lead them up to the cockpit.

Robert had brought in the bow and stern dock lines and looped their coils around the lifelines ready for their next docking. With Sandra behind the wheel she had Robert bring in the forward spring line and slowly reversed the boat making the bow swing away from the dock. Robert freed the aft spring line, told Sandra they were free and she slowly moved *Du-eT* forward. He then pulled up the aft fender and indicated to Ed to do the same with forward one. The middle fender was brought in and the three laid up against the stanchions.

Sandra guided the boat out of the marina harbor into open water and then set the autopilot on the chart plotter putting them on a near westerly path to the first way point, about twenty-one statute miles distance. All could now relax as there was very little boat traffic and the seas were calm. The radar was set at eighteen miles with a warning alarm at five miles but they would be maintaining a visual watch for the entire trip. *Du*-eT would be running at about nine miles per hour over land but when they turned north they would lose about one half a mile an hour due to the southern flowing California Current. The trip mileage to Santa Barbara was about eighty-two miles. They should be there by five o'clock and a reciprocal slip was reserved at the Santa Barbara Yacht Club.

"How about some breakfast up here in the cockpit?" Sandra asked and the crew answered with a resounding, "Yes!"

"We have oatmeal served with brown sugar and coffee. Orange juice will be served first," was Sandra's announcement.

Julia followed Sandra down to the galley and she pulled out the bottle of orange juice and pointed to where the plastic glasses were shelved. She then pulled a container out of one of the lockers and measure out one half cup portions of dry oatmeal in four dishes. Julia looked on some what surprised at this as instant oatmeal seemed a bit simple coming from such a prestigious galley. Hot water was measured and poured over the oatmeal, given one quick stir and then topped with brown sugar. The coffee was in a thermos decanter, cream and sugar placed on the tray with the four cups and the four bowls of oatmeal. Sandra was back up the companion way steps in seconds with Julia following with the orange juices.

They quickly got orientated with Sandra claiming seating that gave her a full view forward and of the instruments. Julia waited as the two men spooned their first portion of the oatmeal and smacked their lips in pleasure. Julia took her first spoonful, smiled to the others and pronounced, "That is the best oatmeal I have ever tasted. Sandra, you will have to tell me where you get this. Just add hot water and it is perfect."

Sandra laughed and looking at Robert responded to Julia's request, "There is a small arrowhead involved in telling where the oatmeal comes from and maybe tonight we will tell you about it."

The day seemed to fly by as far a Ed and Julia were concerned. Around 7:30 am they made the turn to more North and by 10:30 am they passed Santa Barbara Island, the southern most of the Channel Islands, to the port and with Port Hueneme to the starboard. To Julia it was to the west and east but by the time the day neared it's end it was to port and starboard.

Lunch was cheese, cold cuts and crackers. A cold beer for the guys and a glass of white wine for the ladies. They had cookies for a sweet served afterward, again with that knowing smile between Sandra and Robert.

By 3:00 pm they were beginning to prepare for their entrance into the Santa Barbara harbor. The chart plotter showed the entrance in detail and even the location of the side tie dock that was the guest slip for the Yacht Club. It had been a beautiful Southern California day and the seas were quiet with only a slight breeze. If they had been true sailors they would have possibly made the Channel Islands by this time. When time was important, motoring was the way to go. *Du-eT* didn't seem to be offended by this and it had been a very comfortable first day for the newcomers.

Robert announced their arrival to the dock master on the VHF and was welcomed by a friendly voice who offered that the guest dock was open and to tie up as far forward as possible. No other guests were expected for the next few days but leaving room was always a good idea. A roger that and a thank you completed the conversation.

Sandra guided *Du-eT* to the dock and the fenders on the Port side just barely touched it. Robert stepped off the boat with the stern line in hand and made the tie. Ed handed him the bow line and he quickly made it secure. The spring lines were next and in just a couple of minutes they were secure. As Robert stepped back on board he gave Ed and Julia a knowing smile and told them, "It is not always that easy. In fact your first day of cruising has been one of the easiest days I can remember on a boat."

Chapter 16

The weather window showed at least two more days of perfect conditions and the decision was made to spend tomorrow in Santa Barbara and do some sight seeing. They would then make the sometimes hazardous run around Point Conception the following day and try to make it to Moro Bay before dark. Sandra and Robert settled up with Yacht Club for the second night and they had dinner aboard. When the plate of cookies arrived on the salon table the small shadow box holding the arrowhead had been placed in the center.

"I will start our story with how I found my little treasure." Robert said this as he picked up the shadow box and nodded to Sandra. She in turn smiled and laughing, said to Julia and Ed, "Get ready. This takes some getting use to but it happened and this time I was part of it."

Robert started with describing sitting on a rock and with a small twig scratching about in the dirt at his feet. "It was the late afternoon of our second day out and I wanted to have a few minutes by myself so I took a short walk away from the camp. I located an outcropping of rocks and boulders with a good one to sit on. It presented a good view across a valley that extended for miles. Scratching around with the twig up pops this neat little arrowhead. My first thought was that one of the natives, possibly one of those we had seen in the distance that day, may have sat in that very spot and made it. There were chips all around and it was obviously a place some one had sat for hours as he made them."

Robert waited. Both Ed and Julia were thinking about what he had just told them in a rather round about way. Ed was first to comment. "Are you telling us that the arrowhead had been made recently and wasn't ten thousand years old when you found it? Is that what you are saying?" Julia managed a cough and blurted out, "You were there, ten thousand years ago and Sandra was there with you. Your old friend John was there, too?"

They sat around the salon table trading looks. For almost a minute no one said a word. Finally Robert said, "Yes, and yes. It will take a long time to tell the story. We also have some remarkable photos on the iPad to show you. A few Sandra won't let me show but you will find the ones I have picked fascinating. We were back in time for twenty-two days, from July fifteenth to August fifth. When we returned to the present we were at exactly the same place and time as when we went back in time and re-lived those twenty-two days a second time in the present. As John would say, 'Quite a neat trick, don't you think?'"

There was again a prolonged silence as neither Ed nor Julia could think what to say to this and Robert and Sandra realized how impossible it would be for anyone to believe. Robert placed his iPad so they could see the screen and brought up the photo from their approach to the small native village. It was across a golden terrace of wild grasses framed by green shrubs and small trees

leading to a view of the blue Pacific Ocean. In the fore
ground was a small, almost naked native boy frolicking in
the grass and near by a young mother holding a baby.
Next to her was a young man who could only have been
the father. To the opposite side of this beautiful composition were Sandra and Robert, dressed in some type of
outdoor wear, looking at the scene in awe.

Julia was first to comment. "My God, what a beautiful sight. You were there. I can't believe such a place
could exist." She followed with, "I can see why this is going to be so hard for you to tell us but I for one have got to
know the whole story. Please continue!"

Robert and Sandra relaxed at hearing the response
from Julia with Ed nodding his head in agreement. No
doubting or dismissing the possibility of such a thing being possible. A true curiosity and desire to hear every detail. Robert had readied a number of photos to aid in the
telling and the first one he brought up was of Sandra's
look of shock at what she had just seen in front of the
helm. The area was bathed in a mist of green light. "This
is when John arrived on board exactly where and when he
told us he would. He had left his transmission location at
exactly 4:47 pm and was standing, just slightly off balance, in front of the helm at that exact time. The photo of
Sandra on the iPad screen was taken at that moment. John
had traveled back in time ten thousand years.

"Now that is something we will never know how it
was done. Sandra and I met John's five other scientists,
who form the nucleus of this group, but know only their
first names and nothing else about them. It did happen but
even more impressive is how we and the boat were

transported. Sandra was at the helm and I was below taking a nap. It was our fifteenth day out and mid-afternoon when a greenish fog like wall formed in front of of the boat and she called down to me for help. We stood together unable to move. The wind had died down, the boat becalmed and as the wall touched the bow it took on the look of a pane of glass. At the first touch a brilliant green bar, cross way to the center line, moved down the boat, over us, and disappeared off the stern. We didn't feel anything and nothing seemed to have changed. But the sky was a little less blue, the water a bit grayer and it was definitely colder."

"You felt nothing but you were now in an entirely different time. God almighty that is something! What happened then?" was Ed's question but he was asking for much more.

It was Sandra's turn to describe the feelings they both were having at that moment. "I was scared, almost hysterical, but Robert just stood there next to me seeming to be deep in thought. The wind had picked back up, the sails filled and we were again moving. Nothing seemed to have changed but the color of the sky and water were slightly different, as Robert just explained, and it was much colder. Robert had started a call on the VHF and then stopped. I knew at that moment he understood what had just happened. We went below to change into warmer clothes and Robert asked me where we had stored the box of books that the Jacksons had left for us. He found the one he was looking for, titled Hunter-Gathers of Early Holocene Coastal California, and showed me the cover. I knew that era was ten thousand years ago, knew at that moment that was the time we were in and that John, and his group, had transported us there. I didn't want to be there."

Sandra paused for a moment and then inclined her head toward Robert for him to continue. He looked first at Ed and then at Julia. He could see they both were ready for more and said, "John contacted us almost as soon as we had sat down to browse the book. In a matter of minutes we were conversing by voice with him from ten thousand years in the future. I have no idea how this could be done but if they could transport us and *Du-eT* they could certainly make a simple call. I won't go into detail but it didn't take long for John to interest us in what he wanted to do. He gave us time to decide if we wanted to do the exploration. He would join us and provide every-thing necessary for a thirty day stay." Robert smiled at Sandra and continued, "Guess who agreed to go first? I was almost ready to say yes but wavering on whether it was worth the risks. We both said we would do it when he called us back."

Sandra spoke up that she wanted to describe what happened next. "When we agreed John set the time, 4:47 pm exactly, less than an hour later. He would appear in person just in front of the helm. One minute later a large duffel would arrive in the exact same spot. We cleared the bimini and waited. At exactly 4:47, in a green flash, there stood John. He had just enough time to get his balance and receive hugs and handshakes, when the duffel arrived."

Chapter 17

Robert looked at his guests who seemed to be in a trance. He could understand this as to believe what had just been described to them required a suspension of one's own reality.

"Would you like me to continue?" asked Robert in a quiet manner. Both Ed and Julia nodded their head's in the affirmative. "What a story. What happened next?" Julia asked, then added, "Please go on. Fascinating!"

Robert and Sandra shared the next hour describing arriving at the planned anchoring location in the Monterey Canyon with a sixty foot depth. Putting out almost two hundred feet of chain, setting the anchor and readying for up to thirty days on shore. John had thought of everything and told them almost all they needed to know. They would be trekking about one hundred-fifty miles, would carry all they required and had the best in equipment and technology to aid them. The assumption made was that the geography would be about the same so he had modern topographical maps. He would carry one small caliber, collapsible rifle for use only if needed in extreme circumstances. He neglected to tell them of the numerous very small button cameras embedded in their outer wear and caps.

John had spent a good deal of time telling them of the history of the migration from Asia over Beringia, the Bering Land Bridge, as it opened up as the Last Glaciation subsided about twelve thousand years ago. This had been a boyhood interest of his and was still one of his most desired explorations to attain before it was too late for him to accomplish it. None of the other five in his group had any desire to make the visit so he had thought that maybe Robert and Sandra might be interested.

Over the years he had learned some of the modern native languages from the living descendants and hoped that a few words could be understood if they had the opportunity to meet a few of the natives.

"John's excitement was palpable and infected both of us," Sandra said with enthusiasm. "By the time we set off on our first trip to shore Robert and I were just as excited as he was."

It was starting to get late and it had been a long day. Robert offered that maybe it would be a good time to stop and continue the story tomorrow. Ed and Julia showed their disappointment so he offered one more little view of what was in store for them. He looked at Sandra and she smiled, uttered a small chuckle, and said, "It will probably help them sleep better if it is what I think."

Robert touched a few keys on the iPad and a photo lit up the screen. It was of a small pool in the forest with a waterfall cascading over a ten foot cliff into the opal colored water below. There was lush greenery on both sides with several small boulders about and a very small beach in the foreground. Standing with her back turned to the camera was Sandra, sans clothes, her head turned down and to the left. Looking up at her was a very small, dark skinned girl with a woman's body, showing a smile of unmistakable adoration. They stood together, bonded by something only they could know, ten thousand years in time apart.

Julia was first. "That is so beautiful. It is a painting. It can't be real. You have to tell me the story. I can't wait until tomorrow. That wouldn't be fair."

The screen went blank and Robert and Sandra leaned back on the settee cushions and were smiling. Sandra seemed especially moved and a few tears showed themselves. She spoke in a whisper. "That is Meilani. She had given birth to a perfect little girl that morning. I was the midwife and we had bonded. The pool was a short walk from our camp and we were just entering it to bathe. Robert was holding the baby and it was the camera on his cap that took the photograph. I cry every time I see it," and her tears did come.

"We will tell you all about Meilani, her son and husband, the Cotoni tribe and the short time we spent with them tomorrow. It was the highlight of the exploration, for each of us, and lasted only two days. Sandra said it best the night before we left, 'We don't belong here.'"

As Ed and Julia prepared for bed in the aft stateroom he watched as she donned her shorts and T-top. Turning she caught his gaze and smiled asking, "What is my man thinking, now?" Ed answered, "I was picturing you in that pool with the small native girl. It was a beautiful sight which I will keep in my memories for anytime I need a lift in my spirits."

Chapter 18

The next morning breakfast was served in the cockpit. Orange juice, granola with sliced banana, blue berries and raspberries. Coffee followed. It was another brilliant Southern California morning and the conversation flowed effortlessly between these new friends. At first they talked about plans for a walk up State Street and having lunch at one of the restaurants once they reached the pedestrian promenade area. As with most plans they would change and the quiet evening on board discussing Robert and Sandra's trip back in time would have to be delayed.

The walk began a little after ten. It was pleasant as they window shopped along the way and was nearing noon by the time they reached the promenade and started looking for a restaurant. An outdoor table at the Chase Restaurant beckoned them and shortly the guys had their Barbeque Western Burgers and the ladies the Shrimp Caesar Salads. They joked about their choices but were not disappointed. Water was the beverage of choice. The restaurant wasn't crowded so they were able to have a leisurely meal. It was decided that ice cream cones on the way back would suit them for dessert.

As they walked up to the end of the pedestrian area

Julia stopped in front of an empty store front and called Ed over for a look. In the middle of the sizable room was a small grand piano with two men rushing about with polishing cloths doing a thorough dusting. It looked to Ed that it was a Steinway Model C from the 1920s. He had his mother's 1925 in Palm Desert. He couldn't resist and the four of them entered the store. The two men looked up and as if a chorus asked, "What do you want?" then quickly, "We are not open."

Ed pleasantly explained his interest in the Model C and that he owned one. He then clenched the deal when he asked if this was a 1928 to 1930 New York build. The older man straightened up and looked at Ed with a closer stare. He asked, "Do you play? It is a 1928." Ed laughed and replied that he did play a little and Julia tried to hide a grin. Sandra and Robert both did their best not to start laughing.

For a few moments no one spoke. Just when Ed felt they needed to make an exit the older man set his cloth aside and introduced himself as Samuel Barnard, a local representative for Steinway, who worked from his home. The piano had just been restored and brought here for the new owner to hold a christening party for a few hundred of her closest friends. It had just been tuned and was ready to show but he had another big problem. The pianist he had hired had canceled and he had six calls in for a replacement but none had called him back. The party was to start at 5:00 pm and as he was explaining this the caterer arrived with a team of five and started setting up the room.

Samuel Barnard looked at Ed with a almost hopeless expression asked, "Would you like to play something for me."

Ed pulled back the bench and did a few minor adjustments, lifted the fallboard, flexed his fingers a bit and pressed the keys that introduces *Rhapsody In Blue.* The piano was in perfect tune and Ed continued playing for about five minutes. Samuel Barnard was speeches.

Ed looked at Julia, gave her a smile she understood, and they went into their routine with *No Body Does It Better.* Julia had not lost any of her talent as a singer and as the song ended she mussed Ed's hair in their practiced and sexy finish.

"Could I hire you both for four hours, five to nine, with breaks of course, starting at five?" Samuel asked as if his life depended on it. "Name your price as I am desperate," he added almost in tears. Ed took a long look at Julia, then at Sandra and Robert, and all three nodded their heads in approval. Ed looked at Samuel and offered in a serious voice, "Dinner and drinks as served here tonight and a ride to the Yacht Club at the Marina after the party is over!"

Chapter 19

Samuel looked at Ed with disbelief. He had no relationship with God but was sure this group had found their way to him by some kind of divine providence. Just as he was about to speak, Alison Turner made her entrance, as she always did, followed by several women of her age all talking with exaggerated excitement in their voices. Allison Turner was a tall woman, almost six foot, and even in her seventies was a very beautiful lady. Her conservative California slacks and jacket could not cover up a finely tuned and athletic body. Her entourage behind her waltzed about like human butterflies. Her eyes went directly to her newly restored piano and to it she went.

"Oh Samuel, it is beautiful. They did such a good job. I love it! I love it!" She started walking around the piano, letting her hand slide in a caress along the rim. Looking over her shoulder, as if to see if anyone was watching her performance, she saw Ed who was appreciating what he was watching. A stare of a few moments too long and then recognition lit up her face. "Edward Adams, what are you doing here? Samuel, don't tell me he is going to be playing for my guests this evening. There is no way that can be possible. Edward Adams! Samuel?"

Samuel Barnard was now completely in another

world. He had heard the name and read of the LA Phil's extraordinary concert last week but to have the featured pianist standing there beside him was almost too much to process. Ed saved him by approaching Allison and introduced himself, waving to Julia, Sandra and Robert to join him. Calm returned to the group and Allison's entourage quickly found another area to continue on with their own interests. Samuel recovered somewhat, expressed his good fortune and was able to tell Allison that Ed and Julia would entertain. She then had her phone out making several calls, one to instruct the caterers to plan on twice as many people as had been planned for. The excitement in the room grew quickly as the first guest had arrived.

Ed position himself and started playing as a pianist in a high scale hotel lobby would do, only there was a difference. He mixed classical and popular in a way that blended in with the partying guests but it wasn't long before many realized who was playing. When Julia entered singing several of their most popular pieces the crowd quieted and she and Ed entertained as the star attractions. Sandra and Robert blended in and watched in awe as their new friends played to their audience.

Outside the storefront a well behaved crowd began to gather looking through the big windows at the party inside and could just hear the music drifting out their way. Soon a police car drove up and stopped with lights flashing. One of the officers came inside but before he could say a word Allison had taken his arm and was escorting him out the door. A few minutes later a second patrol car came up and they proceeded to close off the one block of State Street between the pedestrian area and where the store was located. Samuel's assistant, who had seemed almost asleep earlier, was quickly setting up speakers and cordoned off the area in front of the store. His real calling was a disc jockey and all his equipment was in his nearby van. Minutes later he was set up just inside the door, had a pair of microphones near the piano and handed Julia a wireless mike. Sitting down in front of his equipment he nodded to Ed and he played a complete *Rhapsody In Blue*. By the time he finished a crowd of over five hundred had gathered outside and would grow to over a thousand by the time he and Julia took their first break.

It was a good and fun time for the invited guests as they became part of the show for those outside. Those outside enjoyed the music and watching the party goers party. Allison Turner hosted them all, both inside and outside. Allison's party on State Street was the front page news the next morning in the Santa Barbara News-Press.

At nine o'clock Allison announced to all that the party was to end after Ed Adams and Julia Renquest did one more song, *Nobody Does It Better*. Julia's sexy mussing of Ed's hair ending brought cheers from both the inside and outside parties. All were satisfied and happily went their way with nothing but smiles and cheers for Allison, Ed, Julia and themselves.

Allison's big limousine pulled up in front of the store at exactly nine-thirty and Ed, Julia, Sandra and Robert were being wished good evening by Allison in front of the Santa Barbara Yacht Club fifteen minutes later. She made them promise that anytime they were in Santa Barbara they must pay her a visit. She then made them promise twice more and they all again agreed that they would. Each of them wanted to see Allison Turner again as she was the kind of person they would like to get to know better. They would and it would be much sooner than they expected.

Chapter 20

The conversation in the limousine on way back to the Yacht Club was as you might have expected. How good it had all turned out and how nice it was to have the outdoor crowd not only enjoy the music but be so well behaved and willing to leave when it was over. Allison mentioned she knew many of the Santa Barbara police officers as she had organized and sponsored numerous charity events over the years had made their acquaintances. "They will help you out on most things if you give them at least a little of the appreciation they deserve," saying this as to why they had helped get the street closed off with nothing more than her asking them to do it.

As they were about to part, Allison asked Julia if she would mind Ed walking her back to the car and Julia replied, "He better be back in five minutes or I will be coming to get him!" They had walked down to the boat and Ed did as he had been requested.

"Ed, I would really like to befriend you and Julia. And Sandra and Robert. You are special people and very rare in today's world. I know hundreds but almost all are just acquaintances, not friends. I married twice and was widowed twice. They were both exceptional men and left me too soon in their lives and in mine. I miss them both and I miss the people that were in their sphere. I hope you will visit. I think you will find me an interesting person and I can tell you are someone I need right now in my life. You do understand what I am talking about. A friendship. Nothing else." She turned, entered the limousine, the door was quickly closed by the driver and she was whisked away as Ed stood watching. He smiled, understanding what she had said and was sure Julia would not only understand but would want to pursue another meeting with this most interesting woman.

Ed was back to the boat just as the others were climbing aboard and they all went below. Robert was on his cell phone and listening to some type of marine weather recording. Sandra went to their stateroom and Julia looked at Ed in a manner that told him that she expected an explanation of his private chat with Allison Turner.

Before Ed could tell his story Robert had broken the connection on the phone and offered, "A change in plans. It appears Point Conception is starting to build up and unpleasant seas are expected tomorrow. They recommend a late night or very early morning rounding." Sandra joined them and asked Robert what he had found out and he repeated what he had just told Ed and Julia. He then continued, suggesting a late afternoon departure for a overnight passing of the Point.

"If we leave here around four o'clock it will put us off the Point about midnight and the seas should have quieted down a lot. We should be in Morro Bay about noon, fuel up and spend the night there. Two days more should put us in San Francisco." Robert looked at Ed and Julia for an answer and Julia didn't hesitate. She answered with, "More adventures sounds fine with me." Ed nodding his head in agreement.

They each had thought it had been a good day and it was time to turn in. They exchanged knowing smiles that showed their friendships had cemented and that their futures could be shared. They headed for their staterooms, neither couple realizing at that moment, by how much and that it would happen much sooner than expected.

Ed and Julia changed into shorts and T-shirts and got themselves comfortable in the bed. Julia moved over towards Ed, rubbed his shoulders and asked, "Okay, tell me the story of the concert pianist and the party giver. Every last detail."

"I didn't think you would be the least bit interested what that tall, good looking woman of the world would have wanted to talk to me about. Your innocent, shy and faithful husband who hasn't ever been approached like that in front you before. Why would you want to know?" Ed said this with humor but he was not laughing. "She wants us, the four of us, to become her friends. Friends!"

Julia looked closely at Ed and he could see immediately that she understood what Allison Turner was asking. "She's lonely. All these people around her but they are not friends. How sad. We will have to give this some serious thought. She is so poised and sure of herself. I will bet you she has an interesting past, is very intelligent, smart and talented. It reminds me of a couple I know. How many close friends do we really have? Why were we so anxious to get to know Sandra and Robert. So sure we would like making this trip with them. Could it be we don't have very many close friends, either?"

"My best friend is here beside me and tomorrow we will be together for another interesting day. Today was special. I wonder what tomorrow will bring?" Ed asking this question putting his arms around her and holding her close. She responding by moving into a familiar position and they were soon asleep.

In the forward stateroom things were not going so smoothly. There was a tension in the air as they prepared for their nights rest. They too were comfortable in shorts and T-shirts when on board. They enjoyed watching each other dress, especially Robert watching Sandra. She was a beautiful woman and had no qualms about Robert looking at her undressed. At the right times it would lead to love-making, enjoyed by both, but many times just the visual satisfaction was enough. Such it was this night.

They climbed into bed, made themselves comfortable and it was Sandra that said it first. "I saw John standing just outside the window. I am sure it was him even though he had grown a beard. What is he doing here?" She let the question hang in the air.

Robert was quiet for a moment, then he rolled over on his side facing her. "I saw him too. He smiled at me and nodded his head. He did not make any attempt to hide that it was him and I am sure he will be in contact with us soon. I have no doubt about that."

Neither moved or spoke. Finally it was Robert who said, "I think it has to do with Ed Adams, not us this time. Ed has this uncanny way of taking you into his world without any effort or thought. You just want to be somewhere around him. Look at the two of us. First is his music, then Julia who is his soulmate, next Wilma Herman and her helper Cindy, and tonight we have met the most interesting Allison Turner. Can you believe there is any way we would meet people like these, all in just one week's time. It takes a lifetime for something like this to happen. John knows this and he wants Ed to take one of his trips. I'll bet you that is what is going to happen. I am thinking we will be involved and I am actually looking forward to finding out what it will be."

Sandra rolled over toward him and pulled him to her. "You're are right, as usual. I was thinking along the same lines. It doesn't frighten me this time and I find it an exciting prospect." She paused for a minute, and then continued, "Robert, what a life we are having. Don't ever think I don't appreciate what we have together. Every day I thank my lucky stars I am with you."

They lay close together, with their own thoughts until sleep came, first for Sandra and then for Robert.

The next morning dawned in beautiful Southern California morning colors. The four new friends had their now customary breakfast of orange juice, granola with fruit and coffee. Sitting in the cockpit the air temperature was just right and a slight breeze kept them comfortable. About sixty miles north and out to sea would not have been so comfortable as the winds had picked up and the swells and waves around Point Conception were forming.

Chapter 21

They sat in the cockpit, relaxed, having a second cup of coffee when Julia posed the question that all four were waiting for, " Robert, Sandra, when are you going to share your story of your trip back in time? You promised you would."

Robert glanced at Sandra and that invisible conversation between couples took place. It was really their story but he answered as would have Sandra, "We could do it now but it is the type of story that should be told in the evening at days end. Also, hopefully, the day after tomorrow we will be docked on the side tie dock at the Moss Landing Yacht Club. I made the reservation last night."

After a pause he then continued, "After John had arrived on board we discussed the plans for the exploration sitting around the salon table anchored about three miles out from where we will be tied up in Moss Landing. The Monterrey Canyon came up near to that point with a depth of sixty-five feet although the actual shore line, north and south of the canyon, ten thousand years ago was about twenty miles out from there. We were able to take the dingy in the channel formed by the small stream, which is now the slough, up to within about a mile of where we will be docked. I think that is where I would like to tell our story. Can you wait until then?"

Julia answered first, with some disappointment in her voice, "I can, but I don't want to."

Robert was ready for this, pulled his iPad out and brought up the screen. He pressed a few buttons and a photograph of the area he had just describe came up. He handed the iPad to Julia who took a long look at what was presented. "My God, look at that!" and shared it with Ed. They both had made a number of drives through the Moss Landing area as they drove up to the San Francisco Bay area, occasionally stopping to buy artichokes and strawberries at the road side stands. They knew the geography and here the photograph showed no human foot print. Just the flats, hills and mountains. Nothing else. Ed looked intently at what had been presented and a frightened expression crossed his face. He then looked at Robert and told him, "I think we should wait until we are sitting in front of this landscape." Julia could sense what Ed was thinking, agreed and then spoke for the both of them, "It all seemed to be a fantastic story, magical if you please, but that," pointing at the iPad, " makes it absolutely real. It's frightening to know it actually happened. Ed's right. Tell us, show us, the story at Moss Landing."

They decided a walk along the promenade would be nice and on the return walked up State Street again as far as the small Mexican restaurant they had spotted yesterday. All agreed some spicy food would taste good. It was a nice walk and the food was good.

Back on board Sandra placed the charts they would be using on the salon table and they went over the route they would take. Actually, the obvious fastest route paying attention to the number of oil platforms as they approached Point Conception. She expected to be opposite the Point around midnight and they should reach Morro Bay mid to late morning. They could continue on but there were no easy ports until you got to Monterey. Getting there early they should be able to get a side tie at the Morro Bay Yacht Club. If not they could take one of the mooring balls and dingy to shore.

The next morning an early departure would have them to Moss Landing before dark. They could rent a car the next day and make a trip up into the hills to Big Basin Redwoods State Park. Robert and Sandra had promised the full story of their trip back in time and they might even be able to find one or two places they had actually been on the exploration. They could retreat to Monterrey harbor and spend the night there. It would then be another early start and they should be able to make San Francisco at a good time. Timing their entrance under the bridge at slack, or in going tide, would be a priority.

As four o'clock neared they pulled in the fenders and this time secured them to the stanchions. Sandra started the engine, checked the gauges and had Robert and Ed bring in the lines. By four they had cleared the harbor and were on course. Robert and Sandra would do the watches as they had crossing the Pacific from Hawaii and Julia and Ed could spend any time they wanted in the cockpit. Life vests would be required at night. The jack lines were set but no one was to leave the cockpit unless there was an emergency.

They hit the first rough seas within a few miles and

it became progressively worse as they took on the more northerly course. Robert and Sandra had expected it would be rough but were worried about Julia and Ed and how they would handle it. Also, their boat speed had to be adjusted down to find the smoothest running. The four stayed in the cockpit together until after eleven o'clock when the sea started to flatten and they passed Point Conception around midnight, right on schedule. Julia was first to go below and she assured all that it had been a fun ride and she was feeling good but was ready for some sleep. Ed made his excuses and followed her shortly afterward. Robert and Sandra sat close together, keeping watch and enjoying each other's company. They were sure of their new friendships and glad they were with them.

Chapter 22

Ed did his duties in the head and then crawled into bed reaching out for Julia. She was waiting for him and they made love in the manner they both enjoyed. "I feel so good tonight. So alive. How is my man feeling out here in this big ocean?" Julia asked in a teasing manner. "Out here in a big ocean? I hadn't noticed as I was otherwise occupied. But to answer your question I like what we are doing, this all new experience, and I am looking forward to tomorrow. There is a beauty out here I have never witnessed before. I like it," Ed replied and he kissed her one more time before laying back.

Sleep came quickly for Julia, as it usually did, but Ed laid awake still thinking of all that had happened in the last week. The motion of the boat didn't bother him nor did the rumble of the engine. The slap of the water on the hull was muted in the aft cabin but it could still be heard. After about an hour he knew he wasn't going to get to sleep so he put on a sweater, life jacket and headed to the cockpit. Robert had gone below and Sandra was concentrating on the chart plotter. Ed stared at this beautiful woman who was completely in control of the big yacht. He marveled at her confidence and was impressed by her obvious skill. He imagined that there was much more about Sandra Williams that he would get to know if their friendships would continue. Robert was also a person he wanted to get to know better and he was beginning to think that somehow their lives would be linked together in the future.

Sandra turned toward Ed and smiled. "Couldn't sleep? I'm not surprised. We had a rough start but the seas have calmed and we are approaching our desired boat speed of eight and half knots. That's a little better than nine miles per hour. In an another hour it should be calm and the ride will be smooth."

Ed kept his gaze towards Sandra but then began to focus on the dark water and realized the sparkling dots in the water were the reflection from the stars above. Looking up he saw a sight he had nearly forgotten, a star lit sky. "It is beautiful out here. I had almost forgotten the stars, even though after the concert last week I told Julia I thought I had touched them. You would understand what I mean by that, wouldn't you?"

"Edward Adams played Rachmaninoff as he would want his music to be played. I think Wilma said that and I am sure she knows of what she speaks. Robert and I are so glad you understood why we wanted to meet you so he could tell you his story. There is going to be more for the four of us and I think you understand that, too. Touching the stars is important. I hope we can all share, some day, what comes from touching them." Sandra then looked away and Ed could see a single tear slide down her cheek.

Robert poked his head up into the cockpit and greeted them both with, "Good morning. All okay up here?" and without waiting for the obvious answer let it be known he would get dressed and be up in a few minutes. Sandra smiled Robert's way with a smile Ed understood as like those he would receive from Julia. He had no doubt of their relationship and was glad to be sure of that as he wanted to be close to these two new friends without concern of that friendship being misunderstood.

Sandra suggested that Ed get Julia up as sunrise was just about to happen and it was always a welcomed sight. She also suggested long pants and sweaters as the temperature was now becoming more northern California than southern. He had already discovered this but still welcomed her advice.

All four were together as the sun rose and as it cleared the mountains to the east is was a spectacular sight as the sea changed it's color from black to gray and then to Pacific blue. The air was clear and the shore looked much closer. Julia was especially taken in by the vistas and shared her thought, "It is good to be alive."

"We should be entering Morro Bay about noon. There will be an incoming tide but it will be almost over so there won't be much of a current as we dock. We have the forward fifty feet of the dock and there isn't supposed to be any other boats on it when we get there. Should be a simple docking." As Sandra said this Robert was smiling and turned to Ed and Julia, "There is no such thing as a simple docking. Sandra will make it look that way but it is never simple."

They had breakfast and coffees as *Du-eT* did as she was built to do. The sea had become flat and there was just a faint breeze. Sandra gave Ed and Julia a little instruction on how to operate the autopilot. You could run the boat from the Chart Plotter but she preferred to use it for course information and use the autopilot buttons to keep the boat on the magenta line with minor adjustments of negative one degree to port or plus one degree to starboard. Use negative or positive ten degrees for bigger moves. Push Standby and take the wheel if you need to move the boat quickly and when back on course touch Auto. It kept you alert to where you were heading and what was ahead of you. A glance at the radar would tell you what is around you and if something was approaching from behind.

They entered Morro Bay Harbor a few minutes after twelve noon with the looming Morrow Rock to port. A quick stop for fuel was made and then as they approached the Yacht Club they could see the long T dock was vacant. Robert had put the three starboard fenders out and arranged the bow and stern dock lines on the stanchions. Sandra made the u-turn to port and brought *Du-eT* up to the front of the dock with the bow slightly inward as the incoming current was slowly moving it toward the dock. She used the rudder and a little throttle to move the stern in and the boat almost moved sideways until the fenders touched the dock. Robert stepped onto it holding the bow line and secured it to the cleat and then walked back to the stern, picked up the stern line and secured it. They had docked and all Ed could think was, "That was simple."

Chapter 23

After a nice lunch was put together by the ladies with cold cuts, crackers, fruit salad and a glass of white wine for each they began to relax. Spring lines, running fore and aft from stern and bow deck cleats, secured their mooring to the dock. An inspection of the boat had them confident for their overnight stay and ready for the early morning departure for Moss Landing. Sandra and Julia said they needed a little shopping time together and took off to scout the Morro Bay front. They were sharing some kind of secret and Robert and Ed decided they needed some time to do nothing. It was Monday, the fourth of April, and the pleasant spring day made it seem to them that it was the right thing to do.

Sitting in the cockpit, once the cushions are in place, is a most comfortable place. In good weather the view is good and when docked in a busy harbor or bay the activity is enjoyable to watch. Especially if that is all you are doing at the time. The conversation was slow to get started until Ed asked Robert the simple question, "How old are you and Sandra?

Robert smiled a barely detectable smile and answered, "Forty-seven, as of three days ago. April first, April Fool's Day."

Ed laughed, responding, "Happy birthday, a little late. Do you think by any chance Sandra and Julia are off finding a little something to celebrate the occasion? That would be my guess." Ed didn't wait for an answer and continued with, "I have until August to be ten years older than you are and Julia is seven years younger than me."

Robert knew Ed was asking about Sandra's age and he didn't know exactly how to answer him. "As for Sandra, at first she only told me she was just a little older than me but eventually that her birthday was December 22, 1973. So forty-eight is close enough. She had a very rough childhood as her parents divorced shortly after she was born and her father, for all intensive purposes, disappeared. Her mother became an alcoholic and died about the time she finished grade school. She had an older brother who had joined the Army and was killed in an Army training accident at eighteen. She spent the next five years going from one foster care home after another. She left her hometown after finishing one year in college." Robert had to pause after this and collect his thoughts. It had become his pain as it was hers.

"She is so smart and intelligent. You will learn that about her, both from me and her, as we get to know each other. You will find out how fortunate I am to have her with me."

Ed was quiet for a time, trying to decide whether he should tell Robert about Julia's parents, and his own, or let that wait for a while. He was saved from the decision as Julia and Sandra returned, laughing like young girls, as they approached the boat carrying an assortment of bags.

"Dinner is somewhere in this bunch. Did we ever

have a good time shopping!" was Julia's greeting. Sandra added, "Robert, Julia is so much fun to be around. What a good time we had. Chinese take out for dinner and we have a special dessert for afterward. We will take care of everything. You two just sit there and we will call you when things are ready."

They hustled below and the laughter and banter drifted up into the cockpit. Then the smell of Chinese food arrived. It was just after five o'clock and Ed was called to come down to help the ladies. Going down the companion way he could see what all the fuss was about. Happy Birthday was strung across the salon table which was set with dinner plates, silverware and fancy happy birthday paper napkins. On the middle of the table was a German Chocolate cake with Happy Birthday Robert spelled out in white icing. Two packages were wrapped and placed near the cake.

"Robert, you need to come down and see this!" Ed called up to him. As his legs showed up the three below started singing the happy birthday to you song which they managed to get through before the laughter started. Sandra put her arms around Robert and kissed him. "Only three days late, but happy birthday. It is about time you had a party that wasn't on April Fools Day."

Robert smiled at first and then they saw on his face that this was much more important to him than just a birthday party. He looked at each of them and in an faltering voice slowly said, "I think this is more than just a birthday party for me. We can joke about it. It is a little bit silly but there is much more to this than having met two interesting fellow human beings. I don't how to describe it but something is going on that will change our lives. Do either of you sense what I am trying to say?" He was looking at and asking Ed and Julia.

Julia answered with no hesitation. "The minute I first saw Ed I had the feeling you just described. That my life was going to change and it would be for the better. It did and it has been. Something is happening that has brought the four of us together and I can hardly wait to see what it will be."

The Chinese take out was surprisingly good and was all consumed in short order. Sandra spoke up with a lighthearted, "It is time for the cake and presents!" and proceeded to serve the cake and placed the two gift wrapped presents near Robert. The cake was excellent and quickly eaten. Robert picked up the first gift and worked on opening it, taking his time.

As the wrapping was loosened Sandra told of how she and Julia had found this nice thrift shop that had all sorts of neat stuff and that Robert wasn't the only one getting a few presents. She added, "This will replace that worn out paper back copy you have," as he finally uncovered the like new hardback book, *The Last Giant Of Beringia by Dan O'Neill.* "It is the first edition and is signed!" Julia offered and Robert was touched by the gift.

The second gift had been found by Julia in the glass display case holding the more valuable items in the store and she had immediately thought it would be perfect for Robert. She had hid it from Sandra after she found the note contained in a small, old envelope pasted on the back. There were three nice arrow heads mounted on a faded velvet backing in a glass fronted frame. The note was typed on an old typewriter, with several over strikes. It read, "I found these near Big Basin Redwood State Park on our camping trip. August, 1954. They are the best ones. John." The paper was thin, almost transparent and fragile.

As Robert saw what the gift was his eyes lit up and he carefully looked at each arrow head and smiled. As he turned the frame over he saw the brown, stained envelop and Julia mentioned he should be careful in opening it. Sandra crowded in and explained, "So that's what you found and wouldn't show me. You are going to have share it with me, Robert!"

Ed sat back and enjoyed the scene. Julia had made a find and both Robert and Sandra were excited about it. Robert carefully extracted the note and opened it. He read it once and smiled and started reading it aloud a second time. When he got to the last word and spoke "John" his demeanor changed and Sandra's immediately did likewise. Neither Julia nor Ed understood what was happening. "It can't be, Robert. It can't be John," Sandra saying this in a whisper.

Chapter 24

Robert looked at Sandra for several minutes, but said nothing. It was Julia that broke the silence. "How could he possibly know I would see those arrow heads and buy them for you? That I would be looking for something like that? That I even know you and Sandra?"

A smile broke on Robert's face. "Julia, a man like John, who with his friends can send you back in time, can easily set something like this up. He can follow *Du-eT's* passage as we have an activated Automatic Identification System transmitter on board. He knows where we are, or at least where our boat is, and probably knows who is on board. That we might be celebrating my birthday along the way. I will bet you he knows you and Ed are on board and that you know about my precious little arrow head. I don't want to even think of how he knew where to leave the arrow heads but I am sure they would have been picked up after we leave here tomorrow if you hadn't bought them and would be back in his possession the next day."

Ed then surprised them all. "You and Sandra saw him on Saturday outside during Allison's party. You have been waiting for him to make contact and this is it. You knew it was coming but this time I think he is after me to make the trip."

The looks on Robert and Sandra's faces showed both surprise and admiration in what Ed had figured out but on Julia's face was fear. Sandra broke the silence. "I don't think we should ever under estimate Mister Edward Adams. We will know what John is planning by this time tomorrow. I think you two will meet him at Moss Landing tomorrow afternoon and we will know what is going on with him and his group. I, for one, can hardly wait."

Julia had moved even closer to Ed and had taken his hand. "I don't want anything to happen to us Ed. Our life is so good right now. Don't you do anything that risks changing it."

After some more small talk and speculation it was left that they would probably find out what was up with John tomorrow and they could listen to what it would be. For Robert and Sandra it was another interesting twist in their lives which now included Ed and Julia. The plan was set to leave before five o'clock and be in Moss Landing well before dark.

Ed parted with, "Robert, you and Sandra should tell us about your ten thousand years before the present adventure before we get to where it started. Or maybe John would like to tell us with you. We would like to know what happened before any new adventure is proposed. Especially if Julia and I are involved."

They said their good nights with hugs and handshakes and parted company for the evening. Almost before Ed closed the aft cabin door Julia asked Ed, "You won't do anything, anything with that man like go back in time. Promise me that!" She paused for a moment, then smiled a curious smile and added, "At least not going back in time without me."

Once in bed they were too keyed up to get to sleep. "What are you thinking? You suspect something is going on that started with us meeting Wilma, and Cindy, after the concert. All this must have something to do with Sergei Rachmaninoff. This cannot be just coincidence." Julia was now sitting up and tapping Ed on the chest as she talked. "Tell me!"

Ed was smiling, both at Julia's intuition and her way of getting his attention. He reached for her and got his hand planted on her backside. With a gentle pull towards him they settled into a comfortable position and he started his summation.

"I think John and his group have come up with another big improvement in their abilities to send people back in time. What they were able to do with Robert, Sandra and the boat, and then sending John himself to join them seems to be such that to imagine more is hard to come to grips with. My guess it is more in line with being able to go back in time for witnessing history while it is happening. Think what that would be like. What do you want to watch as it was happening. Lincoln's Gettysburg Address, the signing of the Declaration of Independence, the Crucifixion of Jesus Christ. You name it and if a person from the present could be there with the needed equipment you could not only witness it as it happens but record it for others to see and be a witness."

Julia was stunned. "That could be disastrous, Ed. What if it didn't happen the way it is recorded in history, or worse yet, what if it didn't happen at all?" She paused and then continued, "We shouldn't go there. To change the knowledge of history could be even worse than actually changing it. No one should do this. Not you, not anyone!"

Chapter 25

As Sandra guided *Du-eT* out of the Morro Bay channel it was exactly 5:00 am. Robert, Ed and Julia had all done their morning duties and were in the cockpit watching as the big sailboat made the turn northward and into deeper water. It had been a good stay and all had adjusted to the thinking that John would be waiting for them when they arrived at the Elkhorn Yacht Club guest dock at Moss Landing, hopefully in about twelve hours.

Robert and Sandra also had trouble getting to sleep the night before, as had Ed and Julia. The idea of John coming back into their lives had both pluses and minus's. What he had provided for Robert, and then with Sandra, had shaped and added much to their lives. He had made it possible to be where they now were, both financially and in life. It was the fear of jeopardizing it all, and the possible involvement of their new friends that had them worried.

"How should we handle another proposition from John. Or advise Ed and Julia if it is for them? It has to be something like that for John to have set up the arrow heads that way. Probably the book was also placed for me to find. I can't believe he could do such a thing." Sandra said this with both surprise and admiration in her voice.

Robert replied, "Remember the sound proof room I found in Jerry Gallagher's little house the day I decided to take the job of managing his gas station in Point Reyes Station. Our little house. The one John later bought and made it possible for us to buy. It led to my visiting history and our writing the Visiting History programs. Then there was the visit we made where we will be tomorrow, ten thousand years ago. I don't know what to expect next."

Sandra asked, "Why do you think Ed thinks he will be involved?" Before Robert could answer she continued, "Ed is such an interesting man. He is one of the premier pianists in the country and you would think he was just a nice guy you might meet at a little league baseball game. Doesn't put on any airs or show any conceit. He definitely truly loves Julia and would never consider doing anything that would hurt her. There is something about him we need right now. I don't know how to describe it. I think he, and Julia, will make our lives much more interesting in a positive way."

"That is a strange way to say it but I get the same kind of feeling you are trying to describe. We will be finding out pretty soon is my guess. Let's sleep on it and see what happens tomorrow. I am looking forward to what it might be. It is time now for sleep my lovely soul mate," saying this as he kissed Sandra and held her close. He was smiling as he thought his life could be no better than it was at this moment.

They ate a lite breakfast of the now usual granola, fruit, orange juice followed by large mugs of coffee. The seas were flat with almost no wind and *Du-et* had approached her hull speed under power. At ten o'clock

Robert's cell phone announced an incoming call. "Hello John, I was expecting your call. Wondered if I would have to return your arrow head collection. How old were you when you found them?" were Robert's first words to the caller. Ed and Julia looked surprised and a bit shocked. Sandra only pleased.

Robert put his phone on speaker and after a short pause a voice said, "Robert, you never disappoint. Always good to hear your voice and I will assume Sandra is there. Also Edward and Julia Adams. I have a proposition for you four and would like to greet you at Moss Landing this afternoon. If the crew bunk is available I would like to make the trip to San Francisco with you. If you plan to spend tomorrow in Moss Landing I have a van available and would like to do a tour up to Big Basin Redwood State Park. There is not much left after the fires but there are couple of places that are recognizable. I have been up there recently and think you both would like to take a look. Not sure if Sandra wants to bathe in that small pool as it is now but it is almost as it was the last time you were there." John fell silent knowing he would have to wait a few moments to get an answer, but he already knew what it would be.

Robert looked to Sandra and she in turn looked at Ed and Julia. All smiled and nodded their heads to agree. Robert answered, "You know the answer already so I will expect you to be on the dock about five to take a line. You are tracking us so you might as well wait and enjoy the Yacht Club's hospitality until we make our entry into the channel. We plan to spend a few minutes near where we anchored *Du-eT* and then make our entrance. See you shortly. Still have your beard?"

"Ah, Robert. Sounds like a plan. I will see you all around five," and the connection was broken.

Chapter 26

It was a nice sail, or more accurately a motor, heading north about eight miles off shore. A clear sky and blue water. They could pick out the small towns and various other landmarks as they moved slowly up the coast. Around four-thirty they started the turn toward Moss landing. They had taken a route closer to shore as they approached Carmel, Pebble Beach, and Monterey but then headed to where Sandra wanted to try to pick out the spot they had anchored ten thousand years ago. Ed and Julia sat back and enjoyed the conversation between them as they tried to use the chart plotter showing the current topography and the depth sounder that could confirm their location.

A relatively flat area appeared at two hundred and twenty feet on the depth sounder and Sandra said that this must be the place. It would mean that around five feet of new bottom material had been deposited since they had been here before. Some math had to be done as ten thousand years ago the ocean was about one hundred and sixty-five feet lower than at present. When they had anchored before the depth sounder had shown sixty feet. The continental shelf was exposed then and now it was covered by over a hundred feet of water. They had taken the dingy up the canyon and then up the small stream until they reached the area that is now the Elkhorn Slough. It was about two miles to the landing point and at the time the shore line was more than twenty miles out. Looking towards shore all was different as there had been no sign of human presence and now it was every where and un-mistakable.

Sandra said in a soft voice, "It was so beautiful then. Untouched. Robert, you remember. We knew what it would become but is was so beautiful then." Ed and Julia could understand what Sandra was saying and Robert was remembering every detail.

She put the boat in gear and they headed for the Slough. Thirty minutes later Robert was handing a rather short man with a gray beard and sparkling blue eyes the bow line and had stepped off the boat with the stern line. The two lines were tied to the dock cleats and Robert greeted John with such enthusiasm and emotion that Ed and Julia, standing above them on the deck, realized that there was much more they would need to learn about this mysterious man. Sandra had stopped the engine, centered the wheel and was soon on the dock repeating the greeting Robert had just given John.

"There is a lot we need to learn," Julia said and quickly continued, "Sandra and Robert have a love for this man. The fear they showed as they knew he was coming into their lives again was not a fear of the man but of what he might offer them as another great adventure into the past. If it is you John is interested in, are you ready to consider it?"

Ed could hear the concern in Julia's voice and it

matched his. "I don't think so but I do have an interest in what it might be. I promised your grandfather, and Little Willy, I would never do anything that would hurt you. I hold that promise as sacred. It is a promise I will never break."

Julia gave Ed a weak smile, put her arm around his waist and said, "Let's get ready to meet John."

The introduction was made as Robert, Sandra and John boarded the boat. Both Ed and Julia received a handshake, a glad to meet you and both were immediately taken by the friendliness and warmth that their new acquaintance showed them. They went below and Sandra served some fresh coffees. Sitting around the salon table it seemed like they had all done this exact thing before. John spoke first.

"I took the liberty of ordering dinner from the Yacht Club kitchen and it will arrive in thirty minutes. I trust this is okay with you as I imagine you are all pretty tired. I have also brought Robert and Sandra a small present which I am sure they will share with you both," indicating this to Ed and Julia. "It is the photos of our trip ten thousand before the present dressed up a bit with my narration and a little music. Have Robert and Sandra told you the whole story already? I hope not because you should see it this way first."

Julia started to laugh and then offered, "They started to but it got delayed and the rest of the story was promised once we got here where it had really begun." She couldn't hide her excitement and John seemed to almost glow with knowing he was going to have a good audience.

"First I must confess to you that I have been following you since your meeting at the LA Phil concert. Allison Turner, who of course you now know, was a childhood friend that I had kept track of. I invited myself to her piano unveiling party but I choose not to come inside when I spotted you four together. I didn't want to interrupt your budding friendships. At least not that soon." John's enthusiasm in telling his story was infectious and Ed began to realize that he had been right about who he was going to approach for his group's next traveler.

"Allison is a very special lady and I will tell you why later, maybe even tomorrow." Turning toward Robert and Sandra he continued, "I would like to make the Moss Landing to San Francisco run with you. I can easily fit in the crew's bunk and will stay out of the way." Looking to Sandra she nodded her okay and Robert said it would be their pleasure.

As if on cue there was a knock on the hull. John jumped up and asked Sandra to set the table with place mats, silver ware, water and wine glasses. and told her that all else would be provided. He enjoyed being the host and couldn't hide his enthusiasm. Ed and Julia were starting to like this small man, with the twinkle in his blues eyes, and were more certain than ever that their lives were going to be intertwined with not only him, Robert and Sandra, but that Allison Turner would be there as would Wilma and Cindy.

Chapter 27

The four in the salon could hear muffled voices and the muted clatter of metal serving containers, but no sooner than the table was set and Sandra was seated, John came down the companion way followed by the young chef dressed in nice slacks and a spotless white apron. He seemed a very happy fellow. John made a quick introduction to the group and the chef turned just in time to receive the five containers from whoever was above. Two more containers were sent down and the chef proceeded to place, with a flare, the filled plates at each place.

Each plate had one half of a perfectly roasted Cornish Game Hen placed on a bed of wild rice sided with sliced carrots, sweet potatoes and onions. Small diced leaves of spinach, pecans and butternut squash were complimented with the rice and just the right amount the hen's glaze included. It was a beautiful dish and the fragrance was every bit as good. John quickly poured some California Cabernet Sauvignon for each, took his seat, and the first tastes were taken of the delicious meal. The Chef had already departed and the compliments would have to be given to him later.

As the last small tidbits were consumed, they sat back and smiles were exchanged. Kudos to the chef and thanks to John were expressed. He then headed to the galley and brought out five small crystal bowls containing plump strawberries and a sixth bowl with powdered sugar was placed between them. Last, he set a small plate that had a pile of thin and crisp ginger snaps. Sandra and Robert started to laugh while smiling at John who was showing a mischievous grin. Sandra explained, "After each meal we had at camp John would bring out a small bag of cookies. Neither Robert or I ever had cookies as an after dinner dessert but since our first day back on *Du-eT* we have craved them. And here we are with John again, relishing these cookies. I love it. Thank you, John!"

The table was cleared, coffee served and John brought out his iPad. The boat's television was turned on and a vacant channel selected. John fiddled with his device and on the screen came an high definition photograph of *Du-eT* at anchor on a almost colorless sea with a title cover of *10,000 Years Before Present. July, 2020.* The background was just slightly bluer than the water and the boat seemed to be almost floating in the atmosphere.

Sandra let out a gasp and Robert sat silent. Both were moved and Ed and Julia didn't know what to say or think. They were going to receive the entire story of this unbelievable journey in the presence of those who had made it.

John took in an audible breath and started his narration. "Ed and Julia, Robert and Sandra will relive our exploration with me. You will be entertained and hope-fully entranced by what you see but will surely not understand how it could possibly have happened. I know, but haven't told anyone how it is done and I and my partners never will. Someday it will be discovered by others, or our secrets will be found, but we will not disclose them. I am hoping you will accept my invitation to tour our facilities and meet my partners after we dock in San Francisco. We can arrange this later. Now sit back and let me take you back ten thousand years in time."

The next image was of the shocked expressions on Sandra and Robert's faces with just a hint of greenish reflection on their skin. The high definition exposure showed a reflection of a human form reflected in their eyes. Close inspection showed John smiling at them.

"Look at that, would you! John's arrival at the exact time and place he said he would be there. It had happened. We had to believe it at that moment. What a start!" Sandra said this with such excitement that it set the tone for the rest of the show.

The photographs were magnificent. One after another. Robert and Sandra had been presented a CD with fifteen hundred pictures but on the HDTV they looked much better and it became clear many had been modified both in cropping and color. The campsite images were good and varied and showed clearly what the geography and environment was like. The landscapes over looking the valleys, hills and mountain were familiar to all five of them. They were devoid of any human sign and they examined and talked about this in detail. Even Ed and Julia had comments on certain areas they recognized that had no signs of any kind.

John had set up his showing such that pauses were done at any point and that allowed the discussion to flow smoothly without distracting from the show. The first photograph of the natives was of a group of women and children crossing an open area of grassland some distance below them. Again Sandra described the scene of the women, young and little girls walking and prancing along a faint trial as if they had no cares in the world. It was the first view of the natives they had other than the far distance ones they could see in the villages. "It was just as if it was a friendly group mothers and children walking along a beach on a sunny day last week in Carmel by the Sea. It was so nice, so innocent. I didn't think I should be watching them. I felt I was spying on them. I guess that was what we were doing." Her voice trailed off as she spoke the last sentence. Robert reached over to hold her hand. He knew what would be coming soon and knew that the tears would come.

Chapter 28

There were a number of photographs of camp life and on the trail scenes. Each was a quality picture, each bringing memories to the three that had been there and entertainment to the two that hadn't. There was an intense photo of a conflict between two boys and three adult males over a slain deer. It was frightening in the prospect of possible violence but a third image showed the boys escaping up a steep hillside.

It was when the first photograph of Sandra standing with an early morning bowl of oatmeal steaming in the chill air and a terrified look on her face that stopped the show for a more careful explanation by John of what had just taken place.

"This was the event that set our entire trip, our purpose to possibly meet with and gain a little knowledge of these people, in motion. What Sandra is reacting to is hearing a painful scream by a young woman coming from the forest a few hundred yards away. We had just started having our morning oatmeal when it came to us. It is still shocking just in it's remembrance." John paused and it was obvious to Ed and Julia he was not exaggerating. Robert had pulled Sandra a little closer and was still holding her hand. Her eyes were starting to well up and the tears would soon follow.

The expression on Sandra's face in the photograph seemed to sharpen even more as John continued the story. "A second scream came and as we turned in the direction it was coming from a little boy appeared. Crying and shaking violently he stared at us not knowing what to do. Sandra stretched out her arms and gave him a comforting smile. At first he seemed ready to run away but suddenly ran into to her arms." John had to pause again and the tears were now running down Sandra's cheeks. The photograph of Sandra holding this small native boy as any mother would was so moving that all had take in a few deep breaths and regroup.

John cleared his throat, tried to control his voice and spoke softly, very slowly. "The little boy is Citali, around four years old and a smart little kid. I need you, Ed and Julia, to know I am a linguist and had studied the Costanoans, the early coastal native Americans, languages. These were gleamed from living relatives many generations removed so were not what we would be hearing here. But as Sandra was holding Citali he kept repeating the word that was similar enough for me to know his was saying mother and he was pointing toward where the screams had come from." This gave John enough confidence to be able to continue his description of the scene.

"We headed in the direction Citlali was pointing and found a young woman laying on the damp soil and leaves with legs spread. A new born baby was writhing in the coils of the umbilical. She was unconscious and Sandra handed Citlali to me starting the mid-wife chores for Meilani." The next photograph was from Robert's cap mounted camera. It was just as the new mother opened her eyes and was presented her new daughter by Sandra. The look on her face and in her eyes conveyed an immediate bond between them.

Again all was silent around the table. The photographs were breathtaking. An occasional bit of music blended in with the visual but did not detract. Sandra was visibly shaken and Julia slid over on the cushion to be closer to her. John selected the next photo and it was the one they had seen before. At the scenic pool with the waterfall in the back ground and the two women entering the water together.

It was a beautiful photograph but having been seen before did not have the impact the next one conveyed. This one showed Robert's face just above the tiny baby he was holding. In the background were the two women bathing. The scene spread out for the viewer in an mystical way but it was Robert speaking to this newborn child that was the focal point. Sandra was still having trouble with this and the expression on Robert's face was such that she started weeping in earnest. Almost unable to speak Sandra whispered to Robert, "What did you say to her? I have to know what you said."

Robert knew how important this would be to Sandra so he tried to collect himself to say it right, just as it had been said. "You should watch this little one, your mother and my woman, two beautiful women bathing together outdoors in a setting that is right for them." Again it was quiet around the table and then Sandra started to smile and looking at Robert said, "That was perfect. I needed it to be perfect. I know what is next so let's go there."

John loaded the next photo which was of the three young native men that had appeared, one armed with a bow and arrow and the others with spears. The next was of Citlati pulling one of the men, his father Raini, towards John and making the introduction. The tension had been broken but Meilani was starting to show some distress. They placed her and the baby inside Robert and Sandra's tent where she, with the baby, and Citlati and Raini would later spend the night.

The show went forward with the whole tribe of about fifty natives visiting the campsite the next morning. The chief, Akikta, invited the three visitors to set up their camp near the tribes small village. As the photographs continued John described the activity as they broke camp and started the walk down the hill and to where the incredible view of the Pacific Ocean was seen. It was the photograph that Robert had already shown them but on the television screen seemed even more impressive. The next day's activities were shown and again John discussed them in enough detail that Ed and Julia almost felt they had been there. He also explained the circumstances that made them decide they should leave the following morning. A single photograph captured the sad event of their departure. It showed their new family standing together in the early morning mist with tears running down their cheeks and little Citlali crying out for John to stay. It was at that remembrance that John had several tears on his cheeks.

The hike back out to *Du-eT* was documented as

well but did not have the impact of meeting up with the natives. There were a few tense moments as a small group of adult males, carrying spears, ran across the flat area between them and where the dingy had been hidden. Fortunately they turned away before the area where their footprints had been left in their retreat to a hiding place.

The last few photographs showed them preparing the dingy for use and then the last image was of *Du-eT* as they approached and tied up to the transom.

They were all tired. It had been a very emotional viewing. Different for each but also very satisfying. John excused himself as he seemed to have over done it that day. He asked them if they would like to take the tour tomorrow that he had planned. He would discuss it with them in the morning. He received their thanks and two very nice hugs from Sandra and Julia that would send any man to bed with nice thoughts until sleep came.

Ed and Julia went to the aft cabin and Robert and Sandra to theirs.

Chapter 29

All were tired. It had been a very long day capped by an emotional presentation of an impossible journey. There was no wind, the sea was quiet and in the slough not even a ripple. The marina was unusually quiet and each on board *Du-eT* were ready, and needed, a good nights rest. Sleep didn't come easily, however, as their minds were still active thinking about all they had learned.

John just fit into the crew cabin bunk. It was not meant for a tall person, really for children as for length, but the mattress was comfortable and so was John as he laid looking up at the bottom of the upper berth. It had been a good day for him as the photographic trip back in time had been well received. Robert and Sandra had cemented a friendship with him of a kind that was rare in today's world. It was not that which was keeping him awake. It was sound of a little boy crying, calling out his name, in a language he couldn't understand, begging for him not to leave. He had never experienced the love of a child before and had never thought what to love one could mean. It had been hard to walk away from and it was still haunting him as something he had missed in his life. He closed his eyes and tried to think of other things.

In the forward cabin Robert and Sandra were

having a like time as far as being able to let sleep come. Sandra was particularly restless and rolled on her side to face Robert, putting her arm around him. "I am still hurting, leaving them there like we did. We had to. We didn't belong there, but Meilani, Citali and the baby. Just two days and I still think of them as my family. That I have lost them. Lost them forever."

Her tears began falling again and Robert held her close. "We had to leave. We couldn't stay as we couldn't risk changing history. John said they would not remember our visit as soon as we were out of sight. That we couldn't do anything that might change their life in any way. I even think helping Meilani with the birth of Liseli was a risk but one that had to be taken. We came back with no changes that I can detect. Even the arrow head was a risk but again didn't seem to make a difference. It was a great adventure. I will live with that and not think of what may have been. We must leave it at that."

Robert held her and soon could hear and feel her even breathing knew she had fallen asleep. What a remarkable woman he was with and what a life he was living with her. That brought a smile to his face. He moved carefully so as not to disturb her and found a good position such he could watch her deep in slumber and eventually sleep came for him.

In the aft stateroom Ed and Julia were likewise having trouble relaxing. Julia was sitting up and giving Ed a back massage that usually helped calm her nerves. It wasn't working at the moment and she started the conversation. "Edward Adams, you lead me into the most interesting things. True love, professional golf, being an entertainer, wealth, motherhood and married to a world class pianist. And now this strange involvement with people who have traveled back in time. Really done it. Would you care to let me know what is about to happen?"

Ed rolled over and gave Julia an appreciative look. She was still a very good looking woman and was a companion he couldn't imagine living without. He felt as much in love with her at this moment as he was the first day they had met. The strange golf clubs he had bought that had been set up by her grandfather, and some of his friends, that had lead him into a year of playing professional golf. Then finding his way back to the piano and her to singing that had them becoming famous entertainers. It had lasted for eight years and earned them wealth way beyond their needs. Having twins, a boy and a girl, now both in college and doing well had brought joy into their lives. Last week, with the LA Phil, he had performed at the level all pianist hoped to some day achieve. And now what was almost certainly going to be an adventure offered that would have to be considered. Their life was so good right now that he could not jeopardize it any way was dominant in his thoughts.

"I am not hearing an answer to my question!"

"My answer is I am not sure but it certainly involves us with our new friend, John. I am sure he has a last name and we should know it before we accept any kind of time travel. And that is what I think is going on right now." Ed could see the cloud of concern and fear come to Julia's face as he made this suggestion so he continued, "It doesn't appear to me that John is setting up something for Robert and Sandra. I think it is what they were afraid of when he made this latest contact but now they seem totally at ease. That leaves the two of us." Ed paused again and now saw curiosity starting to replace the fear in Julia's face and he marveled at the bravery she had to go to other places when it seemed the right thing to do.

"Okay! What do you think it could be. Who and where do you think he wants us to go to see and when?"

Ed had been thinking about this all during John's presentation. It was of course for Robert and Sandra but to set it up while he and Julia were on board could only mean one thing. He wanted them to consider something along that line and the only thing that was obvious would be Rachmaninoff.

"It's Rachmaninoff!" Julia said, just a bit too loud, and Ed could only smile, responding, "I think you are too smart, or is it you can read my thoughts the minute I am thinking them. Yes, it has to have something to do with him. Interested?"

"Maybe," Julia saying it in a conspiratorial manner while laying down and making herself comfortable against him. "I think I will try to get some sleep. Tomorrow will be the start of another day with Edward Adams and I will need to be rested." Rest was postponed for a few minutes but then came for them both.

The next morning Julia was still asleep when Ed heard foot steps on the companionway steps and then felt the slight motion of the boat as someone stepped off onto the dock. A few minutes later a second set of steps went topside but remained on board. Ed was the third to rise and met Robert in the cockpit.

Chapter 30

Good mornings were exchanged. It was cool, almost cold, and was clear with no fog or clouds. Robert sat quietly, seeming lost in thought. Ed respected his silence and looked around the marina and then off toward the mountains to the east. He had seen them many times before but this morning they looked different. Whether it was the clear air or the early morning colors to Ed it had taken on a new look. He was mulling this over when Robert spoke in a soft and restrained voice, "If you look at the hills to the southeast, past the power plants smokestacks, there is a small area that looks devoid of any structures or roads. When we were here before it was all just like that, in temperature, color and look. There was no sign of any human presence. It was silent. Completely empty. I think that is what I took away from that trip with Sandra and John. We each felt it and I think none of us will ever forget what it was like."

Ed stayed silent and let that thought expand until he could almost think it was that way now.

"It wasn't just the beauty of the place, it was the emptiness. To imagine the entire continent before the first humans came, it must have been something like that."

Sandra was next up with a carafe of coffee and

four cups. "I could hear Julia moving about so she should be up in a few minutes," was her morning greeting. She could sense that something had happened between Robert and Ed. See it in how they were looking towards the mountains. "It was that way, Ed. You can feel it, can't you? You saw the photographs and you can now sense what it was like. I know Robert's feelings about this place as they are also mine. We can share it with you but not through your eyes, just in your mind."

Julia was up, smiling and looking as good as Ed had ever seen her. She looked at each of them and then quickly said, "You all are back when there was no one here. I feel it too. Just like the photograph and can see this place as you two and John saw it. How beautiful it was."

John arrived, carrying several tote bags, and stepping aboard greeted them with, "You are all back in time, are you not? Not seeing any of this all around you but just the landscape by itself. Such a good feeling that so few ever get to experience." Looking at Robert and Sandra he asked, "It was worth it, wasn't it?"

They both nodded their heads in agreement and Robert added, "Ed was there for a few moments and I think Julia was too. John, it was worth it a hundred times over."

John set his bags down and rummaged through one bringing out a plastic bag holding five small packets. Sandra broke out in a laughter so genuine that all had to smile. "John, you devil! I will get the hot water ready and bring it up with the spoons. Breakfast will be served in three minutes!"

By the time Robert had explained to Ed and Julia

that the oatmeal they were about to be served was the same as they had eaten almost every morning while on the exploration, Sandra was back. The hot water was poured into each packet and the new ones were instructed how to stir and wait one minute. Breakfast was taken and first Ed, then Julia, commented that it was the best they had ever tasted. John sat back, saying nothing, but his blue eyes were sparkling and his smile showed that his plans for today would work out just fine.

He demonstrated how to roll the packet up and he stowed them in the plastic bag. "We left nothing behind other than footprints, which would soon be obscured by weather. There was no trace of us having ever been there." A sad expression came over his face and then he continued, "The natives would not remember them either. That is part of the science of our transportation back in time. Those we visit will have no memory of our being there. I want to think Citlali would remember, or maybe the chief, but they won't. That we can remember turned out to be a surprise. We didn't think that would happen until Robert had his first visit to history."

He then brightened with, "I have a plan for today that I hope you will want to participate in. I have permission to tour Big Basin Redwood State Park and take a hike a ways down Opal Creek. Does that peak your interest?" he asked looking at Robert and Sandra.

"That sounds like a good idea. Ed and Julia, you would find it worth while," was Robert's quick answer. They nodded their heads in agreement and Julia questioned the conditions at the Park as it was less than two years since the monster forest fire that had destroyed almost everything that had been there.

John answered with a tease in his voice. "You are right Julia, there is not much left there right now. Most of the big redwoods survived and there are a few pockets that escaped. Almost all the man made structures are gone. The roads are passable and they have cleared an enormous amount of downed and dead timber. But I found one small pool on Opal Creek that is in one of those pockets that looks a bit familiar. Maybe, maybe not, but Sandra and Robert need to take look. Might bring back a memory or two."

He seemed pleased with this and leaned back as he watched Sandra's expression. She smiled a smile that the others now treasured and knew was genuine. She was remembering what had happened in that pool as she and Meilani had bathed together a few hours after the birth of baby Liseli. Even Robert was remembering that special time and knew John had set up the day perfectly. He and Sandra would have to see that place again if it was at all possible he had found it.

Julia spoke for herself and Ed that they would like to see it but they didn't have any type of hiking shoes except for their fancy Sperry deck shoes.

John ruffled through the other tote and dragged out four shoe bags. He handed them out after looking at small labels on each bag. Robert's was first and he pulled out a pair of used hiking shoes and started to laugh. "Look at these, Sandra!" he said as he held them up. Sandra was also holding up her pair to show him back.

Ed and Julia pulled theirs out and found brand new ones of the same design. Before they could comment

Robert said, "Don't worry, they will be a perfect fit. John never misses on anything, unless he does it on purpose."

Chapter 31

John's van was more like a limousine, but could still be classed as a van. Two captain seats up front and a group of four more set up to swivel so none in the back felt they were isolated. Robert got the co-pilots chair and Ed was bracketed by the ladies. Soft, high quality leather and the smell was brand new, just out of the dealer's show room. He was a good driver and the conversation was easy and relaxed. Anticipation was in the air but was not being talked about. It would have to wait until they got there, or didn't get there.

They drove through Santa Cruz until they connected with Highway 17, took a short jog west and then onto Highway 9. The traffic was heavy and the whole area seemed over crowded. A beautiful place having become just another big city in California. The sign to Pasatiempo, just as you started up into the mountains, had Ed mentioning that the golf course was one of the great old course designs and that he had played it many times when he played for Stanford. Then he said, "My guess is that if you can get on the course it will be a preserve." But the build up continuing up the highway then gave him some doubts.

It took some time but the sign to Big Basin showed up and once on Highway 236, known as Big Basin

Highway, they knew they were getting close. John knew where they were and when the first signs of the fire came into view all were quiet. Even after almost two years, it was still a depressing spectacle and when he pulled off into the Big Basin Tent Cabins parking area no one said a word.

After getting out of the van they stretched, walked around and didn't know what to say. John took care of that with just a few words. Pointing to what was once a trail he said, "That is the Opal Creek Loop Trail." Robert and Sandra reacted immediately. Almost a duet, "We are back. We know this place. John, how do you do what you do?" John only smiled and offered, "Let us just take a little walk along Opal Creek."

It wasn't a pleasant walk as there was still a lot of ash and even though most of the burnt trees had been removed it was a forlorn landscape. Just as Robert and Sandra were becoming discouraged they came across a small area of greenery that had escaped the flames. Some trees, a good number of large bushes and some grass. John had walked ahead and stopped in front of a lengthy out cropping of rock with a fairly large area of level land leading up to it. Sandra stopped as she spotted John standing near the rock. "How did you know it was here. How could you possibly know?" she called out as she ran into the clearing.

Robert, Ed and Julia came next and could see Sandra hugging John as he laughed and hugged her back in appreciation. "I cheated. My team at home had us on our private GPS type tracking system and had the co-ordinates for our every move. It was easy for me to drive in here yesterday and find this spot. You can see some significant changes but the rock ledge is almost the same as it was ten thousand years ago."

Sandra grabbed Robert's hand and called out to Ed and Julia to follow them. In a few minutes she stopped, looking around and then knelt down, trying not let her voice crack, said, "This is where the baby was born. Maybe a few feet away but it was here." She stood up, trying to hold back her tears and apologized for being so emotional.

Julia went to Sandra and put her arm around her. "It must have been something, having that happen as you described. I can feel it too, like the space is telling me how special it is. It is like a religious experience."

The three men were silent and watched the ladies have their moment. It had a special meaning to each of them. John and Robert had been there, aiding Sandra as she handled the mid-wife chores of seeing the child and mother were taken care of. Ed could imagine the scene that had unfolded here and was also deeply moved by it's significance.

It was John who broke the spell, suggesting they find the pool in the photograph of the two women together bathing and it was quickly located. At least where it had been. The drought had reduced Opal Creek to a trickle, the waterfall was there but the pool had filled in and was a grass covered flat with the creek bed of exposed sand and rocks running through it. It was still an enjoyable spot and John suggested lunch was in order.

He pulled off the small backpack he was carrying and started pulling out a number of packets, three water bottles, a small propane stove and a pot. Again, Robert and Sandra started to laugh. Without a word they collected the three water bottles and headed to the small creek. Filling each through the special filters they were smiling as the memories were flooding back. They knew what was coming next and were anxious to share it with Ed and Julia. They didn't realize it yet, although Ed had his suspicions, that they were being drawn into John's next great experiment.

Chapter 32

The water came to a boil, three packets were added and five minutes later a remarkably good stew was served to each. After enjoying the excellent meal and good conversation the plastic bowls, which conducted no heat, were rinsed off in the creek and all the lunch items were placed back into John's backpack. He had first withdrawn the small tube of cookies which were passed around. The five human beings sat around comfortably in the small forest that remained in the acres and acres of burned out landscape. The sun was shinning at mid-day and the temperature was just right. They were alone and it could have been ten thousand years earlier. John, Robert and Sandra knew this as a fact and Ed and Julia were sure it had been that way for them.

At that moment in time none in this small group, seemingly alone in this vast place, wanted to break the silence. Suddenly there was the sound of an automobile horn in the distance and the spell was broken. John laughed at this interruption of their concentration of the moment and suggested his next plan. "I think a hike of about a mile and a half is in order. Robert, do you want to lead us?" was said as if all knew where they were going. Actually, three of them did and Ed and Julia were anxious to follow.

Robert started off at a moderate pace and headed towards the place of the small native village they had visited those many years ago. The first stop was on a hillside above a big coastal terrace with a spectacular view of the Pacific Ocean. Sandra ran up to Robert and took his hand. "This was the place, wasn't it. It made the trip worth it. Citlali running about through the tall grass. Meilani with her baby standing next to Raini down near some trees and John standing right where he is standing now. The grass is here, and the ocean, but everything else is burnt and gone. I will only remember it as it was," saying this last as she tried to hide her tears.

John came up next to them, "Let's remember it the way it was, don't you think?" Sandra turned and gave him a weak smile that told him that was their thinking, exactly.

Ed and Julia walked up but said nothing. They both knew what was going on between the three of them and it needed no other thoughts being offered to distract them from theirs.

About thirty minutes later they stood overlooking where Opal Creek joins East Waddell Creek and Robert stopped looking intently at the area below. "This is far enough. There no need to go any farther," saying this in a whisper. There were the beginning of green grasses starting their spring time growth but all else was totally destroyed by the fire. A few tree trunks still stood in small groups but looked like charred groupings of tooth picks. There was no sign of any life and of course no sign of human habitation, past or present.

John broke the silence, "I wanted you to see it. I

have no idea what happened to our native family. How long they stayed. Whether they moved on, died out from disease or famine, or ended up being overwhelmed by a larger tribe." He said this with a sadness that reminded Robert of John's demeanor as they hiked out that early morning ten thousand years ago. John had told him then that no young child had ever shown a love for him as Citlali had and his calling out his name as they left was something he wasn't able to handle.

Again John broke the silence, "We should leave now and never come back to this spot. We didn't belong here then and we no longer need to be here again." He turned away, with his shoulders bowed, and started back up the faint path they had left in the new grass. As they did Sandra bent down and picked a small sprig of some thing that looked like the wild oats she had gathered helping the native women that one afternoon. She smiled at the memory and thought the same thought she had thought that day, but this time not reluctantly, "We don't belong here."

They walked quickly back to the van and the re-turn trip to Moss Landing seemed a lot longer than that coming. The conversation was enjoyable but for the most part did not touch on the visit to the past. They hit rush hour traffic in Santa Cruz and it was constant until they were back to Moss Landing. It was a Mexican menu at the Yacht Club and that was perfect for them. The margaritas were good and so was the food. The evening was finished with coffee and cookies on board *Du-eT.* John smiled at this as Sandra had told him how cookies for dessert was now their favorite.

As they sat in the cockpit Sandra said they planned an early morning start, by 6:00 am, and hoped to make the incoming tide through the Gate around four. John then made the proposal all had been waiting for. "My group would like to invite you four to my place for lunch day after tomorrow. We would like to pick you up at ten-thirty and plan on you staying until around four. We have a rental car for Ed and Julia for their trip back to the California Yacht Club which they can leave there for pick-up by the rental company. You can keep it for up to a week as you choose," saying this last as he looked at Ed. "We wish to show you our facility which I think you will enjoy. It is very impressive but unfortunately we will be closing up shop in the next few weeks."

The four invitees could see the hurt in John's eyes and they waited for an explanation. "When we started this grand experiment Stanford had abandoned their Linear Accelerator project. They had no plans for the facility at the time and we made a very good rental agreement with them for some space. Stanford decided to upgrade the facility a few years back and have been working their way up to our location. It was part of the agreement that we would vacate once, and if, they needed it. You will see why we won't try to set up in another location. Also it is time for us to pursue some less demanding pursuits."

Four sets of eyes looked his way and a slight smile had formed on John's face. It was a nice time to call it a day and to look forward to what tomorrow and the next day would bring.

Chapter 33

Julia couldn't wait and as they entered the aft cabin said in a calm voice, "He is setting you up for some kind of trip into the past. I have to be part of it if you accept anything like that. You are not going to go without me!"

Ed was prepared for this and answered, "I am sure something will be proposed. I won't go anywhere without you. Don't you worry about that but it certainly will be interesting finding out what it might be. And what they have developed that would make them try one more trip before closing up shop. Men like these never retire and join a bridge group in a retirement community. It will have to be something very special."

That was good enough for Julia for the moment. They got comfortable in their preferred sleeping positions and after their goodnight kiss she was quickly asleep. For Ed it was not so easy. He was certain he would be making some kind of trip into the past as he also was certain that John would not be going through all the motions if he didn't think it wasn't a sure thing. This brought a smile to Ed's face and he was beginning to think he was living a charmed life. "How could it possibly get any better," was his last thought as sleep came.

In the front cabin Robert and Sandra traded similar

thoughts and agreed it was Ed that John would be trying to convince to go traveling. Robert spelled it out. "Ed will have to take Julia with him, I am sure of that. I think we should stay right here in the present, no matter what John may be cooking up. Something else is coming for us that will be new and totally unexpected. I sense it but have no clue. Some how the four of us, maybe even Wilma and Cindy, will be involved. Even Allison Turner may show up. You have been thinking along those lines, haven't you?"

He smiled at his beautiful partner and she simply answered, "Yes." That was a good enough answer and it had been a long and emotional day. They both wanted a nights rest before the long day tomorrow. Close together, touching each other, sleep came easily.

In the crew quarter's bunk John lay starring at the underside of the upper bunk. As he made himself comfortable a feeling of satisfaction came over him. Things were working out nicely and he felt fortunate that he was among such special people. He thought how they didn't even realize how special they were. Their intellect, aptitudes and abilities they accepted without suspecting how rare these are in the human species. Robert's trip visiting history as it happened having such ease in communicating with Lincoln, daVinci, and Rachmaninoff. Then being able to write it down so well for the television series. With Sandra at his side the two of them doing the fictional versions for three seasons of programs. Ed now one of the premier classical pianists in the world acted as if it was nothing special. Julia was a partner any man would love to have and in her own right had an entertainer's natural presence and a voice so good that their recordings were still being played and enjoyed over three generations.

His thoughts continued with his childhood friend, Allison Turner, coming back into his life. Seven years older and five inches taller her friendship to the short, lonely little boy in San Francisco was again a fond memory. She wanted to be Emilia Earhart, then Janet Guthrie flying airplanes and driving race cars. It almost happened for her but she was too tall, music came into her life, then marriages took her on other paths. She was still a good pianist and could play at an respectable level. Robert and Sandra coming into Ed and Julia's lives was another bonus that had also brought Wilma Herman, and her helper Cindy, into this interesting group that was forming.

John's smile broadened over his face and he had to suppress laughing out loud. None of them knew of his investigators who were busy, even at this moment, putting together files on all of these new friends of Robert and Sandra's. It was leading to his small group's grand finale in the back into history projects. As with all the projects nothing would be done to in anyway change history as that would be much too dangerous. Even the slightest alteration could cause inestimable damage, even altering the possibility of their own existence.

He closed his eyes, concentrating on letting his mind relax it's grip on his body. To finally let sleep come. A last thought came in among the first signs of drowsiness, "It will have to be Sergei Rachmaninoff."

Chapter 34

The aft cabin was directly under the cockpit and just behind the engine room. Both Ed and Julia were just starting to wake for the new day as the footsteps up the companion way into the cockpit brought them to full consciousness. They both felt good and smiles were exchanged with a gentle hug. It had been active day before, with more exercise than normal, but the enjoyment of being with their new friends would more than compensate for a few sore muscles.

By the time they were dressed and into the cockpit the engine had been started, the lines taken in, fenders stored and they were moving out of the slough and into the ocean. Sunrise had just cleared the mountains and the day dawned clear and cool with an almost eerie stillness around them. John was up minutes later and exuded an enthusiasm that infected them all.

Sandra was at the helm and she soon had *Du-eT* on course and the autopilot engaged. Smiling at Robert she had him take over the controls, meaning all he had to do was look out for what was ahead and around them and kept the boat on the magenta line. She nodded to Julia and they both went below. Breakfast was quickly readied and served in short order.

The sea was smooth and they were making good time. In a little over two hours they were passing by Santa Cruz, relatively close to shore, thinking was that too many people were there with all their stuff. After another hour they had put most of that behind them and the land took on a much more pleasant look. Actually beautiful, and it fit the picture and that of their mood.

As ten o'clock arrived they were approaching the area where Waddell Creek descends into an open valley and empties into the ocean. Ed and Julia both could see the looks on John, Sandra and Robert's face grow somber. Looking up the mountain side one could almost pick out the area where the native village had once stood. Now only the fire scarred terrain running up the mountain side was left to hold their attention.

"One can speculate on what happened to our native family. It could have been as I mentioned yesterday or maybe they were lost to a natural disaster like this fire," John said this in a sad voice that all of them understood. No answers were offered and none were needed but the five of them had become a new family of their own.

Five o'clock had them passing Pacifica and two hours later they went under the Golden Gate Bridge. A few minutes later they were docked at the guest slip at the Saint Francis Yacht Club. It had been settled that John would pick them up next morning at 10:30 am for lunch at his place and they would be treated with a tour of his little empire. His five scientist friends would join them and a surprise guest would also be there. He stepped off the boat and walked up the ramp to the waiting limousine.

The tired crew of *Du-eT* decided the short walk to

Fisherman's Wharf would make for a good break and a sit down dinner at one of the more casual restaurants would be a nice way to end the day. They found the restaurant they wanted, ordered sea food platters family style and enjoyed the dinner and the night time view of the bay.

It was Robert who started the conversation after the meal was finished. Fortunately there were a number of empty tables so they didn't feel hurried. "That was a good trip up the coast. All of it. Ed and Julia, I speak for myself, and I think for Sandra, you make excellent traveling companions. On a boat, even one as comfortable as *Du-eT* and having good seas, you can find out what people are really like in a few days out. Both of us want to continue to have you as friends. We hope you feel likewise." He paused, then continued before they could answer, "Then there is John. You can surmise we have become close to him. He does march to his own drum but so far all the assumptions he makes on what we will do with him, and his group, have been correct. He is a manager of almost everything that interests him. Tomorrow you two will be asked to do something which will be beyond your comprehension. I suggest you give it serious thought. We have already told you some of which we have done with him. First I went back in time and then Sandra and I made that trip with him joining us. It couldn't happen but it did."

Robert looked at the others and smiled. He could tell at that moment that Ed and Julia would listen to John and might be willing to take the offered trip of a lifetime. He could hardly wait to find out what it would be and how it would differ from what he and Sandra had done.

Ed looked at Julia and started to laugh. "You are

ready to do this, aren't you? It will be me that may not have the courage to go there but we will have to wait until tomorrow to find that out. Tomorrows are always the best days for new experiences and we will find out about this one then."

It was a nice walk back to the boat and friendly hugs and hand shakes were made before turning in. Tomorrow was going to be a day to remember.

Chapter 35

Morning dawned clear on this most important day, Friday the eighth of April, 2022. Instead of the normal fog and mist covering the bay the Golden Gate Bridge showed herself in all her glory to the four friends on board *Du-eT.* They had finished breakfast, eating in the cockpit, and it was from the jetty near the Saint Frances Yacht Club that this magnificent view was presented. They had taken an early morning walk up to the club using the facilities for bathroom chores and showers. Dressed in their best from the boat they walked back down and onto the ramp to the dock. The four could have graced the cover of any high fashion magazines.

Julia and Sandra wearing light colored slacks, fine cotton tops and deck shoes looked spectacular. Ed and Robert wore dress pants with complimenting long sleeve shirts, also with nice deck shoes, looked as they should be accompanying them. These were two beautiful women, and two handsome men, confident of not only their looks but their abilities. They had been given their looks from their parents but their confidence had been earned.

They were ready for an exciting day and at exactly ten-thirty a big limousine drove up, stopped at the top of the ramp and the chauffeur stepped around the car opening the doors. Minutes later they were skirting the Presidio and then crossing through Golden Gate Park. A run down a congested 19th Ave, passing San Francisco State College to join Interstate Highway 280 heading south. It was a beautiful and scenic drive and before they were ready exited onto Sand Hill Road just short of the Stanford Linear Accelerator. They then turned into Sharon Heights, a very upscale neighborhood close to Stanford University and in the heart of Silicon Valley. After several turns, that had them all lost, they were driven through the gates into John's estate. Robert remembered the scene from his and Sandra's visit a few days after they had docked *Du-eT* having completed their Pacific crossing from Hawaii. He had followed directions given to him online by John and they drove through the gates in their old Honda van. The directions vanished as he parked the van and when they left that evening he eventually found his way back to Sand Hill Road and knew he could never find his way back. He felt the same way as the limo slowly drove into the parking area. The five luxury sedans were in the same place as the last time but the two cars parked in the first slots were a pair of new Porsche 911 Carrea S's.

The first was a bright metallic cinnamon color that was enough to hurt your eyes. Bent down and looking into the shinning silver metallic twin was a tall woman who had just arrived as indicated by the open door of the first Porsche. She straightened up and turned toward the limo and Allison Turner presented a smile that the four in the limo immediately recognized. The chauffeur seemed to know what was going on and stopped so all could exit in the space by the Porsches.

Greetings were exchanged with hugs and kisses to cheeks. The surprise was complemented by them all wanting to see each other again. Just as they got sorted out a small man approached and the excited greetings were repeated with John. "Lunch is waiting so let's head inside. My group is looking forward to today and we have much to do. Ed, the silver thing is your rental to drive to Marina del Rey. Hope the color is okay. It does look a little pale compared to Allison's but you can keep up with her if you want to try,"

Entering the house through the big doors, Robert and Sandra were remembering their last visit so the surprise of the huge great room was left for Ed and Julia. Allison had arrived the day before and had just returned from a quick trip to downtown Palo Alto. She had been impressed by her small friend living in such a big house but to her he filled the space nicely with his intellect and good nature.

Introductions were made to the seated gentlemen in the large leather chairs. Again none would remember their names for some reason that had to do with the nature of what was about to happen. The dining area was toward the back of the room and had a round table that could comfortably seat ten people. Eleven made it a cozy fit. It was almost noon by this time and all were seated and service came from a hidden kitchen. Large plates held thick lamb chops sided with mashed red potatoes and diagonally sliced fresh carrots with a special glaze. Water was served in fine crystal. It was considered by the guests to be one of the best meals they had ever eaten. Dessert was fresh fruit and a large plate excellent cookies.

Ed Adams Touches The Stars

The conversation was eclectic and all participated. Even the five mysterious scientists of John's group joined in with sincere relish. As the last cookie was taken from the platter and every bowl of fruit had been emptied John stood and looked at his guests. "You may wonder why you are here and what it is I want to show you. You may have guessed some of this and Allison already knows. I am sure Robert and Sandra expect what it may be but let me just say for right now this gathering is for Ed and Julia." John said this as he watched their faces and then smiled and continued, "You are both too smart not to have already figured this out so we will now proceed to my little place of science beyond belief."

Chapter 36

John suggested that all who needed to use a bathroom should do so. He pointed out three possible directions and Ed and Julia chose the one just past the kitchen. It was the kitchen they really wanted to see and it did not disappoint. Big and fully equipped with all the best as was expected. What was unexpected was that is was obviously used and was not just a show case. The bathroom was the first door on the left down the only other passage from the kitchen and it too did not disappoint.

Robert and Sandra utilized the powder room and John and Allison headed for his bedroom. Only Sandra had paid attention and an mischievous smile crossed her face. The other five had seemed to disperse by magic and within ten minutes all had returned to the grand main hall.

"Follow me now to a very special place where the unbelievable is accomplished. We have only a few more weeks to use this space and then it will be no more. That is too bad but it is probably for the best. As is true with much in life it is the journey and not the destination that has it's true value." John said this with no remorse and he wanted to show these five special people what he and his scientist friends had built. Not how it worked, but that it did.

He went to one of the doors that had a key pad, quickly punched a six numerical code and there was a just noticeable click. Opening the door he led his group into a large elevator. Only two of the scientists joined them so the eight stood together as the door closed and John pressed the only button on the panel. The descent was short and the door opened into a large, well lit room holding four golf cart style vehicles, each with four seats. John waved at the carts and he and Allison took the first in line. He had Ed and Julia join him, Robert and Sandra took the second and the two scientists took the third. There was only one exit in the room. It was a tunnel wide enough to have two way traffic with the carts. It was also well lit and without hesitation John started down it at a brisk speed. Conversation wasn't an option and there were no sights to raise questions or require explanation.

After about five minutes the sounds of air conditioners reached them and a slight odor of hot electronic equipment was present. A turn in the tunnel brought them into a large room which at the end was the tube of the Accelerator coming in from the right and exiting to the left. John parked in the middle and the two other carts pulled up behind him. It had been a ten minute ride.

John gathered them together and started the tour. "As you can see the walls are covered with computing equipment. You may have seen some television coverage of the Crypto Currency mining equipment and this is similar but much more powerful. I won't discuss numbers of units but it is in the tens of thousands. They run along the walls of the Accelerator tunnel in both directions. We have two large diesel generators to provide enough electricity to run our programs and at this moment they are running at full power. Come with me," speaking to Ed, Julia, Robert and Sandra.

A single door was between two racks and they entered another room set up as a small theater. A dozen big recliner chairs faced a big television screen. John motioned the four guests to take the first row of four seats and he stepped over to a pedestal table facing them. The screen lit up and on a split screen presented a view of some kind of glass chamber surrounded by electronic circuitry. The view was from inside the chamber. The other half of the screen was filled with a frontal view of a house flanked on each side by partial views of similar homes. It was a black and white photographic image of good quality but vintage in appearance.

"Do you recognize the house, Ed?" John asked.

"It is Rachmaninoff's house in Beverly Hills. Had to have been taken in 1942, the year he purchased it. He only had a little over a year to live there as he died in March of 1943." Ed answered with no hesitation.

John smiled, then said to Robert, "Robert, I know you have heard me say this to you several times but I will say it to Ed this time. You never disappoint."

It was then that it all became clear. Allison appeared in the glass chamber dressed in 1940's attire, looking spect-acular. All four of John's guests then knew what was about to happen. Whatever door she had entered from had been closed and she was now surrounded by the circuitry. Julia reached for Ed's hand and held it tight. The right side screen switched to a current view of the property. There was a small dot flashing on the middle of the lawn to the right of the sidewalk running up to the front door. Ed and Julia had stopped breathing. Robert calmly sat transfixed and Sandra stared in disbelief of what she knew was about to happen.

John nodded in the direction of the screen and there was a foggy green flash in the chamber and Allison Turner disappeared. Almost at the same moment the right hand screen showed a view of the house as one would see if standing at the point where the flashing dot had been.

"Oh my God! Oh my God!" Julia cried out. Ed sat absolutely still, mesmerized with what he had just seen and knowing what it was. Robert and Sandra looked almost amused. It was what they had expected but thought they would never actually get to see.

Chapter 37

John faced the four, cleared his throat to get their attention, and continued as if what had just happened was nothing special. "Allison has just been transported back in time to March 14, 1943 which is Sunday. It is 11:48 am and a typical Southern California Spring morning. The Rachmaninoff's were planning one of their Sunday afternoon open houses for friends, and friends of friends, and she will try to pass herself of as a friend of a friend. She is wearing fifteen cameras and what you are seeing now is what she is seeing and what is around her. What you will be hearing when her microphone is on is what is being said as you are watching it happen. A neat trick don't you think?"

John was beaming with the pleasure of sharing this feat with the others. All their work had been held in strict secrecy and he wanted his new friends to be able to not only see what they could do but to have them appreciate and witness what had been done. He had more to say but would wait as Allison had reached the door just ahead of a couple approaching from the street. She rang the bell and a young girl opened it and welcomed her, and the couple behind her, into the house. It was Julia that cried out, "That is Wilma Herman. That is Wilma at fifteen. She has to see this, John! Can she see it soon?"

John waited as Allison had moved to the side so that the three of them walked into the foyer as if they had come together. Wilma escorted them to the right through an open doorway into the living room. It was a big room and the two grand pianos were the main attraction but did not dominate the space. It was colorfully decorated and about twenty people were already there. Allison did her job and circulated around the room, a quick look into the library through the open bi-fold doors and another into the breakfast room with the kitchen beyond. More guests had arrived and were being greeted and then escorted into the foyer by Wilma.

It was obvious some had been there before and others were first time visitors. As Allison made the single tour of the room the big screen had been divided into eight sections and as many views were being projected at the same time. Several conversations were simultaneously being picked up and were hard to understand. Some were in Russian, and others in another foreign language.

"Allison, any time you are ready. Same spot as near as possible. You have gotten what we need. Try for privacy," John said this with extra meaning that Allison already knew was important.

She retreated to the lawn area, checking her location carefully, looking all around her and then nodded her head to indicate all was clear. There was a hint of greenish vapor and the video and sound was gone. In the left screen now showing the chamber, along with the green vapor, stood Allison. She sported a smile that said to all that it had been a highlight in her life. The four guests thought likewise. Two had expected as much but the other two already knew what their answer would be when John asked the question they knew was coming.

John was smiling. He knew what would happen when the four would witness this for the first time. He felt it every time he had witnessed it happen and even as it was of his, and his group's, invention it was still a thrill to know it could be done. He was planning one more trip before they would close down the operation. Maybe some day in the future others could figure out a way to do travel of this kind but he was going to let go of it for now. Too much could go wrong and there was always the danger of affecting the present by altering the past to make it worth while to continue. He was confident his plans for this last trip was safe and his hope was that it would add much to the present without any danger if it happened.

"Let's return to my place, make ourselves comfortable and I will tell you what I would like to do before we remove all this and can not make any more trips back in time," he said this with a wave towards the waiting carts. Allison walked into the room just as he said this, dressed back in her own outfit, and gave John an embrace and kiss that was obviously more than just a thank you.

The short trip back to the house was just the two carts as the scientists had remained in the SLAC area. They spread out around the table, coffee was served by John and a dish of small chocolates was placed in the center. The anticipation was almost unbearable for five of them, with John relaxed but excited with the prospect of presenting his plans.

Chapter 38

John placed five files on the table. In appearance they ranged from somewhat worn to new and from thin to thick. He then said, "You can probably guess what these are, investigation reports, one for each of you here. I am not going to elaborate on any of these. We also now have reports on Wilma Herman and Cindy. Anyone we consider to be involved in our program must be thoroughly investigated. I think you can understand why this needs to be done and I will leave it at that." John said this last as he pushed the pile aside.

He then gave them a smile they all had learned that meant he was now ready to tell them something of importance. This time they were expecting the purpose for their presence.

"As you are aware this will be our last visit to the past. There was never any idea, or desire, to capitalize on this enterprise. As it has become obvious in our current culture when one accumulates enormous wealth through some special new business venture or investment they seek another interest to spend that wealth on, whether wisely or not. My group was here at the very start of Silicon Valley as venture capitalists and managed to turn an initial five thousand dollar investment into several billion. The two physics majors, asleep in the chairs over there, never graduated but dreamed up the idea going back in time travel. My other three partners were more digital engineering types and were able to put the whole thing together with the help of several hundred part time, young super technology geeks. I was the lowly manager. What a trip it has been. But it is about over and it is time for it to be." John sat back and looked at his group of friends. Robert had been the first to actually visit history. It was an out of body experience as it was his mind that had been transmitted and the use of hologram technology allowed the visited to interact with the visitor as if he was actually there physically. It turned out to be too dangerous for the visitor to make more than three trips so the program was abandoned. The encapsulation technique that was developed was the breakthrough that could transport people and objects, such as Robert and Sandra's sailboat with them on board, back in time safely from which they could visit places in person and return with no side effects. This was how Allison had just made the visit to the home of Sergei Rachmaninoff they had all just witnessed.

John now presented his plan for this last trip. It was not really a grand plan by any means. It was more like a pleasant hand shake or kiss on the check as in a fond farewell between close friends. There was a chance of it being much more and he was making a big assumption that it would happen.

John looked first at Ed, then Julia, then back to Ed and pronounced the expected, "Ed, I want you, and Julia if she wishes, to pay a visit to Sergei Rachmaninoff on Sunday, March 14, 1943 at his home arriving at exactly

11:48 am. I also want Allison and Cindy to go with you. Rachmaninoff is in declining health and will be in bed upstairs in pain, fully aware of his fate and of the activities downstairs. He dies only two weeks later on March 28 with his wife Natalia and daughter Irina at his side. He had lost consciousness two days before his death."

John paused and received the response he was expecting, silence. "You have just witnessed Allison's trip and visit. She was sent to see if the arrival spot was suitable and if it would be private enough. You have witnessed that happen and your, Allison and Cindy's arrival will be at the same spot, the same day and at exactly the same time. Wilma will answer the door and the other couple approaching will be right behind you, just as they were with Allison. I want Wilma to be here with the rest of us to witness this visit."

Julia reached for Ed's hand, looking directly at him and nodded her okay. Ed looked at John saying, "You have our interest and if we like what you propose we will go. How does Cindy fit into this and why do you want us to go?"

John was delighted. It was what he expected as was usually the case when he approached people to do things he wanted done. He would tell them most of his plan and could be honest with that part. But he did have this one possibility that may bring value to the trip beside giving Rachmaninoff some peace before he left this life.

Chapter 39

John looked at his guests. The five of them were probably the best looking group of middle aged human beings one could assemble in one place. Allison was actually a senior, but was none the less still a woman whose looks one could admire. It was not their physical appearances that he valued, however, it was their intelligence and abilities that drew him to them. He had worked with some exceptional men and women over the years but in these five he had found the ones he wanted as his friends. Real friends for whatever future he might have. This was his wished for family. He had no others to turn to and no longer wanted to be alone.

"Let me first tell you what we know about Cindy. Unfortunately it is not very much. I haven't met her in person, as it is with Wilma Herman." He slid two of the thin folders over but didn't open them and continued, "We will have to depend on your relationship with Wilma and hope you can make an appraisal of Cindy for us. We will need her for this project to work. We know she is an accomplished pianist, especially gifted and a true student of Rachmaninoff. Her mother pushed her too hard early and eventually was forced to let her go to a special music boarding school. Last night Allison and I were going over what I had on her early years and she told me she had a friend that invited her to a recital given at the school. She was very impressed with Cindy and followed her progress for a few years. She then lost track of this gifted young girl and was wondering what had happened to her. We have one of our investigators on the case and hope we can find a little more of what happened between leaving the music school and starting her working with Wilma."

"Now as for Allison. She was my only friend when I was a little boy in San Francisco. Even being older than I she would play with me, as an older sister might, and made that part of my life so much better."

John waited and enjoyed the looks he and Allison where being given by the others. He didn't mention how he had cried for weeks after her parents, with her in tow, had moved away. She had been his only friend during his childhood and seeing her again in Santa Barbara last week had brought back that long lost desire for her friendship. He felt a bit foolish to have never tried to see her again but had followed much of her life through the newspapers and magazines as her two marriages to prominent men kept her in the public's eye. He sensed he was drifting off course so continued, "Cindy's early childhood was good by most standards. Happy parents, an older brother and younger sister. It was as she finished primary school that things started to fall apart. She started early on separating from her siblings because of her concentration on her interest in music and the piano. Her mother's thinking that they had a prodigy in the family had her concentrate on Cindy to the determent of the rest of the family, including her husband. She started pushing Cindy in that direction much too hard, limiting her time with others. The parent's marriage began to be strained by this and her older brother got into the wrong crowd and was placed in a juvenile facility. Next her younger sister developed leukemia and died at the age eleven. Her parents divorced. Leaving all that behind she somehow managed to be accepted into a school for the gifted in Michigan and never went back home as her family had disintegrated."

John paused as he thought this was a lot to digest, then continued, "As she studied the piano she became infatuated with Rachmaninoff, both his music and especially in the man. Sometime in her second or third year at the school her mental state became so entangled with this obsession she required professional help. Apparently after several years of therapy she was back into music but wasn't able to handle the stress of playing in public. She was able to work in an extended care facility for the indigent and this lead a counselor to match her up with Wilma Herman. We have no information of her time, or where she was, for those years in therapy. As you have seen, it has worked out for both and has brought them into our sphere. You must also understand she is a true master in playing his work. Ed, you have already witnessed this but I don't think you fully understand what she is capable of yet."

Again John thought he should pause. It was Sandra that asked the obvious question. "What happened to her that would require that kind of help?" His investigator had found out with a little unethical snooping and John had decided that at least Ed had to know and saw no harm in trusting the others not to misuse what he was about to tell them.

"Cindy became obsessed with the thought she had gone back in time to when Rachmaninoff was depressed from the poor response to his first concerto and the church forbidding his engagement to Natalia. He was in his early twenties, close to the age that Cindy is now. She had fantasized her relationship with him to the point of not being able to relate to her own time. She could no longer think she was living in the present."

Ed started to speak, then paused and started again. He spoke softly, as if he was telling the others a secret they should not repeat. "When we were at Wilma's, the four of us," he started looking at Sandra and Robert, "I left the table after I finished my meal to watch and listen to Cindy play. I had never heard Rachmaninoff played in that style. It was totally romantic. No Russian bravado with heavy chords and pounding of the keys. I wasn't sure what to say but I was so impressed that I told her that Wilma was becoming part of our family and I would like her to come with her. Be part of our family." Ed let his voice trail off on the last sentence as he couldn't describe why he had made the offer. He just knew that he should.

John listened carefully to what Ed was saying and a small smile showed on his face. His eyes conveyed an understanding of what had just been said and it was exactly what he had expected. He knew that his plans were coming together and that it was time to tell them all what they were. It wouldn't include what he was thinking might happen. That would have to wait until it did.

Chapter 40

John sat very still as he appraised this new group seated around his table. Allison was to his left with Robert next to her and then Sandra and Julia, sitting just a bit closer together than the rest. Ed completed the circle and was to John's right. Missing, of course, were Wilma and Cindy. These were the seven he would be working with on this, his last adventure into the past.

It was time. His partners and he had made their mark in what became Silicon Valley and then moved on into a secretive development of investigating the past in a most unusual way. It brought a smile to his face which was not lost on the five sitting around him at the table. They were waiting, each knowing that they would some how be involved in this last hurrah for John and his group.

"I will now tell you what it is I want to do. You have already seen a demonstration with Allison's visit to Rachmaninoff's home in 1943. That you were able to actually see it in real time, so to speak, as spectators is what my team has developed. We think what we propose now should be the grand finale of our efforts. It is too dangerous to go much further as an accidental change of history could be catastrophic, as you can imagine." John paused at this and could see he had their undivided attention.

"I feel it is safe to make a visit to Rachmaninoff on this date and to interact with those there without changing history in any way. As you know those there will have no memory of our visit as they have already lived that time before. The time we are spending with them has already happened. Although we will have recorded our visit and will remember what happened, those that have already lived that time will not. Robert and Sandra are most aware of this. Since this trip will be an hour at most, those that go will only have that one hour to relive. During that hour they will not remember it except as in a dream. Once that hour is lived it will all come back clearly."

Again John paused not for any questions, none of which were asked, but to prepare for what was coming next.

"I would like Ed, Cindy and Allison to make the trip." John saw Julia reach for Ed's arm and see the alarmed expression on her face. "You may go if you wish, Julia. It won't be a problem and I understand your reasons. If you choose to go you will add to the party as you always do. Robert and Sandra will sit this one out but will be in the audience as will Wilma. She will get to see herself as she was at fifteen and will know many of the people there. It should be an experience of a lifetime for her."

No one said a word. Except for John it seemed if all were holding their breath. All waiting for what was next and John didn't make them wait.

"Cindy will have to be convinced and it will be up to Ed to do the convincing. Being present when Robert played his recorded meeting with Rachmaninoff to Wilma should make her decision an easy one. Wilma will be asked to witness this trip as my guest. It will be her enthusiasm that should help make Ed's effort to secure Cindy's participation. We need her to make the visit." John paused again and then continued, "Rachmaninoff is close to dying. He is in considerable pain and probably on some kind of medication to help him through it. In 1940s there was little hope for someone in his condition and few drugs were available to help with the pain. Cocaine was illegal at the time but was available to those with the right connections. I would guess he had something like that to help him through it. He was in the upstairs bedroom, just at the head of the stairs, and one can assume his door would be open. He will be at least semiconscious when we get there. We need that assumption to be correct."

Ed moved about in his chair and looked at Julia, smiled, took her hand and then said, "John, let me guess what you are about to propose. Cindy and I will seat ourselves at the pianos, play some Rachmaninoff and you are expecting the great man will make an appearance. He will still have the strength to come down the stairs and talk to us. I am, I think Cindy is too, capable of playing to a level that he will have to do that to find out who it is that is playing. My question is what do you hope will happen to make this worth the risk."

John smiled again and shocked them all, "I know what it is I want to happen, and it should happen, but I won't tell you ahead of time. You will know immediately if it does and it may work out such to occupy all of you for years to come. I hope to join you." His smile broadened further and then he continued, "It is time to plan the timing of this project. I have secured from Stanford an extra week. We have at most only two weeks to make it happen. First, Allison has already committed."

Sandra spoke first. "John, I understand that Robert and I will just have to watch this happen. Deep down I want to travel again and would if it had been offered. How do Robert and I fit in here? How we do is intriguing and we will trust you in that we will." She looked at Robert and he nodded back in his agreement.

"Thank you both and be assured if all works out you won't be disappointed in what will be proposed." John said this and was delighted to get the confirmation which would help in convincing Ed, and possibly Julia, to make the trip. He turned to Ed and asked, "It is up to you Ed. Would you be willing to make the trip?" Expecting hesitation on Ed's part he continued, "Let me entice you a bit more before you answer. You saw Allison make the trip and return. Our group will travel to the exact same place at the exact same time. You will all be supplied with the appropriate clothes and you will fit in with those at the house as Allison did. What I want you and Cindy to do is to lure Rachmaninoff to come downstairs to see who is playing his music and converse with them. This will be your chance to actually meet Sergei Rachmaninoff in person. Talk to him, shake his hand and have him sit next to you as he watches you play. For Cindy it will be much more as you will find out when you try to convince her to go. I need you both there to make this trip work."

Julia was now grasping Ed's arm so tight that he had to cover her hand to seek some relief. He smiled a reassuring smile and she relaxed her grip. She knew he would make the right decision for them both and she would be considered in it's making.

"John, I have some questions and Julia and I both have to agree on what we think of your answers. I am willing to go but I must be sure it is worth the risks. Julia and I have too much to loose to risk some thing as far fetched as this. You have skillfully manipulated us into this project. Meeting Robert and Sandra through Robert's trip with Rachmaninoff brought us together as friends. How you could to do this in less than a week is a remarkable bit of management. Most impressive." Ed let this compliment move the conversation back to John.

He smiled, bowed his head slightly toward Ed and was thinking what a pleasure it was to work with people of this caliber.

Chapter 41

John was all business as he began to outline what needed to be done if the proposed visit with Rachmaninoff was to take place. The sooner the better was his thinking and he was hoping it would take place one week from today, Friday, April 15, 2022. Why not income tax day, the thought brought a smile to his face.

"Ed, a great deal is resting on your shoulders. If you decide against making the trip our efforts here will be over. No regrets, for me or my partners, in doing so as it is time to close down this project. But as I have implied it may work out in a fashion that will benefit not only us but music history as well. I realize I am teasing you with that but please bear with me for now. To help in your decision let me propose a time table." John paused here, but his guests sat very still and waited.

"One week from today at four o'clock in the after-noon. In attendance in the viewing room will be myself, my five partners, Wilma Herman, Robert and Sandra, and two others that are part of the technical staff that have been with me for years and are the only others that fully understand how this technology works. They have air tight non-disclosure agreements and also have my trust. Ed and Julia, you may invite your two children."

Again John paused and then continued. "The trip will be for one hour maximum. As mentioned before the period clothing, top to bottom, will be provided and I guarantee a perfect fit. The time of arrival will be exactly as it was for Allison's trip and all three, or four if Julia goes, of you will be transported together. The return can be a little more flexible but you will need to locate yourselves to the same location as your arrival. We will at that time imprint your positions on the lawn and when Allison gives us the all clear sign you will be transported back. Your positions don't have to be exact but must be close to make the transport less time consuming. At first you will not be able to remember anything other than a flash of green mist but as the next hour passes you will have the memories return. We will run our tapes back for you after our evening meal and not only will you be able to see the parts your head camera records, but each other's cameras as well. It should be most exciting."

John decided to wait them out and received the first question from Ed. It was not what he was expecting.

"How are you thinking that Cindy and I can put together a program that can get Rachmaninoff off his death bed to come down stairs with such a short time to prepare?"

"The short answer is that you are a professional at the top of your game. You will know what to do to make it happen. That is why you can do what you do. The other part is that Cindy has a talent that may not be equivalent to yours but the part she will play, literally, will come to her in a natural way as she has prepared for this trip in her dreams for years. In fact, it was what was in those dreams that led her to us."

Allison was next to speak. "John! Why the tease about why we are doing this? Shouldn't you let Ed and Julia in on it. I don't care as you have just saved me from becoming another boring old matron in Santa Barbara. I will take any trips into history you can dream up. What a ride!"

John knew her question would be asked and not only was he ready, he was delighted that her enthusiasm would help get Ed on board. "I need you all to act as normal as possible. Just Sunday guests at a party for the appreciation of music. Very few knew that Rachmaninoff only had a few weeks left to live. They knew he was not feeling well and had to cancel the remaining of his 1943 concert tour. Four weeks before this he had done a recital in Knoxville, Tennessee and upon his return was when he learned of his fatal melanoma cancer.

"Vladimir Horowitz will be showing up a little after noon and will of course then be the center of attention. It would be best for us to be gone from the scene before he arrives." John paused and knowing he had to answer Allison's question, continued, "I don't mean to tease you about the purpose for this trip. I just ask that you and Cindy play the big Steinway's in a manner that will get Rachmaninoff off of his sick bed, come down-stairs and talk with you. It will be in this conversation that if we are successful he will tell, or ask you a question, that you will understand why you are there. If I am wrong about this, which I may be, it will just be a wonderful few minutes for you and Cindy to have a personal visit with a man you both admire."

The five guests sat perfectly still not knowing what to say. Allison didn't care. The excitement of John's trips back into history had lifted her spirits to a level she hadn't had in years, actually never had before. Robert and Sandra could view this with just a touch of envy but felt they had already had their share of the travel already. Ed was intrigued with the possibilities of actually meeting and talking to Rachmaninoff and also thought he knew what John's hope for a result was based on. Julia was scared. Not about the trip but whether she should participate. She believed it would be safe but was thinking she really didn't belong on this one. She would have to decide on that in the next few days.

Chapter 42

It was now getting late in the afternoon. John told his guests he would like their answers by Monday before six o'clock that evening. They said their good afternoons and that he would have his answers before the deadline. Ed and Julia would drive home to Palm Desert in the morning and try to arrange for a stop to see Wilma and Cindy on their way home or plan one for the next day. They would spend one more night on *Du-eT* and leave from there. Robert and Sandra would be moving the boat to their long term rental slip across the bay on Monday and keep in touch online. They planned to be home in Point Reyes Station that evening. Allison stood next to John and waved to their departing guests as the limo picked up Robert and Sandra and Ed and Julia squeezed into the Porsche 911 Carrea.

All four of the departing guests did not miss the sight of John and Allison turning and entering John's house together. Neither Julia or Sandra could suppress polite laughter and likewise neither Ed or Robert could hide knowing grins. All four thought the same thought, "John, you never disappoint."

Ed fumbled with the ignition but got the powerful Porsche engine started in time to get behind the limo as it exited the gated entry. He didn't want to try to find his own way out of the housing development as he hadn't paid attention when they had entered. Forty five minutes later they were in the Saint Francis Yacht Club parking lot. They decided to take a leisurely stroll to Fisherman's Wharf for a take out Fish and Chips. They were back on board by eight-thirty and soon enjoying some coffee and cookies. All were tired but for whatever reason were content. Only nine days had passed since they had left Marina del Rey and their futures were now entwined in John's world. Sandra asked the obvious question of Ed, "Are you going to do it?"

"I haven't decided for sure yet, but probably."

Julia reached for Ed's arm, pulled him toward her and said in a sad manner, "I can't decide if I want to go or wait for you to come back. You have to come back. You have to do that!" She rose and went into the aft stateroom.

"I want to trust John on this. I saw Allison make the trip and return with no effects. I have seen photos of the two of you ten thousand years in the past and return. I have to believe it is safe." Ed said this as he stood to follow Julia.

Robert could sense the uncertainty in Ed's voice and said, "It works. You don't have to worry about getting both there and coming back. John wouldn't send you if there was any chance you would not get back. I would leave that question aside for now and concentrate on working with Cindy on her part in this trip. How you get Rachmaninoff to come downstairs will be what is needed to make the trip work. What John is wanting to happen is fun to speculate on but I can guess. I think you already know." Robert said this last as a question.

"I can make a guess but I will keep it to myself for now. I expect you also have an opinion but let us leave it at that. Let me work with Cindy, get Wilma ready to go to Palo Alto, and settle with Julia on how to handle this. Monday, only three days, is not much time to contemplate a change in your life." Ed was tired, worried and a bit confused. It showed on his face and in his demeanor.

Sandra stood and announced she was tired and it was time to retire, but first said to Ed, "I would go without any hesitation. Robert might think it over a little more, but he would go." She left the salon and Robert stood to do likewise. He turned and looked into Ed's eyes saying, "I would do it. Something big is about to happen. You have to find out what that is. For all of us," and he followed Sandra to their stateroom. Ed headed back to join Julia.

Chapter 43

Ed entered the aft stateroom just as Julia came out from the head. She had put on a T-shirt and boxer shorts for bed. Ed stood still appreciating her looks and thinking she was as beautiful now as she was the day he first saw her some twenty-eight years ago. He smiled a smile that Julia was accustomed to seeing and knew it's meaning. It wasn't sex, it was a love for her that she could depend on. It was something she cherished above all else.

"You are going to tell me all of it right now, aren't you? Every thing you are thinking about this offer to visit Rachmaninoff that makes it worth the risk." Julia said this as she pulled back the covers and climbed into the bed. "Hurry up!" came next.

Once Ed was in bed, made himself comfortable and pulled up the covers Julia slid in close and placed her free hand on his chest. "'Why is John doing this? Why are we involved? What does he expect to find or get that will affect our futures together?"

Ed waited trying to organize his thoughts and how to express them. He then started, "John is a brilliant man, an accomplished manager and wise. He also understands human nature. He and his friends have been able to put this fantastic enterprise together but now it is coming to it's end. Their age, the end of the lease and the thought they should no longer push their luck on not changing history. I can't speak for the other five but John is not ready to retire and grow roses. He wants and needs a new project to pursue. At least one more."

Ed paused and Julia moved closer and asked in a whisper, "You are not ready to give up the music are you? You have just started what can become a path to greatness. You can't let go of that now!"

"No. Don't worry about me leaving the classical music arena. Not for a good while." He paused and then continued, "Here is what I think is going on with John. How he could put it together in only a few days is beyond me but this is what my thinking is. Like all men of real talent as their life comes towards it's end they begin thinking about all the things they wished to accomplish and the things they had started but not finished. John knows, as I do, that Rachmaninoff would have been going through this stage of his life and has suddenly found he has no more time left. He would want someone, or some group, to finish and complete all the music he had post-phoned bringing to life. John is thinking he may present us with what he has started but not finished."

Julia sat up and looked at Ed. "Of course that's it. Rachmaninoff would have boxes of sheet music covered with all sorts of notes, scores, changes and possibly new pieces. All he wished to work on some day when he had time. He needs someone, or several someones, to do it as he knows he won't be able to. That has to be what John is thinking. It will happen or it won't."

Ed pulled Julia down to him and kissed her. "You

see this as clearly as I do. John expects us to figure this out but will not want Cindy to suspect it. He needs her talent and infatuation with Rachmaninoff to lure him downstairs. She plays his music differently. She expresses that infatuation in the way she plays it, totally romantic. He will want to meet her and will come down, sit by her and watch her play. As I play he will recognize my skill but it will be Cindy that will gain his interest. It will be his gift to her if it can be worked out how to make the transfer. This is were Wilma will come into the mix." Ed stopped here as he thought he might have gone to far already.

"Edward Adams you are too smart. I love John's expression, you never disappoint. I won't be going with you. There is nothing I can add to the visit and might even distract from it. You have to come back to me. Don't you dare break my heart." Julia said this with tears forming in her eyes but was still smiling. Ed answered, "I think I have heard that once before," and pulled her closer.

In the forward stateroom the conversation was much more simple and brief. They had prepared for bed and snuggled close together. Sandra then asked a question she had asked Robert several times before, "What is John up to this time?"

Robert smiled at this and answered, "John is trying to do something for Rachmaninoff that will result in a new project for him to manage. I have no idea what that might be but putting together our little group is more about finding a new a project than dealing with us personally. As for Rachmaninoff it must have something to do with him thinking that he would need someone to carry on with his music so that his work would be appreciated for years after his passing. Ed and Cindy are relatively young and are both fluent and skilled in playing his work. He may want to talk to them about something like that. I can't see why he should be concerned. His success had been so obvious how could he have any doubts about it's future."

Sandra moved closer and whispered in Robert's ear, "It isn't that. John has more he wants to do and limited time left to do it. He wants one more big project and this time do it on his own and in the present. Rachmaninoff must still have musical scores laying about that he still wanted to complete and now has no time left to do it. He needs others, and Ed and Cindy are the ones that can make it happen if they can get hold of the music sheets and bring them back. John will want to be in charge of getting the works to the public and will want the story told which is where we may come into this one. This is both for Rachmaninoff and for John."

Robert rolled over to face Sandra. He looked into her eyes and said, "You never cease to amaze me. That is exactly what is going on. How could John have put this all together so in such a short time. We will be involved. I think you are probably right about John wanting some recognition but for the classical music world it will be the music. It would be something very special and good to be associated with. Do you want to go there?"

Sandra kissed Robert, smiled the smile he loved the most of anything in this world, and answered, "Yes!"

Chapter 44

In the big house in Sharon Heights, Palo Alto the rather small owner, dressed in comfortable pajamas, slid into his bed next to the tall woman seven years his senior who was much better looking than most women her age. She was wearing a nightgown that showed her off as the desirable woman she still was. Her gentle laugh was followed with a teasing question, "John, what am I doing here? Was is it just ten days ago I saw you again, for the first time in sixty years in Santa Barbara, and I am now in your bed in Palo Alto. Would you please explain this to me?"

John's smile was radiant. He hadn't felt this good in years. It wasn't that there was a woman in bed next to him, a woman who was just a girlfriend to a small seven year old boy playing in Golden Gate Park sixty years ago. It was the thought of the grand plan that had dropped into his lap just two weeks ago when he attended the Los Angeles Philharmonic opening concert and spotted Robert and Sandra in the audience. He saw their reaction to Edward Adams as he played Rachmaninoff Number 3, followed by Number 2. He had slipped into the post concert donor's party and carefully watched and listened to the interchange of Ed, Julia and Wilma Herman. Then as Cindy helped Wilma out of the gathering their approach to Ed and Julia. He had found the project he was desperately looking for just in time and he knew he would have to put it together at a speed he had never had to work at before. His smile broadened even wider.

Allison voice brought him back. "I don't hear an answer to my question. I am not staying here unless I get one! Oh what the hell, I'll stay the night anyway!"

Her question, and demand for an answer, brought him back to reality from what was as good as any dream he could ever have imagined. He thought about how to answer her and took a little too long.

"Okay my paramour, if that's the best you can do for me tonight I will wait until morning!" was Allison's tease.

"Allison, my answer will take time and I want it to be correct. I think you can understand my feelings about the visit history project for my group coming to an end. It has been a most exciting adventure combining dreams, ambition, dedication, and thousands of hours of work. I think you can surmise I would have some misgivings as this being the end of two decades of intense immersion into an almost fantasy world of science and adventure. Our small group started this with the obscene amounts of money we were able to garner from our venture capital firm. Today's high technology monarchs are dabbling in space travel and electric cars. We chose a different path with no expectations of any financial return. Just doing it to for the joy in the doing. Now it is almost over and done with."

As John was talking Allison moved closer, on her

side and facing him. She fluffed her pillow and position her head so she could look directly at his face. He turned to face her.

"Sixty years ago you were my only friend, your parents moved away and took you with them. I was seven years old and cried for weeks. I never got over it until about two years ago. I want you know about this." John was now serious and was having trouble speaking the words. He then told her of his trip with Robert and Sandra to 10,000 years before this time and the visit with the small tribe of natives they had befriended. It was the small boy, maybe four years old, that had taught him a lesson he needed to learn. He told her of how the boy, in just the two days they were together, became almost family for him and how he had cried and called for him not to leave when they had to go. Allison could see the tears forming in John's eyes as he said, "I was that little boy when you left me and the hurt was almost the same but I am now in my late sixties. I have spent most of my life avoiding that happening again and then it did but it was another small child that was hurting. His name was Citiali. A native boy with brown skin and black hair. A beautiful child from another time but the bond was the same. He does have the advantage as in all of our our trips to the past those we meet will have no recollection of our visit once we return to our own time. We do and in that parting I realized I have missed something very important in life. That family is important and that I have none."

Allison moved closer and kissed John's cheek. She could taste the tears and with a smile she told him, "We will work on that my little friend. You have more to tell me. It can wait but I would like to know. Specifically, how did I end up in your bed."

That provoked a laugh from John. He cleared his throat and answered, "I will tell you how. It is a good story and I want to tell you. Now is the right time."

John relaxed, collected his thoughts and started, "I decided to attend the Concert at the last minute. One of my partners has a donor's membership and wasn't able to go so he offered me the ticket. Talk of serendipity, his reserved seat was in the balcony just opposite where Ed's family had seats. As I took in the scene I spotted Robert and Sandra just a few rows behind them. My interest was piqued and I almost missed the drama of Ed and the conductor's entrance. As you know Ed is a very special human being. He carries himself with much more than just good looks and a confident bearing. He and Julia are special. It wasn't until Number 3 was well underway that the music began to take my concentration. Ed's back was toward me but I thought it extraordinary that the music that he played was done with such apparent ease. It was at that moment that the plan for one last trip into history came to me. It was so clear and had many parts but I knew at that moment I would make it happen."

John took one of his pauses as he readied for what he wanted Allison to understand next. It wasn't conceit but the desire to have her understand that his mind worked much different than most and was capable of collecting large amounts of data and quickly organizing it into a working project. He had lead his group to the visiting back in time from just a youthful wish to reality. The dreams of a seven year old to visit a native village during the first migration into the Americas had been made a reality. He had made it happen. Allison had, just a few hours ago, been transported back to 1943 for a quick visit to the home of Sergei Rachmaninoff, returned and was now laying next to him in his bed.

Allison reached over with her free hand and lightly touched his shoulder. "I remember those days we played together in the park, you running around pointing out areas you were sure the earliest human inhabitants had their villages, always looking for arrowheads or tools. Telling me in the most serious way that you would some day travel back in time to see it for yourself. And you did. I want you to tell me now what you want to do this time and how I can be part of it."

John didn't hesitate and started with the experience Robert had during his visit with Rachmaninoff. How interesting was the personal relationship that was struck between the two men. "It was the music that made me think that anyone that could compose such magnificent scores must have other projects, whole or just as ideas, underway. Either in the mind or on paper. Rachmaninoff was still so busy with active performances on a scale that would preclude him of working on any of these. His 1942-1943 schedule had around fifty performances. These were scattered all over the country and left little time for any new work to be done. It wasn't until after returning by train from his last recital, February 17, 1943 in Knoxville, Tennessee, in failing health did he find out he had lethal melanoma cancer and only weeks to live. I can only imagine his thoughts as he then knew he had no time left. He wasn't done. Some of his best was written but not ready to go public. Others were just in parts and pieces waiting to be put together, some hadn't even made it to paper yet and now he had no way to get any of it done. Depression had to have overwhelmed him and because of who he was he would never tell anyone what caused it. It was at that moment I thought maybe I can change that bit of history without changing actual history in any way."

Allison sat up so quickly she almost fell on top of him. "You are going to try to retrieve his unfinished works and have Ed and Cindy, along with Julia, Robert and Sandra, and the two of us finish them and organize their performances. It won't change history but add to it. My God John, what a great project! I am all in. It is what I need in my life right now. Robert and Sandra are looking for the same thing. You must have something like this to replace trips to the past as it closes down."

She laid back down not taking her eyes off John and then asked the next, obvious question, "How do you do it? How could you get this far so quickly?"

John knew he had Allison with him now and another piece of his plan was securely in place. He had been lucky this time as all the many pieces he needed had fallen into place with hardly any effort on his part. All he had done was put these extraordinary pieces of the puzzle together.

Chapter 45

John was letting these thoughts run through his mind as he looked at Allison. Her eyes had closed and she was breathing in the manner of sleep. She was a very attractive woman, intelligent with a good sense of humor, healthy and tanned. Maybe she could help him find another new interest in life. He watched as she fell further into deeper sleep and a smile came to his face. He was smiling a lot this last couple of weeks and it was because of Sergei Rachmaninoff. He almost laughed out loud at the thought.

He had gone to the concert by the chance of having been given a ticket and having nothing better to do. He liked classical music but it had always been in the background as he had other things to think about. That period of his life now seemed to be coming to it's end. They would be disassembling their huge electronic operation at SLAC after this trip was completed and sale of the equipment would be done by a salvage company. They would reap about ten cents on the dollar and that wouldn't nearly cover their other expenses. Each of them would still have enough money left from their venture capital days and they could start it back up again if need be but at the moment that didn't have any appeal for him. He was starting to have some doubts creep into his thinking about his future. It was as the Los Angeles Philharmonic struck the first notes of Rachmaninoff Number 3 and the entrance of Edward Adams on the piano that things began to change. He had seen Robert and Sandra's intense concentration on this man which lead him to become curious about what had brought them there. He knew them well enough from their time together while exploring 10,000 years before the present that he hadn't expected they had any real interest in classical music. He surmised they had a reason to be here and it had to be Robert's previous visit with Rachmaninoff on the Visiting History program.

At the intermission it was electric in the hall as something special had just happened. He had thought that he had never heard anything to compare with what Ed Adams and the orchestra had just done but he didn't have enough knowledge of music to make the comparison. He did know it must take greatness to write such music and greatness to play it as Ed and the orchestra had just done. He was reading the small, boxed biographical paragraphs of Rachmaninoff on the back of the program as the ovation for the performance subsided when he noted the dates of birth and death, April 1, 1873 and March 28, 1943. He knew then what he wanted to do next and that he didn't have much time to get it done.

He would be seventy in two years and to contemplate death at that age had sent a chill down his spine. He had known the dates from Robert's visit but hadn't placed them in context. It was much too soon for some one to pass on with the talent to still produce such great works. Rachmaninoff deserved more time. Much more time.

It was then, as Ed was playing the introduction of Rachmaninoff Number 2 followed by the familiar theme, that he had thought, "He must have a lot of work almost finished, just started and maybe even completed, that he will have no time to finish or produce. Let's go back and see if we can find them and bring them to life here in our time."

John again smiled, remembering that moment. He was sure it would be there and if they could get it back to the present he thought he had all the talent around him to make it happen. What happened next was like being given the pieces of that puzzle, one at a time and him knowing exactly where they were to be placed.

After the concert he had wandered about the halls trying to find the approach he was certain would be revealed. He had watched Ed meet with his family, bid them good evening and walk away with a very attractive lady that must be his wife. He followed them and they entered a side hall that was filling up with patrons which he assumed were the big donors. He spotted Robert waiting near the Ladies Room and then saw Sandra escorting a finely dressed dowager and the three of them enter the hall. He took out his ticket and presented it to the lady at the door and she welcomed him in. He thanked his friend and his luck.

His new beard, formal attire and platform shoes made him confident that Robert and Sandra wouldn't recognize him unless they made eye contact. In less than an hour he knew he had more members on his team. Wilma Herman was the key. Her words to Ed, "I knew him, you know," brought her into the group. Cindy, her care giver, would be added two days later when his detectives had reported on Wilma Herman's care giver.

The rest was easy as the new friendships between Robert, Sandra, Ed and his wife Julia developed and the four of them had entered the lives of Wilma and Cindy. Their trip up the coast on Robert and Sandra's sailboat opened up another opportunity for him to set up his plan. Allison was gathered in by his following the travels of the foursome. Their stop in Santa Barbara had given him the chance when his computer algorithm displayed her name in the social pages about her downtown party to unveil her newly refurbished Steinway piano. Either by chance, as it had happened, or by the Adams reading about the party he thought he could again see his old friend and perchance see his new foursome. He ended up seeing them both and had decided to at least try to seek out Allison's friendship again, even if was from sixty years ago. Joining them on the boat in Moss Landing gave him the chance to get know Ed and Julia. It worked out so well that he almost thought he didn't deserve such good fortune.

John adjusted his position to help sleep come, turning his head to once more to look at Allison. This time it was a longer gaze. An unfamiliar yearning came over him and he wondered if it was possible more could come his way with this interesting woman. He did worry he wouldn't match up to her expectations if such was to happen. He shouldn't have as the next morning he found he had no need to wonder.

John was still in bed when Allison came out of the bathroom, freshly showered and dressed in a nice casual outfit that fit her just right. She smiled and with no hesitation came over and sat down close to him. "Sometimes life surprises you my young friend. Two weeks ago, in Santa Barbara, I took Ed Adams aside and confessed I wanted to in some way become friends with him and Julia. And with Sandra and Robert. That at this point in my life I needed to have a few true friendships, real friendships with people who have talent and are living interesting lives. I tell you the same thing but I think there is more here with you than just friendship. I want to find out if that's the case. Can we start with that this morning?"

"I think you can be certain of that," John was able to get out before almost losing complete control of his senses. "What is coming together in my life right now is beyond any expectations I could have ever hoped for. I need this now and I need you to share it with me. This next week is going to be so exciting, bringing my plan into reality and you are going to play a major part in it. I want you to be here and we will figure out what we should do about what just happened as it unfolds. One day at a time right now. Is that okay with you?"

Allison gave him a sound kiss and commented, "Don't just lay there, we have big plans to make. Maybe breakfast first would be a good idea."

Chapter 46

At this same time Ed was handing the dock lines to Robert as Sandra started maneuvering *Du-eT* away from the guest slip at the Saint Frances Yacht Club. Breakfast had been the special instant oatmeal with brown sugar, fresh orange juice followed by a cup of coffee taken while sitting in the cockpit. Hugs and hand shakes had been made and the understanding was that Ed was going to make the trip if his recruiting of Cindy was successful. Robert and Sandra had leased a slip at the Brickyard Cove Marina, just across the bay in Point Richmond, and should be able to make it home to Point Reyes Station by early afternoon. It was Saturday the ninth of April, and a very pleasant day in the Bay Area. Beside the climate there was also a tinge of excitement in the air between the four new friends. All had to be accomplished in a week as John's elaborate electronics complex was scheduled to start being dismantled on Monday, April 18th.

Fifteen minutes later the silver 911 Carrea S, with Ed at the wheel and Julia seated next to him entering their home address in the GPS, headed toward Interstate 280. Julia asked, "You don't want to go down on Interstate 5 do you?"

"No!" was Ed's quick answer.

"It will be about nine hours if the traffic is not bad and you obey the speed limits. We should be home by six o'clock. We better try for a visit to Wilma on Monday. I am pretty sure John wants to make the trip on Friday. That's your thinking, isn't it?"

Ed nodded his head in agreement and then had to slow down for the ever present traffic on 19th Street heading south. Thirty minutes later, on Interstate 280, Julia suggested he slow down a bit as he had just gone through the gears and hadn't realized he was doing a little over ninety miles per hour. He smiled at this and thought, "There is slow and then there is slow."

They talked about their new relationships with Robert and Sandra and now the involvement with a person such as John. They still didn't know his last name and as far as they could tell neither did Robert or Sandra and that they didn't care. They both sensed that if the trip back in time to visit Rachmaninoff went as planned this forming group would be part of a new life for them. Ed was already committed to over twenty events but fortunately the first one after the LA Phil was in six weeks and would require very little rehearsal. His next big symphony performance was in July and would again be Rachmaninoff Number 2 and 3.

Approaching Santa Barbara in early afternoon they stopped for an early dinner and drove up State Street and parked in front of the empty store front. It had been just one week since they had stopped to look in the window and saw the Steinway Parlor Grand being polished by two men. Julia took Ed's hand, holding it tight. "You have made my life a dream. I am not afraid of what is coming because I know I will always be with you. It can't be any other way."

Ed bent down, kissed her lips and hummed the opening bars of *The First Time Ever I Saw Your Face*. It had been one of their most popular songs and thought to be almost as good as Roberta Flack's 1972 recording.

In Point Reyes Station Robert and Sandra pulled into the parking space next to their little house. It had been an easy drive from Point Richmond, over the Richmond-San Rafael Bridge and quickly into the hills and over the mountains to home. The old Honda van was still their car as they could leave it anywhere with no fear of loss. It always started and most of the time the brakes worked good enough. Robert had a touch of envy at seeing Ed and Julia in the Porsche but knew two things. It couldn't carry much of anything and certainly you could never leave it in an unsecured parking area for weeks at a time. Besides, a hundred thousand plus dollars seemed a bit pricey for a car.

Their trip south and back on *Du-eT* had taken over three weeks and it was good to be back. Sandra had stopped at the front door as Robert searched his pocket for the key. She moved closer and put her arms around his neck. "Do you remember seven years ago standing right where we are now, opening the door to this neat little house so I could come back into your life. I feel that way every time we come back from any trip. This is home for me and I never want to live anywhere else."

Robert kissed her, opened the door and they went inside. She was right, this was home. He, and they, had taken some remarkable trips back in time, but the crazy part of those trips was that they had actually never been been away from the present. The time spent away was repeated in the present. Ed wouldn't really sense this as Robert hadn't in his thirty minute trips. The trip he and Sandra took back 10,000 years was for twenty-two days but they lived those days again when they came back. Only the memories had any relevance to time.

Sandra understood his silence. "You don't want to go back. Not with Ed, Allison and Cindy. Neither do I, but what do you think our part in this will be. John is planning something that will keep us together. Even Wilma will be involved. Have you any idea?"

"No, nothing I am sure about. John has teased us with what he is planning. I think Ed has figured it out, and maybe Allison knows but I doubt it. It will be really exciting for Wilma to see herself as a fifteen year old."

Sandra waited a moment then offered, "You know, Rachmaninoff was about two years older than John is now when he died. You talked to him when he had only a few days left. What was your impression of this great man who was dying so young?"

It was Robert's turn to wait as he thought about Sandra's question. "Regret. It was regret I sensed. He was annoyed more than mad or upset. Regret, he wasn't finished yet. He had more to do!"

Sandra was excited now. She reached for Robert, pulled him to her and said, "John is going to try to get hold of his unfinished work and somehow bring it back to the present. He wants to finish some of Rachmaninoff's music for him and take it public for the world to enjoy!"

Chapter 47

Jennifer was busy fixing Sunday morning breakfast for herself and Ben as Ed and Julia arrived from their side of the two house complex. Hugs were exchanged and Ben wanted to know how they liked life aboard a boat. "I wanted to try boating. One cold winter day I found a Sail magazine that had a photo of beautiful people out on the water on a beautiful sailboat and I thought that someday I should try that."

"Grandpa, are you sure I didn't tell you about the poster I dragged Ed over to see when we were in Newport Beach. That was twenty-eight years ago." Julia said this as she was hugging him while standing behind his chair. He turned, looking up at her with a love that was apparent too all and answered, "Could be. I never did go out sea. Jennifer, let's put that on our bucket list. Ninety-five is not too old, is it?"

"Ben, let's hear Julia tell us how it went and what new things are going on in their life. I can tell something is! If she won't tell us, Ed will. He doesn't know how to say no when we ask something of him. Julia, you are a lucky girl."

The orange juice, French toast and coffees were served out by the pool and the close family talked of the familiar things that close families always talk about.

Later that morning Ben was in his office, sitting behind his desk reading the Sunday paper. Ed came in and sat in one of the two big chairs opposite the desk and waited for Ben to acknowledge his presence. He lowered the paper and took a long look at Ed, then spoke, "Jennifer told me to ask you what you were up to. She knows something big is going on and expects me to find out what it is."

Ed wasn't the least bit surprised. Since the first day they had met, Jennifer could see through him as if he was a pane of glass. They met when she was a home nurse for Ben after he had a prostate surgery. He and Julia were living together in the house before they were married and soon Jennifer had joined Ben in the same manner. At the time, as it was now, they were four very happy people sharing their lives together in one house. Ben was Julia's only living relative at the time, Ed had none and Jennifer was a widow. Each had a need for the other and those needs were met in a way they all cherished. It was as true now as it had been then.

"Well, Ben, it is quite a story. I could tell you a little but Jennifer should be here so I don't have to repeat it. Why don't I get her to join us. Julia should be here, too." Ed rose and found the two ladies still poolside and Ben's small office suddenly became a little crowded.

He started with asking Ben and Jennifer if they remembered the Visiting History television series and they both indicated they had and had loved them. Ben pointed to the shelf having the presentation box containing the entire series in nine DVD cases holding the three years of programs. Ed stood and retrieved the case that had one, two and three. Pointing at the credits which showed Robert Johnson and Sandra Williams he said, "It was on their boat, named Du-eT, that we were on. They are really interesting people and it was a good trip up the coast."

Ed paused but Jennifer didn't hesitate. "Okay, tell us the the important news. Nothing about sailing, which marina you stayed at or the restaurants you went to. What happened and what is it that is about to happen."

He smiled at her and started describing the events starting after the concert. Their meeting Wilma Herman, who said she had known Rachmaninoff, at the donor's party and then Robert and Sandra introducing themselves to them. Meeting them again in Marina del Rey for brunch, the developing friendship and the decision to join them on their boat for the trip up to San Francisco.

Jennifer could not hold it back any longer and in an excited voice said, "My God, Ben! Robert Johnson actually went back in time and met with Rachmaninoff. I told you it was too real not to have happened. He went back to visit Lincoln and daVinci, too. The rest was made up. I told you that, didn't I?"

Ben started nodding his head in agreement, Julia looked surprised and Ed could only think that he should have known Jennifer would have figured it out. That she had waited before saying so until he got to that point.

"Jennifer, I quote another new friend, you never disappoint. That friend is John. The mysterious John in the series. He is a real person. You are spot on, it really happened. Julia and I are now involved in one last visit. A visit to Rachmaninoff one week earlier this time, March

14, 1943. Our trip will be made next Friday."

It became very quiet in the small space. Julia broke the silence. "I am not going. Ed and I will be trying to recruit Wilma's caregiver, Cindy, to go. She is a true classical pianist and is infatuated with Rachmaninoff, both his music and the man. John's friend Allison Turner will be the third one making the trip. It will be for less than one hour. It is almost unbelievable but John demonstrated how it's done with Allison making a short reconnaissance visit as we watched in the studio theater at his headquarters. I'm not sure Ed should do this. I don't want him to but it is such an opportunity and he thinks there is more to the trip than just a visit. John won't tell us but I am sure we have already figured it out. He is hoping Rachmaninoff wants someone to finish his unfinished works as he knows he has no time left to do it himself."

Again there was a pause. Then Ben cleared his throat and whispered, "We all put off things we want to do until it is too late. For a creator of music it is all he was planning to compose and now it is too late. What an awful thing to happen for him. I think this John fellow is some one I would like."

It was the final day of the Masters golf tournament and all agreed to spend the afternoon watching it on television. They had a big screen TV in the music room in the main house. Ed and Julia sat on the small sofa, close together. She whispered in his ear, "Do you miss it, I do?"

Ed smiled and answered, "Yes I do, but Julia Renquest with Ed Adams was much better." They had met when Ed had bought some special golf clubs designed by an old friend of Ben's that elevated his golf to the level of the professionals during the 1994 season. He had played in a number of tournaments during which another of Ben's old friends had found his mother's Steinway Parlor Grand piano, had it restored and gave it to Ed placing it where it was now in the room where they were sitting. Music had come back into his life and the gift he had to play returned. At the same time Julia's talent as a singer was revived and their eight year career as entertainers had replaced golf. With the birth of their twins that life had been curtailed and Ed went back to his first love, classical piano, specializing in but not limited to Rachmaninoff. He was now thinking he might be able to meet his favorite composer in person via this strange and sudden relationship with Robert, Sandra and their mentor, John. There were a lot of memories and the new prospects of going back in time to think about. He was finding it hard to concentrate on the golf.

Chapter 48

Sunday in Point Reyes Station was a bit different for Robert and Sandra. They had an easy run across San Francisco Bay to Point Richmond the day before and were home as planned. Sunday started with a sticky-bun, fresh orange juice and coffee at the Bakery's community table. Some chit-chat with locals and then they readied themselves for a hike to a special place of theirs in the Point Reyes National Seashores.

It was three and a half miles and after the first mile the Sunday crowds had thinned to just a few. By the time they had found the place they were looking for they were alone. The rolling hillside was covered in golden grasses just starting to turn to green. The small shrubs and trees scattered about looked to be in good health. The view over this landscape down to the blue Pacific Ocean was spectacular. Enough to take your breath away. It was here they had scattered the ashes of Conrad Engstrum. He had been their friend, Robert's former boss, a father figure to Sandra when it was needed and the benefactor that put *Du-eT* into their hands, the first time.

They spread a small blanket and laid down together looking up into an almost surreal blue sky. Eight years ago Robert had accepted the job at Engstrum

Technologies in San Francisco, rented a fabulous apartment and met Sandra. One year later his job was gone, the love of his life had left him to cruise the North Pacific with his ex-boss and he was alone and homeless. Then John came into his life and changed it in a manner that could never be thought of as possible. He rolled over on his side to look at Sandra. Her eyes were closed but she was not asleep. He stared at her face and thought to be here at this moment was good enough. Life was as good as it could be. His next thought was that John was back, but this time he was not worried. Everything he had in the here and now was because of this most interesting man.

Sandra, not moving or opening her eyes, spoke in quiet voice, "You are thinking about John and how we got here. To this spot. Today."

He was never surprised in how Sandra thought about things. He hadn't realized how intelligent and smart she was until long after he had fallen in love with her. It had been a remarkable discovery for him over the last eight years. He had expected as much but the realization came slowly. She never flaunted it but it wasn't just modesty. She had let him find it out in an honest way of exhibition and accomplishment. She had survived a very difficult childhood, limited formal education and early financial difficulties with grace and ethics above reproach. The thought of life without her was unthinkable.

"As you already know this should I ask of you the same?" Robert answered.

She answered, "Okay, but let's talk about what will happen after the Rachmaninoff visit and how will we fit in. You first"

"I think we agree this trip back for Ed, Cindy and Allison is to try to secure some of Rachmaninoff's documents on projects he wanted to work on, complete or take public that have never surfaced and to do that task for him. For the music it will be mostly Ed and Cindy. To make public the results will be the two of us. At least in planning the use of what we may find. Doing it will be Allison's department and Julia will be in the mix somewhere. John will see that all the parts work and are put together correctly. I think Wilma's contribution will be to watch the goings on and to remain alive until it has been accomplished."

"Robert, let's go with that. Just watch it come together," Sandra said this as she rolled over to embrace him and enjoy what life had to offer.

Chapter 49

After John had collected the breakfast dishes and loaded them into the dishwasher he turned to Allison suggesting they get to work. "Now what do you mean by that?" was Allison's response as she slid off her chair and followed him as he was already heading somewhere but hadn't answered her. Another of the doors into the great room was opened and Allison continued to follow John. As he walked through the doorway the lights came on revealing a large room with a single, long table in the middle. It had rows of equally spaced PC monitors and keyboards. A chair was in place in front of each station. A quick count by Allison was about twenty. At the far end was a young man intent on watching three monitors at the same time and making fast key strokes as various blocks of information came on the screens.

John greeted him with, "Good morning, Mike. You almost done? This is Allison. She will be working with us on this project."

Mike glanced their way and said, "Good morning," and returned to his task. John said nothing more and Allison followed him through a second doorway which lead to his office. Allison stopped as soon as she had a full view of the space. The dark paneled walls were spaced by large, floor to ceiling book cases which had between them magnificent paintings and framed photographs. There were no windows but the lighting was such that they were not needed nor missed. She had never been in a space that exuded the success that this room did. The big desk in the middle of the room was surrounded on three sides with leather chairs that begged to be sat in. Behind the desk was a modest sized office chair which John went to and sat down. He motioned for Allison to take the chair closest to him, which she took without hesitation.

John smiled in a cheerful and almost teasing way uttered, "Not bad for a little boy dreamer in Golden Gate Park. Don't be deceived. This is where the real work is done. There are five other offices around the pit, as we call the work station out front. When the trips are being made there are twenty people out there, All six office doors are open and the activity rivals a missile shot at Cape Canaveral. Normally it is just monitoring the fully automated time travel. The real business as the trip is going on is to make sure no possible change in history occurs. I think you might appreciate that even the smallest mistake could cause unbelievable changes to the present. Even to our, and I mean my and your, existence might be jeopardized. This morning would never have happened." This last was said with some humor and a smile but Allison understood exactly what John was saying. She felt a tightening of fear in her chest. She realized she was with someone that was way beyond her in the perspective of a normal life. That he was comfortable with the risks of this travel and was confident he could control them.

As Allison was contemplating this a small printer

on John's desk began printing out letter sized sheets of paper at high speed. By the time she realized what was going on six pages were collated, automatically stapled and slid into an awaiting folder. As John reached for it Mike stuck his head in the door said, "Not much there but it is what we have. See you later," and was gone.

John pushed the folder toward Allison and she picked it up. On the top was Allison Turner in capital letters. Nothing else. She looked at John and he returned her gaze. "There is nothing there you don't already know. On the last page, however, is something you should know about. Why don't you look at that." John, the little boy of her childhood sounded like a corporate executive addressing a favored employee. It was an unfamiliar position for Allison to be in. One she had never experienced before.

She opened the thin file to last page and saw, highlighted, the words she had spoken to Ed Adams in Santa Barbara about staying in touch and the possibility of friendships. As far as she could tell it was verbatim. She looked at John, searching his face, and then asked, "How did you do this? Why did you do this?"

"The how is just that we could. The why is also simple. Ed Adams is the key, assisted by Cindy, to make contact with Rachmaninoff such that he would trust them to bring to life any unfinished work that he feared would be lost with his impending death." John paused and then answered the next question that she was trying to formulate in her mind.

"As I told you, or at least implied, the idea for this project came to me at the concert. Before I had left the donor's party I had Ed, Julia, Wilma and Cindy as the nucleus needed to get it started. Robert and Sandra were added as I expect this to go further if we get the material I am hoping will be there. I therefore contacted my detectives, they prefer to be called researchers, to do their research and Mike just put this together from what he has found about you. I called him from Santa Barbara during your party. By the way, I also had a personal interest which I hope you are not offended by."

Allison sat back in her comfortable chair and stared at the man behind the big desk. A smile slowly spread across her face. "John, you know what, I am not offended. In fact it will let me be me with no qualms. But you, you conniving rascal, better be on your best behavior or I will be gone from here as fast as your transporter transports."

"Let's go for a little tour about the property and see what you think of my humble abode. Then maybe a walk about downtown Palo Alto and lunch at my favorite cafe. After that we will come back here and with your help we will plan the next few days to get our Rachmaninoff treasure from where it now hides onto my desk." John could not hide his happiness, or his excitement, from his new, old friend and she was feeling the same way.

Chapter 50

Ed and Julia left their house in Palm Desert at 8:00 am hoping to arrive at Wilma's place in Beverly Hills by the promised time of eleven o'clock. Interstate 10 heading West was open and Ed was staying with the traffic in the fast lane at just under ninety miles an hour. Occasionally he would pull over into the middle lane to let the faster cars pass. He knew that in the last hour all would slow down, hopefully not stopping completely.

Before they left the house Julia checked for mail on their laptop finding one with the sender I.D. John/Palo Alto. It hadn't been there last night and she noted the time stamp of 11:30 pm yesterday. Touching the download button brought a cover sheet with CINDY on the top. At the bottom of the page was 1/12. She hit the print button and the twelve pages printed quickly. Stapling them together she placed them in her leather attache case and headed to the garage and the Panamera with Ed. After about thirty minutes their conversation turned to Cindy and Julia told Ed about the download from John.

"Interesting he would wait until eleven thirty to send it to us. I'll bet he wants us to read it while we are driving to Wilma's. Don't ask me why I think this, it is just that I am beginning to understand how this man thinks."

Ed let this last bit go as he could sense Julia reaching for her case and understood that she she would be reading it to him within a few minutes.

"Cynthia Anne Ashbaugh is at the top of the page. It then looks like a medical doctors description. We now know she is five foot ten inches tall, weighs one hundred thirty-five pounds, born on July 28, 1998 and is twenty four years old. You will like to know that she exhibits a good temperament, is well coordinated and is healthy. Want any more of this part?"

Ed smiled and was thinking that he would but instead of an a answer he asked "What's next?"

Julia went down the first page and went to the next. It was lab reports from blood and urine tests and she browsed quickly through them and found nothing out of specification. Four pages in was a observation addendum from a psychiatrist.

"I have found the start. Let me read through this and then we can talk it over," Julia offered and Ed accepted this as, while driving, a summary would be better.

Thirty minutes went by and as the traffic was starting slow things down a bit, that is it was traveling at the speed limit, Ed now had more time to hear about the young, healthy, and beautiful Cynthia Anne Ashbaugh.

Julia had been quiet the whole time and had read through the psychiatrist's report twice. She laid it down in her lap and turned toward Ed, "Oh my God Ed, you have no idea what we have got ourselves into. No idea. John must have just gotten this yesterday and that is why we didn't know about it sooner. Cindy is special. Much more than he told us. She was a child prodigy who lost her way.

Her mother drove her there."

Ed glanced at Julia, back to the road and then back to her, as he could see the tears running down her cheeks, falling on the papers she was holding. He spotted an upcoming off ramp and manage to cross to the outside lane just in time to pull into it. He took the first right into a Shell Gas Station. Driving around to the back there was more parking and he found a place sheltered by a big sycamore tree leafed in it's new year splendor. A hedge shut most of the ugly view in all the other directions and he parked, stopping the engine and waited.

Julia found a tissue and mopped at her eyes but couldn't stop the tears from coming. Ed knew to wait and she would tell him when she was ready.

"Ed, do you remember that movie we liked. An Australian film, around 1998, maybe later. It was about a prodigy, a boy, who's father drove him mercilessly until he found his way to another mentor. It was about playing Rachmaninoff Number 3 and his winning a competition in London having mastered it, but losing his mind in the process. With psychiatry, and the love of an older woman, he was able to play again. I cried then, too. That is what we have here with Cindy. And it is Rachmaninoff, again. It was her mother, this time."

"I remember it. Shine, I think that was the title. 1996, we were just starting to hit the big time. At least you were. It won an Oscar that year, remember, and we went to see it right after that. And yes you cried through half the movie. Peter Helfgott was the pianist. I am sure of that. We met him once or twice. Goffrey Rush was the actor that played him as an adult after he recovered. We met him too, I think."

Ed paused to try to figure out what to say to Julia but, as she often did, she solved the problem for him.

"Cindy's life, up to now, is much like the movie except she imagined being in love with Rachmaninoff, and he with her. That is why the romantic interpretations of his music is what she likes to play."

Again Ed had to wait for Julia to continue. She shuffled the papers a bit and set them back on her lap. She was struggling on how to tell Ed what had happened as it was almost too sad to imagine.

"Ed, I am going to read to you what the report says verbatim after I tell you about the report's first paragraphs. Cindy was found sleeping in the Greyhound Bus Station in West Hollywood. The police report was to check on a non-responsive teenager who had no identification papers, showed some bruising about the face, under nourished and had no money, jewelry, or even a watch. When asked for a name she would give none, only saying that she couldn't remember what it was.

"Whoever put this report together stated that no names, other than Cindy's, would be used. His source will not be identified in any way traceable. His source made him promise this and he would honor that promise. He asked to have all copies destroyed after reading. Any electronic transfer should be protected and deleted after sent."

Julia had Ed's attention and as he watched her he knew this would take some time. She looked scared but picked up the pages and commenced reading,

This report is filed April 10, 2022 at 11:05 pm.

All names other than Cynthia Anne Ashbough will be denoted by representative initials. No dates or times will be referenced other than it spans twenty-one months to this date with the subject under care by Dr. A for the first eight months and spending the last thirteen months as a caregiver for WH.

1. *One of the two summoned police officers arriving at the West Hollywood Greyhound Bus depot called a friend about Cindy not responding to her, or to her partner. The subject, Cindy, did not know her own name, where she was from, had some bruising about the face, no money, looked under-nourished, had one small tote bag she guarded and would not let the officers examine. She was wearing gloves and removed them when asked. Her hands were clean and manicured in stark contrast to her outward appearance. No rings or signs of having worn any. Her bus ticket had an origin of South Bend, Indiana and was two days old. When she was asked who she was here visit she answered Sergei Rachmaninoff.*

2. *The police woman's friend, Dr. A, a psychiatrist and amateur pianist, arrived in fifteen minutes and conversed with Cindy for twenty minutes. Then offered professional assistance in helping Cindy find out who she was and where she wanted to go. She would take Cindy to her own home where she could stay until things got worked out.*

3. *The policemen discussed the situation and thought it would be better for Cindy to go with Dr. A than be processed through the normal lost persons*

routine and left the station.

4. *Arriving at Dr. A's small home in Beverly Hills the presence of a Parlor Grand piano in the living room changed her demeanor immediately. Dr. A reported Cindy went directly to the piano, took off her gloves and played a medley of Rachmaninoff themes.*

5. *Lunch was offered and Cindy ate eagerly. At Dr. A's suggestion she showered and let Dr. A wash her clothes. Dr. A showed Cindy her guest bedroom and told her she could stay as long as she needed to.*

6. *After a nap and before dinner Dr. A asked who she had come to visit and Cindy repeated Sergei Rachmaninoff. That he was her friend and she was helping him get over his depression after the first performance of his Symphony Number 1 was panned and the discouraging problems he was having with the church about his engagement to Natalia , his first cousin.*

Julia lowered the papers and looked toward Ed. She had recovered her composure and told him that it went on like this for six pages until she was placed with Wilma as her care giver.

Then Julia told him the most interesting thing was that Cindy is fluent in speaking the Russian language. This was discovered when Dr. A's piano tuner stopped by. He was of Russian descent and commented, as a tease, about Cindy's playing Rachmaninoff in Russian and her answering him in the same language.

Ed was surprised by this but then asked Julia if

they should get back on the freeway so as not to be too late getting to Wilma's.

"Yes, let's do that. I am feeling better now but reading of her sitting on a bench in a Greyhound Bus Station not knowing who she was, hungry, with no money or identification, or what time she was in or where she was going is so frightening to me. I just couldn't process it. Things like that should never happen to anyone. In a way it happened to both of us when we were about her age. The loss of our parents so early was devastating but we knew who we were, had support and could go on with our lives. Cindy is just now making it back."

Ed started the car and quickly got back on Interstate 10. The traffic had slowed even more but the GPS said they would still be at Wilma's before eleven.

Chapter 51

As they turned onto La Collina Drive a smile crossed Ed's face. It was exactly eleven o'clock and the small gate opened as they approached it. Wilma was waiting on the porch, standing with her walker in front of her, waving a welcome. Julia reached over touching Ed's arm indicating that she was fine with being where she was and with what they were doing. The sun was out, the sky an unusual blue and the temperature perfect. Cindy came up behind Wilma and waved a friendly welcome. She looked absolutely beautiful and Ed thought it could be a painting to be framed and kept in one's mind.

Hugs and kissing of cheeks were exchanged and they went inside. The big Steinway Grand Piano in the small living room made it's presence to them and Wilma asked Ed to see if it was in tune. He obliged with the third movement of Rachmaninoff Concerto Number 2. The piano was in tune and when he finished Wilma announced that lunch was ready to be served.

The places had been set, wine glasses filled with water and plates ready to be filled. This time there were four places set because Cindy would be joining them. She was now family.

Cindy brought out a single round platter. On it was

a lamb crown roast with a stuffing of mushrooms, apples, walnuts and cranberries and surrounded by small roasted potatoes and Brussels sprouts. She quickly carved and plated the meal and put aside the serving platter. Watching this as the smells of the roast hung in the air was almost more than the three observers could take. Julia clapped her hands and Wilma and Ed followed her lead. It tasted so good that very little conversation was made while they ate. Dessert consisted of small dishes of vanilla ice cream, raspberries and topped with a whipped cream swirl.

Wilma said in loving tone, "I have gone to heaven and Cindy is my personal angel."

After the dishes were cleared and congratulations to the chef had been made, Ed started the conversation about the purpose of their visit. Cindy stood as if to leave and he asked that she stay as it was to her he wanted to talk. A initial look of fear crossed her face but was quickly replaced with one of curiosity.

"Cindy, you were present when Robert Johnson played the CD of his visit with Sergei Rachmaninoff. Wilma confirmed that it was the voice of Rachmaninoff and she had no doubt about it. The people who made it possible for this to happen have advanced their trans-portation back in time program immensely since then. They can transport the whole being and place him, or her, in that time as if they are in the present. I can be sent, as myself, back to visit with Rachmaninoff in his time. That is what is being proposed to do and I have accepted to do it. I want you to go with me. There will be one other person, Allison Turner, who will join us. She is a very attractive woman, in her mid-seventies, and will serve to lead us into Rachmaninoff's home. She has already made the trip once to make sure the timing and location are correct. She has been in the house and seen who was there."

The frightened look came back in Cindy's eyes and she stared blankly at Ed, afraid to speak. Ed immediately continued with the description of Allison's visit to the house, speaking calmly about the details and the view they had from the theater room. When he told them about seeing Wilma there at age fifteen, he turned to Wilma and told her she could be in the theater to watch if she would like and that he would explain how this would be organized shortly.

Ed, turning back to Cindy, asked, "I would like to talk to you privately. Will you join me in the living room, sit on the piano bench in front of Wilma's piano, and talk? Just the two of us?"

Cindy's face had turned pale and her breathing was coming in gasps. Ed hoped he hadn't played his cards wrong and spoiled this relationship completely when she stood up and offered her hand. They went into the small living room with the magnificent Steinway and sat down on the bench. Ed placed his fingers on the key board and played the first few notes of Pagini's 18, the familiar theme used in the movie *Somewhere In Time*. He smiled at Cindy, moved over enough to make the room she needed and she continued playing it without a pause. As she played Ed could see the color return to her face and that she was playing while other thoughts were in her mind. He thought how beautiful she was and how important it was that he approached this the right way.

"You play that as you want it played. Is that the way you approach all of Rachmaninoff's music? Even his concertos and symphonies?" he asked in a whisper.

"Yes. I knew him. I was in love with him at one time. I know now it was only in my dreams but it was so real I still think it happened. I am not afraid to go with you, I am afraid of seeing him again. Seeing him old and dying." A few tears were sliding down her cheeks and as if to bring herself back she started the forceful beginning of Concerto Number 2. Before Ed could even decide what to say or do next she said in a firm voice, "I will go. I want to see him, not in a dream, but as the real person!"

Chapter 52

Ed spent the next half hour describing the planned trip back in time. Arriving at the Rachmaninoff home at 11:48 am, Sunday morning March 14, 1943. They would would be positioned on the front lawn, walk immediately to the front door, be greeted by Wilma, age fifteen, and escorted into the house. Cindy took all of this in without showing any doubt or asking any questions. She continued softly playing her interpretations of Rachmaninoff themes while Ed talked. He then told her they were planning on traveling this coming Friday, April 15 at 4:00 pm to make the trip. She nodded her head in agreement.

Cindy stopped playing, turned to Ed and said, "He kissed me. Two times. Different times. We were sitting together, just like we are now the first time, and I was playing from a sheet of his hand written music, which ends up in the second movement of Number 2. He bent down his head and kissed me on the lips. I played on as he pulled away and started to apologize saying how he was in love with Natalia, wanted her to be his wife and that he shouldn't have done that. It was a dream, but is so real in my mind that it seemed to have really happened. Can you understand that?"

"Of course I can. That is what dreams are for. To

be able to remember them is something very special and that is one dream I hope you never forget." Ed said this hoping he had said it right. The smile Cindy gave him made him think what he had said was what she needed to hear. Not only that, he believed her.

They continued to share the piano, each playing various parts of Rachmaninoff favorites and after another half hour Ed suggested they rejoin Julia and Wilma.

While Ed and Cindy were at the piano they were talking about some women's things but the sound of the piano being so clear in the dining room there were several times they had to stop to just listen. The back and forth between the two pianists was not lost on either of them, especially Wilma.

"When Rachmaninoff hears this he will have to get out of his sick bed, come downstairs and see who is playing and why they are playing it that way. It's delightful, fun and shows the love for the man who composed it. He will know this and come down to join them. That's why you need my Cindy to go with Ed. To get Mr. Rach down stairs to talk with them." Wilma was excited with this observation but realized Cindy might be leaving her to lead her own life soon. She reached for Julia's hand and expressed this thought.

"You will not be left alone. You will be with us in Palo Alto, watch the trip with me by your side and watch them come back to us. We are a family now and none of us will ever be alone." Wilma's smile was what Julia wanted and it was given to her.

It was getting late in the afternoon as Ed laid out the plans for Wilma and Cindy's trip to Palo Alto. To go by private plane or be driven up in a van were the options. Wilma preferred a van even if meant most of the day. The hassles of boarding a plane, using the restroom and the small space was a bother to her and she had more time than she needed anyway. Ed knew that John would take care of this and the told Wilma that they would all have rooms at his house and how nice they would be. Wilma suddenly looked concerned and said to Ed, "I haven't been away from here overnight since before Ernst died. Even before that, maybe seven years or more. Will my house be okay? The piano?"

Julia calmed those fears by pulling out her cell phone and tapping the speed dial for their son. "BJ, you there. Good, how about house sitting for a friend of ours Thursday, Friday, and Saturday night. Yes this week. It is in Beverly Hills, less than thirty minutes from UCLA. Do you want to come over here right now. We will be leaving in about an hour. Okay, here is the address."

Julia repeated the address as Wilma gave her the particulars and BJ told them he would be there in twenty minutes according to his phone's GPS. Things were going a bit fast for Wilma but she managed a grin and let it be known her life was certainly getting exciting with all this fuss. As Julia described their son taking after his father in height and good looks she caught a look of concern cross Cindy's face. She had turned away quickly but Julia could see that she was not comfortable with meeting some one her age and of the opposite sex.

BJ arrived as he had predicted and was greeted on the porch by Wilma and Julia. Julia explained to Wilma that BJ was an acronym for Ben Junior as he was named after her grandfather Ben and having two Ben's in the same house had been confusing. It had stuck and it was now used by everyone.

Ed was seated at the piano, Cindy sitting next to him as he was explaining to her how they could play opposite each other on the two big Steinway pianos in Rachmaninoff's living room. BJ's whistle at seeing the piano for the first time drew their attention his way. He did look like his father. Tall, an inch taller than Ed, an athletic build and a handsome face. He waved to his father and then saw Cindy, almost hidden behind him. The introduction was made and Cindy managed a smile and muttered a glad to meet you. Wilma knew, as did Julia, that the looks between the two young people had more meaning than just a hello. Ed could sense Cindy's change of emotions and looking at his son brought a smile to his face. He was remembering when he had first seen Julia and thought, "What ever may happen in ones life, that should happen at least once,"

Wilma gave BJ the tour and suggested he would be more comfortable sleeping in Cindy's bedroom than hers which brought forth a chuckle, or two. They would unclutter the single bathroom and supply the kitchen with any food he would like. BJ then told them what they all would remember, "I will just be here for a few nights. You don't need to make a bunch of changes for me."

The extra house key and a fob for opening the gate were handed to BJ and they all headed to the living room. Ed asked Cindy to join him and they played some of what they had earlier, trading positions as the music demanded. It was good, solid Rachmaninoff, and Ed started thinking this strange project of John's would work. He then had another thought, "John's projects always worked."

Chapter 53

The drive back to Palm Desert started a little later than planned and the traffic was heavy. Ed concentrated on the driving and that gave him the excuse to not talk to Julia about the day's events. It wasn't that he wouldn't, he just needed time to put them in order. Everything was falling into place. Cindy was willing, actually said she wanted to go back in time to see Rachmaninoff. Wilma was genuinely excited, would make the trip to Palo Alto and be an observer. The mix of playing the two pianos seemed to have solved it self with an almost effortless playing between himself and Cindy on the big Steinway. Even the schedule was acceptable to all. It had been too easy.

Julia broke his concentration, making him smile, saying, "This is all going together so easily. Everything thing seems to fit with no effort on our part. All but one thing." She left that as a question she wanted answered and to be told that it wasn't her fault if things went badly between BJ and Cindy.

"You saw it too?" Ed asked and answered it for her, "BJ is a good boy, a man, and he will handle it correctly." Ed paused and then continued, "That is how I looked when I first saw you, bending over a putt behind the big cabinet in the Golf Museum. I saw myself in BJ as he first looked at Cindy. It may not turn out the same way, but we shouldn't interfere with what is to come. Cindy has a lot of problems but I like her. Her talent, her willingness to talk to me about her dreams and listen to my opinions. We had a good time at the piano and she is truly gifted. Underlying the melodies she plays with such ease is talent. Possibly greatness. Let's stay back and if need be we can give advice. But not yet."

The traffic finally thinned out and the Panamera was able to show her true colors. Ed quickly realized he should slow that color down a bit and was glad he didn't see any flashing red lights coming up from behind. They pulled into their garage two hours later.

It was good to be home. It was Julia's grandfather's house first and then the addition and remodel of the next door property had given them the sanctuary they needed raising their children. At first it had been for Julia as her mother had moved back in with her parents after her husband had left her soon after Julia's birth. It then became her refuge as first her mother died and then her grandmother one year later. Her grandfather carried the burden raising and caring for Julia until Ed had come into her life. His new love, Jennifer, a younger woman came at the right time for him and the new family had formed. Six years later the twins arrived and the adjacent house was purchased, and the three generations bonded even closer. Their twins would be selecting, or be selected, new mates as the next generation would form their partnerships. Whether they would find their own places to live, or join with their parents, would be as it would be.

Julia's grandfather and Jennifer were in the music room when they arrived. The kitchen and the dining area were also in the main house along with Ben's office and his and Jennifer's bedroom. The second house had a larger living area, small kitchen and dining area and three bedrooms, each with their own baths. Together they made for a comfortable and livable space for the two families.

Jennifer had made a simple but tasty shrimp salad served with a fresh baguette sliced and offered in a basket. On large plates the meal was taken out to the pool area and as it was a nice evening made for a good atmosphere to relax and have dinner. Most of the days events were discussed and Julia even commented on BJ's meeting the interesting and beautiful Cindy. At the mention of this Jennifer spoke up asking how the twins were doing and Ed and Julia, like all proud parents, bragged about BJ and Jan doing so well at UCLA.

After dinner Ed indicated he wanted to spend some time at the piano, Ben wanted to go to his office for a while and the two ladies decided to remain outside. It had been a while since he had touched a keyboard other than the brief playing with Cindy that morning. He had a one hour practice routine he followed for times when he just wanted the touch to be exercised. When he finished he could see the ladies still by the pool and headed down the entry hall to Ben's office. The hall still had Ben's collection of antique golf clubs and memorabilia.

When Ed had first arrived on the scene his office had been a small interior room but comfortable having a big desk and two upholstered chairs. Nothing had changed except the wall facing the hall now had a large curtained window. When the curtain was drawn the view from his desk, on the opposite wall, was of a glassed case holding in a fanned display the twenty-seven Morris Cornith golf clubs. On either side of this case were matching narrow cases each containing a single putter. They were the Cornith Putter and the Julia Putter.

Chapter 54

As Ed entered the office he saw that Ben was staring at the big display case, eyes moist but not really focused. Ed waited a moment, then asked in a whisper, "Ben, are you okay?"

Ben's head moved slowly in Ed's direction. He gave him a weak smile and responded. "Yeah, okay. Just remembering some things worth remembering."

There was another long pause, then he continued, pointing at the Cornith collection, "That was the best year of my life. Well, the second best. The best day was the day I met my first wife at that Paris bakery. That was the best one. I have told you that story at least once or twice, haven't I?"

Ed could see Ben was having trouble putting his words and thoughts together so he made a bit more than necessary getting seated.

"Yes Ben you have, but it is such a good story I would like to hear it again."

"No you wouldn't!" This brought a familiar grin to his face and Ed could see the color coming back to his face, his eyes clearing and regaining their bright and mischievous appearance. "I have been sitting here thinking about my life. It has been good one, even with it's tragic parts. I guess that is what one does as he reaches the end. Just sitting, thinking of the past. But that," pointing at the clubs, "was a good year. Maybe the best year."

Ed knew more was coming so he sat back and waited. It was the year he got his life back and everything that followed was intrinsically related to the man that sat in front him.

"Hank was my boss at IBM and my best friend from then on. We wouldn't be here talking about him if that had not happened. I have no idea where, or even if, I would be if we had not met." Ben paused and Ed moved to get comfortable for he knew he was going to told some things he hadn't heard before and some would be about him.

"When Hank died he willed his big property to Little Willy to either convert or sell for his foster care operation. The *Little Willy Foster Home* has become one of the finest of it's kind as you and Julia know. It was Hank and Morris that got me to move here when I retired. Morris Cornith was here, retired and making golf clubs." This brought an even bigger smile to Ben's face and he gestured toward the display case again. He then asked Ed, "Do you want to know the rest of the story of how we picked you to play them and get you on the PGA Tour for that year?"

It was now Ed's turn as he had never been told why he was selected or how it was that he could play the clubs as he could. No one else, even to this day, could hit even one decent shot with them. For the putters, it was a different story.

"I think that would be a really good thing for me to

know. You are the only one left that knows. I have never had even a clue but it changed my life and I could never wish to have had a better one. So please tell me."

"You know the why. Hank and I promised Morris we would try to find someone who could play them and try to get his name as a club designer known. It was a promise to a dying man who had been a lifetime friend. Hank was the one who made it happen, I managed the program and Little Willy joined us to make it work. You know how I met Little Willy. Him sitting in the breezeway at the golf center one morning, a homeless, broke twenty something black kid. He shagged some balls for me and I then took him to lunch. Had him caddie for Hank and me the next day and then Hank hired him to be his driver and man Friday. Boy did that work out for all of us."

Ed had heard most of this and Little Willy had become an important part of Julia's, and then his life. Morris's passing was the loss of one's immediate family. It was what came next that was what Ed had never known, or even suspected.

"After Morris died his wife moved in with her sister in La Jolla. She took the clubs with her and they were put in the storage area of the condominium. Maureen died not too long after that and Morris's clubs collected dust right where they had been left. We, meaning the three of us, let things slide regarding to the clubs. It was when Harriet's health started to decline and she told Hank that she was going to toss them out that the wheels started to move. Hank needed something to do, Little Willy was busy with his wife caring for a bunch of foster kids and needed some relief, and I was bored stiff. We had a project and settled on the outcome needed first. Find a golfer that could use the clubs at the professional level, get him into the PGA and win one tournament using them." Ben smiled at Ed and said in a soft voice, "You came close Ed, close enough, and using and promoting the putter brought the real name recognition for Morris that is still going on. There have been lots of copies of the design but almost every year there is a Pro that stands there with a trophy that used an original. That is nice."

Ben took a long look at Ed, then started with, "We needed just the right man to pull this off. It was more than his golf game that was important, because no one seemed able to use these clubs. It was a good golfer whose mental state was such that he needed a new lease on life. Hank knew a wide range of people who could do research and each time we had a candidate he would set them on him. Going on our third year we started to think this wasn't going to work. It was then your turn and this time all the pieces fit. We were convinced that Morris had designed something special and it would take just the right person in the right frame of mind to pull it off. You fit the bill and when Hank's research team put all the right pieces on our table, so to speak, we got started."

Ed was now into the moment. For twenty-eight years he had wondered how it was done. He sat forward and could see that Ben was now in his element.

"Okay Ed, here's the story. First understand that Julia, you meeting her and all that has followed had nothing to do with our planning. It couldn't have turned out better for both of you and for me, but it was not planned. What was planned was that knowing you liked to stop at garage sales, that you had a regular Saturday run west of town in the hills and always drove home the same way gave us the place we needed. We also knew of the tragic loss of both your parents while you were at Stanford, that you were on the golf team and also were a classical pianist. After their death you left everything behind except golf. Your winter in Aspen, the many small jobs you had, your lack of any friends or social life fed directly into our needs. The garage sale was set up in the empty Cornith house that still belonged to Hank. He had bought it from Morris's wife after he died and she had moved in with her sister. Harriet pretended to be Morris's widow selling the clubs. Ed, every man at sometime in his life needs to have some magic enter his life. On the day of your first swing with a Morris Cornith golf club you needed that magic in your life and it was that need that set everything in motion."

Ben was then trying to think how to phrase what he wanted to say next. Ed didn't know what to say so he waited.

"You know the role confidence plays in the game of golf. You have to believe that every swing will be perfect even if you also know it won't be. At that moment in your life you needed to believe that something would provide that confidence and that a strange looking golf club might. Hank's researcher thought you were the one that this might work on. Harriet played her part perfectly and by the time you pulled that seven iron out of the bag, the one with the blue tape and the last club Morris had designed, you believed they were special. You know what happened next. You had convinced your self you couldn't make a bad swing. And until you and Julia decided on a different future you never lost that confidence. Would you like to take one of the clubs to the driving range tomorrow and see if its still true?"

Ed could see Ben was having fun at his expense and was enjoying every minute of it. He pondered on his answer and showing a big grin said, "No thanks Ben, but it is nice of you to make the offer."

Just then Julia stuck her head in the door, told Ed she was heading for bed and asked if he wanted to go with her. As Ed rose to follow her he thanked Ben for the conversation and Ben smiled back thinking how well it all had turned out and that he should make a better effort at living each day. He was certain something was now happening that he must be a part of and he would forever be sorry if he missed it.

Chapter 55

It had been a long day and both Ed and Julia were tired. Preparing for bed was done in the familiar routine of a married couple that spent all their time together. Once there neither sensed that sleep would come easy. It was Julia that first started the conversation about Jennifer's comments that Ben was showing signs of losing interest in life. The Concert had seemed to affect him more than anything of late and he had made an revealing comment to her on their drive home. She was driving and as the traffic thinned out and they both began to relax he had told her he thought his responsibility to family was over. That you and I had produced two fine great grandchildren, had formed an unbreakable union, and that you had reached a place in music that he felt was more than most could ever have hoped to have achieved. He had told her, "My part in this life is over. I will just sit around and wait for what is to come next. It is all out of my control and that is how it should be."

Julia paused but couldn't hide the sadness she felt when she told Ed of her grandfather's comment. "I don't want that to be the case. He deserves more and I am not sure what we can do to make it better for him."

"He is living his past now," Ed answered. "We

talked about the Morris Cornith golf clubs. How much he missed Hank and Little Willy. About Morris's wife, her sister. How they helped in the plan for bringing Morris's clubs into the public view. That it had started sometime in 1992 and it wasn't until June of 1994 that I showed up. You remember June of 1994 don't you?"

Julia gave Ed a punch in the ribs for an answer. She then moved to him with an embrace and a passionate kiss. Whispering in his ear asked, "How about a shower together tomorrow morning and see what comes up. That okay with you?"

They got into their sleeping positions and as usual Julia was first to fall asleep. Ed was still awake and was letting the last twenty-eight years flow through his mind. Ben telling him how he had been investigated as to his background and psychological condition before he had been selected as the candidate to play the Cornith clubs. That at that point he had needed something so badly to make his life worthwhile that a bunch of strange golf clubs would instill a mystical confidence in his golfing ability. To make it possible for him to make several top ten finishes on the PGA tour.

The chance meeting of Julia, the same weekend he had found the clubs at the setup garage sale had taken him from deep despair to a height of optimism that was still with him. They had led such a fulfilling life so far, with no real tragedies, he thought he ought not think that way with what was now being planned. He tried to put it out of his mind but it would be another hour before sleep would come.

The next morning would be a very busy one. The

shower was one of the best in months and as they met Jennifer and Ben in the big kitchen their attempt to hide their smiles didn't work. Jennifer let it pass but Ben had to mentioned something like what a nice morning it was with the emphasis on the morning.

Breakfast was Ben's special waffles, cantaloupe wedges and strawberries, dusted in powdered sugar. Fresh squeezed orange juice from oranges off their backyard tree, real maple syrup, butter and coffee filled the tray, all of which was taken out poolside. The early April morning in Palm Desert did not disappoint, nor did the breakfast.

When they finished, and Julia and Jennifer had cleared the dishes and returned with refills of coffee, Ed excused himself to make a few telephone calls. Looking towards Julia he suggested, "Why don't you fill them in on the latest on our little adventure. It won't take me long so save a little bit of the story for me to tell."

Julia could see in her grandfather's eyes that he knew something more was going on and was eager to find out what it was. She thought his expression was just like John's when he was about to spring a surprise on you. They, Ben and John, had a lot in common. Maybe they could meet and share some management stories on how they could find ways to make talented people do extraordinary things.

"We had a good day yesterday with Wilma and Cindy," was Julia's opening to Ben and Jennifer. They waited patiently for her to continue. "Wilma is such a dear and it looks like Ed is ready to adopt Cindy into our family." Again she paused and detected a concerned expression on Jennifer's face. Ben just showed interest and waited patiently.

"They are going to join us. I was surprised how willing Cindy was to go back in time on the visit. She had seemed so shy, or maybe withdrawn is a better word for it, I had thought she might show fear or at least reluctance. She actually was enthusiastic and seemed to come alive at the offer. She is a remarkable pianist and is a very beautiful young woman." Julia again saw the concerned look on Jennifer's face and was hoping she would not see her own concerns about this relationship forming between Ed and this young pianist.

"Wilma, who knew Sergei Rachmaninoff when she was a youngster, was really excited at the idea of being in attendance to watch the trip in the theater room in Palo Alto. That is what Ed is doing now. Setting up the transportation for her and Cindy. Her father took care of his cars and fixed anything that needed to be fixed. He was asked to restore an old Steinway Grand and it was placed in living room of her family's small bungalow to do the work. Her father wasn't able to get it finished before Rachmaninoff died and the family of Mr. Rach, as Wilma called him, told him to keep it. By the time it was restored Wilma had married and they were living with her parents. She is still there and the magnificent Steinway is also still there. Ed played it and it is a sight to see and hear."

Ben and Jennifer were now entranced so Julia went on to what was to happened next. "It will be Ed, Cindy and John's friend Allison Turner that make the trip. This coming Friday, April fifteenth."

Julia took a look at her grandfather and saw an excitement that she didn't want to take from him. She was still thinking how to approach telling them about what else was planned when Ed came back out to the pool and sat down in the seat he had left a few minutes earlier. He could tell that as all three of them were looking at him expecting an answer to the question he hadn't heard.

Looking at Julia he asked, "You told them about our meeting with Wilma and Cindy and that they will join us at John's place for the trip."

"Ed, that is so risky, should you do such a thing?" was Jennifer's immediate response. "Is it really safe to do something like that? Will you come back to Julia, and to us, the same person? Is it worth it?"

"I will answer yes to most of your questions. There is more going on here and I think it will turn out to be much more valuable than just a visit. Let me tell you what I know right now."

Ed then started by telling Julia the van had been reserved for Wilma and Cindy and would pick them up at eight-thirty Thursday morning. They should be in Palo Alto by dinner time. He told Ben and Jennifer about the mysterious man named John who, with his five friends, had developed, built and ran the high technology that made this travel possible. About he and Julia seeing in person his travel mate, Allison Turner, make the exact trip and return. He then paused and focused on Ben.

"Ben, I think you would like John. He is a man-ager, like I think you must have been at IBM and as you were putting together the Cornith golf club project. This is much bigger, complex and enormously expensive. He and his five buddies were early venture capitalists at the very beginning of Silicon Valley, making enormous profits and when that started to bore them they opted to experiment in time travel. Having a cadre of Stanford techno geeks at their beckoning they were able to design and build what was needed to make these trips possible. Robert Johnson was the first to make real trips and it was the mind that traveled, not the whole self. They then discovered how to transport not only humans but physical objects as well. Robert and Sandra, on their big sailboat at sea, were transported back in time 10,000 years to investigate the first natives that arrived in the San Francisco area. John joined them on board. They were there for twenty-two days and came back safely with total recall. I will be traveling, with Allison and Cindy, this Friday afternoon. The trip will be for only sixty minutes."

There was a silence that was becoming awkward. Then Ben asked the question Ed knew was coming, "Can Jennifer and I go to Palo Alto and watch it happen?"

Chapter 56

Ed reached for his cell phone as he looked to Julia, who nodded her head slightly to indicate it was alright with her. He touched a speed dial and moments later John's voice came over the speaker phone. "Hello Ed. I would be delighted to have Jennifer and Ben join us for our little party. And hello to you both, I look forward to meeting you in person. You can have Ed and Julia's room and I will fix up the bunk behind the pantry for them."

The looks were passed around, Julia started the laughter and then all joined in. "That will be fine, John. I had a nice conversation with Wilma, and Cindy, after talking to you and they are ready for Thursday morning to come up to Palo Alto. Wilma is almost beside herself and kept telling me that the last two weeks has been the most exciting time she can ever remember. Cindy confirmed that she had never seen Wilma this happy and she told me she was also happy for the first time in years. It has been a very good day already and we have just finished breakfast."

It was Allison's turn next and she only said that she and John needed to get their day started and breakfast sounded like a good idea. Smiles were passed about and Ed finished the conversation with that they should be there by six o'clock Thursday and said his goodbye.

"Ben, I never mentioned to John that you and Jennifer would like to come and watch the event. Not one mention to him but that wasn't a surprise." Ed saying this with appreciation in his voice.

Ed wanted to spend some time on the piano and stood to make his way there. Ben spoke up and said to him, "I think I want to meet this man named John. There is more to this trip than just the visit. Do you know what it is? You are thinking that, aren't you?"

Ed sat back down and had their attention. He had already told Julia his thoughts and he decided to share them with Ben and Jennifer. "Rachmaninoff had been feeling poorly for sometime. He was advised that a more temperate climate would help and in California first rented a house, and then bought the house in Beverly Hills, near where his friend Vladimir Horowitz lived. He had a full 1942-1943 schedule but during the swing through Florida he had to cancel the remainder of his tour and by train returned to Beverly Hills. His last performance was on February 17, 1943 in Tennessee and he died on March 28 from a just discovered aggressive melanoma."

Ed paused and then looked at Ben and continued, "He was four days short of his seventieth birthday. His life was cut short and I believe he had much more he wanted to do, both with family and his music. I think he has a pile of works in progress, some maybe even finished, that he doesn't want to be lost or forgotten. John hasn't talked of this but since he is about Rachmaninoff's age when he died, I think that is what he expects might be offered to a pair of accomplished pianists that are not famous or too wrapped up in their own lives to not be interested in what he wasn't be able to finish."

Ben sat very still and you could see in his manner that he was thinking about this and about himself. He looked up at Ed and said in a firm tone, "I want to be part of this. I have no idea how or what I might do but I want to be part of it." Jennifer reached over and took his hand. "You stay close to this guy, Ed Adams, and some thing good will happen. It always does. I am right about that, aren't I Julia?"

"She is right, Grandpa. Jennifer told us both that years ago, remember. Let's go with that and try to guess what will happen this time."

Ed wasn't sure what he should say so he excused himself and went to his favorite piano. The one that had once been his mother's and on which she had taught him to play. Hank had found it, had it restored and gave it to him at just the right time for he and Julia to start on the path that had reached its peak less than three weeks ago in Los Angeles. As he sat on the familiar bench, reaching for the keys, he played without thinking about what he was playing. The others sat by the pool and listened to the music coming out to them through the open patio doors. They listened, also not needing to know what was being played. Just to listen was all that was required.

Chapter 57

Tuesday dissolved into Wednesday as the family blended together for meals and conversation. Ed was able to spend extra time on his piano chores, Julia and Jennifer escaped the house pretending they wanted to go shopping but buying nothing, and Ben had some time to do some searches on this mysterious man named John. He didn't come up with much but searching the records of venture capitalist in the Silicon Valley during the 1970s lead him to a group of six Stanford drop outs that had hit the big time. One of the six was named John Smith. This brought a smile to his face as a Ben Shea should feel right at home with a man named John Smith. Their company name at the time was AAA Half Dozen, Inc. but in 1985 it was no longer listed and he could find nothing more about them. He did find that a John Smith was involved in a lease with Stanford Linear Accelerator, Inc in 1995 but with little details. As he sat at his desk he began to look forward to the trip to Palo Alto and to be around a few more very extraordinary people. He knew Ed easily fit in with people like these and he missed their presence in his life.

They were prepared for their departure for Palo Alto and left Palm Desert at eight o'clock after a good breakfast and taking care of all their morning duties. The

Panamera is a extremely comfortable car and those in the backseats have all the room and comfort as those in front. Ed would drive and Ben sat up front with him and the ladies sat in the back.

In Beverly Hills Wilma and Cindy were picked up promptly at eight-thirty by a nicely dressed driver in a luxury van. Captain chairs front and back, a small kitchenette and fully stocked refrigerator. A table could be placed between the rear seats and there was a small enclosed toilet and wash basin in the rear. It had a wheel chair lift and was set up for convenience.

At six-forty that evening the two cars drove through the gates of John's estate. He and Allison stood at the front door to greet them. It had started and all the players were now in place. Robert and Sandra were inside waiting for them while John was introduced to Ben and Jennifer followed by Wilma and Cindy. Wilma wouldn't let go of John's hand until she had told him how excited she was to have the chance to see Mr. Rach again, and maybe even herself at fifteen. That he was such a nice man and treated her and her parents as real friends. She finally let go of his hand as she said, "He was such a nice man. Mr. Rach was such a nice man," with tears coming to her eyes. John gave her a hug and told her she was part of what made this trip possible and thanked her a second time.

As they entered the house the introductions to Robert and Sandra were made and the party entered the great room. Ed was first to see the two Steinway Model D's positioned in the middle of the room. Cindy saw them next and called out to Ed, "Can you believe what I see!"

and taking his hand pulled him toward the pianos. "Which one do you want?" Ed asked and she took the nearest bench and began to play Pagini's 18. Ed walked around to the other end, sat down and they played that most familiar melody together as if they had practiced it for years. The sound in the big room was electric and the rest of the group crowded up around the pianos.

Ed played part of the second movement of Rachmaninoff Number 2 and Cindy followed with the main theme and then another similar one that Ed had never heard before. He was trying to understand what he was hearing when Wilma asked him to play *Nobody Does It Better* and for Julia to sing the words for John. She did and at it's end she went to John, mussed his hair in her practiced sexy way while she kissed his cheeks. Everyone applauded and the group had bonded in an very important way.

John gave the guided tour of the house, including all the bedrooms for his guests. His office was of special interest for Ben and he was able to get a quick look at some of the photos and framed certificates on the wall. John then took Ben aside and told him he could use the office when time permitted and pointed out a small table and chair with a key board and monitor, "Just tap any key and enter your first and last name plus enter and you will have high speed access to the internet," were John's instructions. Ben nodded his head that exchanged his thanks and they acknowledged their respect for each other.

Dinner was an exceptionally good pot roast with all the trimmings. Red wine was offered but little was consumed, John and Allison served and there were no others to assist. Julia was first to note this and asked about who had been the chef. Allison reached over and John had his hair mussed up for the second time. That also answered another question John's guests had and made the evening even more pleasant.

After dessert of ice cream and cookies John presented several gifts to his new team. First to Ed and Julia was a eight by ten framed color photograph of Julia with microphone in hand looking movie star gorgeous with Ed equally as good in the background at the piano but still featured. Both were surprised as they had never seen this shot before and it brought back memories of their time as top entertainers. Next was for Sandra and Robert. It was a similarly framed photograph from their trip back in time with the small family of natives. It was a photo of the six together with a magnificent view of the Pacific Ocean in the background. The colors and fidelity seemed to draw you into the picture as if you were there. Sandra could not hide the tears that came that gave John his thanks. Wilma was presented a similar sized photograph and when she saw the fifteen year old girl standing next to Sergei Rachmaninoff looking at her with love on his face it was her turn to weep. "Oh my! Oh my! That is me with Mr. Rach. He was so nice to me. He was such a nice man." She clutched it to her breast and looked at John in a way a mother might look at her son when she told him what a good boy he was.

They all reassembled to the main hall, listened to some remarkable piano and it was then time to retire.

Chapter 58

Far from the small room behind the pantry, Ed and Julia's room was the same as all the bedrooms, large, well appointed and more than adequate. Actually, one of the finest bedrooms they had ever had been in. Once in bed they moved close to each other, laying on their backs and enjoying the comfort of the bed. Julia was happy. It had been another long day but it had passed quickly and the group was fun to be with. There was no tension between any of them and the extraordinary trip to be taken the next day seemed to be accepted by all as nothing to be concerned about.

"Isn't it strange that none of us seem worried about the trip back in time tomorrow. Not even me about you going there," she asked Ed as she moved even closer to him. Since he didn't answer she continued, "That photograph of us is really a good one. Do you remember where it was taken?"

It was Ed's turn but instead of answering Julia's question he said, "I can't figure out what Cindy was playing just before we did the Nobody Does It Better routine. I am sure it was Rachmaninoff but I have never heard it before. It was too good not to have been used somewhere in one of his major works. I will have to ask her about it in the morning."

Julia put her arm around his waist and pulled him a little closer. "I would think that if you have the woman in that photograph with you in bed you might think of something other than a lost Rachmaninoff theme."

Ed then paid attention but in the back of his mind was what Julia had just been saying about a lost theme by Rachmaninoff. He was sure, now more than ever, that what he was expecting to happen tomorrow was going to happen. What he didn't dare think was where Cindy might have learned to play it, or the possibility that she had helped to compose it.

"You are just short of ninety-five Ben and I am keeping up with you at sixty-seven. What are we doing here in John Smith's guest bedroom. But then how could it be much better?" Jennifer's remarked at seeing in Ben's eyes a look of excitement with life that had been missing for several years. His brush with prostate cancer, which had brought her to him as a home nurse after his surgery, had been twenty-seven years ago. At first they thought he may have only ten years more of health good enough to enjoy life and it had kept him going until he found he had little, in his imagination, left to offer others. He had tried to hide his depression but it was readily apparent and easy to understand.

Ben looked at Jennifer and answered her question, "It can't be. I needed this, to mix with this group. Even think that I am part of it and tomorrow will watch some thing that can't possibly happen. What an exciting adventure to have at the end of one's life. Now I feel each day is so important that I must stay around as long as possible. A couple of weeks ago I was hoping I wouldn't wake up in the morning. Right now I can't wait to wake up to see what will happen next."

Jennifer snuggled up close to the man that had saved her from a period in her life after her husband, a test pilot of military jet aircraft, had been killed in a crash. They had no children but she had lived the life as the wife of a top-gun pilot for twenty years and then one afternoon in the skies over Fallon, Nevada it was over in seconds. Ben had given her a new life of family, friends and a totally different life style that she treasured every day. She gently rubbed his shoulder, kissed his check and waited for his even breathing knowing that sleep had come for him. It would be another hour before she slept but she didn't mind. She was where she wanted to be and thought life couldn't be much better than that.

Wilma got ready for bed. Their room had two rooms, one the main room and the second a sleeping quarter, each with a queen size bed. Cindy took the small room and was quickly in bed trying to relax enough to let sleep come but not having much success. She heard the knock on her door and called out for Wilma to enter. She noisily got the door open and with the walker made it around to Cindy's side of the bed. She seated herself and smiled down at her beautiful, young care giver.

"I'm too excited to get to sleep. You are too, I expect. I will get to watch but you will be there. Not where you were in your dreams of being with Mr. Rach. That must have been earlier in Russia when he was about the age you are now." Wilma paused, hoping Cindy might say something to further the conversation. Then she reached out for Cindy's hand and took it in hers, "I am beginning to believe your dreams were not dreams but really happened. It is not possible, of course, but what will happen tomorrow isn't possible either. For me it will be the most exciting day of my life. Maybe I have already lived long enough but I am sure there is a reason I am here now."

Cindy smiled, squeezed Wilma's hand and told her, "You are here to guide me back from a very dark place and give me a meaning for living. It was you that caused us to meet Ed Adams, Julia and the rest. Being here is because of you and there has to be a reason for it happening. I think when I return with Ed and Allison we will know why this has happened. Then we will know what to do next. I am not worried about my future for the first time in my life."

Wilma bent to kiss her cheek whispering, "Ed Adams is a very special man. Stay close to him, and his family. Trust me on this, dear child," and she clattered her way back to her room.

Down the hall in another of the big guest rooms Robert and Sandra readied for their night's rest. They were comfortable and moved close together as they always did when ready for sleep. Sandra spoke softly, "This time I have no fear about what John has planned. We will be spectators, not participants. The photograph of us with our native family is so beautiful. I think it can be thought that having been there should be enough for a lifetime. Everything that comes next for us will be a bonus."

Robert looked at her closely and could see the emotion that was near the surface. As it was every time he looked at her he marveled at what a beautiful person she was and how much he loved her. "We are developing a family here. New friends and I think our lives are destined to become entwined with theirs. If the trip is for what we were thinking we will have a part in the development of what is retrieved. I am sure John has more going than just to show off what his team can accomplish. He has been up front about this being the last trip back in time for him but he is planning on something to come from it that will involve all of us afterwards. That is what is exciting for me. I plan to go to sleep thinking of what it might be and what will happen tomorrow. You are with me on this?"

With a long and passionate kiss she whispered, "I will be right next to you. With you. Always."

Allison was walking about the huge master suite in a shear nightgown that did not leave much to the imagination. She was a tall woman, proportioned very nicely and not the least bit self conscious. John laid in bed enjoying the sight and marveling as what had happened in his life in such a short time. Allison finally looked his way, caught his intense gaze and only said, "Well?"

John smiled and spoke in a guarded tone, "You are a joy to watch. To look at and wonder on how this could have happened for me. Just when I am coming to an end of my biggest achievement in life you have given me a chance to live a new one. Your timing is exquisite and so are you."

Allison's laughter was taken by John in the way it was intended and minutes later he had another of life's great pleasures to attend to with all his concentration on doing it well. It seemed so natural for him that he regretted having not practiced it more. As he laid back and Allison made no move to get up he turned to her and said, "Some things in life are meant to be. Having you here with me is, at least now, one of those. I want you with me as long as you wish to be there. If tomorrow goes as planned this small group that has formed may be quite busy for some time. I want you to be a part of it."

"My first boy friend. My first little boy friend. Never in my wildest dreams would I have ever thought I might be laying here next you to as satisfied as I feel right now. It is funny how my life seems to be turning out after so many years of trying to make the most of it. I didn't even try to have any of this happen and here I am enjoying my life more than ever. Tomorrow is going to be one more day when it is fun to be alive. I like it!" Allison rolled over, stood up by the edge of the bed picking up her nightgown while looking at John. He smiled and she smiled as she dropped her gown on the floor and climbed back into bed.

Chapter 59

They gathered in the dining room and breakfast had been placed on the breakfront. Fresh orange juice, place mats, spoons, coffee cups and carafes of coffee were already on the table. Ten large bowls were in two rows of five, each having two small packets. Serving dishes had a variety of fruits and banana's were hung on a special stand. Hot water dispensers with a measuring cup were at either end of the table. A small sign read "1/2 cup per packet." Robert and Sandra did not hesitate, emptying two packets in their bowls and fixed themselves fruit in the small glass dishes provided. Ed and Julia did likewise without hesitation as they had this breakfast once before. Ben and Jennifer followed suit. Wilma asked Cindy to fix two packets for her and she dished up fruit for the two of them. John and Allison had watched, then fixed their own last and all were seated as the first tastes were taken. Nothing was said and then Wilma announced what was being expected from the rest, "This is the best oatmeal I have ever tasted."

Breakfast was quickly consumed and several conversations ensued. Around ten o'clock John suggested they get started on the things they wanted to do to prepare for the afternoon's event. He said a buffet lunch would be available at one o'clock and they would leave the house at three-thirty sharp for the laboratory. The trip would start at four o'clock. It would last about one hour and everyone should be ready to spend another hour at the lab before returning to the house.

Ed was first to stand up and asked Cindy to come with him to the pianos so they could do a little preparation. She was eager to go and looked at Wilma, who told her to get going as she had all the help she needed from the other girls. The other girls had a fun time being girls again and rushed to cater to Wilma's needs. John joined Ben at the table and asked him if he would like a tour of the laboratory as he needed to check on a few things that were being done there this morning. Ben was delighted and waved to Jennifer as they hurried off. Robert was left by himself which was fine with him. He had spotted a library just passed John's office. Loving books he was happy to wander off in that direction.

Ed and Cindy shared the piano bench fronting the piano she had chosen when they had arrived. He started explaining what he thought they should do once inside the house and after Allison had introduced them to whomever it was necessary they meet. They would then head to the pianos, Ed first and Cindy to go to the other one and seat herself.

"I will start with the third movement of Concerto Number Two, play it in the shortened piano solo version and end with the Cadenza. You then come in and play the second movement and as you get into the second theme move into Pagini's Variation 18, Hopefully by then Rachmaninoff will have made it down the stairs to find out who is playing his music. When he comes into the room I want you to play the theme you played yesterday. The one I have never heard before." Ed stopped there as he saw a sudden look of fear on Cindy's face. He asked, "Is it the theme that worries you?"

Cindy sat frozen and then reached out for Ed's arm. "I told you about my dreams. Over and over I was told not to think of them but I can't. They were so real and that theme was one of two I helped Sergei develop. He told me they were mine and that he would never use them. He hasn't. Not in any of his works. He was twenty-six and trying to get his life together. Working on the second and third movements of his Symphony 2 at the time. We were sitting close together when he read my score and then played it. He was so handsome, I could smell him and he kissed me. He tasted and smelled of cigarettes. It happened. It was real." She put her head against Ed's chest and started to cry. He waited and Cindy lifted her head. "Tell me you believe me. I can do it. Play anything you ask if you will believe in me."

Ed looked into her eyes and told her he did. He did and was not trying to deceive her. "I want you to do that piece. I want Rachmaninoff to recognize it. The second one you worked on, can you play that for me now and again when we are there. She did and Ed knew he was right. It was Rachmaninoff and he had never heard it before. Cindy murmured that it was the second piece she wrote for him and that he kissed her a second time. Her tears came again.

"Let's play. Just improvise and see how we might pull this off together. I will start as I said before and then let's see what happens." Ed tried to say this lightheartedly and went to the other piano and played through to the Candenza and Cindy took over. He sat and listened. This would work and as Cindy finished the second unfamiliar theme they meshed their skills into a superb collection of Rachmaninoff favorites that filled the big room with even bigger music.

John and Ben took a golf cart down into the SLAC area. As they passed a room with rows computer screens on a big table which with young men and women working on their keyboards and staring at the screens in front of them. There was tension in the air but a confidence that both men were able to recognize. One man, a little older, came up to John and said everything looked as it should. It would be operational in two hours and the simulations should be completed well before time to run the full program. All would be ready at four o'clock. John merely smiled and simply said, "Good."

They then walked into the SLAC area and Ben could see the many banks of computers running in either direction. The smell and humming sounds of the electronics was familiar to him but not at this level. He said to John, "I was at IBM in 1986 when the very first PC was being designed and produced. We were chasing Jobs and Wozniak's Apple and it was then I realized a new generation was taking over. My two best friends, Hank Morgan and Morris Cornith, had retired a few years before and I knew it was time for me to bow out and did likewise. I moved to Palm Desert, played golf and tried to raise Julia after both my wife and our daughter had lost their lives to breast cancer. It was Julia that kept me going then. Golf was no substitute and I had nothing else I wanted to do. In 1994 Ed Adams showed up and it was Morris's crazy collection of golf clubs he had designed and built that brought him into our family. Or more correctly, into Julia and my lives." Ben stopped there and asked John, "You already know all that, don't you?"

"Yes Ben, I do but it is good to hear you tell me. Reading about one's story is okay but hearing it told by him is much better."

Wilma was tiring and asked if the ladies would mind her taking a brief nap. Sandra and Julia escorted her to her room and then returned as Ed and Cindy were playing some extraordinarily good compositions. Sandra had seen Robert head toward John's office and told Julia she would go see what he was up to. Julia found a spot to sit and watch the two pianists. It was strange watching Ed working with the young pianist. It was how they had worked together when they were performing as singer and accompanist. It was seamless in the transitions from one to the other, as if they had practiced together for years. She then remembered how easy Ed had made it for her to sing the words just right and always find the right key and tempo. He was doing the same for Cindy. "This is going to turn out just fine. All the pieces are in place. We need to spend some time with John because he has the same gifts that Ed has," she thought, which let her relax and enjoy the music as it passed over her.

Sandra found Robert in front of a floor to ceiling bookcase studying a long row of books. "Find anything of interest?" Sandra's question startled him as he was intently searching a row of titles and was just then reaching for one of the books. He showed her the title. "This is one of the same books I used in preparing for my Lincoln visit. If you look closely you will see books on every trip we wrote about for the television series. All twenty-seven. They have been read and are not just for show. There is not one book of fiction here," Robert said as he motioned with his hand, "They all look like they have been read. They are not for show, but for education.

"I think we are in the company of a genius here and didn't even realize it. I think it is a good place to be and I hope it will continue that way. This afternoon we will find out a bit more of where it is going. Where we might be going."

Robert replaced the book and they returned to the big room and settled in to listen to the great music being played.

John and Ben made it back and joined the group as it assembled. Allison asked if they had a good time down in the hole and Ben quickly said, "It was great. One of the best mornings I have ever had. I can hardly wait for this afternoon's entertainment."

The clatter of Wilma's walker announced her arrival and now the whole group was together again. John mentioned that the buffet would be set in fifteen minutes and the clock was now running. He and Allison went to the kitchen and set up the buffet.

Ed had come to the end of what he was playing and walked around the two pianos and stood behind Cindy. He watched as she played one of her favorite Rachmaninoff themes and smiled at the thought of her own compositions knowing that there would be more for them to work together on in the future. He touched her shoulder as she finished and as she looked up, her face shined and her eyes were bright with excitement. She took his hand and they walked together, joining the others as they entered the dining area.

Chapter 60

Three-thirty had arrived. Everyone had taken care of what was necessary and Ed, Cindy and Allison had all changed into their 1943 outfits. Allison was particularly stunning in a white jacket and matching mid-calf skirt. The shoulder pads showed off her long torso and legs to advantage. High heels of white tipped in black toe and heels added to the elegance. Red lip stick and her gray hair topped by a rakish hat completed the look.

Ed wore a light tweed tan three button suit coat. It's shoulder pads gave his already broad shoulders an even wider look. A complimenting tie, perfectly tied, with a white collared shirt blended in nicely. His pants were belted high up and pleated with wide cuffs looked per-fectly in style for the occasion. Polished brown leather shoes and a period hat set at an angle completed the look.

It was Cindy's look that took their breath away. She was wearing a black dress with three quarter sleeves, v-neck top and pleated skirt. The material was lightweight but had a shine that seemed to reflect the light in every direction. The fitting was tight at the waist, such that her figure was shown off, and the v-neck also exposed just enough to realize the shape that was hidden. The skirt came just below the knees exposing very nice legs and the black, strapped high heels matched the outfit perfectly. She wore no hat, gloves or makeup and the only jewelry was a small string of pearls about her neck. Eight of the group took a collective gasp as she walked into the lighted area. Allison just admired this young woman as she had helped Cindy dress.

It was time to head to the SLAC center. They loaded into the golf carts and fifteen minutes later were taking their seats in the theater. The big screen was operating and split as before with the transfer chamber on the left and the photo of the Rachmaninoff's lawn and house on the right. John escorted the three travelers around to the rear of the chamber and they were positioned inside by one of the white lab coated assistants. One last check by John and the chamber door was closed and secured. John came back to his seat in the theater room. A large clock with hour, minute and second hands was above the chamber and as the hands showed 3:59 a digital clock came on for the count down.

The three inside appeared calm. All had been done so efficiently and well that they hadn't had time to become apprehensive. The same was true of the seven seated in the studio chairs. At T-minus ten seconds Julia felt a chill and reached for John who was seated next to her. He smiled a calm smile which helped. Sandra was next to Wilma and was holding her hand, it wasn't in fear but excitement. Ben and Jennifer were holding hands and were mesmerized to the point of having no feelings.

At 000.00 on the digital clock a green mist appeared in the chamber, then a flash and the three inside had disappeared. At 000.01 they stood in the same positions on the lawn in front of the house except this time the big screen separated into four sections and the views varied as the cameras in their clothing were showing multiple views. The technical crews running the camera views started to sort out the pictures and soon a major view was surrounded eight smaller views.

The group relaxed as Allison moved toward the front door. A couple had entered from down the street and walked up behind them and the five arrived at the door together. Allison rang the bell and the door was opened. The main view showed a young girl greeting them and asking them to come in.

Wilma's cry was not loud or frightened, "That's me. Oh my God, that is me. I am fifteen years old there, I am ninety-six here. Oh my God in heaven."

As they entered the house Wilma guided them from the foyer into the large living room. The scene was exactly as Robert, Sandra and Julia had seen it before but for Wilma, Ben and Jennifer an all new experience. For John it was very familiar as this was the fourth time it had been done. He had gone twice. The time and place was determined by those two trips. The first time he had almost been placed next to a group of four that had just entered the house. He had seen the couple but they were down the street and had about ten seconds to walk to where they would be able to see the flash and sudden appearance of others on the lawn. Allison's trip had verified the time and place that was safe and her entrance being accepted left them confident of at least gaining entry. What would happen next was new to all involved.

Allison led them in as if she was a valued guest

and any friend of hers would have been a friend of Sergei Rachmaninoff. Wilma lead them in and around the two big pianos. Natalia was at the end of the room opposite the pianos and barely looked up as they approached. Wilma didn't try to do introductions, just said that these people just arrived and left them going back to the door as the bell had just rung again.

Allison introduced Ed and Cindy, introducing Cindy as Cynthia, and that they were from out of town but professional pianists, specializing in playing her husbands music. She spoke as an aggressive agent would lauding Ed as being thought to be a competitor of Vladimir Horowitz which brought a weak smile to Natalia's lips. Cindy was spoken of as an up and coming prodigy developing into a world class pianist. Again Natalia was trying to hide her annoyance and to spare her this suggested Ed play the piano nearest them as that was the one Sergei liked the best of the two. As they turned toward the pianos Cindy said something to Natalia that made her offer a genuine smile and they conversed with a few more pleasantries. Ed didn't understand at first and then realized Cindy was speaking in Russian. She looked at Ed and let out a gentle laugh. "So you don't know everything about me," saying this as she headed for the far side piano.

There were about thirty people in the room and more were showing up. Ed sat down and ran up and down the keys getting a feel for pressure and sound and found he liked what he felt and heard. Cindy was doing the same at the other piano and also liked the piano. Ed nodded her way and he started with the third movement of Concerto Number 2, solo Piano. It went well and half the people in the room stopped talking and began to listen.

Natalia was making small talk with the next cluster of guests but her attention went to this handsome man that was playing Sergei's favorite Concerto so well. She felt maybe today might turn out a little better than the last several as her beloved husband was laying in pain upstairs knowing he had only a few days left.

As Ed finished the cadenza Cindy, with perfect timing, started the second movement. It was after the first few bars had been played that Natalia realized something special was happening and the rest had stopped their conversations to listen.

Upstairs in the bedroom at the top of the stairs Sergei Rachmaninoff lay in his bed awake. The pain was getting worse. He ached all over, especially on his left side. His bones ached, his breathing was difficult and the ever present headache seemed to be worse than ever but he could clearly hear the music coming from downstairs. His first thought was that his friend Vladimir Horowitz had arrived and was entertaining his guests. He knew immediately it wasn't him but whoever was playing was a good pianist. He listened carefully. He liked how the third movement of Concerto Number 2 was being played and when it was finished another pianist started the second movement on his other piano. He knew that it was a woman playing and that she was good, every bit as good as the man.

Rachmaninoff struggled to get up off his bed. He wanted to go downstairs and meet these people. He had changed into his daytime clothes of slacks, collared shirt and light sweater that morning but was so weak and in such pain he had just laid back down on his bed. He had wished he hadn't wakened and would have passed away in his sleep but now he wanted meet these pianists that were playing his compositions. His clothes were wrinkled and a quick glance in the bathroom mirror showed an old man near death. Dark circles under his eyes, his skin pale, blotched and covered with small bumps. His thoughts were why could he not have died and got it over with when Paganini Variation 18 floated up to him. The start of a smile formed on his face and he knew that he had to make it downstairs.

A quick wash of his face and brushing what little hair he had left he then shuffled out of his room. Hanging onto the railing he made one careful step after another until he made to the foyer. Looking into the living room he could see who it was that was playing and in his blurred vision she was the most beautiful woman he had ever seen. She turned toward him and smiled. Not looking away she started playing the piece she had composed with him in her dreams. He winced as he listened then made his way to the piano. Sitting on the end of the bench facing away from the keyboard he continued listening and said nothing.

Ed could see this happening and moved slightly to get a better view. Cindy was almost finished with her first piece and Rachmaninoff was sitting absolutely still. His emaciated back bent forward in an awkward position but his concentration was intense. Cindy started the second piece, the one she had written herself and had played for him in her dreams.

Rachmaninoff slowly moved, turning towards her,

and speaking in an strained and hoarse voice said, "I know you from a long time ago. You played that for me. For me alone. I was young, healthy, working on Concerto Number Two. In Russia. You played me both of those pieces and I told you how good they were. I was engaged to Natalia but in those few moments I fell in love with you. How can this be happening now. I am dying. Old. Almost helpless and you are as beautiful as I remember you."

A tear ran down his cheek but he didn't try to wipe it away. Cindy had finished as he told of his love and she reached over and wiped his tear away. "I knew it wasn't a dream. It happened and I want you to know I was in love with you then. I have your music now and that is enough for me. Know that."

Ed had started to play the first movement but started quietly as the first theme develops. Rachmaninoff tried to stand up, staggered but caught himself. "I have some things you must have. You and your partner must have them. Come with me. They are in the library closet."

He took Cindy's hand and they walked together to get Ed. He had no idea what was being said as Cindy and Rachmaninoff were both speaking Russian but he understood by their gestures he was to go with them.

Chapter 61

In the theater room all sat mesmerized by the unfolding scenes on the screen. The conversation between Cindy and Rachmaninoff was being translated into English so they knew what was being discussed between them. A satisfied look was on John's face as he was anticipating what was about to happen. He was sure of what would be on Rachmaninoff's mind, as it would be on any creative person's when life was leaving them too soon. He wasn't finished. He would have other things he wanted to create, finish or were even ready to bring public and now he had no time left. For Rachmaninoff it had been his drive to make his life, and his family's, back to the wealth and position as they had been in his early youth in Russia. His father had squandered almost all his inherited wealth on crazy schemes and what had been left for him was then taken by the communists when they ransacked his homes following the revolution.

After they had fled Russia and immigrated to the United States he had booked an unending schedule of concerts and recitals in an attempt to gain the wealth to return his family to the standard of living he was striving for. At the time he had become sick he was one of the highest paid entertainers in the world but now he had no time left. It had been the time he should have valued more than the money.

It was when Rachmaninoff asked Wilma, speaking in English, to go find her father and have him come to help him without delay. "He's out in front of the garage working on my car. I saw him there this morning. Tell him not to even wash his hands. I need him right now. Hurry up now!" When Wilma heard this she couldn't contain her excitement and loudly said, "I am on my way, Mr. Rach!" just as she was saying the same thing, as a fifteen year old, on the screen.

Those in the theater room all looked her way and could barely contain their own excitement in what was happening. All but John who sat with a big smile that he couldn't hide any longer.

Ed was following Rachmaninoff and Cindy into the library which was just off the dining room. There were several guests there and as they saw them enter they bowed their heads towards their host and went back into the living room. Rachmaninoff hurried to a single door, opened it and pulled Cindy in after him. It was a small store room and one side had shelves loaded with labeled boxes. He started his search but with failing eyesight and exhaustion was having trouble locating what he was look- ing for. Ed could see Cindy was also searching but he, even though he thought he knew what they were trying to find, couldn't help as all the labels were in Russian.

Just then Wilma and her father pushed into the room, which was now getting very crowded and before they could ask what he needed Rachmaninoff had pulled out a box, about twelve by eighteen inches and six inches in height. Almost dropping it, Wilma's father grabbed it and Rachmaninoff pointed to two more that were the same size and asked him to bring them out to the table in the library. He then asked Wilma and her father to wait outside and closed the door behind them.

John could hardly control his thoughts as Cindy and Ed's cameras were picking up the video and sounds of what was happening. Rachmaninoff was talking to Cindy as if Ed wasn't there.

"I remember you from before. You wrote those two themes I just heard you play. I want you to have what is in these boxes. They contain what I have written, some only started and never finished and others almost ready to release. I was going to do it when I had time. I have no time left and I want you to do it for me. Will you do that for me?"

Cindy seemed to straighten, looked directly into his eyes and said, "Yes, I will do it. I want to do it more than anything I have ever wanted to do. I want to do it for you."

Ed was almost embarrassed by the love shown between these two people who never could have met before. He did know that there was no way they could transport any thing like the three boxes back to their own time, but had an idea of how it might be done.

"Cindy, Cynthia, the only way we can get the boxes home is to have Wilma's father take them and store them for us until we get there. Get them to Wilma's house. Do you understand what I mean?" Ed was talking directly to her but Rachmaninoff either understood why it had to be done this way or thought it was just a way to have them picked up later, maybe that afternoon.

"I will have Alfred take them right now and you can pick them up there. Do this for me, otherwise all I planned to get done in my last years will be lost when I die."

Cindy took Rachmaninoff's hands, pulled him down toward her and kissed him on the cheek. "I will take care of these and my life's work will be to finish them as you would like them to be. I can do this. You know I can. You have taught me with your music and I want there to be more of it to share with others."

Ed had gone into the dining room as Cindy talked to Rachmaninoff and standing next to the door was Wilma and her father. Ed said to him, "Mr. Rachmaninoff wants you take the boxes home with you and store them in a safe place until we come to pick them up. He is starting to tire so if you will take care of them right now I am sure he will be much relieved."

In the theater room the digital clock was counting in real time and had reached 044.58. John sat relaxed as he watched Wilma's father carrying the three boxes out of the library, around the corner and through the kitchen. Ed's main camera showed him exiting outdoors through the kitchen's backdoor.

Rachmaninoff's face had gone pale and he started to stagger. Cindy put her arm around him and they walked back into the dining room. Wilma had gone to the front as the bell had sounded and in walked Vladimir Horowitz and a half dozen of his friends. The excitement of his entrance allowed Cindy, now joined by Natalia, to steer Rachmaninoff into the foyer. Horowitz joined them there, a short discussion ensued and then Vladimir and Natalia helped the tall, slumped man up the stairs. It would be the last time he would be downstairs in his beloved home.

Ed put his arms around Cindy as the tears came and she was having trouble standing. Allison had been watching this and was at their side telling them both it was time to leave. They left out the front door and assembled on the lawn standing as near as possible in the footprints in the grass where they had arrived. Cindy had recovered somewhat and Ed nodded they were ready. Allison looked around in every direction and seeing no others raised her right hand with her thumb and index finger in a circle indicating the okay sign.

There was a flash, the digital clock stopped at 052.37, and through a mist of green vapors in the chamber the three travelers were back.

Chapter 62

All in the theater sat in silence staring at the three in the chamber. The rear door opened and the white coated attendant quickly hustled them out closing the door as he left. Again it was quiet in the theater until Cindy, Ed and Allison appeared around the corner of the room entering the theater. Those seated stood, clapping their hands in relief. John had been standing and was watching his three travelers, enjoying the sight of their return. It was the last of his group's travels to the past but this time something was brought back in the only way that it could be without changing history. The three boxes containing the unknown works of Sergei Rachmaninoff had stayed in their own time and if they, as John was expecting, had been placed by Wilma's father in his workshop garage they would still be there now. There was no history that they had been dis-covered. John's researchers had thoroughly searched every avenue possible and had found nothing.

His answer came in the next few minutes as Cindy had gone to Wilma and knelt down in front of her reaching for her hands. Her tears were again flowing as she said, "I saw him, I touched him, Wilma. He knew my com-positions. He remembered them. He remembered me. He once loved me. He wants me to finish his work. It was not in my dreams. It happened."

Wilma pulled her to her, cradled her head on her breast. It was then John had his answer as Wilma said in a calm and clear voice, "I know where the boxes are. How could I have forgotten. They have been on a top shelf in the workshop. Ernst mentioned it to me once or twice after my father passed away but I had forgotten all about it. We were supposed to give them to the right people when they showed up. That was over fifty years ago. I don't even remember exactly what was said about who would come for them. We can get them when we get home."

John had made sure he was near Wilma when Cindy went to her and heard the entire conversation. He had thought it would have been Ed that Rachmaninoff would have gone to bring his unfinished work to life. He had thought when Cindy was telling them about her dreams of being with Rachmaninoff, and of composing with him as he developed his Second Concerto, that they were just her dreams. It was not possible she had actually been there, but it had been Cindy that Rachmaninoff had selected to be the one to make it happen. He had clearly said that he remembered her and her compositions. John thought he had been right about most of what would happen but he now thought he had more to learn about going back in time. For now, however, if what he thought was in the boxes was there he knew his new group, sitting here in the theater, would have something to occupy their time for years to come. As would he.

He moved to face the group and watched as they positioned themselves to listen to what he was about to say. He spoke first at how successful the trip had been and how satisfied he was with how it had turned out. He then asked if all of them were comfortable to spend some more time here in the theater room so he could expand on what the trip meant to him personally and what might it be in the future for each of them. All nodded their heads in approval and gave him their full attention.

"First I want you all to know how good this went, start to finish. It couldn't have worked out better. You also know this was the last trip into history that will be made from this facility or with this equipment. It will be my last effort, and my groups last effort, in anything of this nature. On Monday the removal and liquidation of every thing of ours here will start and it has been promised nothing will remain of ours in the SLAC area. We have no plans to save anything except the transfer chamber and even it will be disassembled and stored.

John then made his most important point clear, "We obtained my goal for this trip exactly as I had hoped. That was obtaining some boxes that contained works of Rachmaninoff that he wished to complete later when he had the time. Not only that, he made the offer to give them to us but that he accepted, without any hesitation, the only vehicle that we could use to get them to us without chang-ing history. We have Ed's quick thinking to thank for that."

He paused and then looked at Cindy and said, "It was Cindy that made this work. I had thought Ed would be the one to get it done, but it was Cindy and her two compositions, themes, that got his attention and which made him confident that she had the skills to complete his unfinished pieces at a level he would be comfortable with.

Also, Cindy could speak Russian. I had forgotten about that detail although I now remember it was mentioned in one of the reports. Her dreams apparently are not the dreams we thought they were and I now believe that without them we would just be returning to the main house, maybe feeling it had been a nice experiment but having nothing to go with other than the memories."

Again he paused but couldn't hide his enthusiasm, "The boxes are in the garage workshop at Wilma's house, just as I had hoped they might be. That worked perfectly. Four weeks ago I was sitting in my office trying to think of what I could do now that the back in time experiments were over. I want you all to understand that I couldn't think of a thing and the usual depression one gets coming to an end of something that has brought so much pleasure in accomplishing is not enjoyable. By chance I was given a ticket for Ed's symphony performance and decided to attend. I flew down Thursday afternoon and went straight to the Walt Disney Center. Arriving early I was able to observe the patrons as they entered. Spotting Robert and Sandra was a surprise and needless to say I tried to not let them see me but I did kept a close watch on them. They seemed to have more than a casual interest in Ed and it was then I put the first two pieces of the puzzle together. The visit to Rachmaninoff by Robert and the way Ed played his music. It was a phenomenal performance and I decided to discretely follow my new interest. I was able to get into the donor's party with my ticket and watched as Ed and Julia met Wilma. I over heard her tell them she had known Rachmaninoff when she was a young girl. That her father had worked for him and they had been to his home.

Then Robert and Sandra approached Ed and Julia and I eaves dropped on their conversation."

John had to stop to collect his thoughts. He knew most would not understand his thinking at the moment he had seen the connection of these five people but he had sensed an opportunity he would be following less than an hour later. "I secured a room at the hotel and set up my laptop to get my researchers going on their mission. You can call them spies if you want but I prefer researchers. I will confess to you that the night before, while sitting at my big desk in my big house I was trying to think of what to do next. At that moment I had nothing to plan and nothing to do. I did have a kind of bucket list of things to pursue, one of which was to write an autobiography. An interesting life, but maybe it was only of interest to me. Twenty-four hours later as I watched Ed, Julia, Robert, Sandra and especially Wilma some pieces started to come together. I had noticed Cindy but other than her attractiveness and relation to Wilma, it had made no impression on me yet. It didn't take long to realize she would be instrumental in the project as the first research reports came in."

John could not stop smiling and his obvious happiness was infecting those who he was speaking to. "My bucket list thinking was replaced by Rachmaninoff. He had to have a number of things he had wanted to accomplish when he had the time to do them but he was given no time to do any of them. Especially his music. Someone with that talent in composing would always have new ideas floating through his mind and surely he would write them down in their musical form. I could imagine pages and pages of sheet music stuffed in con-venient boxes that he would keep near him. Always near by so if the mood struck him he could pull out something and work on it at that moment. He would have them there and Wilma was the connection that was needed to secure them."

Again a pause and then John teased them saying, "Shall I continue now or after we have dinner up at the house?"

Chapter 63

It was unanimous that he should continue. Even Wilma, who had missed her afternoon nap, was adamant that he continue. "At my hotel room the research team was alerted, even at that late hour, and by morning I had information including that Ed and Julia had been invited to lunch at Wilma's home and that two days later they would have lunch in Marina del Rey with Robert and Sandra and be invited aboard their sailboat, *Du-eT.* I wasn't sure what would happen at Wilma's but I did know about the piano in the living room. It was easy for me to guess that Ed and Julia would be told of Robert's visit with Rachmaninoff when on board *Du-eT.* I had a new project and just time enough to put the pieces together if everything would go right. It went together even better than I could have hoped for. Ed and Julia going with Robert and Sandra up the coast on their boat gave me the chance to meet them and work on that part in person. Then in Santa Barbara the mini concert for Allison's refinished piano set another thing in motion for me. Talk about your bucket list being taken care of."

John had to stop this time as he almost couldn't talk for a minute. "Let me see, where was I now. Oh yes! Cindy, I have to apologize to you," directing this to her, "as sometimes we take liberty with private matters when time is of the essence. I hadn't paid enough attention to you until Ed told me of hearing you play your compositions from your dreams of being with Rachmaninoff. I won't disclose how we found out about this or about the psychiatrist who befriended and helped you. Just that when we learned these things you became a very important person in our planning." John stopped to think this over and then continued, "I have to be honest, there were no others in the planning. You being fluent in Russian surprised me and we had a moment of panic when you started speaking in Russian with Natalia. I had forgotten that bit of information and we hadn't set your mike up to be translated from Russian into English missing a couple of sentences."

A quiet came over the group as they began to truly appreciate how John had managed to arrange the trip to accomplish the recovery the boxes of Rachmaninoff's papers. Even thinking they would be there and contain things he wanted to work on when time permitted. Ed had suspected as much and had told Julia after the trip to visit Rachmaninoff had been suggested. Robert and Sandra had also guessed as much but were sure they would only be spectators. Ben had an inkling but had kept it to himself. They all knew, including Cindy, that it might have not worked without her playing her two compositions and all of them had this feeling that more than just John's plan was involved. That would be partially answered later but at this time Cindy's confidence was building and she had never before felt this good about herself.

"Now to our plans," John's positive declaration

brought everyone back to the present, "I will ask Wilma and Cindy to find the boxes, bring then into Wilma's house and carefully, I mean carefully, open each one and see what is there. Only the top few sheets. Look for content and condition. If it is what we are hoping for I ask you both to let me know what you see and then wait until we all come down to go through a complete evaluation. I will provide curator's equipment for each of us so we can make an initial sorting and hopefully divide some items for each of us to spend time analyzing on how to proceed. It may be just sheet music and that will be for Ed and Cindy to work with but I am hoping there will be notes, dates and names that will require different skills to analyze. Ed and Julia can drive over and Allison and I will fly down and arrive by limo. Robert and Sandra can come down once we find out what we have. How does Monday the eighteenth work for every one? Ben and Jennifer are welcome, of course, and it may turn out they will have a significant part in what what may happen. It is my guess we may have a tiger by the tail here if what I anticipate we are going to find is in those boxes."

John then suggested it was time to head back to the house. Dinner would be Chinese cuisine which he had already ordered from his favorite Palo Alto restaurant. Allison would confirm the order when all were ready and it would arrive ready for the table in one hour.

As they assembled around the golf carts he asked Allison to share one of the carts so he could spend another thirty minutes in his office before coming back up. She understood and rode back with Ben and Jennifer.

John walked out into the SLAC area and looked up

and down along the long row of computers lining both sides of the big accelerator tube. Large banks of computers were furiously blinking their data signal LED's as the data and programs were being cleaned from the hard drives. His face showed the sadness he felt as thousands of hours of work was being erased. The blinking would stop and the power LED would blink twice and then go dark. This was being repeated in blocks of computers at a time. Immediately another block would then start signaling their cleansing. He turned away and went to his small office, sat down in his chair and closed his eyes. It had been the most exciting period of his life and now it was over. This time next week there would be nothing left except the recordings of the visits. To make anymore visits back in time would be up to others and they would have to figure out how it could be done on their own. All of his, and his groups, knowledge was in the computers and soon all that stored information would be gone.

There was a knock on the open door of his office and he slowly looked towards the doorway. His eyes focused and he saw Ben leaning on the door jam staring at him.

"I hope you don't mind my coming back to make sure you are okay, John. Allison told us you wanted to spend a little time by yourself and she was worried about you. If I am intruding I will head back up to the house. I know what you are feeling. It is universal for men like us when the important things in our life are finished, or over. It is like losing loved ones, a part of one's life that can never be replaced. Sometimes we are fortunate to find another so life can go on again but the hole that is there remains."

John sat very still, thinking this over for a minute, not answering him. Then motioned for Ben to take the chair facing him across his desk. "I think you might be the one I should talk to right now. You understand what I am going through as this part of my life is certainly ending."

Ben took the seat and offered, "I was about your age when my daughter, Julia's mother, died and one year later her mother, my wife, passed away. You probably know this already, so be it. I raised Julia from her grade school days until graduate school in college. It was then Ed came into our lives through an odd combination of two old friends trying to find someone that could play the golf clubs a third old friend had designed and made. He had died and we had promised his widow we would try to see he got some recognition for his efforts. During this time I found out I had a rather aggressive form of prostate cancer and for a short period thought I wasn't going be around to be with Julia. That brings me to Ed Adams. You keep close to him and Julia. They will make your life better and that will go a long way in making up for what you are losing now. Let them become your family. Trust me on this. You will find out I am right."

John again sat very still, looking directly into Ben's eyes but seeming to not be seeing him. He then surprised Ben with his answer. "Ben, you can trust me that I already knew this and it is not just a coincidence that the ten of us are gathered here together now."

Chapter 64

Dinner was excellent, as all there had been sure it would be. Afterward Ed and Cindy went to the pianos and played a variety of Rachmaninoff favorites followed by Julia joining with Ed doing some of their old repertoire of songs. It was a nice evening and as they departed to their separate rooms for the night's rest all were confident a close family had formed. None was more thrilled than Wilma as she knew she would not leave this world alone and that Cindy now had a future to look forward to.

The next morning the departures were made with the excitement of a new adventure in the offing and the knowledge of togetherness that they all desired. It was when the limousine had delivered Wilma and Cindy home, and they found BJ standing on the porch to great them, that the wheels began to turn. Wilma insisted they go to the garage first and as the limo backed out of the driveway, the gate closing behind it, they discovered both the big garage door and side door were locked. Wilma stated somewhat embarrassed that she had not been in the garage since, and maybe even many years before, Ernst had died. They entered the house and the hunt for the keys began.

The first look wasn't successful and darkness was coming so it would have to wait until the next morning.

Wilma was tired and begged off to bed. Cindy went through her chores to get her ready and once settled in her bed she pulled Cindy over to sit with her for a while. "Cindy, you sweet child, I have had the best few days I can ever remember and you have become the most important person in my life. I don't want to be a burden to you as I can tell your life is just beginning again. You have to follow where it will lead you and I want you to go there when it arrives. You have an important purpose in the pursuit of Rachmaninoff's unknown works that John is expecting to find in those boxes. Some of it will be done here but soon it will have to be done elsewhere. You are to go there. I will survive just fine with other help if it turns out that way. There is also BJ in the living room. I know the looks he gives you, and that you return them. Don't rush what may happen. If it is meant to be it will be. You have time to make sure. Give me a kiss and go talk to that nice young man."

While Cindy was with Wilma, BJ had been looking for the keys. He didn't bother with the places they had already looked but decided on the obvious. That was the back door that opened to the walkway to the garage. The keys should be close by there and on the wall near the door would be the place you would expect them to be. They had looked there but not seeing them had started in other places. Carefully examining the wall behind the stove that was next to the door he spotted what seemed to be a small nail hole with some smudging about it. He looked behind the stove on the floor and still saw nothing. Getting down on hands and knees he still didn't see them but sliding the long handle of a wooden spoon under the stove he heard the metallic rattle of keys moving across the linoleum. He had the keys in hand moments later.

When Cindy returned he waved the keys at her and asked, "Shall we take a look, or do the right thing and wait until tomorrow so Wilma will be with us?"

"We will do the right thing," she said quickly and wasn't sure what to say next. She knew what he was probably thinking but she didn't want to go there, at least not yet. He was tall and good looking, just like his father, and for the first time, maybe ever, she was attracted in a way she wasn't prepared for. He solved her dilemma by saying he would like to spend the night to be here in the morning to help find the boxes and that he could sleep on the couch if he could borrow a pillow and blanket. He had been sleeping in her bed the last two nights and wanted to sleep there tonight but knew he should let that be her decision.

"I will get them for you from my bedroom." Coming back she handed him the blanket with the pillow on top. She looked into his eyes and could see his desire. She pulled his head down to her and kissed him on the lips. Backing away she asked of him, "Don't break my heart, BJ. Give me some time to sort things out." She turned away and went back into her room closing the door behind her.

BJ stood rooted to the spot. His mother had told him, several times, about the first time she had kissed his father, "Don't you dare break my heart," she had said and left him standing on the doorstep of her grandfather's house as she went inside closing the door.

The trip back to Palm Desert was actually good for the four of them. Ed always enjoyed being with Ben and

Jennifer, and they with him. Julia was the one who really bound the four together and all had enjoyed all that life had brought to them, especially their twins. They talked of both and Julia took pleasure in telling them about the looks that BJ had given Cindy at Wilma's house and the reaction she could sense in Cindy receiving them. It was Jennifer that posed that the trip to Rachmaninoff had visibly changed her. That she showed more confidence and seemed more at ease with them. "I think we are going to want her to be around us for years to come. It would be nice if she and BJ could become friends." Julia smiled at this, knowing what Jennifer was implying, and that she was thinking the same thing. Ed didn't offer his opinion but knew Cindy was destined to become a classical pianist of merit and was hoping his son would be able to live with that if it happened.

Ben had his eyes closed but was listening to the conversation. He had already thought there was no doubt they would be seeing a lot of Cindy for the rest of their lives. She was very special and fit in with his family quite nicely. Jennifer was thinking the same as Ben and she gave him a nice squeeze on his thigh. He only said, "What?" and fell back into his pretending to being asleep.

Robert and Sandra had the three hour drive back to Point Reyes Station and it went smoothly. They could have slept on the boat but decided home would be better. As they got to the curvy road approaching Point Reyes Robert said a Porsche would be a lot more fun to drive, as he said every time they were on this road. This time Sandra asked, "What color do you want?"

"Silver with black interior. A 911 would do just

fine and it doesn't need to be brand new." He laughed at their common joke but this time Sandra responded in a serious tone, "I like silver too and we will start looking for one tomorrow. Although I sort of liked Allison's color. We don't really need the turbo."

In the big house in Palo Alto it was very quiet. John and Allison cleaned up the dishes and John took the trash out. It seemed lonely with no one else in the house and it was John who mentioned it first. "It was fun having them all here at once. It is a good group. To have all that talent around you is what I want most. My venture capital group was like that. In a different way of course, but every day was an exciting one. I spoiled it somewhat by moving us in the direction of traveling back in time but the experimenting, designing and building the program was what kept us together so long. That is now over and we are separating by interests but not in friendship. They are good people, good to work with and enjoy, but with the time that is left each of us have some things we want to do individually."

Allison came over to John and wrapped him in comforting hug, kissed him hard and told him, "You are on the edge of a great adventure. If those boxes have what you think they do our new group is going on a ride of a life time. I can hardly wait for it to start. How you did it and how these people have come together is beyond belief. You know this and I think each of us know it, too. It is my guess that by tomorrow afternoon we will be heading to Wilma's little house and will be looking at sheets of paper with our future written on them by a man named Sergei Rachmaninoff. I can't wait, so let's go to bed and you can tell me how you are able to do something like this, giving me something I need so badly right now. Each of us that was here today and saw what happened is feeling the same way. You, I am sure, more than any of us."

Chapter 65

Wilma was up first and with her walker clattered out into the dining room where BJ was sleeping, half on the small couch. He was still dressed in what he had been wearing the day before, woke and slid the rest of the way off the couch to the floor just as Cindy came out of her room to check on Wilma. As soon as she saw that Wilma was dressed and BJ was awake she realized she was still dressed in her usual bedtime outfit, panties and cotton T-shirt. It covered her adequately, but didn't hide much. BJ was now fully awake, sitting up and staring at her. He kept looking at Cindy, unable to take his eyes off her, but managed to say to Wilma, "I found the keys. They were under the stove."

"Get dressed and let's go get the boxes," were Wilma's first words to them not paying any attention to either Cindy or BJ's looks and what was being thought and acknowledged by them both. The spell was broken and five minutes later the big garage door was opened. It was actually a work shop as no cars had been inside in over fifty years. It was crowded with tools and the walls covered likewise. On the back wall were shelves above a long workbench. Everything was neat but covered in dust and the air was heavy with smells that had been locked up for years. They were not smells of decay or rot but of sawdust. On the top shelf, on the left end, was the shape of a box tightly wrapped in a dust covered, black plastic looking material. Wilma pointed to it and said in a reverent tone, "That's it. I remember now. After about ten years, might even have been longer, my father told me if nobody was going to come by for Mr. Rach's boxes he better pack them up good. It could be yesterday he told me that. Why is it I only remembered this now?"

BJ found a small ladder, climbed up and retrieved the big box placing it on the workbench. He looked at Wilma and she answered his question without him having to ask it, "Let's see what's here," putting her hand on the dusty box.

In the second drawer under the bench BJ found a utility knife and tried to slice the wrapping along the top edge. It was some kind of tough woven fabric with a thin rubber type coating. He decided to cut the tape instead which sliced apart easily. Once the fabric was loose he was able to unwrap the cardboard carton. Wilma managed to squeeze her walker up close and Cindy pressed against BJ on his other side. He opened the carton and lifted the top, tight fitting smaller box out. It was one of the ones that was taken from Rachmaninoff by Wilma's father. BJ didn't know what he was holding but Wilma and Cindy did. "That's one of the boxes, Wilma. We have them! Here! They are here!" Cindy cried this out, putting her arms around BJ's waist and hugging him so hard he yelped out a cry for mercy.

It took only a minute more to have the other two boxes out of the carton and on the bench. Cindy remarked that they looked exactly as they had when they had picked them up. It was then BJ's turn to ask, "What are you two talking about. Rachmaninoff has been dead for eighty years. How did Wilma end up with the boxes here? Cindy, what are you talking about that they look like the ones Rachmaninoff gave to Wilma's dad? How could you have seen that?"

Wilma turned to BJ and said in a voice so calm that it startled both him and Cindy, "We need to be careful with these boxes. Very careful. You two carry them up to the house. Put the lid down on the piano and cover it with a blanket. We will the open one and see what we have. We must be very careful in handling them. John wants us to look at only a few pages and then call him. We need to be careful with what ever is inside."

BJ and Cindy did as asked and they had the three boxes lined up on the covered piano. Wilma asked Cindy to wash her hands and dry them thoroughly. She then had BJ lift the lid off the box on the left and the three of them took their first look at was inside. On the top was a music sheet heavily marked in notes and small written passages on the side margin. Cindy carefully lifted it out and placed it on the cover. The next sheet looked very much the same as the first but was only half filled. At the top of the first sheet was something in Russian with a recognizable numeral seven and a dash and a numeral one.

Cindy stared intently at the musical notations. "I think this the first page of a concerto number seven. That one in the box is page two. We better call John."

She went into her bedroom and returned holding a brand new cell phone. "John gave this to me. He showed me how to turn it on and said to touch the phone icon and then contacts. Then touch his name." She said this looking at BJ as if asking for help as she followed John's instructions and on the first ring it was answered.

"We have the boxes, opened one and music sheets are inside. The first two look like the beginning of a concerto or symphony. They are in pencil with some notations in Russian and what looks like sheet one and two. I can read a few words but speaking the language is one thing and reading Rachmaninoff's handwriting is another." Cindy was looking at Wilma as her confidence grew and when John asked her if she could play what was on the first sheet she handed the phone to Wilma and carefully placed the sheet on the music rack. Studying the first four bars she pressed the keys as was written. It was unmistakably Rachmaninoff and John's reaction was immediate. "Allison and I will be there in a few hours. We will fly into Santa Monica Municipal, have a car waiting and should be there by two o'clock. I will call Ed and Julia and they can drive over. Robert and Sandra may want to come down but I think they may be okay with coming down later. See you shortly," and the phone went dead.

They looked at each other but didn't know what to say. The phone was set to speaker so Wilma and BJ knew what had been said. It was Cindy that broke the silence, "Let's put this sheet back and see what's on top in the other two."

Wilma agreed, and was happy to see Cindy taking charge. BJ knew very little of Cindy's past but was liking the feelings he was having for her. The first sheet was placed back in the box but before putting the top back on

Cindy pointed out the several notations that had been changed. The eraser marks showed and there were slight replacement of note locations.

The second box was nearly full but had the first three sheets with only a few bars filled in on each and a number of hand written notes added in various spaces. It looked organized, as was the first, and after replacing the sheets they had examined put the top back on. The third box was opened and it was more a collection of papers, envelopes and single sheets of standard letter paper. Cindy took out a half dozen items and laid them on the covered piano. Almost all were in Russian handwriting and she wasn't able to make much sense of them. Many had dates and recognizable locations in English. A few were in English and one was a confirmation of a concert date.

Again Cindy lead the discussion, "This may be the most interesting box as the items there are likely ones Rachmaninoff thought special and worth saving. He must have had thousands of correspondences over the years and saving these would make you think they are important. The one on the concert date doesn't seem to be of significance by itself but who knows. I bet you that John gives this box to Robert and Sandra to go through. What fun this will be. Wilma, you will have to be the adviser. You knew him, probably the only person left that did."

Wilma thought Cindy might be right about that but she knew at that moment that waking up tomorrow would be something she would cherish. No more thinking it was time to let go of life. Her excitement was added to by watching the relationship between the two youngsters mature.

"Let's fix some breakfast and take a little time getting the house in order for going through what we have here. I think I need to sit a while so Cindy you take charge and tell BJ what you want him to do. I will watch you two do the work. I am good at that."

Chapter 66

After they had breakfast Wilma suggested Cindy and BJ make a trip to the grocery store to stock up on a few items that her pantry was lacking and get anything they thought might be good for snacks. BJ said he would like to make a quick stop at his apartment as he had been wearing the same clothes for the last three days and hadn't planned on being here longer. He didn't add that he was planning on staying as long as possible and wanted some clean and better looking outfits. Wilma would take a nap while they were gone because she was certain once John arrived she would want to see everything that was going on.

BJ drove an older Volkswagen Beetle convertible and as it was a nice morning had put the top down. Cindy liked the little car and it was fun for her to lean back, close her eyes and let the wind blow through her hair. She knew she was attractive and that BJ would be looking at her now and then. He did and was falling in love with this unusual and talented woman. He also knew there was more he needed to know about how she had ended up a care giver hiding away from life caring for Wilma. His mother and father knew, as John did. Something had happened in her life that had placed her here where they would meet. He smiled at the thought and Cindy caught the sight of that smile and asked, "What are you smiling at now? I have seen you do that several times and I like it."

He answered and wasn't embarrassed about his answer, "I like looking at you. Trying to figure out what you are thinking. I want to know and I plan to find out."

Cindy's answer was a smile and she thought she would wait to tell him when the time was right. It wasn't now but it wouldn't be much longer. She was happy and it felt good. She couldn't remember the last time she had felt this way and she wanted that good feeling to become part of her life.

BJ had pulled into the parking area of an attractive apartment building and told Cindy he wanted to get some fresh clothes as today was going to be a long one and with so many people crowded into Wilma's small place he didn't want to offend. Cindy laughed at this, opened her door and jumped out to go with him.

It was a nice apartment and that he shared with his twin sister. Two bedrooms, each with a bathroom, a large comfortable living room and nice kitchen. Just blocks from the campus had made it a nice living arrangement for their college years. Now, with both in graduate studies and living different lifestyles, it had still worked out and his sisters fiance living in was not a problem. They all liked him and assumed it would be a permanent relationship.

BJ opened the door and as they entered the living room Cindy told him she would wait for him there. He nodded his head okay and took about five minutes to change clothes and pack a few extra items in a small tote bag. Coming out Cindy surprised him by asking to let her look at his bedroom. She said quickly, "Don't get the wrong idea. I just want to see how you live. Do you mind?" It was a quick peak and she saw what she had wanted. His bed was made and the room was kept neat. She had no family, no friends, no money and nowhere to go when Wilma no longer needed her. Everyone in this group she had come to know she liked and she was comfortable in their presence. The intelligence, the talent and the music was where she wanted to be. BJ was the first man she had ever met that she felt comfortable with. It was too soon to be in love but this was what she thought it must be like. She wanted to be sure before it went to far.

As they walked back to the car Cindy reached over and took BJ's hand. "It is a beautiful day to go to the grocery store, don't you think?"

BJ was thinking just that and smiled the smile she was getting used to seeing. She liked that, too.

By two-thirty that afternoon seven people were crowded around the giant Steinway piano which was now covered by a surgical spread and the first box was placed in the center. John passed out sterile white gloves to every one except Ed. He suggested Ed be at the keyboard to play various pieces they might be curious about. He wanted Cindy to give opinions as they sorted through the sheet music. Allison was going to keep notes of identification on sheets they would like to come back to if need be. Julia would handle the sheets as they finished with them keeping the order in which they had been stored. Wilma was to be ready if they found something referenced in the Beverly Hills house or on anything she thought of as they discussed what they were looking at. BJ was to do whatever was asked of him which seemed to please the others if not him. John would observe and instruct.

The first three sheets of music were passed to Ed. He read the first few bars and started. It sounded just as when Cindy had played it but he played through to the end. About seven minutes.

All had stopped what they were doing to listen and each heard exactly the same thing. It was Rachmaninoff at his best. Ed played the theme a second time and then stopped not able to speak. Wilma said it for them, "That Mr. Rach was the best, the very best that ever was."

The second three pages went on through what was obviously the second movement. And was followed by the music for the third. It was Concerto Number 7 for Piano. It could rival his Number 2. No one had heard this before, at least no one who knew what they were hearing. Sheet music for two more concertos were uncovered and then another surprise was what appeared to be the music for the Concerto Number 2 for Piano. Other sheets with music filled the remainder of the box.

It was Julia that made the most important discovery of the day. She had been stacking the sheets of music such that when they would be placed back in the box they would be in the same order they had been when taken out. They had only gone through about one third of the contents of the box and as she started to carefully replace them she noticed the top sheet in the box had a different format of the staffs than those they had been playing from. She set what she was holding aside and lifted out the sheet from the box to take a closer look.

"Look at this Ed. It is different than the others.

Look at all the staffs and the markings next to them on the side. Is it what I think it is?"

Ed glanced at what she was holding. He took a second look and almost choked trying to get out, "My God, look at this!" He started to reach for the sheet and remembered he didn't have gloves on and his hesitation allowed Allison to reach for it and hold it up.

"It is the music for the full orchestra. The full scoring. Oh my God, it can't be!" Allison almost shouting this out. By this time all were pushing around Ed and Allison to see what was all the excitement was about.

Julia took out several more sheets and the Russian notation across the top could not be read but the numeral 7 was recognizable. They all knew what they had and knew what they would now be able to do, much sooner than they had thought possible. Even John, who wasn't familiar with musical scores, understood what had just been dis-covered.

It was five o'clock when they finally placed the cover on the first box that held a treasure beyond belief. John had sat down on the piano bench next to Ed and Cindy was sitting on the opposite side. Wilma was in her small chair at the dining room entrance and Julia, Allison and BJ were standing, leaning on the piano.

Cindy suddenly stood and went to her bedroom. Ed had sensed her starting to cry but wasn't certain what he should do. The emotions of hearing such music was unnerving to each of them, but to each in their own way. John knew what they had here and his mind was already seeking some pathway to take it public. Ed was thinking how would he play it good enough to honor the composer.

Julia was with Ed on this thinking as she had never heard anything as good. All could be deemed Rachmaninoff's best. Allison was with John in thinking about how they could go public in a manner to do justice to the music.

BJ seeing Cindy suddenly stand and head to her bedroom with tears on her cheeks was his concern and he wanted to follow her but Wilma was already entering her room and had closed the door behind her. Cindy was face down laying at an angle on the small bed and Wilma left her walker, sitting down next to her, placing her hand Cindy's shoulders in a gentle massage.

"I saw him composing number two. It wasn't a dream Wilma, I was there. I can feel his presence in those pieces. It is the same as before, I can smell the cigarette smoke, the odor of his clothes, the taste of his mouth when he kissed me. I can't stop thinking that it happened. I don't want to go crazy again, Wilma. I don't want to go back here."

Chapter 67

John suggested that he and Allison get some take out so they could have dinner and then go through the second box. They planned to spend the night and had hotel reservations at the nearby Hilton. Julia asked if she and Ed could go with them and that they would also stay overnight rather than drive back to Palm Desert. She was also thinking that letting BJ be here alone with Cindy for a short time might help Wilma find out what was bothering her. John had already told them about her infatuation with Rachmaninoff and her thinking she had actually spent time with him in the past. John didn't mention to the others that he was starting to think that it was something more than just dreams. His recognition of Cindy and his conversation with her during the visit, even in translation, made it seem to be more than just in her dreams. It was rather clear, in fact, that he knew her and that, of course, was not possible.

Wilma thought that it was a good idea to get take out as she was tiring and she had given Cindy all the comfort she could for now. The house became very quiet and Wilma told BJ she would go to her room to rest. She then gave him some advice, "Treat her gently, she is reliving a past she is trying to forget. At one time she was convinced she had been with Rachmaninoff when he was first coming out of his depression following the poor reception of his symphony number one. Also his engagement to his first cousin was being challenged by the church. What we heard Ed play this afternoon brought it all back. It is all true to her again. She needs love and understanding, and nothing more."

BJ knew what Wilma meant by the last and entered Cindy's room with some doubt as to what he should do. There was no chair or any place to sit except on the bed. Cindy was curled up in the fetal position with her back toward him so he sat at her feet and waited.

"BJ, I need you to believe in me. I need someone to believe I was there. I was there with him. I wrote music in his house, with him sitting next to me. I played his piano. He kissed me twice and was embarrassed when he did as he was engaged to Natalia." She rolled over to face him and her tears broke his heart. Touching her shoulder had her reach out for him and he then lay down next her and kissed her gently on the lips. Nothing was said. Or needed to be said. They lay perfectly still and soon BJ realized she was sleeping. They stayed that way until the sounds of the returning group and the call for dinner being served reached them. Cindy stirred and looked into BJ's eyes. She saw what she wanted to see so badly and gave him the smile he wanted.

Chinese had been selected again as it was easy to serve and easy to eat. When they finished all the trash was bagged, hands thoroughly washed and the white gloves donned. The second box was put on the covered piano and opened. The first sheet was placed by Ed on the piano rack and he played the short theme. It was unknown, beautifully romantic and definitely one hundred percent Rachmaninoff. It went on like this for over an hour, one after another of unconnected short and long compositions of brilliant music that was exhausting the listeners. Then it all came to a halt.

Ed was handed three sheets that appeared to be together and as he examined the first few bars it had a familiar look, as if he had heard it before. The structure of the notations was also different. He then placed his fingers on the keys and pressed the first few notes. They all knew immediately what they were hearing was the composition that Cindy played that had drawn Rachmaninoff's interest and resulted in them having it in their possession. He played through to the end. The only sound in Wilma's small house was the sobs from Cindy as she had sat down on the floor next to the piano bench, covering her face with her hands and was quietly crying.

Ed looked up to the top of the page. It was in a different hand than Rachmaninoff's and on the top sheet was written *1899 Cynthia.*

Wilma, with her walker, pushed herself up so she could see what Ed was staring at and then saw the name and date. She got out a frightened, "Oh my God!" and she began to lose her balance. BJ reacted first, helped Wilma get settled on the dining room couch and was trying to hide his concern as Wilma had gone silent. Cindy was still crying softly sitting on the floor with her hands covering her face. BJ knelt before her holding her shoulders and she lowered her hands and whispered, "I was there. It happened. It wasn't dreams, I was there. I wrote that composition with Sergei. He kept them all those years. There are two of them, each three sheets."

John heard this, as the rest did, in the small room with the antique grand piano covered with the sterile white cloth on which sat one of the boxes containing unknown Rachmaninoff sheet music and another composition that couldn't be there. He had no answer and couldn't move.

Julia did make the move and withdrew the next three sheets from the box. Looking at the top she read out loud, "1899 Cynthia."

Chapter 68

John was the only one in the room that was active as he was setting up his laptop and a device that looked like an iPad to be used as a camera atop a frame facing down. He asked Julia to hand him the six sheets of Cindy's compositions and the sheets that came before and after them from the box in that order. He photographed the back of the sheet that came before Cindy's top sheet and then the top of her first sheet. Then it was the back of the last sheet of Cindy's music and the top of the sheet that followed. All were watching as he manipulated the images on his lap top.

He turned to Cindy and asked her to come over to see what he had found. Now all were interested and they gathered around the two of them. Wilma stayed sitting on the couch but was paying close attention.

"I want you to look closely at the two images, one is of the first page of your composition and the second is the page that was facing it. Here," pointing at a very faint dot on the facing page, "is a smudge from this penciled note on your page that was pressing on it in the pile in the box. There are a number of these." John pointed out several more and then switched the images to the back pages and pointed to similar smudges. "This is absolute proof that your compositions were placed in the box as we found them. You do understand what I am saying to you. They were in the box in this order in 1943 when Rachmaninoff handed it to Wilma's father."

Cindy immediately knew what this meant as she had not even been born yet. Ed and Julia, as did Wilma, understood. The only one confused was BJ, but then even he suddenly realized the only way they could have gotten there was if Cindy had actually been with Rachmaninoff when she had said she was there.

Again there was silence in the room. John was smiling and said, "There is more evidence of the timing. Look at the G Clef on your sheet music. See this slight rounding at the start. It is different from the G Clef on the adjacent sheets. The paper is also just enough different in appearance and feel to tell they are not the same. It is still old and correct for the dating of the other works in the box but it does not match yours. Now if Julia will get one of the Concerto Number 2 sheets out of the first box we will have absolute proof of when you wrote those compositions."

Julia quickly opened the first box and found a sheet of Concerto Number 2 and handed it to John. He placed the two sheets side by side. The G Clefs were identical.

Cindy's tears started again but these were tears of relief. She hugged John and said in a breathless manner, "I don't care that it couldn't have happened. There is no way it could have, but two days ago I was with Rachmaninoff in 1943, so some how I was with him in 1899."

It was Wilma that asked what they were all

thinking, "So what are we going to do now?"

Ed answered without hesitating, "We are going to bring all this music to life. We have to make it possible to give this music to the world to enjoy as it would have been had Rachmaninoff lived long enough to have done it himself. That was why he gave us these three boxes and we owe it to him to do it, and do it right."

BJ watched his father and realized one more time what a special person he was. He didn't care in the least what it could mean financially to this group but the music must be shared solely because of what it was. He thought to himself, "I now know what I want to do. I want to be part of this, and I want to be part of Cindy's life. It makes no difference what it is I am able to do, I just want to be part of it."

Ed then surprised them when said as calmly as if saying let's go for a walk, "I think I know what we should do and all of us, including Robert and Sandra, can contribute." He turned to Wilma and told her, "You must hang around a little longer, Wilma. You have a major roll to play in what I think should be done."

He could see they were all looking at him and also noted a slight expression of anxiousness cross John's face. He knew what it meant so he started there. "I have committed to a number of concerts this year and it is not my forte to manage anything like what I am about to suggest. John is the one to do this. We all know he can do the impossible so this should be easy for him to put together. Also I think it would be good to get Robert and Sandra in at this point so let see if we can get them on a Zoom meeting." One minute later they were on John's laptop screen. They were on their boat and had been waiting to learn what had happened. The greetings were exchanged and John gave a short summary followed by announcing, "Ed is now going to tell us how we are going to pull off one of the greatest feats in classical music history!"

Chapter 69

Ed surveyed the room and looked at Robert and Sandra's expectant expressions on the laptop's screen. "John knows how to set things up. And he is right about what this will mean in the classical music world. Three unknown concertos by one of the world's most famous and loved composers being found in some small boxes in a garage that once belonged to his automobile mechanic. Can you make up a story as good as this."

He then added that if what they had been able to tell so far about the three concertos was that they may be of the same quality as Concerto Number 2. If so it would be even more impressive. He suggested that to perform one of these with a big time symphony orchestra might pose problems in both timing and expense and that he had another idea that might work.

"When Julia and I were doing our tours as entertainers we did a couple of shows in Palm Desert at the McCallum Theater. It's a small, thousand seat theater with a very good sound system and is the home for the Desert Symphony Orchestra. The Orchestra has about fifty professional members. They have a conductor but I think they would be willing to accept another if we felt this would work better for us. We could negotiate with the Los

Angeles Philharmonic, of course, but I would like to go with the idea of making this a discovery in a way that would make the surprise even more of an Alice in Wonderland story. It would set the stage for international coverage and almost guarantee demand for the discovery to be followed by a long line of top marquee symphony performances."

Ed didn't see anything but enthusiasm so he continued, "There is the copyright problems but again we are fortunate. I think that the original copyrights will have run out as it is usually seventy years after the death of the composer if the work has not been made public or if there was a copyright that was never renewed. I think we are safe on both counts but once the news is out the value of what we have in the three boxes will be such that we will need legal help. Things could get complex in a hurry. My thinking is that we work on the financial rewards later and make Rachmaninoff's last works available to those qualified to properly play them at little, or no cost."

Again Ed paused and again all waited. "My next question is to Cindy. Would you consider being the pianist for the first concert if I was to choose to be the conductor? Your two themes will be the encores." Cindy at first looked frightened, then calmly looked directly at Ed and said, "Yes! I want to do this."

"Alright, I have made my pitch. John will be the manager of the project. Cindy and I will handle the piano, orchestra and probably the choice of what will be played. I want Allison to join Cindy and me in the piano effort as we also want to take a close look at all the short compositions he has given us. I think there will be some gems in those. Julia will be the conservator and BJ can help in taking care of making the copies for the working sheet music. We'll need to be extremely careful to not damage the originals. Robert and Sandra will take the third box and see if they can figure out why Rachmaninoff placed im-portance on its contents. I think there is a lot to learn from what is in there and will provide a story to be told. I would like Wilma to share her stories of knowing Rachmaninoff as a teenager and that will help bring his later years into focus. Why it was her father that was asked to get the music sheets to the right people. I want BJ to also do all the errands, dirty jobs and high tech ones until he finds his place in management of what I think will be years of interesting challenges. I would like it if we can include Ben and Jennifer in this as well. If they have an interest, also my daughter and her fiance. We have become a large family and we have something important to accomplish."

The wheels were now turning. Each of them had talents to contribute and each were looking for something to do to utilize those talents. Here was what each needed in their life at this moment in time and each knew what an exciting and important project it would be.

John's eyes were sparkling again. Five weeks ago this coming Thursday he was seated in the Walt Disney Center Symphony Hall depressed by the ending of his Visiting History project and the dissolving of the group he had been part of for most of his adult life. They had all decided with the time they had left they should pursue the things they had set aside to do now before it was too late. He had no other friends and no idea what to to do next. He now had a new family of friends and a project so exciting and valuable that it would surpass anything he had done before.

Allison was smiling, almost laughing at herself. A couple of weeks ago she had no idea if her life was only going to be that of a matronly widow of Santa Barbara with a bunch of boring acquaintances. Now here she was, seventy-five, twice widowed and sleeping with a short, inexperienced lover seven years her junior who was once a childhood friend. She was embarking on an adventure in music that may turn out to be one of the most important chapters in classical music history. Looking around she could sense that each of them, even Robert and Sandra on the Zoom screen, were thinking similar life changing thoughts.

Ed and Julia had a life to live, and this was going to interfere with it, but both knew that what was about to happen would not only change that life but be it's highlight. So great that nothing else in the current world of classical music could compare. A challenge, but with a reward that would be far greater than any that could be imagined.

Cindy was beside herself with a happiness she had never felt before. It was a sense of confidence she had never experienced. Ed Adams had somehow brought it forth just by his words and presence. She would not question any of this and accept what came as it happened. She looked at BJ and could see his thoughts were elsewhere at the moment but that didn't bother her as she was certain where their relationship was going. She almost sang out her thinking that she was in love.

Wilma sat on the small couch and looked about at her new family. A few weeks ago she was waiting to die. She had Cindy but otherwise was alone. She was certain the day would come that she would have to go into some kind of care facility and then she would truly be alone. She wanted to die in her own bed, the bed she and Ernst had shared those many years. She missed him and never had any hope of being truly happy again. Cindy had saved her from despair and now she had something to live for. She prayed she would wake the next morning and would be there when Cindy played Rachmaninoff's number seven, or six, or five and her own compositions. She couldn't remember ever being as excited about life as she was now.

BJ was in total confusion. A few days ago he had been lost as far as direction. He liked college life, even graduate school. Science was enjoyable but for the rest of his life it seemed to fall short of what he wanted. Space was his real interest and he had been angling his studies in that direction but the last week had changed everything. He was in love for the first time and it had confused him in his thinking. Watching his mother and father in this new environment, and how the easily they adapted to it, was a true revelation. He was going to follow them hoping it would keep him close to Cindy and reveal the path he should take.

On *Du-eT,* in San Francisco Bay, Robert and Sandra were smiling at each other and Sandra said, "I take it back. John has snared us into another project and this one I want to be a part of. I am not sure what we will find in that box but I think it will lead us into writing another interesting story. Maybe even a book, or two. We have some new friends that are going to provide us something we need right now and I can hardly wait for it to get started."

Robert took a long look at Sandra and thought the same thought he always had, what a beautiful woman she was and that was exceeded many times over by her intelligence and wisdom. He told her, "You won't believe me but I was sure we would join John in whatever was his next plan and when we started to see the others being drawn into it I was sure we would be, too."

It was time the new group went to their respective homes and get organized for what was coming. All knew their lives would be changing in the next few years and all were eager to get started.

Ed and Julia would take possession of the boxes for now and safely store them at their home in Palm Desert. John and Allison would return to Palo Alto in the morning and make plans for staying in Palm Desert for a few weeks to get things started. Robert and Sandra would try to make plans to do the same.

It was decided that Ed and Cindy would be the ones to go through the box with the concertos and symphonic scores. Allison was to continue to go through the second box of sheet music, that had Cindy's compositions, assess it's contents, play what she liked best and provide a summary. John would meet with Robert and Sandra in San Francisco and discuss with them about the contents of the third box. It was hoped it would provide a wealth of unknown personal information about the central figure in all this, Rachmaninoff.

Chapter 70

As Julia and Ed headed back to Palm Desert the next morning it was Julia who was first in initiating their conversation and it had little to do with music. "What do you think about BJ and Cindy?" Ed chuckled at this and reached over to touch Julia's thigh, then give it a gentle squeeze. "Does it remind you of a young couple meeting about twenty-eight years ago?" Julia took his hand, moving it up and down on her thigh in a sexy manner and laughingly said, "Touche, Ed Adams. Touche!"

Ed then began expressing his thoughts on how to organize their end of the project. That he would have to work with Cindy on which of the three concertos they should concentrate on that would be best for both her playing and his conducting. He had been involved in much of the rehearsal aspects of a conductor's responsibilities and thought he could handle that part. In fact he felt comfortable directing a small orchestra like the Desert Symphony and was hoping it could be worked out with the board and the musicians. They should be able to organize the sheet music, using a camera and computer to generate the sheets for print out. Once they had that done they could archive the originals and store them safely. They continued to plan and the miles went by quickly.

As Ed pulled into their driveway Julia mentioned that the house on the other side of her Grandfather's had a for sale sign up and a sold banner showing. The house had been vacant for several months and the Zillow information showed a nice floor plan. It had been a long term rental for the last two years. The price seemed high but as all prices were going up it was not surprising it had sold. A Realtor, an attractive young lady, was exiting the front door and they approached her asking about who had bought it.

"It was the fastest sale anyone in our office had ever witnessed. A man from Palo Alto called in last night, said he would pay full price cash, wanted it furnished if possible and no inspection necessary. He wanted occupancy next week. If closing would take longer he would rent it for the next month." She was smiling at this and said the market was crazy and was starting to become worrisome. She added, "I can't tell you more but he seemed to be very pleasant and efficient. He told me the occupants would be moving in the next week and there would be two couples at first, himself and his spouse, both seniors, and a second middle age couple. All were professionals and they would be good neighbors. The money arrived in escrow this morning and the papers were signed electronically. It is a new world I guess," saying this as she rushed off to her car and drove away.

"What's it going to be like having John as a neighbor?" Ed asked Julia. She smiled back and said, "Very interesting."

Interesting was an understatement. The next morning as Ed and Julia were having their customary breakfast with Ben and Jennifer poolside the door bell rang. Jennifer jumped up with a who could that be and went to the door. Ed looked at Julia and mouthed the word, "John," and she nodded her head in agreement. They were beginning to learn how he operated and knew for certain he would be front and center in everything that happened for the next few months, and maybe for years to come.

"We don't mean to interrupt your breakfast so just a quick hello and we will be off," John was saying as he and Allison made their entrance to the pool area. Hellos and welcomes to Palm Desert were said. Ed was unsure how to handle the interruption but needn't have worried. The immediate offer to join them came from both Jennifer and Julia and the three women headed to the kitchen to fix additional breakfasts. Ed looked at Ben, who had remained seated, and saw a look of what could only be joy on his face. He answered Ed's inquiring look in one sentence. "He reminds me of myself when I was a top executive at IBM and a new and exciting project was just starting."

Ed waited for more and then could see that Julia's grandfather was going to have one more chance to participate, even if only as a spectator, in a new product development akin to some of his best at IBM with his old and now deceased friends, Hank Morgan and Morris Cornith. He understood, maybe better than any of those involved other than John, what was about to happen. He had a reason to live a little longer and now desperately wanted to.

John didn't wait long to bring them up to date. The new neighbors would be in residence for the duration of the project. Robert and Sandra should arrive this afternoon and would also stay until their part in the program was completed. He asked a very big favor of Ben and Jennifer if they would house Wilma and Cindy until the concert was performed. That he had already found a UCLA music student who would house sit her house while she would be here. He thought Cindy needed to be here working with Ed on their part of the program.

There was another doorbell chime and John jumped up and said he was sure that was the movers bringing down the Palo Alto things they needed and he was off to the door. Allison didn't bother to get up but looked at Jennifer, then towards Ben and back to Jennifer. "What can I say. He has been like this since I made that little visit to Beverly Hills, nineteen forty-three. I thought it was some kind of strange joke at first but he made it out that it would be a fun thing to do. My life had become a bore, he knew that of course, but when it actually happened I then had to accept to being part of his plan to try to get Rachmaninoff's treasure of unfinished works. He was certain there had to be some and with Wilma's connection he had a vehicle to transport them to us. God, that little man is a genius."

The ball was now rolling faster and a few days later everyone was in place. The print shop, as it was to be known, was located against the wall opposite the glass wall of the music room fronting the pool area in Ben's house. Ed and Cindy would do their work at the Steinway Parlor Grand piano that was there. John would be every where but his command center was in the office set up in his just purchased house. Allison had the living room with the piano brought up from her home in Santa Barbara. She also had two tables set up for examining the contents of the second box and a copy and printer setup.

Robert and Sandra would be staying in John's guest room and would use the second guest bedroom to do their work on the contents of the third box. Wilma had accepted the idea of coming to Palm Desert with Cindy and they would be staying with Ben and Jennifer. BJ would take the rest of the year off from pursuing his Master's degree and would be in his old room.

In three days all was in place and they were underway. Jennifer mentioned to Julia that she hadn't seen Ben as excited as he was now in years. That she was so happy to see him that way. Getting old was no fun for a man like him who wished he could be the man he used to be but knew he wasn't anymore. It would turn out that he just happened to know, or knew someone that did, every one they would need to put their ambitious program together in Palm Desert.

Chapter 71

It happened that BJ was computer literate and he had Julia's print shop up and running quickly. The computer was one of the one's John had in Palo Alto. He had brought down ten of them and added flat screen monitors and key boards. They each had their own, all were connected to a wireless network and each had high speed internet. BJ had them all running in half a day and started the task of getting those who weren't savvy able to use them. It was especially fun to watch Wilma use one as she learned to do internet searches.

Julia had removed the sheet music bundle for Number 7 and started the process of photographing the sheets. She would place one on the holder bed, tap the photo key, store the image in memory, remove the sheet and place the next one and repeat the process. There was one hundred and twenty-three sheets using only one side of each page. They were in full orchestra scores having seventeen staffs with eleven and twelve for the piano. Words were in Russian but the musical notations were familiar. Once Julia had six pages stored she printed them out using both sides of the blank paper John had provided. Boxes of quality paper, eleven by seventeen inches and of typical weight for sheet music. The first three sheets were spit out in a fast print on both sides and were of excellent quality. The two HP Laser Jet 5200DTN printers they were using could handle the over sized paper easily and the both side printing was flawless.

Ed had been sitting on the piano bench with Cindy while Julia made the first copies. She interrupted their conversation by handing Ed the three sheets. He looked up with a surprised expression and Julia's first reaction was that she had better ask him what they had been talking about. He recognized what was being handed over and was immediately back to the present. Looking over the top page he turned it over to page two and then handed page one to Cindy. After all six sides had been examined by both Ed moved to the center of the bench and placed the sheets on the music rack. He had already played the first three and went through all six. It was similar to Concerto 2 in that the piano started solo for six bars but in a dream like melody and then burst into life with what could only be imagined with the orchestra in full pursuit. He smiled and was thinking what would come next as Rachmaninoff had left no doubt that you must find that out.

Ed looked at Cindy and moved aside to let her have the playing position. She treated Ed to what he had just played and it was every bit as good. He nodded his head in approval and she bowed in the manner of a thank you. Julia watched this exchange and hoped that it was only professional courtesy she was witnessing between them.

He left Cindy at the piano and went over to where Julia was going through the routine of photographing and downloading the rest of the concerto. Ed picked up one of the original pages and examined it carefully. It was all done by hand, in pencil by Rachmaninoff himself. In almost a whisper he told Julia, "This is in Rachmaninoff's own hand, in pencil. All of it. This score is worth millions of dollars to collectors. We will have to let John know about this and find some suitable way to store them."

Julia stopped what she was doing and a look of fear came over her face. Her thoughts about the relationship developing between Ed and Cindy disappeared and the idea of having millions of dollars worth of pages so casually being handled and stored brought a whole new worry for her.

As if called by magic, John walked into the room. Cindy was playing the last part of what she and Ed had just played and Ed was holding the seventh original page. John glanced at what Ed was holding and commented, "You had better handle that carefully. At a good auction house it might go for half a million. Scary thought, isn't it."

As if it was of no concern he continued, "I have had one of my techs set up our computers programmed as Rachmaninoff and will be linked to our satellite. Your cell phones will be linked as paging devices so you will always know when there is a reason to communicate on the system. I have my fire proof safe from Palo Alto and it will be securely installed in my office tomorrow. The box of binders for the musical scores should arrive today, as will the punch. I will have my lawyer start whatever copyright protection is available to us." John said all this as if answering all the questions that hadn't been asked.

Ed and Julia smiled having expected something

like this would happen. Robert and Sandra weren't even surprised when Julia had described John's visit to them as they had expected he would be at full speed ahead once the boxes had been handed over to Wilma's father. Even though they had been left in a garage some seventy-nine years ago he had been sure there would be boxes of works to be completed and his bet had paid off. John was back in business and every day was going to be spent making what he was expecting to happen, happen.

Allison was in her music room, the living room which was very similar to Ben's and for that matter Ed and Julia's. Her piano was close to the exterior glassed walled back of the house and her table and printer were against the opposite wall. She was appraising each sheet and then placing them face down on the covered table top. Allison could read music and when she saw one she found of particular interest she would place it such the top extended out enough to mark it's place in the pile. Continuing this way until reaching the point where Cindy's composition had been, almost a third of the sheets were offset so she turned over the pile and took the first of the offset sheets to the piano.

Allison read the music twice then placed her hands in position and played through the twenty-four bars. She then did it once more. Sitting very still her eyes began moisten. She knew that right in front of her was some thing that was so good that it had to brought out in a formal presentation to the public. She also was sure she was faced with hundreds of such pieces. Enough to form dozens of concertos and symphonies. For the first time in years she was scared that she wouldn't be able to meet the challenge. She would need help. Lots of it.

Robert and Sandra were in John's third bedroom. They had a small covered table and were sorting through the piles of small papers that were in the third box. None of them seemed to make much sense and several piles were increasing in size. Dating, much of it in Russian, could be figured out and was what they started with. So far the oldest was a receipt dated 1901, the most recent in English was 1943.

It was a hotel receipt of February 17, 1943 from a hotel in Knoxville, Tennessee and had a note on the back in Rachmaninoff's hand. Later, using a translator service, they found out it was probably written on the train heading back to Beverly Hills with him bemoaning how bad he was hurting. That he couldn't think straight and wanted to die. They stopped what they were doing when Sandra had picked it up, telling Robert, "These are re-minders. Each of these pieces of paper were saved to remind Rachmaninoff of what had happened around the time when he had paid for something, such as this last hotel billing in Tennessee."

They then knew what they had to do and it would be an enormous task. An excursion into another mans life by dates on pieces of paper and what ever was noted about that time in his own hand. Each piece, by date and mes-sage, could be related to avenues of known events in his life and a personal touch could be attached to the im-personal biographies, newspaper articles and magazine stories. They looked at each other and acknowledged they had the path to follow. It was what they could do and was a path they were now ready to take.

BJ had been busy with setting up the computer stations and was in and out of each of the houses. He was back in his old room and for the first couple of nights felt more lonely than he could ever remember. Cindy was in the small bedroom in his great grandfather's house, just a few steps away. The houses had been connected to form a family complex when he and his sister had been born. He knew exactly where she was sleeping and he wanted to be there next to her.

Cindy was thinking how good she was feeling the last few days. She had a future and those around her now wanted for her to be successful. Even more important was that she believed they truly wanted that for her. She also had someone that wanted something more than that and she was thinking how she could balance the feelings she had for him with the opportunities that were now being presented. "Tomorrow," she thought it would be best to just let tomorrow happen.

Chapter 72

John was sitting in his small office in his new house in Palm Desert. Not even a week had passed and he was letting the incredible progress that was occurring sweep through his mind when there was a knock on the open door. He looked up to see Ben standing there waiting permission to enter. "Come in, Ben. I was just now thinking how good things were going and it was time to meet with you," saying this in a cheerful and meaningful way. "You knew that of course, now didn't you?"

Ben smiled a genuine smile as he knew John was treating him as an equal despite the fact that he had slowed down. "Thank you for asking that question. So to get to the point, I wanted to know when you would want to make the first contact with the Desert Symphony board, take a look at the McCallum Theater, and meet with the representatives of the orchestra. I assume you will want Ed and Cindy to go with you and I would like to make the introductions. Julia tells me the first scoring is ready for the seventh concerto. Sixty two pages in all. That is a lot of music."

"Yes to all of that. Come in and sit awhile. Let's talk a bit about the big plans and how to do the small ones right."

As the end of April approached the team, as they now called themselves, had made a great deal of progress. All three concertos had been photographed, stored in memory and one complete score printed and bound in a multi-ring notebook. The originals were carefully packaged and stored in John's safe. Cindy's two short themes were likewise prepared and the originals were also in the safe. Allison had picked a variety of partial works to prepare and kept them grouped in a large binder. All the originals had been been through the copying process and the originals packaged and stored.

Robert and Sandra's task was taking more time but they were delighted by their progress. John had arranged for any writings needing translation could be sent as email downloads and the translations would be in hand within twenty-four hours. The review of the contents of the entire box was nearing completion with copies made and the originals stored. They were almost certain a book could be written with what they were learning first hand from the copious notes Rachmaninoff had left behind. They would arrange them in a chronological order and then could make some comparisons with the existing biographies, articles and newspaper files into a informative and interesting story of this great man's life.

The first meeting with the Desert Symphony director, two members of the resident orchestra, and John, Ben, Ed and Cindy was at 2:00 pm on Thursday, April 28 at the director's office. Ben knew the director and Ed had met him him several times over the years but only in a social environment. The director sat at his desk and the orchestra members, the principal violinist and clarinetist, at his side. The team members were in a semi circle opposite.

John lead the discussion, "We are here to make you an offer. I say it that way and I think you will understand why in just a moment. We want to perform a symphony in the McCallum Theater with your orchestra, Ed as the conductor and Cindy the pianist. It is what we want to perform that you will have trouble believing at first but is what you will want so badly to be performed by your orchestra here in Palm Desert."

John handed the director the Symphony Number 7 binder and waited for the expected response which came almost immediately, "There is no Rachmaninoff Concerto Number 7. Why are you wasting our time?"

Taking the first page original in its protective cover out of his briefcase he handed it to the director and asked the two musicians to also look at what it was. "Please be very careful of what you have in your hands. The binder contains the photocopies printed out that can be played by the Desert Symphony for the first time in the history of classical music. Handwritten entries like on this first page are found on many of the sheets and can easily be verified by handwriting experts. We are also in possession of Concerto's Number 5 and Number 6 and a large number of other works." Looking at the two musicians he continued, "The two of you should be able to quickly recognize Rachmaninoff but you will also notice you have never heard anything like this before. Take your time."

Ben sat silently enjoying John's approach in the making the presentation. He knew he would have these three in the palm of his hand in minutes and they would start the plans for the performance within a few days. The director was not particularly impressed by what he was holding but did look closely and carefully then handed it to the violinist. She looked at it first thinking it was a joke and then started humming the first few bars. Then stopped and began again, this time singing the notes. She handed the sheet to the clarinetist and he surveyed the empty staff and asked for the binder and went a few pages further until the first clarinet solo showed up. It carried over twelve bars and when he finished he put the binder on the desk. "It is not possible. It can't be. No chance that this is real," he said in a voice that was shaking and so weak that Ben thought he was going to faint.

John stood, smiled at the three that were trying to get their composure back and gently said, "We will leave the binder with you. You can be assured it is copyrighted and we have all the originals. I will need the first page back now but if necessary we can provide it and several others. I think if your musicians would play several parts they will recognize what we have here. And by the way, you won't be disappointed in either Cindy or Ed. Here's my card and enjoy what I have given you and think what will happen if a small symphony orchestra in small hall brings a lost Rachmaninoff Concerto back into the world of classical music."

The team left the office and the three left behind weren't able to speak or move for fifteen minutes. The principal violinist finally spoke, "It's Rachmaninoff. I am sure it is Rachmaninoff."

The call came to John the next day.

Chapter 73

As was becoming a habit after John had parked his car in the driveway at his house, they walked next door and went into Ben's, down the hall entrance to the music room. The entire team had gathered together and seated themselves in the comfortable chairs that were scattered about the room. It had been the living room but when Hank Morgan had found Ed's mother's piano, had it restored and gave it to him it had been converted to the music room and had been left that way ever since.

Ed and Cindy took their seats on the piano bench and the rest, except for BJ who stood nearby, were all seated. John merely said, "It went well, I think."

Ben commented, "As usual John thinks a master stroke of salesmanship is nothing special. Would anyone care to set up a pool on how long it will be before he gets the call for the go ahead for the concert. I want twenty-four hours, before two o'clock tomorrow afternoon."

After a bit of wagering it was decided to wait and see how close Ben's prediction would be. Ed stood up and went to the table against the wall that had the photography and printer set-up and picked up one of the sixty binders they had printed and bound for the orchestra members. Rachmaninoff Concerto Number 7. He placed it on the music rack on the piano, opened it to the first page and asked Cindy to play the parts they had been working on. She nodded okay, but before she started he had her come over to the hall with him where they had a short conversation. With a smile on her face she gracefully strode over to the piano with Ed walking a few paces behind her. He positioned himself to the right of the piano and a few feet away while Cindy took her seat facing the keyboard, adjusting her position on the bench and then looking at Ed nodding her head in the manner that said she was ready. Ed acknowledge her signal and raised his hands facing across the piano as if to an orchestra. Cindy began playing the first soft, single notes of Number 7. One could imagine the sounds of the first rain drops of a rainstorm that was coming and then it turned into melody so romantic it was enough to melt even the most hardened heart. Ed then raised his hands, bringing in the imagined strings to compliment the piano and Rachmaninoff Concerto Number 7 was underway. Cindy played through the first twelve minutes with such skill that all in the room knew that Number 7 would be judged as good, or maybe even better than, as what many thought was the best concerto ever written, Rachmaninoff's Concerto Number 2.

She had one fourth of Number 7 memorized already and there was no question that she would have the rest done quickly. None in the room had any doubts this concert would be a success. Jennifer was sitting close to Ben and was squeezing his hand. She whispered in his ear, "I told you when I first met Ed Adams that he has some thing about him that brings out the best in people. Could Cindy play any better than that. Not just that but the look she has of happiness from doing what she is doing, and doing so well."

Ed could see what had happened in the room. He was now sure the concert would be well received and in turn knew John's plans would work. As the word spread of the lost Rachmaninoff scores being discovered the entire classical music world would explode.

He then made another suggestion and that was that the ladies of the group should take a day to find several outfits for Cindy to wear both at the piano and to other events that would follow. He went on to say that maybe they should be a bit more conservative than the current young female star, the incredibly gifted and attractive Chinese pianist Yuja Wang. But he privately thought, maybe not.

Ed did one more thing as the team began moving about to go their separate ways before the now customary pot luck style dinners served around Ben and Jennifer's pool. He went over to his son and suggested he and Cindy take a walk up and down El Paseo, which was just a few blocks away. Go by the old apartment building where he was living when he met his mother. Maybe even get an ice cream cone to share as they walked by the store fronts. Ed looked at BJ and told him that was where the best days of his life had begun.

BJ didn't hesitate and minutes later he and Cindy were walking towards El Paseo. It was another spring afternoon with bright sunshine and warm temperature. Just before reaching El Paseo BJ suggested they head over to where he could show her where his dad had been living when he met his mother. As they stood in front of the apartment building he pointed out the second floor apartment his dad was renting and described the Lazy Boy chair, single bed and table which had been his furnishings. Cindy took his hand and leaned against him. "Tell me the story of how they met. They are so right for each other and are such nice people. My parents were different, their marriage ended badly and by the time I was in high school I had no one left to call a family."

BJ looked down at her and could see the tears forming. He reached out with his free hand, lifted her face to his and kissed her. Then Cindy asked, "Take me to where they met. It was at the College Golf Center, wasn't it. Just a couple of blocks from here?"

They went trough the portal to the driving range. BJ had spent many hours there on his own. His mother, father and sister would do most of their practicing at the country club but he liked the rough nature of the range and the average Joe feel of the place. There were still some tables outside and they found a small round metal one with two chairs and sat down. Cindy looked around, smiled and said, "I like it here. It is comfortable."

"My dad had come here on a Sunday afternoon and the range was closed but the Golf Museum that was here then was open. He went in and could hear someone behind a big cabinet practicing putting. He stepped around it, saw my mother and fell in love with her at first sight. There is more to the story but I can tell you that later."

"BJ, I know you don't have much to do in the project right now and that I am the focus of how this will all come out. It is easy for me to say, and understand what

I am trying to tell you. It doesn't make any difference to me. I need you to be with me now. Wilma gave me some advice the night after the trip to see Rachmaninoff. She could see we were attracted to each other and she said don't let anything get in the way of love. If it turns out to be a mistake, so be it and hope for another chance. Don't let love get away because it may be the right one and you will never know if you don't try to find out if it is."

Cindy stood and pulled Ben out of his chair. "Let's go find that ice cream cone your Dad suggested and when we get back to the house figure out how we can find some time for ourselves."

BJ had never had better ice cream and had never felt as good as he did sharing the cone with Cindy as they walked down El Paseo. He knew his parents were special, and that there was something about his father that made him so good with the people around him. He hoped he might have inherited at least some of that trait to help him with the one special person in his life right now.

Chapter 74

That night as Ed and Julia readied for bed Ed could sense something was bothering her so he waited to ask her about it until they were comfortably snuggled together in a routine they did most nights. He turned his head toward her, kissed her on the cheek and asked, "Is my time with Cindy bothering you? I know you caught my startled look when you came over to the piano."

"Now that you mention it, yes," Julia answered surprised, then caught herself as she shouldn't have been. Ed always knew what was going on around him so he would have seen the expression on her face.

"I think Cindy has become a troubled daughter to me. We were discussing stage fright and she wasn't sure she if she would have it when she had to perform in public again. She was telling me how she had talked to Sergei Rachmaninoff about it and he said it often happened to him when he approached the piano at a big event. He told her to tell herself something like, 'I play for myself and the way I think it should be played. I don't care what you may think.' She was so serious and was describing this in such detail I couldn't doubt that it had happened. I believed it had and that was the look I had on my face when you came up to us."

"I thought it might have been something else. You have never, even once, made me suspicious and I didn't want it to be that."

"You have never had a reason to think that of me and never will. I promised you that the first time we made love and I promise you that again."

In BJ's bedroom he lay awake staring at the ceiling. He could see the shadows cast by the textures in the paint and let his eyes trace their images trying to put the hurt and loneliness out of his mind. Cindy was next door in the small guest room in his great grandfather's house. The two houses had been connected and the enclosed walkway was a nicely designed hall of mostly glass bringing the outdoor landscaping and pool area indoors. The need for him to be with her was becoming unmanageable and he was tempted to go to her room. He didn't want to spoil things by pushing the relationship too fast but she had indicated she also wanted it to happen.

He was just about to get out of bed when the door opened and Cindy walked in wrapped in her bed sheet. She raised her hand and placed her index finger to her lips in the universal sign for silence. BJ sat up on the edge of his bed, dressed only in his briefs, and watched her come to him letting the sheet fall to the floor. They didn't speak and BJ knew he wouldn't be able to say what he wanted to in any case.

Cindy put her arms around his neck and pulled him to her and then whispered, "It is time for me to love you. Unconditionally love you."

The next morning Cindy borrowed his bathrobe, kissed him one more time and left the room. BJ laid still and watched her as she put on his robe, turning to give him a smile as she went out the door, closing it silently behind her. He had never had an experience like this and could only think that this would be remembered as the best thing that had ever happened to him. That no matter what may be in his future, whether good or bad, this memory would always be with him to make life matter.

The five of them had their usual breakfast pool side. The conversation was enjoyed and it seemed Wilma, in particular, was the most happy with life. Each knew what had happened last night. Wilma had heard Cindy's restlessness in her room and then her quietly leaving it and not coming back until early this morning. For Ed and Julia it was the demeanor of their son and Cindy that you would have to have been blind not to recognized what had happened between them. BJ and Cindy could not stop looking at each and smiling. It seemed it was a very nice morning in Palm Desert and it would continue that way for many years to come.

Ben and Jennifer came out with their breakfasts in hand and greetings were exchange. Jennifer started to smile as she too recognized what must have made this part of family so contented. Ben pretended not to notice that which was so obvious to all and they weren't fooled by his nonchalance. Just after nine o'clock the door bell rang and John and Allison were soon added to the group.

John looked at Ben and said, "You were a bit of a pessimist Ben, we are meeting with the orchestra reps and the Desert Symphony director, Alan Parker, at two o'clock this afternoon. I will have to give you credit on that twenty-four hour prediction. That okay with you?" Before

Ben could answer John asked another question, "Why are all of you looking so happy this morning, do you know something I don't?" Allison seeing the color rise in BJ's and Cindy's faces poked John in the ribs hard enough to cause him to grunt and then he said, "Oh!" and was off discussing what was to be expected at the afternoon visit that had their futures at stake.

The meeting was at the McCallum Theater office this time and in addition to John, Ben, Cindy and Ed were Julia and BJ. Alan and the two musicians were there and also attending was the full time conductor, Maxwell Harvey. It was crowded in the office but as soon as the introductions were made it was suggested they go to the concert hall. When they entered the hall from the lobby entrance, the Steinway Grand Piano was on the stage in the symphony position, flood lit as it would be in the concert and was the focal point.

"I hope you don't mind but we would like to hear Cindy play what she has memorized of Rachmaninoff number seven," was the Alan's request. John smiled, Ed looked at Cindy and could see she knew what was being asked and she looked completely at ease.

Ben simply said, "That would be nice. Can we sit in the first row and have Cindy and Ed make an entrance for us?" It was not really a question and Ed and Cindy went up on the stage and the rest seated themselves in the front row.

Cindy walked in from stage left and Ed followed, as the conductor would, a few paces behind her. Although dressed quite simply in Palm Desert attire of sleeveless top, matching shorts and thong sandals, the flood lights highlighted her beauty as she strode confidently up to the big piano. She seated herself gracefully and lightly ran her fingers over the keys. Ed turned to the audience and announced the first movement of Rachmaninoff Number 7 Concerto would be played followed by two themes composed by the pianist, Cynthia Anne Ashbough. He turned to Cindy, bowed his head slightly and in return Cindy nodded her head. Ed raised his hands and Cindy began to play.

The two musicians and Maxwell had been given binders. They started following the score but soon put the binders down to just watch and listen. They were mesmerized by what they were watching and hearing. Cindy was a beautiful woman playing in an relaxed manner that showed off her skills and her confidence. The romantic theme dominated throughout but Rachmaninoff brought in his Russian signature tests of the pianist's skill which Cindy handled effortlessly. It was twelve minutes of the best piano music any of them had ever heard. Cindy finished with her two compositions which complimented what she had just played. The sales pitch was now over. How to make the presentation to the classical musical world was now on each of their minds. That was true for all there but for one and that was BJ who had no idea how, or what, he could do to deserve someone like Cindy.

Chapter 75

May was fast approaching, or more accurately was just a few days away. On the McCallum Theater schedule there were limited dates open. It was thought that three weeks were needed to prepare the orchestra and Cindy needed almost that much time to be ready to play the full score. Even that was pushing things fast so Thursday, June the sixteenth was picked as the target date. Rehearsal dates were available the entire week before and as the Desert Symphony had played Rachmaninoff, especially Concerto Number 2, many times it was thought by Max that Number 7 would come easily. Ed hoped he would be ready and in a private conference with Max he explained about Cindy's insecurities which seemed to have left her after he had volunteered to conduct. He apologized about taking the conductor's role and requested he be present at the rehearsals and attend any and all meetings with the orchestra.

Next was the negotiation of the fees. Alan was pleased that John requested a single fee for Cindy and it was settled at three thousand dollars. Ed's time would be volunteered as would all other expenses for their team's contribution. John proposed a quality recording be done and a fractional royalty worked out for Cindy. Again, Ed would waive anything for himself. John explained, "We, those of us involved in bringing this Rachmaninoff trove to light, are not after wealth or fame. Most of us have had, or have, successful careers and money is not the driving force. We want Cindy to benefit professionally. Ed can benefit from exposure which will aid him in the future as he chooses to use it. The rest of us are just along for the ride, so to speak." There was no comment but Alan wasn't sure if this was too good to be true. John addressed this as he would also have suspected something wasn't right in their offer. "We expect your side to take care of all the normal expenses for the venue, salaries, publicity, recording and what ever else comes up. I am sure you understand what will happen once word gets out about what you are planning to present. To put it politely, all hell will break loose. I suggest all your members be given seats with the understanding they must be present in person or donate their tickets for the symphony to resell. You will also need to consider security. You understand when the news of unknown Rachmaninoff concertos gets out there will be thousands that will try any method possible to gain information and attendance. We will have to protect not only what we have in archive but probably our physical selves. This is going be a really big deal in the classical music world."

By the first of May most of the preliminary scheduling and planning was done. John had the sixty copies of the music sheets bound for the orchestra members. Each had it's serial number stamped on each page. It was asked that they be kept in the personal possession of each participant and not shared or copied. Maxwell understood what John was asking and handed out these prized copies to each of the fifty-five musicians that would form the orchestra. All were excited to be part of this concert and also understood what was being asked of them.

John and Allison were taking the next week off to return to Palo Alto as John had a number of things to take care of with the dismantling of the Visiting History equipment. He had decided to sell his big house and would be readying it to be put on the market. The agent he had contacted already had a buyer who was so anxious to have it that an offer above what John had desired had already been made. He and Allison had come to the agreement that the house here in Palm Desert and her home in Santa Barbara would be shared for the time being. John was thinking he now, for the first time in his adult life, had a family he wanted to be with. He also had a new project to manage that would have world wide attention if it was carried out correctly. He was as excited about his life as he had ever been and was looking forward to every minute he had to live it.

John asked Ed and Julia for a few minutes before he and Allison left for the airport. They sat in his small office and John solved a problem Ed and Julia had been worried about concerning their son and his relationship with Cindy. John came right to the point, "Your son is in love with a beautiful young woman who will undoubtedly become a star. He will need to be part of her life if their relationship is to last but that will put him in a very difficult position. The two of you have been able to do it but you are very special people. The finest couple I have ever known. You have been able to compliment each other in individual achievements and supported each other's fame. That is something special. BJ will need your help to discover how to do this and as at first it is going to be all Cindy's show."

"John you are the wise man in our midst," was Julia's immediate response and she then continued, "Ed and I have been mulling this over and we haven't really thought of how we can help him. BJ and Cindy's romance is almost identical to how ours started. We were both lost souls to some extent, were immediately attracted to each other and in less than a week were living together with my grandfather in his house. If BJ and Cindy can have half as good of lives as we have had that should be enough for them. But what will happen after this first concert will put an enormous strain on their relationship. What we are thinking is advising a partnership of a sort with BJ acting as her manager. Would that be possible?"

John smiled at them both. "That is where I would start. It is a difficult relationship but BJ's technical back ground, requiring logic and reason, might be just right to free Cindy to be the artist she will become with out the stress of all the details and organization needed to live in that complex world of music and performances."

Ed and Julia's talk with first BJ, and then including Cindy, was a good start in having them work together. They told Cindy of Ed's success in professional golf using the magic, at least for him, of the Cornith golf clubs and Julia being his caddie helping out. This being followed by their discovering that Julia was a singer and that Ed could be her accompanist which lasted for eight years was even more impressive for Cindy. And now Ed making, by his hard work, to the ranks of the finest concert pianists showed both of the youngsters that much was possible if you were willing to help, without resentment, each other when help was needed.

When BJ and Cindy indicated they wished to be able to spend their private time together it was Wilma that eagerly solved that major problem by suggesting they share BJ's bedroom. By setting up their cell phones she could easily call for help when it was needed. Wilma told them that she was feeling so welcomed here, by Ben and Jennifer, that she didn't think that the nights would be a problem for her anymore. She also later took Cindy aside and suggested she be careful and pay attention to the months. Cindy didn't tell her she had already taken care of that as first Julia mentioned it to her and then Sandra had. The team ladies were taking care of one of their own and being in love with love was universal among them.

Chapter 76

It was now time for Cindy and Ed to concentrate on the music. They planned to spend four to six hours each day practicing all parts of Concerto Number 7, Cindy at the piano and Ed concentrating on the conductor's role. Ed also had his practice schedule to maintain and starting in July had several commitments to prepare for. This posed the first serious problem, there was only one piano and it was in the music room, formally the living room, in Ben and Jennifer's home. In addition the kitchen and pool area had become the meeting area for the group. Six to eight hours a day of piano in the music room was going to be a bit too much.

It was BJ that solved that problem and solved another at the same time. "You need to get a digital keyboard. For practice, composing and generating scores they have become so good UCLA has equipped half their practice rooms with them. A friend and I set them up as it is mostly computer geek kind of stuff. Everyone so far thinks it is every bit as good as a regular piano for practice time and it is great for composing as with the right apps you can download the score and then play it back to see if you like what you have done. You can, with other apps, compose other instrument's scores using the piano and download complete orchestra scoring. At least I think you can do that."

Ed looked at his son. He had been hearing a lot about digital keyboards and how you could use them for practice. That they were portable but he hadn't realized how much technical improvement had been made. Then he asked BJ, "How long would it take to set up one of those in the music room?"

"Do you want the full setup. A good keyboard, PC, maybe a Sibelius program, and all the cables? It might cost around four thousand, or a bit more if you want the very best. How long, I could probably find everything here in Palm Desert so should be able to have you playing by tonight."

Ed took a second look at BJ. Had he grown up in the last few days and had he missed it. Ed handed him his credit card and told him, "See you later. Get the best that is practical."

Cindy asked Ed if she could go with BJ as she knew a little about keyboards and the good ones had key functions that could replicate the touch of the grand piano which she wanted.

They headed to Palm Desert Piano as it was close and had a good website. It was a nice store with a large inventory. BJ thought for a moment no one was there and then looking at Cindy, and then himself, he was thinking they probably didn't look like they would be in the market for a Steinway Model D.

A salesman did come out from a back room and when BJ said they were looking for a digital keyboard, he smiled and said come with me.

In the back room was a man about Ed's age who was just finishing the hook up a keyboard mounted on a stand with a triple pedal assembly attached. On the music rack was an iPad connected to one of the jacks in the back.

The salesman made the introduction to Andy Lehto and paused to let BJ and Cindy introduce themselves. Andy smiled at hearing BJ Adams and asked, "Are you Ed Adams son. I did the recordings for Julia Renquest with Edward Adams years ago."

BJ acknowledged he was and that he knew Andy's name from his Mom and Dad talking about their entertainment days. A little more conversation led to what they were looking for. It was now time for the salesman to smile. He asked Andy if what he had been doing with the just arrived Yamaha P515 and this other stuff, the Sibelius and Symphony applications he had installed, were ready for a demonstration. Andy looked at BJ, then Cindy, and asked her, "Would you like to play, or should I do the honors." Cindy stepped forward and said, "Since I will be using it the most, let me be the one. You will have to turn it on and show me how to get started."

Andy went to another open carton and pulled out the matching bench and set it in place for Cindy. She took the seat, positioned herself and touched several of the keys. "These really feel nice. Just like a real piano's. I'm ready," was said and the sale was almost made.

Andy touched the power button and the various panel lights came on and the small screen lit up with the Yamaha signature. another touch by Andy and CFX GRAND appeared on the screen. He looked at a few other indicators and then told Cindy to go ahead.

Cindy started with her favorite composition and the P515 did not disappoint. In fact, the salesman and Andy Lehto stood transfixed by what they were hearing. Andy knew classical piano enough to realize he was hearing something about as good as anything he had ever heard by any pianist on any piano. The salesman knew it was good but not how good it really was. He did know he had a sale and all he had to do was determine the price he should charge.

Cindy finished the theme and played the Cadenza of the third movement of Rachmaninoff Number 3. Turning to BJ she said, "Give him your Dad's credit card."

The price was fair but at straight list for each piece, including the iPad and applications. Andy would deliver it and do the final setup at Ed and Julia's and asked them to let it be a surprise when he showed up. It had been about ten years since he had last seen them and he was looking forward to seeing them again.

BJ signed the billing, delivery would be made at two that afternoon and Andy would have his assistant to help bring over the piano. He would set everything up and running in a short time. In the next day or so he could come back and help with Sibelius and Symphony Pro applications if they wanted to start using them.

BJ and Cindy were back for a late lunch flush with excitement at having found just what they were looking for on the first try and just a little under the four thousand dollars BJ had estimated. Julia detected that they were hiding something from she and Ed but would not spoil what ever it was by asking. At 2:00 pm exactly the doorbell rang and Julia answered it.

Julia's greeting, "Andy! Andy Lehto, how good to see you!" came down the hall into the music room and then so did Andy. Ed's greeting was just as enthusiastic and once the how are you and how has things been going were over the Yamaha P515 found it's place in the music room. It took less than thirty minutes to set things up and with Andy's promise to come back and get Ed and Cindy up to speed on the two applications and spend some time talking over the good old days he was off to another delivery.

Cindy began playing one of her themes. It sounded surprisingly good and a gathering formed as everyone in the two houses came into the music room. Julia and Jennifer had been in the kitchen which was open to the music room and were doing preparations for the evening meal, Ben came in from the hall as he had been in his office when he heard the first notes. Wilma was next, coming from her bedroom, using her walker with her now ever present smile at being so welcomed.

BJ thought he could use the Sibelius to enter the notations for what was being played. Once he had verified it was working he asked Cindy to start her theme over again. A few minutes later there was the sheet music stored in memory and the wireless printer was busily clattering away in Ben's office. BJ was back and handed Cindy the three pages of her theme. "They may not be perfect but the program is easy to edit and you can change things as you want. If you want to play it back you will like this feature." A couple of clicks and the theme was played back as a vertical line on the screen followed the music along the two staffs on the iPad screen.

It was Ed's turn and he played through the first movement of Number 7 and the Sibelius program stored the score. Tomorrow they would compare the scores with the copy of the originals. After dinner the two pianists would play Concerto Number 2, making a game of playing parts and then pausing for the other to continue. Cindy was on the keyboard and Ed was on the Steinway.

It was a great way to finish an eventful and enjoyable day. They wished John and Allison had been with them but they had much to do in Palo Alto to ready for their move to Palm Desert. Robert and Sandra were in Point Reyes Station to get the computers they used to write manuscripts with and whatever else they would need for the month they planned to be here with the team.

It was going to happen. They were all ready and excited by the prospect but none had anticipated what was about to happen. All but two. Ben suspected and John was sure that once the concert was done, the real game of fame and celebrity would commence. It was their job to protect the rest of the group from it, especially Cindy.

Down the hall in her bedroom, Wilma had a somewhat similar foreboding. But her concern was for BJ as it would be Cindy that became the star and handling that might be more than her lovely care giver would be able to handle. She would try to protect them both.

Chapter 77

The next three weeks went by in a whirlwind of activity. Ed and Cindy were concentrating on learning Rachmaninoff Concerto Number 7. Both were memorizing the complete Concerto for the piano with orchestra. Ed was also working towards being able to conduct the fifty-five member Desert Symphony. They spent two to four hours each day at the Steinway and the keyboard, which with headphones both could be used at the same time. Ed's preference was the piano, but as the days went by he started to like the keyboard as well and they switched between the two instruments. Both were using the same technique, reading three or four bars of the piano's two staffs, the lines having the musical notations, play the lower bass staff first and then do the same the treble upper staff. When satisfied with both they would play them together. If there was a difficult portion, they would play it again and again until it was mastered. Once satisfied they would go back several pages and played through it again until they had it down to that point. Repeat, repeat and repeat.

Cindy had a head start as she had already memorized the first movement. Ed had more experience in memorizing scores but still had to put in more hours than

Cindy to catch up. He also had work to do for several upcoming commitments along with some normal every day practices he did to keep up his skill level. It meant long hours but he enjoyed what he was doing.

The discovery of a new style in Rachmaninoff's composing was exciting but it was still unmistakably Rachmaninoff. BJ was with them full time. He spent most of his time at the keyboard and was teaching them both how to use the software to their advantage. For Ed it was blending in the synthesized instruments with the piano playing that was helping him most. Each instrument type had a single staff with the bars aligned. When there was a flute solo it would show up on the top single staff above the two piano staves and the first note was aligned in the bar in the position relative to where the piano notes were. The PC would show the piano's two staffs and the flute's single staff and when selected would enter the flute. A vertical line that indicated where the piano's time position was would pass over the score as he played up to the flutes entrance. It would sound exactly like what would be expected if the flutist was playing along side of him. Once he got the technique down he started experimenting with the other instruments and by the end of three weeks he had half the orchestra playing along with him.

Cindy, with BJ's help, seemed able to catch on to the technique much faster than Ed and when she played with the speakers on, Number 7 began to come to life. By the last week of May every member of the team was in "The House" as they were referring to the three homes side by side. The three working at playing the music would concentrate on what they were doing and many times would look up to see an audience of four or five sitting around enjoying whatever was being played. They were learning how it should sound and their excitement was building as the music was being developed.

Ed did noticed that occasionally, when just the three of them were in the piano room after a long session, either Cindy or BJ would take a look at the other and they would quietly leave the room. An hour later they would return looking like they were hiding a secret only the two of them could ever know. It brought back memories to Ed of the first few years he and Julia were together, living in this same house with Ben and Jennifer being there. He was sure they knew when he and Julia had sought out time for themselves. His only hope for BJ and Cindy was that it would turn out as good for them as it had for him and Julia.

John and Allison had spent two weeks in Palo Alto with the house sale and selecting what they wanted to bring down to their Palm Desert residence. Allison was surprised on how little John had and chose to keep. He had a big collection of books and the bookcases to house them. A row of nice wood file cabinets, desk and desk chair. He had a closet of clothes, shoes and outer wear. A good bedroom set that would fit nicely in the master bedroom. Most of the living room furniture was over sized as was the dining room set. The kitchen utensils and dinner ware were good quality which would meet all their requirements in his new home so it was packed. He had a big, wheeled tool chest that had all the tools he wanted and that was the garage's contribution. He had a dozen fine paintings and several sculptures he wanted to have with him in the new house and they were readied for the movers. A single large moving truck was big enough and it was loaded early the day of the move and by late that evening had been unloaded in Palm Desert. They slept in his bed that night after having wakening in it that same morning in Palo Alto. It was a very efficient move and as was being discovered by Allison, John was a very efficient man.

Allison lay awake early the next day and watched John as he slept soundly. It puzzled her as it had been what seemed like just a few days since she had accepted his invitation to come up to Palo Alto and take a quick trip back in time. She was now laying next to him, in his bed in Palm Desert, not having any idea what would happen next. She had led an interesting and fun life around extra-ordinary people but nothing like this. She was trying to think of how she should handle her relationship with John when he woke and turned to face her. The smile he gave her had her thinking, "I don't care how this will turn out. Day by day, just let it happen." And happen it did with an enjoyment she had never experienced with another man.

Robert and Sandra's trip was much simpler. They had just wanted some time at home in Point Reyes Station and a few days on *Du-eT* to take care of maintenance and take it out for a day sail about the bay. It was a good break from the fast pace and changes coming about after their first meeting with Ed and Julia. John did not disappoint as usual and now they were involved in this most interesting relationship with one of Robert's visits back in history. It had been on May 24, 2015 that he had visited Sergei Rachmaninoff on the date of March 22, 1943. Seven years had passed since that visit, his last one, and his and Sandra's lives couldn't have been better. The success of the Visiting History series had brought them some fame and income to make their current life style easily affordable.

John had recruited them for his expedition going back in time 10,000 years to seek out information on the early Americans migration from East Asia into North America. That was in June-July of 2020. Less than two years later they were now in another venture with him, totally different but equally exciting. On their day sail, they had anchored behind Angel Island, just opposite the Angel Island Visitor's Center. It was a nice day and Sandra had prepared lunch that was served in the cockpit.

"What are you thinking about our position in this Rachmaninoff discovery. I think we have been used by John to make it happen but, you know, I like being part of it," was Sandra's comment to Robert.

It was a very pleasant day and Robert had been thinking a nap before heading back would not be bad but he answered, "I like it. We have a book, at least one, to write. It will be a challenge, fun to do and will bring us into a totally different genre than we are use to. It will not take too long. We have the structure with all the notes in his own hand and they are for the most parts on dated scraps of paper. All we have to do is make it interesting and not get sued for defamation of character."

Sandra laughed at that and gave Robert a gentle kick. "Let's go below for a short nap and then head back. Maybe go out under the bridge a ways and then back to the marina." It was a short nap, they didn't sleep much and by the time they were back under sail in the bay it was time to head back to their dock in Brickyard Cove.

They were back in Palm Desert four days before John and Allison returned and by then had made them selves comfortable and set up the third bedroom for their office. They had a big board with all the copied notes pinned up in order of dates and were planning the outline.

John and Allison's return had the team now all in place. Ed and Cindy were well on their way to the complete memorization and were playing entire sections of Rachmaninoff Concerto Number 7 in a way to make all that heard it think that Number 2 now had a competitor to represent his best work.

It was time to meet the Desert Symphony orchestra members.

Chapter 78

Meeting with the full orchestra was set for Tuesday May 17, 7:00 pm at the McCallum Theater. Ed, Julia, Cindy, John and Ben were the team members and were met in the lobby by Alan Parker and Maxwell Harvey. The symphony director and principal conductor seemed very excited about this meeting and as soon as the greetings were completed rushed them into the concert hall.

They were greeted by the applause of fifty-five musicians, in place with instruments ready and the grand piano in it's place centered with the conductor's platform just behind it. Alan could barely wait for the applause to die down before he explained, "Everyone here tonight has no doubt about what is being offered to them. Already the rumors are going through the classical music grape vine about the discovery of unknown works by Rachmaninoff. We all know that we will be the first to bring Concerto Number 7 to the public. They," waving at the standing musicians, "are sure of what has been put in front of them and want to do it justice. They would like to work into the first movement this evening and will have your complete attention," this last being directed to Ed and Cindy.

Ed had Cindy on his left and Julia, holding his hand, on his right. Cindy had just grabbed his other hand

and was squeezing it so tightly he was almost afraid to look at her fearing she was scared. He was mistaken, as she looked radiantly happy.

Ed looked around and saw all were looking at him and he didn't disappoint. "I will have to borrow a baton and one of the music binders. You all appear ready and I will assume you have looked over all of your parts as Rachmaninoff has scored them. Cindy is ready, so let us see what happens!"

"I don't believe this!' was all Alan could say as Maxwell handed Ed the baton. Ed, Cindy and Alan walked down the isle and up the steps to stage left. Ed motioned for Cindy to make her entrance and then followed behind with Max in tow. He shook the hand of the principal violinist, waited for Cindy to adjust to the piano and then mounted the conductor's podium.

He turned to Cindy and asked her to run through a few bars until she felt comfortable with the keyboard and then turned to the musicians. "I trust you have been told that I have never conducted a full orchestra before and none of us has ever played this special piece as a symphony. Expect a lot of stops and starts. Even some major mistakes. I have Max up here to help me out. Let's see what it sounds like. We will start at the beginning if it is all right with you."

Ed motioned for them to be seated and looked toward Cindy. He couldn't have been prouder as her look of total confidence helped him gain some for himself. The first six bars were for the piano only and when Ed nodded to Cindy she started to play. Everyone in the room knew immediately that it wouldn't be Cindy that would need any help. Ed kept the tempo with very small movements of the baton and pointed at the principal violinist and lifted the baton at the exact instant the violins were to make their entrance. They did and as Cindy continued he used his left hand to indicate he wanted a small increase in volume from the strings which was done.

With only a few minor lapses they continued on. The flute solo came quickly at bar sixteen with Cindy leading into it and the flutist matching her notes until she left him alone. Ed did only a few motions with the baton keeping the tempo, thinking he didn't even need to be there. They made it almost half way through when Ed made the first error calling in the brass late but Cindy had made a quick chord addition that almost covered it for him.

He stopped the play and smiled at those around him. "I think we should take a moment here to talk about what we just did and what we are about to do. First, I want to thank all of you for accepting that this is exactly what it is. If you didn't we could never had played this far on a first try. I firmly believe we have some magic with us and we will put on a concert that will be referenced in classical music lore for years to come. We have four weeks to rehearse and I expect, with your help, that Concerto Number 7 as first played by The Desert Symphony will become the premier standard for all symphonies offering Rachmaninoff." Ed paused and then said what some had expected but what none could believe. "We have, in the format you have in front of you, Rachmaninoff Concerto Number 5 and Number 6 ready to be played. If this works out successfully we may have a busy summer season."

There was a gasp, then applause and conversations among the musicians. These were professional musicians but almost none made a living at the concert level alone. Most taught music, either privately or in a school setting. Others worked in other professions but it was the love they had for music in the symphony that brought them true joy in their lives.

They made it through the entire first movement with enough success that it was decided on four rehearsals in the next two weeks would be sufficient to tell if much more would be needed. They had a little over five weeks before the concert date. Alan had told Ed that the principal violinist was the concert master and would take care of leadership of the entire orchestra. He also mentioned that everyone in the orchestra loved playing together and this chance to be in on this particular adventure had them all wanting to do it beyond their best.

After the final notes were played Cindy was given an ovation and Ed asked her to play one of her compositions. By demand she played her second and it became a favorite to all. It had been a very good start and Alan and Maxwell were relieved to see the relationship become what was needed.

Ed and Cindy made the rounds within the still seated musicians. They had cased their instruments and covered those that stayed in place. They didn't want to leave. Cindy held Ed's hand as they mingled and Julia couldn't help to notice the relationship that was building between them. John was standing next to her and taking her hand said, "That is a very nice thing to witness. BJ and Jan now have a new sister. You do understand what is happening between them. Cindy never had a loving father and her mother had treated her as a prodigy but not as a daughter. Julia, Ed is a very special person and by the time the concert is performed every one in this room will want him to be their friend."

Julia looked at John responding, "John, you do seem know everything. I have three very special men in my life right now. Grandpa was first, then Ed and now you. My life can't get much better."

Chapter 79

It was after ten by the time they left the Theater. They had thought before hand that they would go out for dinner after meeting with the orchestra but the late hour had them changing plans. Julia had called BJ to tell him that the meeting was going to be considerably longer than planned and suggested he eat in with Wilma and let Robert, Sandra, Allison and Jennifer make plans or eat in as they chose.

They decided that a breakfast style meal at home would be fine and they were there in fifteen minutes. Wilma wanted every detail and her eyes shown bright with excitement. Cindy described how smoothly it went and that they had played most of the first movement. The musicians had prepared, were all wanting to play and gave her and Ed an ovation as they walked in. Another when they finished. Ed had passed the test as a conductor and she felt she had played very well.

Wilma took her hands in hers and looking into her eyes whispered, "Was he there with you?"

Cindy tried to look away but couldn't, saying, "Yes! Right next to me the whole time. I could sense his presence, smell his scent. He didn't speak but he was there. Ed was with me, you were too." Cindy could say nothing more and bent to hug Wilma and kissed her cheek. Only Julia and Jennifer noticed this exchange and both were sure they knew what had been said.

The cereal and fruit dinner was capped off with ice cream and cookies. Then it was time to retire for the evening's rest. It had been an excellent event. Perfect in every possible way. A confidence had developed, in each other, in the music, and in what could be expected in the way of rewards.

The team was tired and after the good evenings and see you tomorrows had been said they headed off to their individual spaces in the three houses, side by side. Their lives were now intertwined, each needing the adventure and companionship at this particular time in their lives. What they were embarking on was something that only dreamers can ever dream. Each new day was becoming the most important day of their life which was a nice way of greeting the new one each morning.

Ed and Julia's house was to the left of Ben's when facing it from the street and John's new purchase to it's right. From the street all three houses looked about the same and all had been built the same year in the nineteen seventies. The entrance hallways led back to the open dining, kitchen and living room areas. A large master bedroom fronted the house opposite the garage side and beyond it were the two additional bedrooms with Jack and Jill bathrooms between them. A powder room and office completed the floor plans. Each had been modified somewhat, especially Ben's with the living room at the rear having a glass wall across the entire back opening to the view of the swimming pool and cabana. Ed and Julia's was connected to Ben's by a glassed in walkway and the two families shared both houses.

This night found Ben and Jennifer having Wilma occupying one of their guest bedrooms. Ed and Julia were now sharing their home with BJ and Cindy in BJ's old bedroom. John's house had he and Allison in the master bedroom with Robert and Sandra in one of the guest bedrooms. They had spread out as needed in the extra space in the house to carry on their parts of the project. Ben's music/living room became the meeting area and coupled with the pool area became the main social and dining gathering place. It was working together efficiently and most satisfactorily.

Robert and Sandra were using the third bedroom as their workroom and had two large cork board panels mounted on the wall. To one side was a long office table and two office chairs. They each had a laptop PC and shared a printer. They were using their personal iPads for reference searches and keeping printed notes in three ring binders.

The cork boards were divided in columns by dates, 1900 to 1950 in five year increments. They had pinned the copies of the pieces of paper from the third box that had a recognizable date in the respective column. Those that didn't have a date were pinned at the bottom of the column that seemed to be the most logical choice.

This evening they were not that tired so they decided to spend a little time going over what they had organized on the cork boards. Over the previous week they had compiled a batch of notes by Rachmaninoff, all in his handwriting in Russian and had sent them to the interpreter John had recommended. They had matched the notes to the ones on the boards and they now had a working group in English.

The notes ranged from old fashioned receipts to partial music sheets with double staffs having one to six bars, all hand written. Sandra had taken 1900 and Robert started with 1910 leaving room for Sandra with 1905 between them. They found a number of notes that showed dates giving some relation to what they would need for getting an idea of what they could do with them. They knew Rachmaninoff must have had a purpose for keeping these items but at first glance they hadn't discovered what it could be.

Sandra gasped when looking at one of the music staffs having six bars. "Robert! Look at this! Look here," pointing at the interpreter's translation and reading it out loud, "I hope C will visit me tonight. I could use her help on this." It was placed in he 1905 column.

Chapter 80

Ben was up early as was his usual routine only now instead of the small, two cup coffee maker he prepared the larger twelve cup. He mixed some waffle batter using the Bisquick recipe on the box he thought was as good as any and had the waffle iron hot when Julia and Ed arrived from next door. His first thought was, as it always was, how pretty Julia looked. Just as her mother and grandmother always looked when he greeted them in the kitchen fixing their breakfast as he was now doing for Julia and Ed this morning.

He savored that memory for a moment then it was back to the present. Jennifer came in next and he poured the waffle batter into the hot iron and in a few minutes the morning orange juice had been consumed, coffee cups filled and the syrup poured on the first waffles. Their morning fast had been broken and the conversation of a close family was being carried on.

They were just finishing up when Robert and Sandra made their entrance and more waffles were started. When Sandra had finished and had her second cup of coffee in hand she handed Ed the music sheet she had found the night before. She had folded it in half as had been he original. Ed unfolded it and glance at the contents.

His brow furrowed and he took a closer look at the notes and one could see him concentrate on what was there. He looked up at Sandra and said, "This is not quite right. It is from the middle of the first movement of Number 2 but it is not what we now play. Actually it doesn't sound very good either. Rachmaninoff must have changed it later."

Sandra cleared her throat and struggled to say, "Look at the translation at the top left of the page. This had to have been written in nineteen hundred and if I have the right timing it is when he was composing Number 2."

Ed became almost stoic, a look of fear was on his face. He tried to speak, then cleared his throat first and managed to get out, "I hope C will visit me tonight. I could use her help on this."

The room went silent. All knew of Cindy's thinking that she had actually been with Rachmaninoff about this time and they were beginning to be convinced it may have actually happened and was not just in the dreams of a young girl infatuated with her idol. Ed wasn't sure what he should do but he did want to play what he was holding and compare it to what was now accepted for these few bars in Number 2. He went directly to the piano and played the accepted score, then played the one on the photocopied staff. The difference was obvious and the accepted one was much better.

"I helped him with that," was Cindy's sleepy introduction on her entrance into the music room. "I heard you playing the part he was . . . ." she paused when she realized what she was saying the tears came. Julia reached her first and held her close.

The clatter of Wilma's walker startled them and

when she got close to Cindy she reached for her and spoke softly, "It's okay dear child. There is a reason for everything in one's life and sometimes it's best not to try to find out the why."

"Wilma, I was there. I wrote over those notes." saying this as she had picked up the sheet from the music rack when she had come in and was now staring at them.

Ed stepped over to Cindy and asked of her, "Let's play around with this. I will play the Number 2 bars and you play the ones you wrote." They did this a few times and it seemed to calm Cindy. She seemed to accept the situation and asked if there were any waffles left. BJ showed up, dressed at least, but not yet totally awake. Cindy commented to him that Sandra had found a note written by Rachmaninoff that described something like what had happened in her past and even mentioned some one as C.

Ben handed Cindy a plate with a steaming waffle quarter and fruit on the side. She thanked him with a smile but her hands were shaking.

John and Allison made their appearance and more waffles were served. Ed waited until they had settled in the music room with plates in their laps to approach John with the morning's session with Cindy. She and BJ were then having their breakfast out by the pool so Ed felt comfortable in sharing the discovery with them. "Cindy seemed okay with it after talking with us about being with Rachmaninoff and her helping on that small part in his composition. Wilma was very helpful but it was left with it having happened. I think it goes much deeper than that. We have to accept that Cindy somehow was able to learn to play those two themes, or that the written scores that were in the box with her name and 1899 noted on the top are authentic. Even more troubling is that Rachmaninoff recognized not only the themes but her on our visit. What do you know that I don't?" was Ed's question to John.

John had finished his breakfast and asked Ed to take a walk with him so they could talk. Outside they started down the street and John was quiet at first then filled in with what he thought and what he knew. He started by asking Ed if he and Julia had read the background report on Cindy he had sent them. Ed answered in the affirmative and he then summarized the part of her arriving in Beverly Hills at the Greyhound Bus depot not knowing who she was, with no identification, no money and thinking she was there to visit Sergei Rachmaninoff. How a psychiatrist friend of the policeman came to get her and that Cindy had lived with her for almost a year. The psychiatrist convinced Cindy that she was imagining this affair with Rachmaninoff in her dreams, and as a pianist herself, was able to get Cindy back on track. She had set Cindy up with Wilma through an elder care placement service and that Ed knew most of the rest of the story.

"This needs to be handled carefully, John. It is not over and although she seemed okay with how we left it, I don't think she really believes anything other than she was actually there with him. I don't want to do anything that drags her back into a bad place. She has become like a daughter to me. The music will go on without her but it will never be as good as it is with her now." Ed had said what he wanted to and waited for John to respond.

They walked a little farther then John stopped and

faced Ed, "I will have a talk with her. I won't talk of dreams, or that she has really has been with him in person, but that life does have some surprises that cannot be explained. That what she has experienced with our group is likewise not explainable but it did happen. That we are about to give the classical music world an inestimably valuable gift. That she will be an integral part in doing this and we need her to make it successful. That she has had this relationship with Rachmaninoff can be cherished but kept as her secret. I will tell her that we are her family now and will always be with her both in being and in our thoughts the rest of her life. She will never be alone again."

Ed looked at John for a long moment and then said to him, "You are a good man John. It is a privilege to be in your company. Let's get this done."

Chapter 81

That afternoon Ed and Cindy wanted some practice time and told the rest of the team they needed four to six hours every day in the music room until the concert was given. All understood their need but knew they were welcome to take a seat and listen. Also to use the kitchen, even though it opened into the music room, as they needed. Ed would plan a break each day to have lunch and would like their company. It would work out well for all and, with Ed and Cindy stopping each day by five o'clock, they would meet in Ben's kitchen for the evening meal preparation. This would become the routine, broken a few times for dinners out in Palm Desert.

The first afternoon went well. John had won over Cindy's trust and she was comfortable with his reasoning, just as Wilma had suggested, "Some things just can't be explained." He had discussed the Visiting History program he and his fellow scientists had created sending just the mind back, and using imagery to converse with people of interest, that couldn't be thought to be possible. That the transportation of objects and humans back in time was even more unbelievable, but she had just made such a trip. Believing she had actually been with Rachmaninoff on occasions was not that much of a stretch as far as he was concerned. It was this that gave her peace of mind and with Ed next to her she felt a new confidence that all would go as planned.

Their practices were going good and the work on Number 7 was showing excellent results. By the third rehearsal with the orchestra everyone was confident of their performance. The excitement of what they were about to perform was so great that each wanted perfection. This enthusiasm made each member of the orchestra want to do their part better than best.

Alan's job had increased ten fold. The word had spread and the desire to attend was overwhelming. He asked Ed and Cindy if they would consider a second concert, and a matinee in the afternoon before it. John was in charge of this part of the effort and, with Ed and Cindy's approval, set the ambitious plans in motion. The response was immediate and all three concerts were sold out in two weeks. The Desert Symphony would have a windfall that would support them for years to come. The musicians would have a pay day that gave solace to their souls for all the times they played for just the joy of performing.

Robert and Sandra were also putting in long hours on their project but were still uncertain on how to pursue it. All the bits and pieces with messages, long and short, were giving them a great deal of information about this man but much had been covered in the many biographies, newspaper and magazine articles. They did come across an interesting partial sheet of five staffs that had written at it's top, in Rachmaninoff's own hand, "Is it possible for me to be in love with two women at the same time. One is real and is here all of the time, the other comes and goes, but is always here when I need her. This is what she wrote for me. How can I not love her."

When they showed the sheet to Ed it took him only a second to recognize Cindy's theme from one of her compositions. It was his turn to take time before speaking. While he caught his breath he also noticed the notations were not of Rachmaninoff's style and he was certain they would match as how Cindy would have written them.

"Why don't you hold onto this for a while. I think it would be best to wait until after we get the concerts played and we see where this is going. Show it to John and I assume he will ask you to do the same. You know what this is so I also assume you understand why am asking you to wait."

"It's incredible, but the fact we are here now is just as incredible," Sandra said this knowing it couldn't be but John had shown them that it could have been.

Ed and Julia's lives became more complicated as Jan, with her live in boy friend, had decided to spend the Spring Break in Palm Desert. UCLA's spring quarter ended June 10 but their finals were over so they showed up two days before that. It was felt best that they would take the other guest bedroom in Ben's house and try not to bother Wilma too much with the shared bathroom. Jan and Daniel Westin had been together for over two years so would probably be quieter than BJ and Cindy. Wilma was a bit disappointed in this as silence in the night was not always her friend. She could understand the logic and did appreciate the courtesy.

There was now only one week left before the big

first night. Alan Parker was beside himself in that all three concerts had sold out and most of the seats were going at premium prices. There were even a number of international attendees and the press coverage was going world wide. It was starting to cause some nerves to jangle in Palm Desert but Ed had gone into his normal demeanor of confidence to the point it seemed unreal to all those who didn't know him. He had infected Cindy and she was feeling a similar confidence about her skills and herself.

The last rehearsal was on Tuesday, the fourteenth, and once everyone was in place Ed took charge and again it seemed his confidence infected the entire orchestra. They had a flawless playing of Rachmaninoff Number 7. Max was first to congratulate Ed and he expressed being glad that it was Ed and not himself conducting for this event. They agreed that the encore would be the theme at the beginning of the third movement and would finish with an unannounced playing of Cindy's favored composition. It had an almost magical finish that left most thinking that it was so good that you shouldn't ask for more. They were ready.

The team would have the best seats for the opening performance and the ladies were determined to be dressed for the occasion and have their men dressed good enough to be worthy of sitting with them. They had been preparing for this for several weeks and by the last rehearsal had their wardrobes selected and made sure the men had theirs as well.

Chapter 82

Thursday, June 16, 2022 had arrived. The sun came up as it should in Palm Desert, on time with clear skies and a promise of a warm afternoon and evening. It seemed an excitement was in the air that was unusual for this time of the year. The high season was almost over but the town had the vibration of a special event in the offing. The hotels were busy and the clientele seemed a bit different from the golf and tennis crowd the locals were used to seeing during the winter months. The focus was on the MaCallum Theater and as the sun dipped behind the mountains to the west a rather large gathering of well dressed patrons had formed.

Filing in thru the backstage entrance a number of nicely dressed musicians, many carrying their instruments, were moving about the stage in a routine that was most familiar to them. There was an anxious expectation that a special performance was about to happen. One they hoped to remember the rest of their lives. Joining them on the stage were Ed and Cindy. Some whispered conversations were being made and a professional calm was exhibited. Maxwell Harvey and Alan Parker were walking about the theater checking that all was ready for opening of the main doors at 7:00 pm and welcoming those lucky patrons with tickets into the hall. The staff was in place, the theater set up perfectly and the time had arrived.

By seven forty-five every seat in the house was occupied. No one would be late tonight. In the front row of the orchestra seats were eleven people who were the guests of Ed and Cindy. Those being Julia, Wilma, John, Allison, Robert, Sandra, Ben, Jennifer, BJ, Jan and Daniel. Eventually this group would gain fame as the team that brought to the world of music the unknown works of Sergei Rachmaninoff. But this night they were just seen by most as very good looking and nicely dressed VIPs.

As the last ticket holders had taken their seats the orchestra members began the warming up of their instruments, readying the music scores and talking softly to each other. Then the principal violinist stood and tapped on her music stand. The oboist played the A note, repeated it once more as the other musicians matched it and then all fell silent.

Exactly at eight the house lights dimmed slightly to a pleasant level and a beautiful young woman walked onto the stage followed by a handsome man a few paces behind her. In turn they greeted the principal violinist, turned to the audience together for a bow of appreciation and then the young woman approached the Steinway Grand Piano taking her seat and the man ascended the conductor's podium. The applause had started as they had made their entrance and seemed especially exuberant this night. It then quieted as everyone was now in position.

At the opposite side of the stage Alan Parker, microphone in hand, made a brief statement introducing Ed and Cindy and announcing the program of Sergei

Rachmaninoff's Concerto Number 7. He then added that it had recently been discovered in one of several boxes stored in a garage in Beverly Hills and that it had been authenticated along with a collection of other scores, sheet music, notes and memorabilia. That tonight the concerto's three movements would be played without breaks and was fifty-seven minutes in duration. The encore would be a replaying of the extraordinarily beautiful third movement and then followed by two themes, solo piano, not written by Rachmaninoff but from the same boxes and dated 1899. He welcomed all to this historic event and nodded to Ed it was time, leaving the stage and taking his seat.

Ed looked at the orchestra, acknowledged the nod of the principal violinist, and turned to look at Cindy. He couldn't suppress his smile, or hide the fondness he had for her. She bowed her head slightly, indicating she was ready. He turned back to the orchestra and the first piano notes of Rachmaninoff Number 7 were played.

Unlike Rachmaninoff's popular Concerto Number 2, this one started with a softly played theme that would be revisited through out all three movements. It used all his well known combinations of keys and cords being allowed to continue as the next notes were laid on top of them, tenuto in piano speak, which increased the beauty of the sound. Legato, playing one melody with one hand while overlaying a second melody with the other hand was worked into the very first few bars establishing the theme in more detail. Then with an unusual combination of chords, building on the theme, until a dynamic tension developed to bring in the strings, first just discernible and then in full voice as the rest of the orchestra joined in. It was Rachmaninoff at his best and Cindy was playing it as he would have wanted it played.

It would later be written, and rightfully so, that Cynthia Ashbough played with a grace that was refreshing. She played with such skill that only her hands needed be watched as her fingers moved over the keys. No exaggerated movements of arms, head or body was required for this talented newcomer to play at the highest level. Although it was not noticed by most, all in the orchestra had by this time realized that Ed Adams's purpose was to guide the musicians to perform what Rachmaninoff would have wanted and nothing more. He may have been the leader, but it was who were being led that was important.

As Rachmaninoff Number 7 finished there was, at first, an unusual silence in the theater. Those that knew classical music realized they had just heard what might be the greatest symphony ever composed and that it had been magnificently played. Others were just awed by it in a way that made making any sound might cause what they were feeling to be taken away. As when awaking from a wonderful dream one does not dare think about what was dreamed because it would then be gone from memory forever. Finally someone called out a whispered bravo, then a second and the applause and cheering started. Cindy then stood and bows were taken. First by Cindy, then by Ed going to her for a hug and kiss on her cheek, then bowing together. This had the patrons cheering even louder. Ed and Cindy turned toward the orchestra and clapping their hands showing their approval. Then raising their hands asking them to stand and take their bows as the applause continued.

Cindy and Ed then took their positions for the encore, the patrons quieted and the third movement was played a second time. Following the triumphant cadenza and the finale there was again a silence of appreciation and Cindy immediately began the first of her two compositions. Her finish of the second was met with the same enthusiasm from the patrons only this time it was the part of the concert that would be remembered by everyone as the best part of the great program they had just witnessed.

In the front row there were no dry eyes. Wilma was smiling with tears running down her cheeks, not because of the music but to see her sad and withdrawn care giver turning into the beautiful and talented woman she had been hiding. John also had moist eyes that were from watching what was a performance way beyond his expectations.

Two others in the team had different emotions at that moment. Julia was having a fear that her place in Ed's life may be lessened. It was not jealousy, or even envy, but Cindy was now part of his life and in his way he would help her find the meaning in her life that would define her happiness. He had done it for her with her singing career where he was satisfied being her accompanist. He would still be hers and she was not worried about that. She had felt the same way, to a lesser degree, as their children grew and the many hours he spent with them subtracted from the hours they could spend together. They were well spent hours and she loved him even more on how he had spent them. It would be the same as he helped Cindy.

BJ had a different fear. Cindy was a star. Not

would someday be one, but was one now. Where was he to fit into her life. As he watched his father with her he realized how effortlessly he was able to guide her and give her the confidence she needed. He wanted to be that person in her life. He loved her so much he didn't think he would be able to live without her.

John had moved over from his seat and sat down next to BJ as he was thinking this and speaking softly said, "She is a very beautiful young woman, isn't she?"

BJ was surprised at the question and that John had come up next to him had asked it in such a personal way. "Yes," was all he could get out but he looked at John and could see that more was coming.

"She will become a star. A celebrity. It is already happening and she is going to need a lot of help to not let it destroy her. Watch how your father is protecting her, never leaving her more than a few steps away. See how she turns toward him and takes his hand whenever she needs that protection. You are going to have take on that responsibility if you want your relationship to last. She is talented and has confidence in that talent but has less confidence in herself as a person. When we are back at the house I want to talk to you about her history. You will have to decide on how you can become the man she needs by her side. Your father can do this without even thinking what it is he is doing but for most of us we have to attempt to do it the best way we can."

John stood and looked down at the bewildered young man and thought how hard it would be for him to make himself the kind of person his father was and he was hoping he could help BJ get there in time.

Chapter 83

It seemed no one wanted to leave the hall. All wished there had been more but also realized it was better to feel that way than wishing there had been less. Ed could tell Cindy was tiring and managed to extract her from the small group that had surrounded them on the stage. They politely made their apologies and made their way down to the first row. Wilma was trying to get her walker in place and Cindy was with her the minute she saw what was happening. She turned to Ed and saw he was motioning them to come with him as Alan Parker was guiding them out a side entrance. BJ had brought up John's car and helped Wilma get seated. Then with Cindy and Allison, John drove them home. Ed and Julia, with Robert and Sandra, decided the short walk back would be a nice way to end the evening. Ben and Jennifer took their car home as even short walks were no longer an option for Ben. BJ, Jan and Daniel thought a stroll along El Paseo and ice cream cones would be nice but then BJ thought he needed to get back and be with Cindy so he took off on his own.

He was about half way back when a feeling of depression overcame him. He was opposite the College Golf Facility and he walked around to the range side and found one of the worn plastic chairs and sat down. It was eerily quiet, the only sound was an occasional car driving past. The stars shown bright and when he looked up toward them his tears came. He was sure he was going to lose Cindy. She had a life to live that he didn't think he could be part of. John had given him some hope but at this moment, alone, sitting in a ratty plastic chair next to a somewhat run down driving range didn't allow him to recognize what he had just witnessed and what was to come next for this group he had joined. He sat still, holding his head in his hands and wept. When the tears finally had stopped he wiped away the dampness from his face, forced himself out of the chair and continued his walk home.

As he entered the house it was dark and he wondered if something was wrong. Going to his room he opened the door and in the dim light he could see Cindy in bed sitting with pillows behind her back. She had a frightened look on her face and she asked, "Where have you been? I waited up after everyone had gone to bed but it was getting so late."

BJ looked at her, then at the bed stand clock showing 1:58 am, and then went to her sitting on the edge of the bed. "I thought I was going to lose you. You looked like a star, you are a star, standing up on the stage with a thousand people cheering. You will be famous by the end of the week. I was thinking I have nothing to offer you now and sat down at the driving range and felt sorry for myself. I lost track of the time. I am sorry."

Cindy reached for him and pulled him to her. "I need only one thing from you and that is for you to love me. To know you will always be there for me me. Nothing else matters."

They lay together until sleep came for both and the next morning brought the new day in as it should for a young couple in love.

It wasn't quite so simple for Ed and Julia that evening. First, although they had told Cindy not to worry, they worried about their son not being home. They knew what was troubling him as a new world would be opening up for Cindy and this would put a severe strain on their relationship. If he had been away at college, not knowing he hadn't made it back to his apartment would not have been a concern. They could have discussed the evening's success instead of waiting for the front door to open that would announce his return.

Julia then rolled over to face Ed and asked, "What do you think is about to happen?"

Ed reached out and ran this fingers along her cheek and smiled saying, "The same thing I always say to you when you ask me that. It will be good and we will do it together." He continued looking at her face and into her eyes trying to think how to say what he was thinking. He knew she was afraid for their son being left out of what he knew was coming for Cindy. It was like what was between them at this moment as his major success with the Los Angeles Philharmonic had put him in a position to enter the ranks of sought after classical pianists. Cindy would be there immediately and have with her the overwhelming mystic of the Rachmaninoff publicity. It was just too good of a story to not give her instant fame which is the hardest to handle.

"We will need to help Cindy. I am sure it will be

John that will pull this project together in a way that will work out best for her and the rest of us. Rachmaninoff is the driving force. The discovery of the concertos and the other scores and items in those boxes will be the stars that will touch our lives now. When I told you after my LA Phil performance I thought I had touched the stars, maybe I was was wrong and that it was that they had touched me. We will find out in the next few days if that was so."

They heard the front door open and close, BJ walking down the hall and entering his bedroom. It was quiet and they could hear his and Cindy's muffled voices but not the words they were saying. Quiet descended in the house and Julia kissed Ed in a manner that promised him she would travel the road wherever it led. Ed kissed her back and it was time for sleep and it came.

Wilma lay awake. It was always hard to go to sleep when you were never sure if you would wake again. A few weeks ago she didn't care but now she had to have a little more time with these wonderful people. Almost overnight her whole life had changed. Meeting Ed and Julia after his concert with the LA Phil had given her a reason to live and each day made it more and more important to stay around a little longer. A smile came to her face as Cindy tucked her in and she told her, "Your life is about to change but don't let it change you. Be true to yourself and the good things will give you the happiness you deserve. That is what is important in life."

Ben looked at Jennifer and was having the same thoughts that Wilma was having down the hall. For the first time in months he was truly happy. He could hardly wait until tomorrow came and his last thought before falling asleep was, "Don't take this away from me now!"

Allison was watching John as he readied for bed. He was a friend, a true friend. He wanted the best for those around him and that had been the driving force in his life. It was exactly what she needed right now to make this part of her life even better. She was not sure where Rachmaninoff was going to take her but it was going to be the most exciting ride she had ever taken.

John was sure he knew the path to take and how to make it the right one for his new team. This was what he was made to do in life and he knew this would be a trip of a life time for all of them. He was ready and tomorrow it would all start in earnest. He knew what would happen and he knew what to do when it did. Most would not be able to sleep but for John this confidence made it come easily. The smile Allison showed him made his relaxation complete and seconds later he was at rest.

Chapter 84

John was up early and in bathrobe and slippers he had walked out to the driveway to look for the morning paper. He looked around and a smile crossed his face. Even the Desert News was now e-filed and one more of life's pleasures had been taken away. On his iPhone was the front page with a spectacular photo of Cindy, with Ed close to her just after he hugged her and bestowed the kiss on her cheek. Her smile was so radiant that only the coldest heart would not melt when seeing it. The headline was Rachmaninoff Meets His Match. At the bottom was the first few lines of the story but almost all of the front page was the photograph. It had begun and John was not the least bit surprised.

He and Allison dressed, had breakfast, did their bathroom chores and then headed next door. Ben's door was unlocked by this time, which had become the practice, and they entered and walked down the hallway to the music room. Wilma was up and greeting the new day with a fresh cup of coffee. She and Ben had been talking about last night and how glad they had been there to see it happen. Jennifer came in from the kitchen, still in her bathrobe, with her cup coffee and sat in one of the over stuffed chairs.

John took out his iPhone and with a ROKU type device that BJ had set up on the large screen TV soon entered the front page from the the Desert News. The only comment was Wilma's, "Oh My!"

They sat and admired the beautiful young woman that had given all of them such pleasure playing the truly great music as it was meant to be played.

Ed and Julia came in next from their house through the walkway and stopped in their tracks at the sight on the TV. Ed finally looked at John and repeated his words from last night, "It has begun John. We better get ourselves ready for what is coming."

Just then John's phone rang and after listening for a moment responded, "Yes Alan, we have Cindy up on the screen at Ben's house. You have had a few calls already, I assume," adding some laughter to the conversation, then continued, "We will start the planning, you and Max included, in a few days. Just put off any decisions other than tomorrow's matinee and the evening concert. It will take some careful planning to keep it under control. We will talk later today. Okay," was the end of the call.

Next Robert and Sandra entered. They had taken an early morning walk and their faces were flushed from the exercise. On seeing Cindy's photo on the TV Robert got out an expression he used a lot around John, "You never disappoint, John."

It was when Cindy and BJ came into the room that the atmosphere changed. They were in shorts and T-shirts, barefoot and obviously just out of bed. A little flushed in the face but not from an early morning walk. Seeing herself on the TV looking like a runway model took her by surprise and she reached for BJ. He put his arms around her as a look of panic crossed his face. All that he had feared last night came back to him and he turned away from the TV and held Cindy even tighter.

John spoke immediately, "I should have warned you. Or taken it down before you came in. We will talk about this later but don't worry about what you are feeling right now. Cindy, you will have to share more than just your talent as a pianist so your audience can share the music you play. We will help you and BJ will be with you. This is going to work out just fine and Rachmaninoff and all his friends will be eternally grateful for what we are going to give them. Trust me on this for right now and you will see what I am saying is true.

"Since we are are all here let me pose a suggestion or two. If Jan and Daniel want to join in later, that will be fine." John knew he was to lead this part and the others welcomed him to do it. "First in importance is to bring Number 5 and Number 6 to the public. As Cindy and Ed put this together we will see if we find additional smaller works to include in the performances. Next is to decide if other things in the boxes have historical importance other than the music." He stopped there for the moment and then continued, "What is already happening is the public wanting to know the story of how we found these treasures. Who, when and how. We will all be hounded by a wide assortment of people, both good and bad, and it will get very intense. I will be the point man with Allison at my side. All of you can defer to me and Allison. Be very careful who you talk to and schedule any interviews such that I can be present.

"This can have a dangerous side so I propose for the next few months that we all stay here, close together. I especially want Wilma to be here and we will continue to provide a house sitter for her at her home in Beverly Hills. There is a potential for a considerable amount of monetary value to be generated with the Concerto scores, memorabilia and the recordings we may be producing. As I understand it last night's symphony is being formatted as we sit here. The financial details will be hammered out later. And speaking of that brings up that we may face some legal battles as well."

Jan and Daniel made their appearance and John was quick to describe what was happening and that if they wished to join the team they could do so. It was left at that as the young couple seemed more interested in breakfast than the goings on in the music room. They would change their minds later.

John turned to Robert and Sandra asking if they had found anything to pursue that needed their immediate attention. Indicating they hadn't John was direct, "We need a press release. I suggest starting with Ed and Julia meeting Wilma at the post LA Phil concert party and her invitation to have lunch with her the next day. Then with you two sharing the Visiting History script of the visit with Rachmaninoff with Ed and Julia and in turn with Wilma. It would be at this point Wilma could offer the story of the three boxes that Rachmaninoff had given to her father with his promise to give them to someone who would know what to do with them. You two should be able to make a good story of it I would think."

Sandra was first to exclaim that they would have

the draft ready before lunch. Robert's eyes had also lit up with the prospect as he and Sandra had not yet found the path to use all the material they had and were starting to think that a fictionalized book would be a better tack to pursue. It was now clear to him that this was the way to approach using the material they had in hand.

"Ed and Cindy have Number 5 and Number 6 to master and coordinate with the Desert Symphony. Julia, you, Ben and Jennifer have the three households to take care of and more importantly to care of who are in those houses. BJ, I have a project for you and I want some of your time this morning to talk to you about it.

"I am done for now. Questions are for after lunch," saying this as he headed down the hall with BJ in tow.

Chapter 85

BJ had grabbed a pair of sandals and pulled them on as he tried to keep up with John. They went to John's house, down the hallway and into his office. It was a small room cramped with a big desk, office chair, book cases floor to ceiling and a huge safe that had been built in and secured in an almost comically way making it look like you would have to tear down the house to remove it. There were two stuffed leather chairs and John pointed to one. BJ sat down and waited. He suddenly felt small and out of place. Being in shorts and a T-shirt didn't help.

"BJ you have been brought into this adventure, I like calling it an adventure, in an oblique manner and have become a most important part of it by your relationship with Cindy. I find nothing wrong with this and think it is a good thing." John stopped to let what he had just said take effect, then continued, "When I get involved in a program I need to know everything about who I am working with. Not knowing can lead to bad outcomes and since in life you sometimes only get one chance to do it right, it is best to eliminate as many problems as possible ahead of time. You are not a problem and I am hoping you will help us avoid what could become one."

BJ squirmed in the big chair as this was an unusual

approach, if that was what it was.

"Yes sir. I am listening." He started to ask what he would be doing when John cut him off.

"This is about Cindy." Again John made him wait, then told him what Cindy's past had been like and that she must be treated carefully when that past came into the present. John told of her arrival in Beverly Hills, alone, penniless, without any identification or even knowing her name at the Greyhound Bus station, saying that she was there to see Sergei Rachmaninoff. BJ had heard some of this but not presented in such a clinical way. His mother, as had Wilma, had spoken of something in that respect, but just casually and he hadn't given it much thought. He now sat frozen trying not to let his emotions show.

John continued on how Cindy had ended up with Wilma Herman as a care giver and between the piano in Wilma's living room and all her stories of knowing Rachmaninoff during the short time he lived in Beverly Hills helped her recover some of her interest her music and herself. It was when his mother and father entered her life that recovery began in earnest. Next was Robert and Sandra with his meeting Rachmaninoff in his Visiting History trip which was the real tipping point.

"What you may not know BJ is that Cindy firmly believes she went back in time and was with him during his recovery from depression and while he was composing Concerto Number 2. That was around 1900. She thinks she worked with him, side by side, in some of it's composition. She is convinced it happened. She even remembers his smell, his handsome looks as a young man, and that he had kissed her two different times. She even remembers the taste of those kisses." John paused, then added, "Your father and I both think her visits happened but not in a real way. There is no way of explaining this as she was, of course, not living at the time. What we have found in the boxes and what she can play only verifies that something did happen, but it couldn't be as she remembers it. Let this be our thinking for now and let it be her secret."

BJ was not only silent, but now thoroughly frightened by what John had just told him. John looked directly into his eyes and scared him even more, "Again, I believe that what she has described actually happened but not actually to her. And that, for the time being my young friend, is to be kept between you and me. I want you to understand what I just said. Between you and me!"

BJ choked out, "Yes, Sir," and sat still, lost for words. Finally, after what seemed an eternity, John continued, "She is a remarkable young lady. Talented beyond belief and at this moment in an excellent position. You are the key to her staying there. Keep her close, be patient and love her without asking more of her than she is willing to give you. That is asking a lot and will not always be easy but the reward will be worth it for you many times over."

"Now for what you can do now to make this project a success." John was smiling as he said this and BJ started to relax and marveled at the way he was able to change subjects with such ease. It was his first experience with a high level manager but later, as the pieces of the project came together, he would begin to realize that his great grand-father Ben had been made of the same cloth.

"You are supposed to be learning something about technology and scientific thinking so here is a problem for you to solve. Robert and Sandra are trying to figure out what the contents of third box with all the bits of paper Rachmaninoff chose to save mean. They appear to date back to 1900 and some are as recent as 1943, the year in which he died. They have sorted them as best they can on bulletin boards by dates, and guessed at dates, but can't find the story that he is trying to tell us. I want you to work with them on this and here is my suggestion on where to start."

BJ was now alert and eager to find a place for himself in the project. Cindy would be spending much of each day with his father at the pianos and he had no place in that world. What John then presented was in his world. He told BJ of the Rachmaninoff Performance Diary on the internet that lists all his performances by date, place, type and sometimes other information, from 19-Nov-1886 until his last 17-Feb-1943 in Knoxville, Tennessee. Thousands and thousands of dates and places.

"We know from all his biographers that he almost stopped composing once he had moved to the United States. He did several works while at his Villa Senar in Switzerland but few, if any, otherwise. He was consumed by touring and making money. He also thought leaving his beloved home country of Russia had him leaving his composing talent there. I think that was not the case. What we have in those boxes is what he composed in his hours of travel time between his performances and which he never was able to finish or bring to the public."

BJ sat up straight in the chair and his eyes lit up. John could see he had set things up and waited.

"Most travel was by train back then. Some by

plane but he still must have had many hours to kill. Days between performances, hours in hotel rooms. He couldn't have spent it all socializing at parties and the like. If I can work up a data base that plots the times and distances between performances and the social activities from newspaper clippings, I could make up a list of periods where he had time slots that Robert and Sandra could concentrate on. Maybe then what they have would start to make more sense." BJ was now excited and he had some thing he could do that had some value.

John smiled again and then added, "Pay attention to how we all work in managing the next two programs for Concertos five and six and you may find this will be your place to be in Cindy's future." BJ was beginning to understand this man and what a great manger he was.

"Get started on this and let's see where it leads." John said this as he stood up and BJ was off to assemble what he would need and to talk with Robert and Sandra.

John sat back down in his big desk chair, leaning back and closing his eyes remembering the look in Sergei Rachmaninoff's eyes as he handed Wilma's father the three boxes. He wondered if when his time came would he have three boxes to hand someone to finish up with whatever he hadn't had time to do.

Chapter 86

The matinee and evening concerts went every bit as good as the opener. Full houses, excellent performances by both the orchestra and the featured pianist. Ed had conducted with a seeming ease that let the music be the show. Cindy played so well most thought it was perfect. And it was. Julia and BJ attended both as did Robert and Sandra. Wilma was tired and was satisfied to stay home, as did the rest of the team.

John was busy on the phone as the calls started Friday morning as the news of Number 7 spread. Most were newspaper journalists just hoping for an interview, photos, background, anything they could write about and publish. They were all disappointed as he told them a press release would be coming out in the next week and it would be on the internet. There were two calls that were encouraging enough to maybe call back, one from the Library of Congress in Washington DC and the other, not surprisingly, from the Serge Rachmaninoff Foundation in Lucerne, Switzerland. It had started and he was ready to plan the details with the team on how they should go about it.

All were home by midnight. Cindy went to see Wilma as soon as she returned. "You are such a beautiful young woman. You have been my friend and I will always think of you that way. Even when you become famous and have no time for yourself, or for an old lady hiding away in her bedroom. Was he there with you tonight?"

Cindy sat down on the bed, took Wilma's hands in hers and whispered, "Yes Wilma, he was there. Not in being but drifting in and out as I played. It was just a sense, a good feeling like confidence gives you when you play it the way it should be played."

"He was such a nice man. I have told you that before. He visits me sometimes. Just to say hello and how are you. He is coming more often lately. Go to your young man and tell him you love him," Wilma saying this as she closed her eyes and fell asleep.

When Cindy returned to the music room all had gone to their rooms except for Ed who was seated at the piano. He had a single sheet of music on the stand and was softly playing the score. Cindy walked up behind him and suddenly stopped, placing a hand on his shoulder. In an emotion laden voice she asked, "Where did you find that? How can you know that piece?"

"Sit next to me and I will play it again for you. The way you wrote it for Sergei," Ed answered and Cindy did as he had asked. As he played she started quietly sobbing and when he finished he reached for her hands, pulling her closer and telling her, "Somehow you were there. It can't be, but this was found in the box Allison is going through and is on the same paper used in your other compositions. The notation style is also the same. The bottom portion is missing and it appears it was torn off long ago. It is your composition and it was saved in that box for a reason."

The room was quiet and they sat close together, both staring at the score reading the music in their minds. Ed then asked Cindy if she could read what Rachmaninoff had written on the top.

"No, it's in Russian. When he spoke to me it was usually in Russian and I understood what he was saying as I could speak the language, but I can't read it. Do you know what it says?" she asked pointing at the script.

Ed paused, then slowly answered, "Yes. Translated it reads, 'Is it possible for me to be in love with two women at the same time? One is real and is here all the time, the other comes and goes, but is always here when I need her. This is what she wrote for me. How can I not love her?'"

Ed, looking at Cindy, could see her tears forming as she managed to say that she had written on the bottom of the sheet that this was for him and for him to remember her whenever he played it. Ed moved to face her and wiped away her tears with his fingertips. He then gently kissed her on her cheeks where the tears had just been.

Julia having been unable to sleep and missing Ed had just entered the music room from their house when she saw him kissing Cindy. She stood still not knowing what to do as the silence was broken by Ed playing this short and beautiful melody again that she had just heard moments before as it had drifted into their house through the walkway.

"Do you think that can be true, him loving two women at the same time?" Cindy asked in a sad voice.

"Yes, I am sure it was true. That was what he was feeling at the time." As Ed said this, using his hand, he gently guided Cindy's face up towards his. "Cindy, I love you as a daughter but when I kissed you, just for those few seconds, it was more than that. It was a kind of love that can be shown with a kiss, the soft touching of an arm, or a gaze into an other's eyes. It is an expression of a love, not in the romantic sense, but in the appreciation of who you are and for me the wanting you to be part of my life and my families lives. At the time he wrote that note Rachmaninoff was truly in love with you but was also in love with his new wife, Natalia. How could he not be in love with you both?"

Julia hearing this went back to their bedroom and waited for Ed to come to her as she knew he would. Eventually, after Cindy had left and Ed playing several more melodies, he came back to their room, dressed for bed and joined her. She moved to him, received the kiss she wanted and nestled into the position next to him that was the most comfortable for their sleep.

Cindy had looked at Ed for a long time then gently touched his face and whispered, "Thank you." She kissed him on the cheek and left him sitting at the piano as she went to what was now her and BJ's bedroom. She slipped out of her concert dress and carefully hung it up, smiling, thinking how nice it was and how well it fit. Removing the rest of her clothing she put them in their place and then slipped into bed next to BJ. She felt his hand lightly slide over her shoulder and then continue it's caress. She thought how good it was to be loved and that the love of one man was enough. But occasionally having a moment of the affection Ed had just shown to her by another would be nice.

Chapter 87

For what ever reason this Sunday morning every one in the three houses wound up in Ben's kitchen at the same time. It was a big kitchen, but not that big. Jennifer took over and started putting glasses, cups, dishes and plates out. Julia put the orange juice and milk containers on the counter along with several plastic boxes of berries and bananas. The spoons, of several sizes, appeared and BJ and Cindy put out the cereal boxes from the the pantry. By some kind of magic all had servings and they had assembled in the poolside patio. BJ had brought out additional folding chairs and even Wilma, with a little help from Sandra, was comfortable enjoying her bowl of fruit topped frosted shredded wheat.

John's phone chirped and he touched something and after a quick look touched something else. "Call number fifteen so far since five this morning. We will meet after breakfast for a short time and then take the rest of the day off."

The meeting took a little longer than the short time that had been mentioned but a more satisfied group of people could not be found. Each in their own way. Ed and Julia seemed specially close this morning as their talk that morning about Cindy's entrance into their lives had gone well. Julia had told Ed she had seen him kiss her and then listened to him explain what his feelings were for her. She wasn't threatened by this and it drew her even closer to this remarkable man she was spending her life with.

John was almost beside himself as to the way everything was coming together. They had a number of truly magnificent works to bring to life and he believed his team were the very people that could do it. And now he had Allison with him, a total surprise, filling a place in his life that had been empty for years. He was genuinely happy. He hadn't thought it possible he could ever have such happiness which made it even better.

Robert and Sandra had a different outlook. To be involved with this group and have the project satisfy their needing something more than just enjoying their every day life style had come at just the right time. They were thinking about writing Rachmaninoff"s story, but not as a biography but as a fictional novel based on his persona and take the liberties that were afforded them to make it both interesting and epic.

John had asked BJ to work with Robert and Sandra and use the online Rachmaninoff Performance Diary to do some research. Using his computer skills he sorted the information by place, date, distance apart. hotels, travel time and most importantly the possible free time between performances. Free time when a great man of music could compose.

BJ offered that Rachmaninoff must have had hours of time on his hands while on his concert and recital tours and that he would have certainly created new works during much of that time. From the box that Robert and

Sandra were working with they should be able to co-ordinate time and place for some of it's content and maybe even find ways to associate his activities and how he spent his free time. Even the many fine pieces Allison was discovering could possibly be placed in time and place by notes Rachmaninoff appeared to like to add to his sheet music. It was a daunting puzzle and they all were looking forward to working on it's solution.

BJ had to share with the team one of the newspaper articles he had found written about Rachmaninoff and his ever present piano tuner that traveled with him. They were on their way to a recital in Toronto when Rachmaninoff remembered he was supposed to perform "God Save The King" before starting his program. He had forgotten the melody and asked his piano tuner if he knew it. He said he did and then was asked to whistle it. Rachmaninoff whistled it back and then the two whistled it together. He played the opening perfectly.

Wilma was so glad to be alive she had a perpetual smile on her face and listened to every word spoken. BJ's story of the piano tuner elicited a chuckle and she offered, "That was Mr. Rach. That is exactly what he would do. He was such a nice man."

Cindy and BJ were seated on the Cabana's love seat as close together as possible. They were trying to pay attention to the conversations going on around them but they were for the moment in their own world. BJ could see that John was positioning himself to talk to the group and pulled Cindy closer. "I am not supposed to share this with you but I have too. John and my father are certain that somehow you were with Rachmaninoff back then. It wasn't just your dreams that you were remembering. The scores in the boxes and you knowing them prove that someway you knew them from before. How it could be they have no idea. Neither do I, nor do you. I believe somehow it happened and I want you to know that. I think Wilma thinks you were there but won't admit it and my mother is coming to the same conclusion. I think it best we just let things happen and take what life offers us for the time being."

Cindy reached for BJ, kissed him and then she said what he would remember the rest of his life, "You are so like your father. Life is going to be good for us."

John had taken the floor by standing and moving to where he could face them all. They could see this rather small man was in reality a giant. He had pulled it off in such a way that each of them would benefit from his efforts. The potential financial rewards would be dealt in the future. It was the reward to their own lives that was what was now important to each of them.

"We did it! We absolutely did it! Thursday evening with Cindy playing Rachmaninoff Number 7 and Ed conducting the Desert Symphony was the payoff for our efforts. My chance attendance at the LA Phil concert, the curiosity of seeing Robert and Sandra there and following them into the donor's party. Ed and Julia's conversation with Wilma when I heard her say she had known Rachmaninoff. And then Robert and Sandra introducing themselves to Ed and Julia wanting to talk with them about Robert's Rachmaninoff visit. That was the catalyst that I needed." John paused for just a moment and then continued, "It is so simple to see now. A life of a great man cut short and my own life's work ending soon with no prospects of what there would be for me to do next. The thought that Rachmaninoff must have had many great works running about in his mind, many of which he must have written down and stored to bring together later. And then not be given the time to do it. It was that simple thought that was with me as I left the concert hall that night. I couldn't sleep that night and on the flight back up to Palo Alto the next day I made the plans that we have now carried out. All of this has happened in just a short three months. How about that!"

For a minute all sat still and then they began to clapping their hands as a salute to John. John then joined in with his salute to his team.

Chapter 88

The sun was now fully up and the temperature, still quite comfortable, was going to later rise to almost hot. Sunday, June 19 was a particularly nice day and those sitting around the patio of Ben's backyard pool and cabana were comfortable, both with the temperature and with the circumstances in their own lives.

Ben was still stretched out on his chaise lounge with Jennifer sitting next to him, holding his hand. He was enjoying listening to John's presentation and knew what was coming next. John reminded him of himself when he was one of the top executives at IBM those many years ago. At least it was how he wanted to remember those days. Efficient, confident and getting things done the right way. It was a gift few had and he thought he had never seen anyone better than this interesting man who had so many secret ways to make the impossible happen. Ben leaned toward Jennifer and whispered, "He will now tell us what this summer will have in store for us and what our futures may be like."

The congratulations had ceased and John had their attention again. "We have much to accomplish this summer. Ed and Cindy will prepare for the concerts debuting Rachmaninoff Concertos Number 5 and 6. This should occupy most of their time and of course Ed has several commitments to attend to so they will be busy. I would like to add a thought for their future as collaborators. Allison has found so many excellent compositions in her box that several concertos are waiting to be put together. In fact the two pieces of Cindy's work obviously need a home. I think, even though it may not be as apparent to him now, that BJ should take a look at the mechanics of seeing this gets done. Time is a precious thing and in many cases even the wisest of us waste too much of it. Many things one chooses to do oneself can be better done by another. Such as working in the confluence of technology and music.

"Next is that I think Robert and Sandra's idea of a fictional book on this part of the Rachmaninoff saga is an excellent idea and maybe even include details of our part in it. If you want another thought, I am now speaking to Robert and Sandra again, one could think the adventures of the concert pianist's life on tour could be blended into a series of stories about time spent when not on the stage."

John stopped for a few moments then continued as his audience was waiting. "For Wilma and Ben, you both deserve to sit back and watch what happens. However, when you see one of us wander off the tracks, distracted by some shiny object, please mention it to us. Not just a knowing smile of what is about to happen, but a nudge to take a second look and avoid it happening. Life's lessons are sometimes easy to forget and hard to remember. Share some of that precious wisdom and save us some of that precious time. Wilma, I will always remember your words to Ed at the patron's party, 'I knew him, you know.' If you hadn't told him that I would probably be sitting alone in a big house in Palo Alto wondering what I should do that day and whether it was even worth getting out of my chair. I can't tell you how enjoyable it was for me waking up this morning with Allison there and the day that is today just getting under way. Such as it should be for each of us."

Again John took some time to form the words to tell what he was expecting for their futures. He started with himself and Allison. "Allison and I have been invited to visit Villa Senar as quests of the Serge Rachmaninoff Foundation. It is an open ended invitation made to sell us on the idea of donating the Rachmaninoff papers to the Foundation. It will be considered but for now it is only one of the options. This will be something we, our team here, will decide on later. There are many avenues to take and it is my hope we can determine the right one. I think all the originals are secure and protected in the vault as they are now stored and have twenty-four hour security monitoring. We will make our trip to Switzerland for ten days leaving one week from today. It will be my first trip to Europe. What a sheltered life I have lived.

"Next I will give some advice to the youngsters in our group, namely Cindy and BJ here and to Jan and Daniel if I have that opportunity. A few years back, could it be forty or fifty years ago, there was a popular writer, professor and philosopher named Joseph Campbell who coined and promoted his guide to life as to 'follow your bliss.' In a word, happiness. Do those things that result in your happiness. Follow your bliss always sounded a bit odd to me but achieving your happiness does not."

John started to take a seat, then stood and addressed his audience once more, "Julia mentioned to me that Ed had told her after his performance with the Los Angeles Philharmonic that he thought he had touched the stars that night. If one can have that thought even once, touching the stars, you should deem your life a success."

Later that night Allison rolled over onto her side to look at John and saw that he was staring intently at the ceiling. "What are you thinking about now. Can't you close that mind of yours down, accept what has happened and fall asleep."

"There is no way Cindy could have been there with Rachmaninoff. No way possible. But there has to be an explanation of what we have absolute proof of what could not have happened, happened. I am going to find out how it did. I will tell you in the morning how I plan to do this."

Allison was silent for a few moments while she continued to stare at John. She was having trouble comprehending how he could jump from the near finish of one his greatest achievements to planning another, seemingly impossible to achieve, in just a manner of minutes.

"You shouldn't go there! Not now, maybe not ever. Cindy's life has just begun again. You can't jeopardize that in any way!" Allison had responded rather sharply but after long pause coyly said, "It's an interesting dilemma, isn't it. Since I will be right here in the morning I might as well listen to you tell me how you are going to do it."

As Allison drifted off to sleep, John turned to look at her and thought, "I have absolutely no idea how I am going to do this but tomorrow is another day. Maybe I will have a dream tonight that will give me the answer."

ABOUT THE AUTHOR

Art Myers was born in 1935 and grew up in the small southern California town of La Mesa. He graduated from San Diego State College in 1958 with a BS Degree in Engineering. Several employments in the Military Industrial Complex lasted until the end of 1969. His first layoff was in 1961 and he spent the fall months working as construction labor in Mammoth Lakes, CA and the winter of 1962 skiing in Aspen, Colorado. Another stint in engineering and a second layoff occurred which found him with a wife, daughter, house payments and just beginning what became a thirty year career as a professional sculptor. Interspersed in that thirty years were a variety of residences and occupations for both he and his wife. Retiring in 2002 they bought a sail boat and spent ten years living aboard and cruising both US Coasts. They have lived in a variety of places including Saratoga, CA, Aspen and Loveland, CO, Lake Forest, IL and currently Vero Beach, FL.

His first book was an autobiography, *My Story, How A Young Boy From California Ended Up An Old Man In Florida*, written for family and friends in 2015. He has now completed five works of fiction, *Andrew's Piano, Ed Adams Chases A dream, A New Life For Robert Johnson, 10,000 Years Before Present and Ed Adams Touches The Stars.*